Zona Gale

Miss Lulu Bett

Birth

Introduction by Dianne Lynch

Waubesa Press
P.O. Box 192
Oregon, WI 53575

Contents

Introduction

by Dianne Lynch

At the time of her death in 1938, Zona Gale's life story embodied all of the elements of the stereotypic feminist heroine of the late nineteenth century: After an idyllic childhood in a tranquil Midwestern farming village, Gale earned a graduate degree at the University of Wisconsin, worked as a newspaper reporter in Milwaukee and New York, attained some recognition as a writer of popular novels, and in 1921, earned a Pulitzer Prize for drama.

She was a staunch supporter of women's rights; one of the most steadfast followers of Robert La Follette in a state that would ultimately consider him its finest citizen; an independent thinker and outspoken advocate of liberal causes; and an avid pacifist. She supported her elderly parents on her earnings as a professional writer, and she remained unmarried until the age of 53, at which time she adopted two daughters, ages 19 and 3. She was, by all accounts, the epitome of the "new breed" of women who emerged at the turn of the century: educated, professional, a suffragist, and a political progressive.

Zona Gale was all of these things, but she was far less an ideal figure than a complex, conflicted woman of her times. For if she was the embodiment of modern womanhood in the 1890s, she was, as well, a model of the obedient daughter and small-town spinster. A domineering mother and Gale's own acquiescence to traditional social mores surrounding family responsibility and authority — and not a driving ambition to push the boundaries of women's social roles — prompted her pursuit of a career, her extended singlehood, and her social activism. Like millions of other educated women of her day, Gale spent her adult life struggling to align society's new conceptions of women's roles with her own values and life experience. Hers was not a dramatic struggle, but a silent one, played out in a thousand decisions about what she would study; where she would work; how she would live; whom she would, and would not, marry. It was expressed in her daily letters home to Portage during the years she lived and worked as a reporter in Milwaukee and New York, and in her final decision to break off her engagement with Ridgely Torrence and return home to the small farming village of her childhood to pursue her life's ambition to be a "real writer." And it is reflected in the stories that she chose to tell — from the sentimentalized fables of small town life published as *Friendship Village,* to her stark portrayal of the tender tragedies of inconsequential lives in *Birth* and *Miss Lulu Bett.* It is this conflict, these contradictions in her character and her experience, that make Gale a fascinating and compelling figure in feminist history in general, and in women's literature in particular.

A Writer's Life

The world Zona Gale was born to was one of social upheaval and economic flux. Alexander Graham Bell's telephone patent in 1876 changed the nature of interpersonal communication forever, just as the rotary press had transformed the notion of mass circulation publication a year earlier. At the same time, Charles Darwin's *On the Origin of the Species* (1859) and *The Descent of Man* (1871) were triggering a re-evaluation of established truths in history, law and psychology. James Dewey and William James were preaching the tenets of pragmatism, a viewpoint which stressed the tentative nature of truth, tested not by logic but by experimentation and results. And while the nation's intellectuals pondered its origins and its future, the country's working poor struck back at their corporate exploiters in the Great Railroad Strike 1877. Called American's first national strike, the events of July 1877 were a portent of an increasing level of labor unrest and a gradual shift in worker-management relations that would leave the two sides adversaries.

Against this backdrop of national expansion, innovation and social stress, Zona Gale's childhood was uneventful and serene, undisturbed by events occurring outside Portage village limits. She started writing at the age of seven, printing her first short story in pencil and submitting it to her mother for approval. By the age of 13, she was sending out stories to magazines and newspapers; despite a continuous flow of manuscript submissions, not one was ever accepted for publication. That didn't deter Gale — or her mother, who had high hopes for her only child.

There was never any question that Zona would attend the University of Wisconsin and then pursue a career; Eliza Gale had decided that her daughter should become an English teacher. Upon her graduation from Wayland Academy in Beaver Dam, Gale enrolled at the university campus in Madison, arriving there in 1891. It was her first extended stay away from her parents, and all three felt the separation keenly; Zona was a frequent passenger on the train that ran between Madison and Portage. After four years in which she did "very well in English courses, and not at all well in anything else," Gale was named class poet and awarded a bachelor's degree. She went home to Portage, but by summer's end she had decided to go to Milwaukee in search of newspaper work. "Like most people, I thought the far fields were greener than those at my feet," she wrote later. "There wasn't any romance in Portage. . .my one idea was to escape from what seemed to me an unpromising field."[1] After months negotiation and pleading with her parents, she finally acquired their permission. Determined to succeed — and to find the independence and romance she believed essential to the writing of good fiction — Gale left home in September 1895, to find a reporting job in Milwaukee.

She stayed for two weeks with Edith Pollard, a friend from school. "Every morning of my stay," Gale wrote later, "I calmly deserted her and went down to the newspaper offices to ask if there was an opening for me..."[2] For fourteen days, she went to the city editor of the *Evening Wisconsin;* he refused her each time. But Gale persisted, despite her dread of the morning encounter. "The chief thing that I can recall about those mornings was the intense wish that the elevator which was taking me up to the city room would turn out to be the elevator taking me back down again," she wrote. "In my ignorance, I always managed to arrive when the city room was full of reporters, a fact that made my embarrassment the more acute."[3] Finally, after two full weeks, the editor relented — Gale surmised that he did so out of sheer exhaustion — and asked whether she might be able to cover a flower show. "I have never put such emotion into anything I have written," she recalled.[4]

As in all of the momentous occasions of her life, Gale shared her early successes with her parents. Upon receipt of her first $15 weekly paycheck she drew grinning faces across the envelope, sealed it shut and mailed it off to Portage, contents intact. "It wasn't that they needed the money. But I was like a dog that wants to bring every treasure, every find to show to the person he loves," she remembered.[5] Once Gale had established herself in Milwaukee, Charles and Eliza Gale closed their rambling home in Portage and moved to the city to live with their errant daughter; the family was together once more and Zona's independence had been short-lived. She switched newspapers in 1899 and began to cover city society for the *Milwaukee Journal;* in

[1]Keene Sumner, "The Everlasting Persistence of this Western Girl," *American Magazine,* June 1921. Transcript in August Derleth Papers, State Historical Society of Wisconsin, Madison, Wisconsin.

[2]Ibid.

[3]Ibid.

[4]Zona Gale to Grant Overton, Feburary 1919, Zona Gale Papers, SHSW.

[5]Sumner, "This Western Girl."

two years there, she never strayed from covering "women's news." At a time when successful female reporters prided themselves on their thick skins and their ability to outsmart and keep pace with their male counterparts, Zona was ever the perfect lady. She was her mother's daughter to the core.

Despite her successes in Milwaukee, however, Gale grew increasingly restless. By 1901, she was ready to move on. She knew her parents would never consider a move to the East Coast, and she was well-educated enough to know that successful writers made their contacts in New York City. There was a world of interesting people to meet and fascinating sights to see — and Gale was ready to leave home, finally, in search of them. What had worked in Milwaukee would work in New York. Each morning after her arrival in the city, Gale presented the office boy at the *New York World* with a list of story ideas. The city editor checked those he found interesting; these she would do on speculation in hopes that he might purchase them on a piece basis. Sometimes he did; more often he did not. But Gale refused to give up and, finally, after months of pestering him, he gave her a job on the staff. She loved her work, and raved about her successes in her daily letters home to Portage. But her reporting career was, even then, nothing more than a way to earn a living as she pursued her "real" writing. "I was still trying to write beautifully of things wrapped in an atmosphere of remoteness," she said of those early days. In addition to the contacts she made in the course of her reporting work, Gale began to socialize with several of the leading figures on the New York literary scene. Through Richard LeGallienne, Gale met Edmund Clarence Stedman, an American poet and anthologist who was often referred to as the literary dean of his day. Stedman invited her to attend the weekly meetings of the Sunday Night Club at his home in Bronxville. There, Zona was introduced to Edward Arlington Robinson, winner in 1921 of the first Pulitzer Prize for poetry; Harriet Monroe, founder and editor of *Poetry: A Magazine of Verse;* playwright William Vaughn Moody; and poet Ridgely Torrence, who would become the true love of her young life.

Undoubtedly these acquaintances wielded considerable influence on Gale's political opinions and intellectual development. Added to the stimulation she received from them was her own experience on the streets of New York. Confronted by abject poverty, by the rigid social mores that defined and confined women, by the cruel realities of the city's slums and the blatant indifference of society's well-to-do, Gale began to question her own philosophical and political leanings. Her liberal stance on women's roles, suffrage and, later, Progressivism, was grounded in the teachings and influence of her parents. But in New York, for the first time, Gale's life experiences prompted an exploration of her own stance on social issues.[6]

---

[6]"Zona Gale, Noted Poet, Author, Brought Fame Back to Portage," Capital Times, May 30, 1974.

Central to that exploration was Gale's position on women's roles in society. She was an atypical woman in 1900 on several scores: she was a college-educated, unmarried professional, working in a field considered by most to be a man's domain. She was strong-willed and persistent, and she had the courage to move alone to the nation's largest metropolis in search of work. In 1924, long after she had left New York for the quiet and solitude of Portage, Gale wrote a piece for the *Milwaukee Telegram* on the issue of whether women who worked outside the home should be married. She was at the time a middle-aged woman who lived with and supported her elderly parents; although she had been involved in a series of romances throughout her adult life, she had remained unmarried and her observations about the wedded state reflect frustration with what she saw as the pigeonholing of women.

Society was prone to proposing unrealistic alternatives, Gale wrote, thereby limiting its citizens' opportunities. "Shall women have a career or shall they marry?" was one such proposal; the question unreasonably required a choice between the two. The actual choice that confronted a woman of the middle class was more fundamental, Gale wrote: "'Shall I marry and be a cook, maid, laundress, sumptress combined?' Or 'Shall I marry, and also be a painter, or a lawyer, or a writer, or a businesswoman or a member of any one of the 119 gainful occupations in which women are now engaged?'"[7] Women should choose a profession, Gale argued; among her choices was the role of a housekeeper, but it was not the only, or even the most attractive, option. "The profession of housework, which she has now in addition to marriage, will be exchanged for a profession not thrust upon her, but chosen," she wrote.[8]

Gale's position on working women was molded by her own single status, by her observations of working women in New York City, and by the views and writings of such feminist reformers as Elizabeth Cady Stanton and Charlotte Perkins Gilman; in fact, Gale concluded her column on working women with a reference to Gilman's *Women and Economics*. At the heart of Gilman's philosophy was her contention that all the roles a woman was permitted to play derived from her sexual functions. A man could build a career, enter politics, develop relationships outside the home. But a woman could only marry and have children. In effect, sex became a woman's economic way of life; while "men worked to live. . .women mated to live."[9] The economic status of a man determined his social standing, his value as measured by his peers; it followed logically, then, Gilman argued, that the woman who labored in the home was unsalaried, had no economic status, and was therefore a social nonentity. "The labor of women in the house, certainly, enables

---

[7]"Shall Woman, Wife Choose One of Alternatives to Houework?" *Milwaukee Telegram,* Jan. 13, 1924.
[8]Ibid.
[9]Charlotte Perkins Gilman, *Women and Economics,* (Boston, 1898), p. 71.

men to produce more wealth than they otherwise could; and in this way women are economic factors in society," she wrote. "But so are horses."[10] Gilman's answer was the socialization of housework: professional house cleaners, communal kitchens, dining rooms and day nurseries for children.

Gilman's radical views could be considered the extreme end of a spectrum of public opinion that was as widely divided on the role of women in America. While most women would have opposed the socialization of housework, thousands willingly exchanged the home and hearth for paid positions in the workplace. For new immigrants and for lower-class women in general, this process brought the dubious emancipation of domestic service, the sweatshop and the shirtwaist factory. But for their wealthier sisters, increased leisure time and education enabled more women to enter the professions and to exert their energies in the cause of social justice. Zona Gale was probably typical of the majority of her peers: She was not a radical feminist determined to make inroads into a male-dominated profession. She was, instead an intelligent and educated professional who had been raised by politically liberal parents to believe that, although of "the weaker sex," she was capable of succeeding.

That success was to be measured not in news column inches but in the publication of her fiction and poetry. Newspaper work had always been nothing more than a means to an end; she had toiled as a reporter because it was a ticket into a world she longed for, a world of intellectual discussion, the arts, and the writing scene of the country's most exciting city. In 1902, she left the *New York World* to move one step closer to that literary scene as the personal secretary to Edmund Clarence Stedman. For two years, she struggled to sell her own work as she typed and edited his.

Finally, in 1903, her fiction began to sell. Between 1903 and 1910, she wrote and sold 83 stories about life in small-town America, her "Friendship Village" tales. In 1911, she entered *Success* Magazine's short-story contest, one of 15,000 submissions; her story, "The American Dawn," took first prize and, with the $2,000 prize money in hand, Gale returned to Portage to live the life of a writer. Throughout the next eight years, she continued to write predictable stories of small-town lives; her work was met with scant public response or critical attention.

And then in 1918, Zona Gale surprised her readers and the country's literary establishment with *Birth*, a major departure from the simplicity and romance of her earlier works. In *Birth*, Gale presents to her readers a painfully realistic portrait of an uncertain little man named Marshall Pitt, a pickle salesman whose most compelling characteristic is his refusal — or inability — to recognize the cruelty and selfishness of those he loves. Even as his wife abandons him, even as his son grows ashamed of him, Pitt proves incapable

---

[10]Ibid, in *Feminism: The Essential Historical Writings*, ed. Miriam Schneir (New York:Random House, 1972), p. 233.

of rejecting or rebuking them. In the name of love, he absorbs their anger and their disgust, certain that his own inadequacies merit their scorn. In *Birth*, Gale presents the classic human conflict between independence and commitment, between responsibility and freedom. Pitt is the ultimate martyr, a man who dies without ever having challenged those who oppressed and ridiculed him. His final words reflect his anguish and despair: "Then at dawn he opened his eyes full upon the room. It was lit by the naked flame of an unshaded lamp, and in that unwonted light, at that unwonted level, there may have seemed many people present. An odd, thin-drawn sound broke from Pitt, and he threw up his hands in their shapeless bandages. 'Say!' he whispered, and the words came like whistling. 'Am I going to die — like a fool?'" Gale's implicit answer is a resounding yes.

Two years later, in 1920, Gale returned to the themes she introduced in *Birth*. *Miss Lulu Bett* is the story of the tyranny of a family, of the superficial niceties that can mask stupid pettiness. In the character of Dwight Deacon, dentist, deacon and head of the house, Gale has created one of fiction's most obnoxious and banal of brothers-in-law; it is Deacon's chief delight to taunt Lulu Bett, to remind her as frequently as possible that she is a spinster dependent upon his goodwill for her keep. When, in an unexpected twist of fate, Lulu finds herself married to Deacon's brother Ninian, she rejoices that the marriage offers escape — from her life as a spinster, from her brother-in-law's home, from the judgmental eyes of her neighbors. But her freedom is short-lived and, when the marriage turns out to be a farce, Lulu once again must choose between her family's needs and her own. Unlike Marshall Pitt, Lulu is no martyr. As she agrees to marry Neil Cornish, she reclaims her self-respect and dignity; not surprisingly, the novel ends with hope and expectation: "The street door was closed. If Mrs. Bett was peeping through the blind, no one saw her. In the pleasant mid-day light under the maples, Mr. and Mrs. Neil Cornish were hurrying toward the railway station." Ironically, Lulu Bett has achieved a personal freedom that Zona Gale would not know until after the death of her own parents in 1923.

As readers and critics mark the 120th anniversary of Zona Gale's birth, her work continues to offer us insights into the social and familial conflicts that surrounded women's roles at the turn of the century. Like so many of the educated, middle-class women of her era, Gale's personal and political lives were a study in contradictions: She was a traditionalist and a ground breaker; a submissive, obedient daughter and an outspoken feminist; a professional newswoman and a writer of stylized romantic fiction; a political progressive and a Midwesterner wedded to the perspectives and mores of small-town America. She was, in short, the embodiment of the dilemma faced by so many women of her day, women forced to balance their education, independence and ambition against the very real demands of their families, their history and their circumscribed place in her world. For Zona Gale, like millions of her nineteenth century sisters, it was a very real dilemma, and *Birth* and *Miss Lulu Bett* resonate with its tensions. For that reason alone, these works merit our attention and our recognition.

-- Dianne Lynch chairs the Journalism Department at St. Michael's College in Burlington, Vt. Zona Gale was the subject of her master's thesis at the University of Wisconsin in Madison.

Publisher's Note

This special edition of *Birth* and *Miss Lulu Bett* is published to mark the 120th anniversary of the birth of Zona Gale in August 1994. It is the first of three volumes to be published by Waubesa Press. The second volume, focusing on Zona Gale's later works, will be published in 1995. The third volume, a collection of Friendship Village stories, is scheduled for publication in 1996.

A goal of this series is to give modern readers the opportunity to appreciate Zona Gale's work. Many of her works, such as *Birth*, have been out of print for over half a century. Some libraries still stock the older editions, but their copies often are tattered or missing pages.

In this edition, we have used modern typography and updated some spellings. Some words used by Zona Gale, such as *dray* (a wagon) or *challie* (a lightweight wool fabric) may be unfamiliar to today's readers. These have been left intact and they provide a flavor of her times.

Miss Lulu Bett

April

The Deacons were at supper. In the middle of the table was a small appealing tulip plant, looking as anything would look whose sun was a gas jet. This gas jet was high above the table and flared, with a sound.

"Better turn down the gas jest a little," Mr. Deacon said, and stretched up to do so. He made this joke almost every night. He seldom spoke as a man speaks who has something to say, but as a man who makes something to say.

"Well, what have we on the festive board tonight?" he questioned, eyeing it. "Festive" was his favorite adjective

"Beautiful," too. In October he might be heard asking: "Where's my beautiful fall coat?"

"We have creamed salmon," replied Mrs. Deacon gently. "On toast," she added, with a scrupulous regard for the whole truth. Why she should say this so gently no one can tell. She says everything gently. Her "Could you leave me another bottle of milk this morning?" would wring a milkman's heart.

"Well, now, let us see," said Mr. Deacon, and attacked the principal dish benignly. "*Let* us see," he added, as he served.

"I don't want any," said Monona.

The child Monona was seated upon a book and a cushion, so that her little triangle of a nose rose adultly above her plate. Her remark produced precisely the effect for which she had passionately hoped.

"*What's* this?" cried Mr. Deacon. "No salmon?"

"No," said Monona, inflected up, chin pertly pointed. She felt her power, discarded her "sir."

"Oh now, Pet!" from Mrs. Deacon, on three notes. "You liked it before."

"I don't want any," said Monona, in precisely her original tone.

"Just a little? A very little?" Mr. Deacon persuaded, spoon dripping.

The child Monona made her lips thin and straight and shook her head until her straight hair flapped in her eyes on either side. Mr. Deacon's eyes anxiously consulted his wife's eyes. What is this? Their progeny will not eat? What can be supplied?

"Some bread and milk!" cried Mrs. Deacon brightly, exploding on "bread." One wondered how she thought of it.

"No," said Monona, inflection up, chin the same. She was affecting indifference to this scene, in which her soul delighted. She twisted her head, bit her lips unconcernedly, and turned her eyes to the remote.

There emerged from the fringe of things, where she perpetually hovered, Mrs. Deacon's older sister, Lulu Bett, who was "making her home with us." And that was precisely the case. They were not making her a home, goodness knows. Lulu was the family beast of burden.

"Can't I make her a little milk toast?" she asked Mrs. Deacon.

Mrs. Deacon hesitated, not with compunction at accepting Lulu's offer, not diplomatically to lure Monona. But she hesitated habitually, by nature, as another is by nature vivacious, or brunette.

"Yes!" shouted the child, Monona.

The tension relaxed. Mrs. Deacon assented. Lulu went to the kitchen. Mr. Deacon served on. Something of this scene was enacted every day. For Monona the drama never lost its zest. It never occurred to the others to let her sit without eating, once, as a cure-all. The Deacons were devoted parents and the child Monona was delicate. She had a white, grave face, white hair, white eyebrows, white lashes. She was sullen, anemic. They let her wear rings. She "toed in." The poor child was the late birth of a late marriage and the principal joy which she had provided them thus far was the pleased reflection that they had produced her at all.

"Where's your mother, Ina?" Mr. Deacon inquired. "Isn't she coming to her supper?"

"Tantrim," said Mrs. Deacon, softly.

"Oh, ho," said he, and said no more.

The temper of Mrs. Bett, who also lived with them, had days of high vibration when she absented herself from the table as a kind of self-indulgence, and no one could persuade her to food. "Tantrims," they called these occasions.

"Baked potatoes," said Mr. Deacon. "That's good — that's good. The baked potato contains more nourishment than potatoes prepared in any other way. The nourishment is next to the skin. Roasting retains it."

"That's what I always think," said his wife pleasantly. For fifteen years, they had agreed about this.

They ate in the indecent silence of first savoring food. A delicate crunching of crust, an odor of baked potato shells, the slip and touch of silver.

"Num, num, nummy-num!" sang the child Monona loudly, and was hushed by both parents in simultaneous exclamation which rivalled this lyric outburst. They were alone at table. Di, daughter of a wife early lost to Mr. Deacon, was not there. Di was hardly ever there. She was at that age. That age, in Warbleton.

A clock struck the half hour.

"It's curious," Mr. Deacon observed, "how that clock loses. It must be fully quarter to." He consulted his watch. "It is quarter to!" he exclaimed with satisfaction. "I'm pretty good at guessing time."

"I've noticed that!" cried his Ina.

"Last night, it was only twenty-three to, when the half hour struck," he reminded her.

"Twenty one, I thought." She was tentative, regarded him with arched eyebrows, mastication suspended.

This point was never to be settled. The colloquy was interrupted by the child Monona, whining for her toast. And the doorbell rang.

"Dear me!" said Mr. Deacon. "What can anybody be thinking of to call just at mealtime?"

He trod the hall, flung open the street door. Mrs. Deacon listened. Lulu, coming in with the toast, was warned to silence by an uplifted finger. She deposited the toast, tiptoed to her chair. A withered baked potato and cold creamed salmon were on her plate. The child Monona ate with hocking appreciation. Nothing could be made of the voices in the hall. But Mrs. Bett's door was heard softly to unlatch. She, too, was listening.

A ripple of excitement was caused in the dining room when Mr. Deacon was divined to usher some one to the parlor. Mr. Deacon would speak with this visitor in a few moments, and now returned to his table. It was notable how slight a thing would give him a sense of self-importance. Now he felt himself a man of affairs, could not even have a quiet supper with his family without the outside world demanding him. He waved his hand to indicate it was nothing which they would know anything about, resumed his seat, served himself to a second spoon of salmon and remarked, "More roast duck, anybody?" in a loud voice and with a wink at his wife. That lady at first looked blank, as she always did in the presence of any humor couched with the least indirection, and then drew back her chin and lower lip in her gold-filled teeth. This was her conjugal rebuking.

Swedenborg always uses "conjugial." And really this sounds more married. It should be used with reference to the Deacons. No one was ever more married than Mr. Deacon. He made little conjugal jokes in the presence of Lulu who, now completely unnerved by the habit, suspected them where they did not exist, feared lurking entendre in the most innocent comments, and became more tense every hour of her life.

And now the eye of the master of the house fell for the first time upon the yellow tulip in the center of his table.

"Well, *well!*" he said. "What's this?"

Ina Deacon produced, fleetly, an unlooked-for dimple.

"Have you been buying flowers?" the master inquired.

"Ask Lulu," said Mrs. Deacon.

He turned his attention full upon Lulu.

"Suitors?" he inquired, and his lips left their places to form a sort of ruff about the word.

Lulu flushed, and her eyes and their very brows appealed.

"It was a quarter," she said. "There'll be five flowers."

"You *bought* it?"

"Yes. There'll be five — that's a nickel apiece."

His tone was as methodical as if he had been talking about the bread.

"Yet we give you a home on the supposition you have no money to spend, even for the necessities."

His voice, without resonance, cleft air, thought, spirit, and even flesh.

Mrs. Deacon, indeterminately feeling her guilt in having let loose the dogs of her husband upon Lulu, interposed: "Well, but, Herbert — Lulu isn't strong enough to work. What's the use. . . ."

She dwindled. For years the fiction been sustained that Lulu, the family beast of burden, was not strong enough to work anywhere else.

"The justice business—" said Dwight Herbert Deacon— he was a justice of the peace — "and the dental profession-" he was also a dentist — "do not warrant the purchase of spring flowers in my home."

"Well, but, Herbert—" It was his wife again.

"No more," he cried briefly, with a slight bend of his head. "Lulu meant no harm," he added, and smiled at Lulu.

There was a moment's silence into which Monona injected a loud "Num, num, numly-num," as if she were the burden of an Elizabethan lyric. She seemed to close the incident. But the burden was cut off untimely. There was, her father reminded her portentously, company in the parlor.

"When the bell rang, I was so afraid something had happened to Di," said Ina sighing.

"Let's see," said Di's father. "Where is little daughter tonight?"

He must have known that she was at Jenny Plow's at a tea party, for at noon they had talked of nothing else; but this was his way. And Ina played his game, always. She informed him, dutifully.

"Oh, *ho*," said he, absently. How could he be expected to keep his mind on these domestic trifles.

"We told you that at noon," said Lulu. He frowned, disregarded her. Lulu had no delicacy.

"How much is salmon the can now?" he inquired abruptly — this was one of his forms of speech, the can, the pound, the cord.

His partner supplied this information with admirable promptness. Large size, small size, present price, former price— she had them all.

"Dear me," said Mr. Deacon. "That is very nearly salmoney, isn't it?"

"Herbert!" his Ina admonished, in gentle, gentle reproach. Mr. Deacon punned, organically. In talk he often fell silent and then asked some question, schemed to permit his vice to flourish. Mrs. Deacon's return was always automatic. *"Herbert!"*

"Whose Bert?" he said to this. "I thought I was your Bert."

She shook her little head. "You are a case," she told him. He beamed upon her. It was his intention to be a case.

Lulu ventured in upon this pleasantry, and cleared her throat, She was not hoarse, but she was always clearing her throat.

"The butter is about all gone," she observed. "Shall I wait for the butter-woman or get some creamery?"

Mr. Deacon now felt his little jocularity lost before a wall of the matter of fact. He was not pleased. He saw himself as the light of his home, bringer of brightness, lightener of dull hours. It was a pretty role. He insisted upon it. To maintain it intact, it was necessary to turn upon their sister with concentrated irritation.

"Kindly settle these matters without bringing them to my attention at meal-time," he said icily.

Lulu flushed and was silent. She was an olive woman, once handsome, now with light, bluish shadows under her wistful eyes. And if only she would look at her brother Herbert and say something. But she looked in her plate.

"I want some honey," shouted the child, Monona.

"There isn't any, Pet," said Lulu.

"I want some," said Monona, eyeing her stonily. But she found that her hair ribbon could be pulled forward to meet her lips, and she embarked on the biting of an end. Lulu departed for some sauce and cake. It was apple sauce. Mr. Deacon remarked that the apples were almost as good as if he had stolen them. He was giving the impression that he was an irrepressible fellow. He was eating very slowly. It added pleasantly to his sense of importance to feel that some one, there in the parlor, was waiting his motion.

At length they rose. Monona flung herself upon her father. He put her aside firmly, every inch the father. No, no. Father was occupied now. Mrs. Deacon coaxed her away. Monona encircled her mother's waist, lifted her own feet from the floor and hung upon her. "She such an active child," Lulu ventured brightly.

"Not unduly active I think," her brother-in-law observed.

He turned upon Lulu his bright smile, lifted his eyebrows, dropped his lids, stood for a moment contemplating the yellow tulip, and so left the room.

Lulu cleared the table. Mrs. Deacon essayed to wind the clock. Well now. Did Herbert say it was twenty-three tonight when it struck the half hour and twenty-nine last night, or twenty-one tonight and last night twenty-three? She talked of it as they cleared the table, but Lulu did not talk.

"Can't you remember?" Mrs. Deacon said at last. "I should think you might be useful."

Lulu was lifting the yellow tulip to set it on the sill. She changed her mind. She took the plant to the woodshed and tumbled it with force upon the chip pile.

The dining-room table was laid for breakfast.   The two women brought their work and sat there. The child Monona hung miserably about, watching the clock. Right or wrong, she was put to bed by it. She had eight minutes more — seven — six — five.

Lulu laid down her sewing and left the room. She went to the wood-shed, groped about in the dark, found the stalk of one tulip flower in its heap on the chip pile. The tulip she fastened in her gown on her flat chest.

Outside were to be seen the early stars. It is said that if our sun were as near to Arcturus as we are near to our sun, the great Arcturus would burn our sun to nothingness.

In the Deacons' parlor sat Bobby Larkin, eighteen. He was in pain all over. He was come on an errand with civilization had contrived to make an ordeal.

Before him on the table stood a photograph of Diana Deacon, also eighteen. He hated her with passion. At school she mocked him, aped him, whispered about him, tortured him. For two years he had hated her. Nights he fell asleep planning to build a great house and engage her as its servant.

Yet, as he waited, he could not keep his this eyes from this photo-graph. It was Di at her curliest, at her fluffiest, Di conscious of her bracelet, Di smiling. Bobby gazed, his basic aversion to her hard-pressed by a most reluctant pleasure. He hoped that he would not see her, and he would not see her, and he listened for her voice.

Mr.. Deacon descended upon him with an air carried from his sup-per hour, bland, dispensing. Well! Let's have it. "What did you wish to see me about?" — with a use of the past tense as connoting something of indi-rection and hence of delicacy — a nicety customary, yet unconscious. Bobby had arrived in his best clothes and with an air of such formality that Mr. Deacon had instinctively suspected him of wanting to join the church, and, to treat the time with due solemnity, had put him the parlor until he could attend at leisure.

Confronted thus by Di's father, the speech which Bobby had planned deserted him.

" I thought if you would give me a job," he said defenselessly.

"So that's it!" Mr. Deacon, who always awaited but a touch to be either irritable or facetious, inclined now to be facetious. "Filling teeth?" he would know. "Marrying folks, then?" Assistant justice or assistant dentist — which?

Bobby blushed. No, no, but in that big building of Mr. Deacon's where his office was, wasn't there something . . . It faded from him, sounded ridiculous. Of course there was nothing. He saw it now.

There was nothing. Mr. Deacon confirmed him. But Mr. Deacon had an idea.   Hold on, he said — hold on. The grass. Would Bobby con-sider taking charge of the grass? Though Mr. Deacon was of the type which cuts its own grass and glories in its vigor and its energy, yet in the time after that which he called "dental hours" Mr. Deacon wished to work in his gar-den. His grass, growing in late April rains, would need attention early next month. . . he owned two lots — "Of course property is a burden." If Bobby would care to keep the grass down and raked . . . Bobby would care, accepted this business opportunity, figures and all, thanked Mr. Deacon with earnestness. Bobby's aversion to Di, it seemed, should not stand in the way of his advancement.

"Then that is checked off," said Mr.. Deacon heartily. Bobby wavered toward the door, emerged on the porch, and ran almost upon Di returning from her tea-party at Jenny Plow's.

"Oh, Bobby You came to see me?" She was as fluffy, as curly, as smiling as her picture. She was carrying pink, gauzy favors and a spear of flowers. Undeniably in her voice there was pleasure. Her glance was startled but already complacent. She paused on the steps, a lovely figure.

"Oh, hullo," said he. "No. I came to see your father."

He marched by her. His hair stuck up at the back. His coat was hunched about his shoulders. His insufficient nose, abundant, loose-lipped mouth and brown eyes were completely expressionless. He marched by her without a glance.

She flushed with vexation. Mr. Deacon, as one would expect, laughed loudly, took the situation in his elephantine grasp and pawed at it.

"Mamma! Mamma! What do you s'pose? Di thought she had a beau—"

"Oh, papa!" said Di. "Why, I just hate Bobby Larkin and the whole school knows it."

Mr. Deacon returned to the dining room, humming in his throat. He entered upon a pretty scene.

His Ina was darning. Four minutes of grace remaining to the child Monona, she was spinning on one toe with some Bacchanalian idea of making the most of the present. Di dominated, her ruffles, her blue hose, her bracelet, her ring.

"Oh, and mamma," she said, "the sweetest party and the dearest supper and the darlingest decorations and the gorgeousest — "

"Grammar, grammar," spoke Dwight Herbert Deacon. He was not sure what he meant, but the good fellow felt some violence done somewhere or other.

"Well," said Di positively. "they *were,* Papa, see my favor."

She showed him a sugar dove, and he clucked at it.

Ina glanced at them fondly, her face assuming its loveliest light. She was often ridiculous, but always she was the happy wife and mother, and her role reduced her individual absurdities at least to its own.

The door to the bedroom now opened and Mrs. Bett appeared.

"Well, mother!" cried Herbert, the "well" curving like an arm, the "mother" descending like a brisk slap. "Hungry *now?*"

Mrs. Bett was hungry now. She had emerged intending to pass through the room without speaking and find food in the pantry. By obscure processes her son-in-law's tone inhibited all this.

"No," she said. "I'm not hungry."

Now that she was there, she seemed uncertain what to do. She looked from one to another a bit hopelessly, somehow for foiled in her dignity. She brushed at her skirt, the veins of her long, wrinkled hands catching an more intense blue from the dark cloth. She put her hair behind her ears.

"We put a potato in the oven for you," said Ina. She had never learned quite how to treat these periodic refusals of her mother to eat, but she never had ceased to resent them.

"No, thank you," said Mrs.. Bett. Evidently she rather enjoyed the situation, creating for herself a spotlight much in the manner of Monona.

"Mother," said Lulu, "let me maybe you some toast and tea."

Mrs. Bett turned her gentle, bloodless face toward her daughter, and her eyes warmed.

"After a little, maybe," she said. "I think I'll run over to see Grandma Gates now," she added, and went toward the door.

"Tell her," cried Dwight, "tell her she's my best girl."

Grandma Gates was a rheumatic cripple who lived next door, and whenever the Deacons or Mrs. Bett were angry or hurt or wished to escape the house for some reason, they stalked over to Grandma Gates — in lieu of, say, slamming a door. These visits radiated an almost daily friendliness which lifted and tempered the old invalid's lot in life.

Di flashed out at the door again, on some trivial permission.

"A good many of mamma's stitches in that dress to keep clean," Ina called after.

"Early, darling, early!" her father reminded her. A faint regurgitation of his was somehow invested with the paternal.

"What's this?' cried Dwight Herbert Deacon abruptly.

On the clock shelf lay a letter.

"Oh, Dwight!" Ina was all compunction. "It came this morning. I forgot."

"I forgot it too! And I laid it up there." Lulu was eager for her share of the blame.

"Isn't it understood that my mail can't wait like this?"

Dwight's sense of importance was being fed in gulps.

"I know. I'm awfully sorry," Lulu said, "but you hardly ever get a letter—"

This might make things worse, but it provided Dwight with a greater importance.

"Of course, pressing matter goes to my office," he admitted it. "Still, my mail should have more careful—"

He read, frowning. He replaced the letter, and they hung upon his motions as he tapped the envelope returned regarded them.

"Now!" said he. "What do you think I have to tell you?"

"Something nice," Ina was sure.

"Something surprising," Dwight said portentously.

"But, Dwight, is it *nice?*" from his Ina.

"That depends. I like it. So'll Lulu." He leered at her. "It's company."

"Oh, Dwight," said Ina. "Who?"

"From Oregon," he said, toying with his suspense.

"Your brother!" cried Ina. "Is he coming?"

"Yes. Ninian's coming, so he says."

"Ninian!" cried Ina again. She was excited, round-eyed, her moist lips parted. Dwight's brother Ninian. How long was it? Nineteen years. South America, Central America, Mexico, Panama "and all." When was he coming and what was he coming for?

"To see me," said Dwight. "To meet you. Some day next week. He don't know what a charmer Lulu is, or he'd come quicker."

Lulu blushed terribly. Not from the implication. But from the knowledge that she was not a charmer.

The clock struck. The child Monona uttered a cutting shriek. Herbert's eyes flew not only to the child but to his wife. What was this, was their progeny hurt?

"Bedtime," his wife elucidated, and added: "Lulu, will you take her to bed? I'm pretty tired."

Lulu rose and took Monona by the hand, the child hanging back and shaking her straight hair in an unconvincing negative.

As they crossed the room, Dwight Herbert Deacon, strolling about and snapping his fingers, halted and cried out sharply:

"Lulu. One moment!"

He approached her. A finger was extended, his lips were parted, on his forehead was a frown.

"You *picked* the flower on the plant?" he asked incredulously.

Lulu made no reply. But the child Monona felt herself lifted and borne to the stairway and the door was shut with violence. On the dark stairway Lulu's arms closed about her in an embrace which left her breathless and squeaking. And yet Lulu was not really fond of the child Monona, either. This is a discharge of emotion akin, say, to slamming a door.

May

Lulu was dusting the parlor. The parlor was rarely used, but every morning it was dusted. By Lulu.

She dusted the black walnut center table which was of Ina's choosing, and looked like Ina, shining, complacent, abundantly curved. The leather rocker, too, looked like Ina, brown, plumply upholstered, tipping back a bit. Really, the davenport looked like Ina, for its chintz pattern seemed to bear a design of lifted eyebrows and arch, reproachful eyes.

Lulu dusted the upright piano, and that was like Dwight in a perpetual attitude of rearing back, with paws out, playful, but capable, too, of roaring a ready bass.

And the black fireplace — there was Mrs. Bett to the life. Colorless, fireless, and with a dust of ashes.

In the midst of all was Lulu herself reflected in the narrow pier glass, bodiless looking in her blue gingham gown, but somehow alive. Natural.

This pier glass Lulu approached with expectation, not because of herself but because of the photograph on its low marble shelf. A large photograph on a little shelf easel. A photograph of a man with evident ears, evident lips, evident cheeks — and each of the six were rounded and convex. You could construct the rest of him. Down there under the glass you could imagine him extending, rounded and convex, with plump hands and curly thumbs and snug clothes. It was Ninian Deacon, Dwight's brother.

Every day since his coming had been announced Lulu, dusting the parlor, had seen the photograph looking at her with its eyes somehow new. Or were her own eyes new? She dusted this photograph with a difference, lifted, dusted, set it back, less as a process than as an experience. As she dusted the mirror and saw his trim resemblance over against her own bodiless reflection, she hurried away. But the eyes of he picture followed her, and she liked it.

She dusted the south window sill and saw Bobby Larkin come round the house and go to the woodshed for the lawn mower. She heard the smooth blur of the cutter. Not six times had Bobby traversed the lawn when Lulu saw Di emerge from the house. Di had been caring for her canary and she carried her birdbath and went to the well, and Lulu divined that Di had deliberately disregarded the handy kitchen taps. Lulu dusted the south window and watched, and in her watching was no quality of spying or of criticism. Nor did she watch wistfully. Rather, she looked out on something in which she had never shared, could not by any chance imagine herself sharing.

The south windows were open. Airs of May bore the soft talking.

"Oh, Bobby, will you pump while I hold this?" And again: "Now wait till I rinse."

And again : "You needn't be so glum" — the village salutation signifying kindly attention.

Bobby now first spoke: "Who's glum?" he countered gloomily.

The iron of those days when she had laughed at him was deep within him, and this she now divined, and said absently:

"I used to think you were pretty nice. But I don't like you any more."

"Yes, you used to!" Bobby repeated derisively. "Is that why you made fun of me all the time."

At this Di colored and tapped her foot on the well-curb. He seemed to have her now, and enjoyed his triumph. But Di looked up at him shyly and looked down. "I had to," she admitted. "They were all teasing me about you."

"They were?" This was a new thought to him. Teasing her about him, were they? He straightened. "Huh!" he said in magnificent evasion.

"I had to make them stop, so I teased you. I-I never wanted to." Again the upward look.

"Well!" Bobby stared at her. "I never thought it was anything like that."

"Of course you didn't." She tossed back her bright hair, met his eyes full. "And you never came where I could tell you. I wanted to tell you."

She ran into the house.

Lulu lowered her eyes. It was as if she had witnessed the exercise of some secret gift, had seen a cocoon open or an egg hatch. She was thinking:

"How easy she done it. Got him right over. But *how*, did she do that?"

Dusting the Dwight-like piano, Lulu looked over-shoulder, with a manner of speculation, at the photograph of Ninian.

Bobby mowed and pondered. The magnificent conceit of the male in his understanding of the female character was sufficiently developed to cause him to welcome the improvisation which he had just heard. Perhaps this was the way it had been. Of course that was the way it had been. What a fool he had been not to understand. He cast his eyes repeatedly toward the house. He managed to make the job last over so that he could return in the afternoon. He was not conscious of planning this, but it was in some manner contrived for him by forces of his own with which he seemed to be cooperating without his conscious will. Continually he glanced toward the house.

These glances Lulu saw. She was a woman of thirty-four and Di and Bobby were eighteen, but Lulu felt for them no adult indulgence. She felt that sweetness of attention which we bestow upon May robins. She felt more.

She cut a fresh cake, filled a plate, called to Di, saying: "Take some out to that Bobby Larkin, why don't you?"

It was Lulu's way of participating. It was her vicarious thrill.

After supper Dwight and Ina took their books and departed to the Chautauqua Circle. To these meetings Lulu never went. The reason seemed to be that she never went anywhere.

When they were gone Lulu felt an instant liberation. She turned aimlessly to the garden and dug round things with her finger. And she thought about the brightness of that Chautauqua scene to which Ina and Dwight had gone. Lulu thought about such gatherings in somewhat the way that a futurist receives the subjects of his art — forms not vague, but heightened to intolerable definiteness, acute color, and always motion — motion as an integral part of the desirable. But a factor of all was that Lulu herself was the participant, not the onlooker. The perfection of her dream was lot impaired by any longing. She had her dream as a saint her sense of heaven.

"Lulie!" her mother called. "You come out of that damp."

She obeyed, as she had obeyed that voice all her life. But she took one last look down the dim street. She had not known it, but superimposed on her Chautauqua thoughts had been her faint hope that it would be to-night, while she was in the garden alone, that Ninian Deacon would arrive. And she had on her wool challie, her coral beads, her cameo pin. . . .

She went into the lighted dining room. Monona was in bed. Di was not there. Mrs. Bett was in Dwight Herbert's leather chair and she lolled at her ease. It was strange to see this woman, usually so erect and tense, now actually lolling, as if lolling were the positive, the vital, and her ordinarily rigidity a negation of her. In some corresponding orgy of leisure and liberation, Lulu sat down with no needle.

"Inie ought to make over her delaine," Mrs. Bett comfortably began. They talked of this, devised a mode, recalled other delaines. "Dear, dear," said Mrs. Bett, "I had on a delaine when I met your father." She described it. Both women talked freely, with animation. They were individuals and alive. To the two pallid beings accessory to the Deacons' presence, Mrs. Bett and her daughter Lulu now bore no relationship. They emerged, had opinions, contradicted, their eyes were bright.

Toward nine o'clock Mrs. Bett announced that she thought she should have a lunch. This was debauchery. She brought in bread and butter, and a dish of cold canned peas. She was committing all the excesses that she knew — offering opinions, laughing, eating. It was to be seen that this woman had an immense store of vitality, perpetually submerged.

When she had eaten she grew sleepy — rather cross at the last and inclined to hold up her sister's excellencies to Lulu; and, at Lulu's defense, lifted an ancient weapon.

"What's the use of finding fault with Inie? Where's you been if she hadn't married?"

Lulu said nothing.

"What say?" Mrs.. Bett demanded shrilly. She was enjoying it.

Lulu said no more. After a long time:

"You always was jealous of Inie," said Mrs. Bett, and went to her bed.

As soon as her mother's door had closed, Lulu took the lamp from its bracket, stretching up her long body and her long arms until her skirt lifted to show her really slim and pretty feet. Lulu's feet gave news of some other Lulu, but slightly incarnate. Perhaps, so far, incarnate only in her feet and her long hair.

She took the lamp to the parlor and stood before the photograph of Ninian Deacon, and looked her fill . She did not admire the photograph, but she wanted to look at it. The house was still, there was no possibility of interruption. The occasion became sensation, which she made no effort to quench. She held a rendezvous with she knew not what.

In the early hours of the next afternoon with the sun shining across the threshold, Lulu was paring something at the kitchen table. Mrs. Bett was asleep. ("I don't blame you a bit, mother," Lulu had said, as her mother named the intention.) Ina was asleep. (But Ina always took off the curse by calling it her "si-esta," long i.) Monona was playing with a neighbor's child, you heard their shrill yet lovely laughter as they obeyed the adult law that motion is pleasure. Di was not there.

A man came round the house and stood tying a puppy to the porch post. A long shadow fell through the west doorway, the puppy whined.

"Oh," said this man. "I didn't mean to arrive at the back door, but since I'm here —" He lifted a suitcase to the porch, entered, and filled the kitchen.

"It's Ina, isn't it?" he said.

"I'm her sister," said Lulu, and understood that he was here at last.

"Well, I'm Bert's brother," said Ninian. "So I can come in, can't I?"

He did so, turned round like a dog before his chair and sat down heavily, forcing his fingers through heavy, upspringing brown hair.

"Oh, yes," said Lulu. "I'll call Ina. She's asleep."

"Don't call her, then," said Ninian. "Let's you and I get acquainted." He said it absently, hardly looking at her.

"I'll get the pup a drink if you can spare me a basin," he added.

Lulu brought the basin, and while he went to the dog she ran tiptoeing to the dining room china closet and brought a cut-glass tumbler, as heavy, as ungainly as a stone crock. This she filled with milk.

"I thought maybe. . ." said she and offered it.

"Thank *you!*" said Ninian, and drained it. "Making pies, as I live," he observed, and brought his chair nearer to the table. "I didn't know Ina had a sister," he went on. "I remember now Bert said he had two of her relatives—"

Lulu flushed and glanced at him pitifully.

"He has," she said. "It's my mother and me. But we do quite a good deal of the work."

"I'll bet you do," said Ninian, and did not perceive that anything had been violated. "What's your name?" he bethought.

She was in an immense and obscure excitement. Her manner was serene, her hands as they went on with the peeling did not tremble; her replies were given with sufficient quiet. But she told him her name as one tells something of another and more remote creature. She felt as one may feel it in catastrophe — no sharp understanding but merely the sense that the thing cannot possibly be happening.

"You folks expect me?" he went on.

"Oh, yes," she cried, almost with vehemence. "Why, we've looked for every day."

"See," he said, "how long have they been married?"

Lulu flushed as she answered: "Fifteen years."

"And a year before that the first one died — and two years they were married," he computed. "I never met that one. Then it's close to twenty years since Bert and I have seen each other."

"How awful," Lulu said, and flushed again.

"Why?"

"To be that long away from your folks."

Suddenly she found herself facing this honestly, as if the immensity of her present experience were clarifying her understanding: Would it be so awful to be away from Bert and Monona and Di — yes, and Ina, for twenty years?

"You think that?" he laughed. "A man don't know what he's like till he's roamed around on his own." He liked the sound of it. "Roamed around on his own," he repeated, and laughed again. "Course a woman don't know that."

"Why don't she?" asked Lulu. She balanced a pie on her hand and carved the crust. She was stupefied to her own question. "Why don't she?"

"Maybe she does. Do you?"

"Yes," said Lulu.

"Good enough!" He applauded noiselessly, with fat hands. His diamond ring sparkled, his even white teeth flashed. "I've had twenty years of galloping about," he informed her, unable, after all, to transfer his interests from himself to her.

"Where?" she asked, although she knew.

"South America. Central America. Mexico. Panama." He searched his memory. "Colombo," he super-added.

"My!" said Lulu. She had probably never in her life had the least desire to see any of these places. She did not want to see them now. But she wanted passionately to meet her companion's mind.

"It's the life," he informed her.

"Must be," Lulu breathed. "I — " she tried, and gave it up.

"Where you been mostly?" he asked at last.

By this unprecedented interest in her doings she was thrown into a passion of excitement.

"Here," she said. "I've always been here. Fifteen years with Ina. Before that we lived in the country."

He listened sympathetically now, his head well on one side. He watched her veined hands pinch at the pies. "Poor old girl," he was thinking.

"Is it Miss Lulu Bett?" he abruptly inquired. "Or Mrs.?"

Lulu flushed in anguish.

"Miss," she said low, as one who confesses the extremity of failure. Then from unplumbed depths another Lulu abruptly spoke up. "From choice," she said.

He shouted with laughter.

"You bet! Oh, you bet!" he cried. "Never doubted it." He made his palms taut and drummed on the table. "Say!" he said.

Lulu glowed, quickened, smiled. Her face was another face.

"Which kind of a Mr. are you?" she heard herself ask, and his shoutings redoubled. Well! Who would have thought it of her?

"Never give myself away," he assured her. "Say, by George, I never thought of that before! There's no telling whether a man's married or not, by his name!"

"It don't matter," said Lulu.

"Why not?"

"Not so many people want to know."

Again, he laughed. This laughter was intoxicating to Lulu. No one ever laughed at what she said save Herbert, who laughed at *her*. "Go it, old girl!" Ninian was thinking, but this did not appear.

The child Monona now arrived, banging the front gate and hurling herself round the house on the board walk, catching the toe of one foot in the heel of the other and blundering forward, head down, her short, straight hair flapping over her face. She landed flat-footed on the porch. She began to speak, using a ridiculous perversion of words, scarcely articulate, then in vogue in her group. And,

"Whose dog?" she shrieked.

Ninian looked over his shoulder, held out his hand, finished something that he saying to Lulu. Monona came to him readily enough, staring, loose-lipped.

"I'll bet I'm your uncle," said Ninian.

Relationship being her highest known form of romance, Monona was thrilled by this intelligence.

"Give us a kiss," said Ninian, finding in the plural some vague mitigation for some vague offense.

Monona, looking silly, complied. And her uncle said my stars, such a great big tall girl — they would have to put a board on her head.

"What's that?" inquired Monona. She had spied his great diamond ring.

"This," said her uncle, "was brought to me by Santa Claus, who keeps a jewelry shop in heaven."

The precision and speed of his improvisation revealed him. He had twenty other diamonds like this one. He kept them for those Sundays when the sun comes up in the west. Of course — often! Some day he was going to melt a diamond and eat it. Then you sparkled all over in the dark, ever after. Another diamond he was going to plant. They say — He did it all gravely, absorbingly. About it he was as conscienceless as a savage. This was no fancy spun to pleasure a child. This was like lying, for its own sake.

He went on talking with Lulu, and now again he was the tease, the braggart, the unbridled, unmodified male.

Monona stood in the circle of his arm. The little being was attentive, softened, subdued. Some pretty, faint light visited her. In her listening look, she showed herself a charming child.

"It strikes me," said Ninian to Lulu, "that you're going to do something mighty interesting before you die."

It was the clear conversational impulse, born of the need to keep something going but Lulu was all faith.

She closed the oven door on her pies and stood brushing flour from her fingers. He was looking away from her, and she looked at him. He was completely like his picture. She felt as if she were looking at his picture and she was abashed and turned away.

"Well, I hope so," she said, which had certainly never been true, for her old formless dreams were no intention — nothing but a mush of discontent. "I hope I can do something that's nice before I quit," she said. Nor was this hope now independently true, but only this surprising longing to appear interesting in his eyes. To dance before him. "What would the folks think of me, going on so?" she suddenly said. Her mild sense of disloyalty was delicious. So was his understanding glance.

"You're the stuff," he remarked absently.

She laughed happily.

The door opened. Ina appeared.

"Well!" said Ina. It was her remotest tone. She took this man to be a peddler, beheld her child in his clasp, made a quick, forward step, chin lifted. She had time for a very javelin of a look at Lulu.

"Hello!" said Ninian. He had the one formula. "I believe I'm your husband's brother. Ain't this Ina?"

It had not crossed the mind of Lulu to present him.

Beautiful it was to see Ina relax, soften, warm, transform, humanize. It gave one hope for the whole species.

"Ninian!" she cried. She lent a faint impression of the double *e* to the initial vowel. She slurred the rest, until the *y* sound squinted in. Not Ninian, but nearly Neenyun.

He kissed her.

"Since Dwight isn't here!" she cried, and shook her finger at him. Ina's conception of hostess-ship was definite: A volley of questions — was his train on time? He had found the house all right? Of course! Anyone could direct him, she should hope. And he hadn't seen Dwight? She must telephone him. But then she arrested herself with a sharp, curved fling of her starched skirts. No! They would surprise him at tea — she stood taut, lips compressed. Oh, the Plows were coming to tea. How unfortunate, she thought. How fortunate, she said.

The child Monona made her knee and elbows stiff and danced up and down. She must, she must participate.

"Aunt Lulu made three pies!" she screamed and shook her straight hair.

"Gracious sakes," said Ninian. "I brought her a pup, and if I didn't forget to give it to her."

They adjourned to the porch — Ninian, Ina, Monona. The puppy was presented, and yawned. The party kept on about "the place." Ina delightedly exhibited the tomatoes, the two apple trees, the new shed, the bird bath. Ninian said the unspellable "m-m," rising inflection, and the "I see," prolonging the verb as was expected of him. Ina said they meant to build a summer-house, only, dear me, when you have a family — but there, he didn't know anything about that. Ina was using her eyes, she was arch, she was coquettish, she was flirtatious, and she believed herself to be merely matronly, sisterly, womanly . . .

She screamed, Dwight was at the gate. Now the meeting, exclamation, banality, guffaw . . . good will.

And Lulu, peeping through the blind.

When "tea" had been experienced that evening, it was found that a light rain was falling and the Deacons and their guests, the Plows, were constrained to remain in the parlor. The Plows were gentle, faintly lustrous folk, sketched into life rather lightly, as if they were, say, looking in from some other level.

"The only thing," said Dwight Herbert, "that reconciles me to rain is that I'm let off croquet." He rolled his *r*'s, a favorite device of his to induce humor. He called it "croquette." He had never been more irrepressible. The advent of his brother was partly accountable, the need to show himself a fine family man and host in a prosperous little home — simple and pathetic desire.

"Tell you what we'll do!" said Dwight. "Nin and I'll reminisce a little."

"Do!" cried Mr. Plow. This gentle fellow was always excited by life, so faintly excited by him, and enjoyed its presentation in any real form.

Ninian had unerringly selected a dwarf rocker, and he was overflowing it and rocking.

"Take this chair, do!" Ina begged. "A big chair for a big man." She spoke as if he were about the age of Monona.

Ninian refused, insisted on his refusal. A few years more, and human relationships would have spread sanity even to Ina's estate and she would have told him why he should change chairs. As it was she forbore, and kept glancing anxiously at the over-burdened little beast beneath him.

The child Monona entered the room. She had been driven down by Di and Jenny Plow, who had vanished upstairs and, through the ventilators, might be heard in a lift and fall of giggling. Monona had also been driven from the kitchen where Lulu was, for some reason, hurrying through the dishes. Monona now ran to Mrs. Bett, stood beside her and stared about resentfully. Mrs.. Bett was in best black and ruches, and she seized upon Monona and patted her, as her form of social expression; and Monona wriggled like a puppy, as hers.

"Quiet, pretty," said Ina, eyebrows up. She caught her lower lip in her teeth.

"Well, sir," said Dwight, "you wouldn't think it to look at us, but mother had her hands pretty full, bringing us up."

Into Dwight's face came another look. It was always so, when he spoke of this foster-mother who had taken these two boys and seen them through the graded schools. This woman Dwight adored, and when he spoke of her he became his inner self.

"We must run upstate and see her you're here, Nin," he said.

To this Ninian gave a casual assent, lacking his brother's really tender ardor.

"Little," Dwight pursued, "little did she think I'd settle down into a nice, quiet married dentist and magistrate in my town. And Nin into — say, Nin what are you, anyway?"

They laughed.

"There's the question," said Ninian.

They laughed.

"Maybe," Ina ventured, "maybe Ninian will tell us something about his travels. He is quite a traveller, you know," she said to the Plows. "A regular Gulliver."

They laughed respectfully.

"How we should love it, Mr. Deacon," Mrs. Plow said. "You know we've never seen *very* much."

Goaded on. Ninian launched upon his foreign countries as he had seen them: Population, exports, imports, soil; irrigation, business. For the populations Ninian had no respect. Crops could not touch ours. Soil mighty poor pickings. And the business — say! Those fellows don't know — and, say, the hotels! Don't say foreign hotel to Ninian.

He regarded all the alien earth as barbarian, and he stoned it. He was equipped for absolutely no intensive observation. His contacts were negligible. Mrs. Plow was more excited by the Deacons' party than Ninian had been wrought upon by all his voyaging.

"Tell you," said Dwight. "When we ran away that time and went to the state fair, little did we think—" He told about running away to the state fair. "I thought," he wound up, irrelevantly, "Ina and I might get over to the other side this year, but I guess not. I guess not."

The words give no conception of their effect, spoken thus. For there in Warbleton these words are not commonplace. In Warbleton, Europe is never so casually spoken. "Take a trip abroad" is the phrase or "Go to Europe" at the very least, and both with impressment. Dwight had somewhere noted and deliberately picked up that "other side" effect, and his Ina knew this, and was proud. Her covert glance about pensively covered her soft triumph.

Mrs. Bett, her arm still circling the child Monona, now made her first observation.

"Pity not to have went while the going was good," she said, and said no more.

Nobody knew quite what she meant, and everybody hoped for the best. But Ina frowned. Mamma did these things occasionally when there was company, and she dared. She never sauced Dwight in private. And it wasn't fair, it wasn't *fair* —

Abruptly Ninian rose and left the room.

The dishes were washed. Lulu had washed them at break-neck speed — she could not, or would not, have told why. But no sooner were they finished and set away when Lulu had been attacked by an unconquerable inhibition. And instead of going to the parlor, she sat down by the kitchen window. She was in her chally gown, with her cameo pin and her string of coral.

Laughter from the parlor mingled with the laughter of Di and Jenny upstairs. Lulu was now rather shy of Di. A night or two before, coming home with "extra" cream, she had gone round to the side-door and had come full upon Di and Bobby, seated on the steps. And Di was saying: "Well, if I marry you, you've simply got to be a great man. I could never marry just anybody. I'd *smother.*"

Lulu had heard, stricken. She passed them by, responding only faintly to their greeting. Di was far less taken aback than Lulu.

Later Di had said to Lulu: "I suppose you heard what we were saying." Lulu, much shaken, had withdrawn from the whole matter by a flat "no." "Because," she said to herself, "I couldn't have heard right."

But since then she had looked at Di as if Di were some one else. Had not Lulu taught her to make buttonholes and to hem — oh, no! Lulu could not have heard properly.

"Everybody's got somebody to be nice to them," she thought now, sitting by the kitchen window, adult yet Cinderella.

She thought that some one would come for her. Her mother or even Ina. Perhaps they would send Monona. She waited at first hopefully, then resentfully. The grey rain wrapped the air.

"Nobody cares what becomes of me after they're fed," she thought, and derived an obscure satisfaction from her phrasing, and thought it again. Ninian Deacon came into the kitchen.

Her first impression was that he had come to see whether the dog had been fed.

"I fed him," she said, and wished that she had been busy when Ninian entered.

"Who me? You did that all right. Say, why in time don't you come in the other room?"

"Oh, I don't know."

"Well, neither do I. I've kept thinking, 'Why don't she come along.' Then I remembered the dishes." He glanced about. "I come to help wipe dishes."

"Oh!" she laughed so delicately, so delightfully, one wondered where she got it. "They're washed —" she caught herself at "long ago."

"Well then. What are you doing here?"

"Resting."

"Rest in there." He bowed, crooked his arm. "Senora," he said, —
his Spanish matched his other assimilations of travel — "Senora. Allow me."

Lulu rose. On his arm she entered the parlor. Dwight was narrating
and did not observe that entrance. To the Plows it was sufficiently normal.
But Ina looked up and said:

"Well!" — in two notes, descending, curving.

Lulu did not look at her. Lulu sat in a low rocker. Her starched white
skirt, throwing her chally in ugly lines, revealed a peeping rim of white embroidery. Her lace front winkled when she sat, and petulantly she adjusted it.
She curled her feet sidewise beneath her chair, her long wrists and veined hands
lay along her lap in no relation to her. She was tense. She rocked.

When Dwight had finished his narration, there was a pause, broken
at last by Mrs. Bett:

"You tell that better than you used to when you started telling it,"
she observed. "You got in some things I guess you used to clean forget about.
Monona, get off my rocker."

Monona made a little whimpering sound, in pretense to tears. Ina
said "Darling — quiet!" — chin a little lifted, lower lip revealing lower teeth
for the word's completion; and she held it.

The Plows were asking something about Mexico. Dwight was wondering; if it would let up raining *at all*. Di and Jenny came whispering into
the room. But all these distractions Ninian Deacon swept aside.

"Miss Lulu," he said, "I wanted you to hear about my trip up the
Amazon, because I knew how interested you are in travels."

He talked, according to his lights, about the Amazon. But the person who most enjoyed the recital could not afterward have told two words
that he said. Lulu kept the position which she had taken first, and she dare
not change. She saw the blood in the veins of her hands and wanted to hide
them. She wondered if she might fold her arms, or have one hand support
her chin, gave it all up and sat motionless, save for the rocking.

Then she forgot everything. For the first time in years someone was
talking and looking not only at Ina and Dwight and their guests, but at her.

June

On a June morning Dwight Herbert Deacon looked at the sky, and said with his manner of originating it: "How about a picnic this afternoon?" Ina, with her blank, upward look, exclaimed : "To-*day?*"

"First class day, it looks like to me."

Come to think of it, Ina didn't know that there was anything to prevent, but mercy, Herbert was so sudden. Lulu began to recite the resources of the house for a lunch. Meanwhile, since the first mention of picnic, the child Monona had been dancing stiffly about the room, knees stiff, elbows stiff, shoulders immovable, her straight hair flapping about her face. The sad dance of the child who cannot dance because she never has danced. Di gave a conservative assent — she was at that age — and then took advantage of the family softness incident to a guest and demanded that Bobby go too. Ina hesitated, partly because she always hesitated, partly because she was tribal in the extreme. "Just our little family and Uncle Ninian would have been so nice," she sighed, with her consent.

When, at six o'clock, Ina and Dwight and Ninian assembled on the porch and Lulu came out with the basket, it was seen that she was in a blue-cotton house-gown.

"Look here," said Ninian, "aren't you going?"

"Me?" said Lulu. "Oh, no."

"Why not?"

"Oh, I haven't been to a picnic since I can remember."

"But why not?"

"Oh, I never think of such a thing."

Ninian waited for the family to speak. They did speak. Dwight said: "Lulu's a regular home body."

And Ina advanced kindly with: "Come with us, Lulu, if you like."

"No," said Lulu, and flushed. "Thank you," she added, formally.

Mrs. Bett's voice shrilled from within the house, startlingly close — just beyond the blind, in fact :

"Go on, Lulie. It'll do you good. You mind me and go on."

"Well," said Ninian, "that's what I say. You hustle for your hat and you come, along."

For the first time this course presented itself to Lulu as a possibility. She stared up at Ninian.

"You can slip on my linen duster, over," Ina said graciously.

"Your new one?" Dwight incredulously wished to know.

"Oh, no!" Ina laughed at the idea. "The old one."

They were having to wait for Di in any case — they always had to wait for Di — and at last, hardly believing her own motions, Lulu was running to make ready. Mrs. Bett hurried to help her, but she took down the wrong things and they were both irritated. Lulu reappeared in the linen duster and a wide hat. There had been no time to "tighten up" her hair; she was flushed at the adventure; she had never looked so well.

They started. Lulu, falling in with Monona, heard for the first time in her life, the step of the pursuing male, choosing to walk beside her and the little girl. Oh, would Ina like that? And what did Lulu care what Ina liked? Monona, making a silly, semi-articulate observation, was enchanted to have Lulu burst into laughter and squeeze her hand.

Di contributed her bright presence, and Bobby Larkin appeared from nowhere, running, with a gigantic bag of fruit.

"Bullylujah!" he shouted, and Lulu could have shouted with him.

She sought for some utterance. She wanted to talk with Ninian.

"I do hope we've brought sandwiches enough," was all that she could get to say.

They chose a spot, that is to say Dwight Herbert chose a spot, across the river and up the shore where there was at that season a strip of warm beach. Dwight Herbert declared himself the builder of incomparable fires, and made a bad smudge. Ninian, who was a camper neither by birth nor by adoption, kept offering brightly to help, could think of nothing to do, and presently, bethinking himself of skipping stones, went and tried to skip them on the flowing river. Ina cut her hand opening the condensed milk and was obliged to sit under a tree and nurse the wound. Monona spilled all the salt and sought diligently to recover it. So Lulu did all the work. As for Di and Bobby, they had taken the pail and gone for water, discouraging Monona, from accompanying them, discouraging her to the point of tears. But the two were gone for so long that on their return Dwight was hungry and cross and majestic.

"Those who disregard the comfort of other people," he enunciated, "cannot expect consideration for themselves in the future."

He did not say on what ethical tenet this dictum was based, but he delivered it with extreme authority. Ina caught her lower lip with her teeth, dipped her head, and looked at Di. And Monona laughed like a little demon.

As soon as Lulu had all in readiness, and cold corned beef and salad had begun their orderly progression, Dwight became the immemorial dweller in green fastnesses. He began:

"This is ideal. I tell you, people don't half know life if they don't get out and eat in the open. It's better than any tonic at a dollar the bottle. Nature's tonic — eh? Free as the air. Look at that sky. See that water. Could anything be more pleasant?"

He smiled at his wife. This man's face was glowing with simple pleasure. He loved the out-of-doors with a love which could not explain itself. But he now lost a definite climax when his wife's comment was heard to be:

"Monona! Now it's all over both ruffles. And mamma does try so hard . . ."

After supper some boys arrived with a boat which they beached, and Dwight, with enthusiasm, gave the boys ten cents for a half hour's use of that boat and invited to the waters his wife, his brother and his younger daughter. Ina was timid — not because she was afraid but because she was congenitally timid — with her this was not a belief or an emotion, it was a disease.

"Dwight darling, are you sure there's no danger?"

Why, none. None in the world. Whoever heard of drowning in a river.

"But you're not so very used —"

Oh, wasn't he? Who was it that had lived in a boat throughout youth if not he?

Ninian refused out-of-hand, lighted a cigar, and sat on a log in a permanent fashion. Ina's plump figure was fitted in the stern, the child Monona affixed, and the boat put off, bow well out of water. On this pleasure ride the face of the wife was as the face of the damned. It was true that she revered her husband's opinions above those of all other men. In politics, in science, in religion, in dentistry she looked up to his dicta as to revelation. And was he not a magistrate? But let him take oars in hand, or shake lines or a whip above the back of any horse, and this woman would trust any other woman's husband by preference. It was a phenomenon.

Lulu was making the work last, so that she should be out of everybody's way. When the boat put off without Ninian, she felt a kind of terror and wished that he had gone. He had sat down near her, and she pretended not to see. At last Lulu understood that Ninian was deliberately choosing to remain with her. The languor of his bulk after the evening meal made no explanation for Lulu. She asked for no explanation. He had stayed.

And they were alone. For Di, on a pretext of examining the flocks and herds, was leading Bobby away to the pastures, a little at a time.

The sun, now fallen, had left an even, waxen sky. Leaves and ferns appeared drenched with the light just withdrawn. The hush, the warmth, the color, were charged with some influence. The air of the time communicated itself to Lulu as intense and quiet happiness. She had not yet felt quiet with Ninian. For the first time her blind excitement in his presence ceased, and she felt curiously accustomed to him. To him the air of the time imparted itself in a deepening of his facile sympathy.

"Do you know something?" he began. "I think you have it pretty hard around here."

"I?" Lulu was genuinely astonished.

"Yes, sir. Do you have to work like this all the time? I guess you won't mind my asking."

"Well, I ought to work. I have a home with them. Mother too."

"Yes, but glory. You ought to have some kind of a life of your own. You want it, too. You told me you did — that first day."

She was silent. Again he was investing her with a longing which she had never really had, until he had planted that longing. She had wanted she knew not what. Now she accepted the dim, the romantic interest of this role.

"I guess you don't see how it seems," he said, "to me, coming along — a stranger so. I don't like it."

He frowned, regarded the river, flicked away ashes, his diamond obediently shining. Lulu's look, her head drooping, had the liquid air of the look of a younger girl. For the first time in her life she was feeling her help-lessness. It intoxicated her.

"They're very good to me." she said.

He turned. "Do you know why you think that? Because you've never had anyone really good to you. That's why."

"But they treat me good."

"They make a slave of you. Regular slave." He puffed, frowning. "Damned shame, *I* call it," he said.

Her loyalty stirred Lulu. "We have our whole living—"

"Add you earn it. I been watching you since I been here. Don't you ever go anywheres?"

She said: "This is the first place in — in years."

"Lord. Don't you want to? Of course you do!"

"Not so much places like this —"

"I see. What you want is to get away like you'd ought to," He re-garded her. "You've been a blamed fine-looking woman," he said.

She did not flush, but that faint, unsuspected Lulu spoke for her:

"You must have been a good-looking man once yourself."

His laugh went ringing across the water. "You're pretty good," he said. He regarded her approvingly. "I don't see how you do it," he mused, "blamed if I do."

"How I do what?"

"Why come back, quick like that, with what you say."

Lulu's heart was beating painfully. The effort to hold her own in talk like this was terrifying. She had never talked in this fashion to anyone. It was as if some matter of life or death hung on her ability to speak an alien tongue. And yet, when she was most at loss, that other Lulu, whom she had never known about, seemed suddenly to speak for her. As now:

"It's my grand education," she said.

She sat humped on the log, her beautiful hair shining in the light of the warm sky. She had thrown off her hat and the linen duster, and was in her blue gingham gown against the sky and leaves. But she sat stiffly, her feet carefully covered, her hands ill at ease, her eyes rather piteous in their hope somehow to hold her vague own. Yet from her came these sufficient, insouciant replies.

"Education," he said laughing heartily. "That's mine, too." He spoke a creed. "I ain't never had it and I ain't never missed it."

"Most folks are happy without an education," said Lulu.

"You're not very happy, though."

"Oh, no," she said.

"Well, sir," said Ninian, "I'll tell you what we'll do. While I'm here I'm going to take you and Ina and Dwight up to the city."

"To the city?"

"To a show. Dinner and a show. I'll give you *one* good time."

"Oh!" Lulu leaned forward. "Ina and Dwight go sometimes. I never been."

"Well, just you come with me. I'll look up what's good. You tell me just what you like to eat, and we'll get it—"

She said: "I haven't had anything to eat in years that I haven't cooked myself."

He planned for that time to come, and Lulu listened as one intensely experiencing every word that he uttered. Yet it was not in that future merry-making that she found her joy, but in the consciousness that he — some one — any one — was planning like this for her.

Meanwhile Di and Bobby had rounded the corner by an old hop-house and kept on down the levee. Now that the presence of the others was withdrawn, the two looked about them differently and began themselves to give off an influence instead being pressed upon by overpowering personalities. Frogs were chorusing in the near swamp, and Bobby wanted one. He was off after it. But Di eventually drew him back, reluctant, frogless. He entered upon an exhaustive account of the use of frogs for bait, and as he talked he constantly flung stones. Di grew restless. There was, she had found, a certain amount of this to be gone through before Bobby would focus on the personal. At length she was obliged to say, "Like me to-day?" And then he entered upon personal talk with the same zest with which he had discussed bait.

"Bobby," said Di, "sometimes I think we might be married, and not wait for any old money."

They had now come that far. It was partly an authentic attraction, grown from out the old repulsion, and partly it was that they both — and especially Di — so much wanted the experiences of attraction that they assumed its ways. And then each cared enough to assume the pretty role required by the other, and by the occasion, and by the air of the time.

"Would you?" asked Bobby — but in the subjunctive.

She said : "Yes. I will."

"It would mean running away, wouldn't it?" said Bobby, still subjunctive.

"I suppose so. Mamma and papa are so unreasonable."

"Di," said Bobby, "I don't believe you could ever be happy with me."

"The idea! I can too. You're going to be a great man — you know you are."

Bobby was silent. Of course he knew it — but he passed it over.

"Wouldn't it be fun to elope and surprise the whole school?" said Di, sparkling.

Bobby grinned appreciatively. He was good to look at, with his big frame, his head of rough dark hair, the sky warm upon his clear skin and full mouth. Di suddenly announced that she would be willing to elope *now*.

"I've planned eloping lots of times," she said ambiguously.

It flashed across the mind of Bobby that in these plans of hers he may not always have been the principal, and he could not be sure . . . But she talked in nothings, and he answered her so.

Soft cries sounded in the center of the stream. The boat, well out of the strong current, was seen to have its oars shipped; and there sat Dwight Herbert gently rocking the boat. Dwight Herbert would.

"Bertie, Bertie — please!" you heard his Ina say.

Monona began to cry, and her father was irritated, felt that it would be ignominious to desist, and did not know that he felt this. But he knew that he was annoyed, and he took refuge in this, and picked up the oars with: "Some folks never can enjoy anything without spoiling it."

"That's what I was thinking," said Ina, with a flash of anger.

They glided toward the shore in a huff. Monona found that she enjoyed crying across the water and kept it up. It was almost as good as an echo. Ina, stepping safe to the sands, cried ungratefully that this was the last time that she would ever, ever go with her husband anywhere. Even Dwight Herbert, recovering, gauged the moment to require of him humor, and observed that his wedded wife was as skittish as a colt. Ina kept silence, head poised so that her full little chin showed double. Monona, who had previously hidden a cookie in her frock, now remembered it and crunched sidewise, the eyes ruminant.

Moving toward them, with Di, Bobby was suddenly overtaken by the sense of disliking them all. He never had liked Dwight Herbert, his employer. Mrs. Deacon seemed to him so overwhelmingly mature that he had no idea how to treat her. And the child Monona he would like to roll in the river. Even Di . . . He fell silent, was silent on the walk home which was the signal for Di to tease him steadily. The little being was afraid of silence. It was too vast for her. She was like a butterfly in a dome.

But against that background of ruined occasion, Lulu walked homeward beside Ninian. And all that night, beside her mother who groaned in her sleep, Lulu lay tense and awake. He had walked home with her. He had told Ina and Herbert about going to the city. What did it mean? Suppose. . . . oh no; oh no!

"Either lay still or get up and set up," Mrs. Bett directed her at length.

July

When, on a warm evening a fortnight later, Lulu descended the stairs dressed for her incredible trip to the city, she wore the white waist which she had often thought they would "use" for her if she died. And really, the waist looked as if it had been planned for the purpose, and its wide, upstanding plaited lace at throat and wrist made her neck look thinner, her forearm sharp and veined. Her hair she had "crimped" and parted in the middle, puffed high — it was so that hair had been worn in Lulu's girlhood.

"*Well!*" said Ina, when she saw this coiffure, and frankly examined it, head well back, tongue meditatively teasing at her lower lip.

For travel Lulu was again wearing Ina's linen duster —the old one.

Ninian appeared, in a sack coat — and his diamond. His distinctly convex face, thick, rosy flesh, thick mouth and cleft chin gave Lulu once more that bold sense of looking — not at him, for then she was shy and averted her eyes — but at his photograph at which she could gaze as much as she would. She looked up at him openly, fell in step beside him. Was he not taking her to the city? Ina and Dwight themselves were going because she, Lulu, had brought about this party.

"Act as good as you look, Lulie," Mrs. Bett called after them. She gave no instructions to Ina who was married and able to shine in her conduct, it seemed.

Dwight was cross. On the way to the station he might have been heard to take it up again, whatever it was, and his Ina unmistakably said: "Well, now don't keep it going all the way there"; and turned back to the others with some elaborate comment about the dust, thus cutting off her so-called lord from his legitimate retort. A mean advantage.

The city was two hours' distant, and they were to spend the night. On the train, in the double seat, Ninian beside her among the bags, Lulu sat in the simple consciousness that the people all knew that she too had been chosen. A man and a woman were opposite, with their little boy between them. Lulu felt this woman's superiority of experience over her own, and smiled at her from a world of fellowship. But the woman lifted her eyebrows and stared and turned away, with slow and insolent winking.

Ninian had a boyish pride in his knowledge of places to eat in many cities — as if he were leading certain of the tribe to a deer-run in a strange wood. Ninian took his party to a downtown cafe, then popular among business and newspaper men. The place was below the sidewalk, was reached by a dozen marble steps, and the odor of its griddle-cakes took the air of the street. Ninian made a great show of selecting a table, changed once, called the waiter "my man" and rubbed soft hands on "What do you say? Shall it be lobster?" He ordered the dinner, instructing the waiter with painstaking gruffness.

"Not that they can touch *your* cooking here, Miss Lulu," he said, settling himself to wait, and crumbling a crust.

Dwight, expanding a bit in the aura of the food, observed that Lulu was a regular chef, that was what Lulu was. He still would not look at his wife, who now remarked:

"Sheff, Dwightie. Not cheff."

This was a mean advantage, which he pretended not to hear — another mean advantage.

"Ina," said Lulu, "your hat's just a little mite — no, over the other way."

"Was there anything to prevent your speaking of that before?" Ina inquired acidly.

"I started to and then somebody always said something," said Lulu humbly.

Nothing could so much as cloud Lulu's hour. She was proof against any shadow.

"Say, but you look tremendous to-night," Dwight observed to her.

Understanding perfectly that this was said to tease his wife, Lulu yet finished with pleasure. She saw two women watching, and she thought: "They're feeling sorry for Ina —nobody talking to her." She laughed at everything that the men said. She passionately wanted to talk herself. "How many folks keep going past," she said, many times.

At length, having noted the details of all the clothes in range, Ina's isolation palled upon her and she set herself to take Ninian's attention. She therefore talked with him about himself.

"Curious you've never married, Nin," she said.

"Don't say it like that," he begged. "I might yet."

Ina laughed enjoyably. "Yes, you might!" she met this.

"She wants everybody to get married but she wishes I hadn't," Dwight threw in with exceeding rancor.

They developed this theme exhaustively, Dwight usually speaking in the third person and always with his shoulder turned a bit from his wife. It was inconceivable, the gusto with which they proceeded. Ina had assumed for the purpose an air distrait, casual, attentive to the scene about them. But gradually her cheeks began to burn.

"She'll cry," Lulu thought in alarm and said at random: "Ina, that hat is so pretty — ever so much prettier than the old one." But Ina said frostily that she never saw anything the matter with the old one.

"Let us talk," said Ninian low, to Lulu. "Then they'll simmer down."

He went on, in an undertone, about nothing in particular. Lulu hardly heard what he said, it was so pleasant to hear him talking to her in this confidential fashion; and she was pleasantly aware that his manner was open to misinterpretation.

In the nick of time, the lobster was served.

Dinner and the play — the show, as Ninian called it. This show was "Peter Pan," chosen by Ninian because the seats cost the most of those at any theatre. It was almost indecent to see how Dwight Herbert, the immortal soul, had warmed and melted at these contacts. By the time that it all was over, and they were at the hotel for supper, such was his pleasurable excitation that he was once more playful, teasing, once more the irrepressible. But now his Ina was to be won back, made it evident that she was not one lightly to overlook, and a fine firmness sat upon the little doubling chin.

They discussed the play. Not one of them had understood the story. The dog kennel part — wasn't that the queerest thing? Nothing to do with the rest of the play.

"I was for the pirates. The one with the hook — he was my style," said Dwight.

"Well, there it is again," Ina cried. "They didn't belong to the real play either."

"Oh, well," Ninian said, "they have to put in parts, I suppose, to catch everybody. Instead of a song and dance, they do that."

"And I didn't understand," said Ina, "why they all clapped when the principal character ran down front and said something to the audience that time. But they all did." Ninian thought this might have been out of compliment. Ina wished that Monona might have seen, confessed that the last part was so pretty that she herself would not look; and into Ina's eyes came their loveliest light.

Lulu sat there, hearing the talk about the play. "Why couldn't I have said that?" she thought as the others spoke. All that they said seemed to her apropos, but she could think of nothing to add. The evening had been to her a light from heaven — how could she find anything to say? She sat in a daze of happiness, her mind hardly operative, her look moving from one to another. At last Ninian looked at her.

"Sure you liked it, Miss Lulu?"

"Oh, yes! I think they all took their parts real well."

It was not enough. She looked at them appealingly, knowing that she had not said enough.

"You could hear everything they said," she added. "It was —" she dwindled to silence.

Dwight Herbert savored his rarebit with a great show of long wrinkled dimples.

"Excellent sauces they make here — excellent," he said, with the frown of an epicure. "A tiny wee bit more Athabasca," he added, and they all laughed and told him that Athabasca was a lake, of course. Of course he meant tobasco, Ina said. Their entertainment and their talk was of this sort for an hour.

"Well, now," said Dwight Herbert when he was finished, "somebody dance on the table."

"Dwightie!"

"Got to amuse ourselves somehow. Come, liven up. They'll begin to read the funeral service over us."

"Why not say the wedding service?" asked Ninian.

In the mention of wedlock there was always something stimulating to Dwight, something of overwhelming humor. He shouted a derisive endorsement of this proposal.

"I shouldn't object," said Ninian. "Should you, Miss Lulu?"

Lulu now burned the slow red of her torture. They were all looking at her. She made an anguished effort to defend herself.

"I don't know it," she said, "so I can't say it."

Ninian leaned toward her.

"I, Ninian, take three, Lulu, to be my wedded wife," he pronounced. "That's the way it goes!"

"Lulu daren't say it!" cried Dwight. He laughed so loudly that those at the near tables turned. And, from the fastness of her wifehood and motherhood, Ina laughed. Really, it was ridiculous to think of Lulu that way . . .

Ninian laughed too. "Course she don't dare say it," he challenged.

From within Lulu, that strange Lulu, that other Lulu who sometimes fought her battles, suddenly spoke out:

"I, Lulu, take thee, Ninian, to be my wedded husband."

"You will?" Ninian cried.

"I will," she said, laughing tremulously, to prove that she too could join in, could be as merry as the rest.

"And I will. There, by Jove, now have we entertained you, or haven't we?" Ninian laughed and pounded his soft fist on the table.

"Oh, say, honestly!" Ina was shocked. "I don't think you ought to — holy things — what's the *matter*, Dwightie?"

Dwight Herbert Deacon's eyes were staring and his face was scarlet. "Say, by George," he said, "a civil wedding is binding in this state."

"A civil wedding? Oh, well—" Ninian dismissed it.

"But I," said Dwight, "happen to be a magistrate."

They looked at one another foolishly. Dwight sprang up with the indeterminate idea of inquiring something of someone, circled about and returned. Ina had taken his chair and sat clasping Lulu's hand. Ninian continued to laugh.

"I never saw one done so offhand," said Dwight. "But what you've said is all you have to say according to law. And there don't have to be witnesses . . . say!" he said, and sat down again.

Above that shroud-like plaited lace, the veins of Lulu's throat showed dark as she swallowed, cleared her throat, swallowed again.

"Don't you let Dwight scare you," she besought Ninian.

"Scare me!" cried Ninian. "Why, I think it's a, good job done, if you ask me."

Lulu's eyes flew to his face. As he laughed, he was looking at her, and now he nodded and shut and opened his eyes several times very fast. Their points of light flickered. With a pang of wonder which pierced her and left her shaken, Lulu looked. His eyes continued to meet her own. It was exactly like looking at his photograph.

Dwight had recovered his authentic air.

"Oh, well," he said, "we can inquire at our leisure. If it is necessary, I should say we can have it set aside quietly up here in the city — no one'll be the wiser."

"Set aside nothing!" said Ninian. "I'd like to see it stand."

"Are you serious, Nin?"

"Sure I'm serious."

Ina jerked gently at her sister's arm.

"Lulu! You hear him? What you going to say to that?"

Lulu shook her head. "He isn't in earnest," she said.

"I am in earnest — hope to die," Ninian declared. He was on two legs of his chair and was slightly tilting, so that the effect of his earnestness was impaired. But he was obviously in earnest.

They were looking at Lulu again. And now she looked at Ninian, and there was something terrible in that look which tried to ask him, alone, about this thing.

Dwight exploded. "There was a fellow I know there in theatre," he cried. "I'll get him on the line. He could tell me if there's any way —" and was off.

Ina inexplicably began touching away tears. "Oh," she said. "What will mama say?"

Lulu hardly heard her. Mrs. Bett was incalculably distant.

"You sure?" Lulu said low to Ninian.

For the first time, something in her exceeding isolation really touched him.

"Say," he said, "you come on with me. We'll have it done over again somewhere, if you say so."

"Oh," said Lulu, "if I thought —"

He leaned and patted her hand.

"Good girl," he said.

They sat silent, Ninian padding on the cloth with the fat of his plump hands.

Dwight returned. "It's a go all right," he said. He sat down, laughed weakly, rubbed at his face. "You two are tied as tight as the church could tie you."

"Good enough," said Ninian. "Eh, Lulu?"

"It's — it's all right, I guess," Lulu said.

"Well, I'll be dished," said Dwight.

"Sister!" said Ina.

Ninian meditated, his lips set tight and high. It is impossible to trace the processes of this man. Perhaps they were all compact of the devil-may-care attitude engendered in any persistent traveller. Perhaps the incomparable cookery of Lulu played its part.

"I was going to make a trip south this month," he said, "on my way home from here. Suppose we get married again by somebody or other, and start right off. You'd like that, wouldn't you — going South?"

"Yes," said Lulu only.

"It's July," said Ina, with her sense of fitness, but no one heard.

It was arranged that their trunks should follow them — Ina would see to that, though she was scandalized that they were not first to return to Warbleton for the blessing of Mrs. Bett.

"Mamma won't mind," said Lulu. "Mamma can't stand a fuss any more."

They left the table. The men and women still sitting at the other tables saw nothing unusual about these four, indifferently dressed, indifferently conditioned. The hotel orchestra, playing ragtime in deafening discord, made Lulu's wedding march.

It was still early next day — a hot Sunday — when Ina and Dwight reached home. Mrs. Bett was standing on the porch.

"Where's Lulie?" asked Mrs. Bett.

They told.

Mrs. Bett took it in, a bit at a time. Her pale eyes searched their faces, she shook her head, heard it again, grasped it. Her first question was:

"Who's going to do your work?"

Ina had thought of that, and this was manifest.

"Oh," she said, "you and I'll have to manage."

Mrs. Bett meditated, frowning.

"I left the bacon for her to cook for your breakfasts," she said. "I can't cook bacon fit to eat. Neither can you."

"We've had our breakfasts," Ina escaped from this dilemma.

"Had it up in the city, on expense?"

"Well, we didn't have much."

In Mrs. Bett's eyes tears gathered, but they were not for Lulu.

"I should think," she said, "I should think Lulie might have had a little more gratitude to her than this."

On their way to church Ina and Dwight encountered Di, who had left the house some time earlier, stepping sedately to church in company with Bobby Larkin. Di was in white, and her face was the face of an angel, so young, so questioning, so utterly devoid of her sophistication.

"That child," said Ina, *"must* not see so much of that Larkin boy. She's just a little, little girl."

"Of course she mustn't," said Dwight sharply, "and if *I* was her mother—"

"Oh stop that!" said Ina, *sotto voce,* at the church steps.

To every one with whom they spoke in the aisle after church, Ina announced their news: Had they heard? Lulu married Dwight's brother Ninian in the city yesterday. Oh, sudden, yes! And ro*man*tic . . .spoken with that upward inflection to which Ina was a prey.

August

Mrs. Bett had been having a "tantrim," brought on by nothing defin-able.

Abruptly as she and Ina were getting supper, Mrs. Bett had fallen silent, had in fact refused to reply when addressed. When all was ready and Dwight was entering, hair wetly brushed, she had withdrawn from the room and closed her bedroom door until it echoed.

"She's got one again," said Ina, grieving. "Dwight, you go."

He went, showing no sign of annoyance, and stood outside his mother-in-law's door and knocked.

No answer.

"Mother, come and have some supper."

No answer.

"Looks to me like your muffins was just about the best ever."

No answer.

"Come on — I had something funny to tell you and Ina."

He retreated, knowing nothing of the admirable control exercised by this woman for her own passionate satisfaction in sending him away unsatis-fied. He showed nothing but anxious concern, touched with regret, at his failure. Ina, too, returned from that door discomfited. Dwight made a gal-lant effort to retrieve the fallen fortunes of their evening meal, and turned upon Di, who had just entered, and with exceeding facetiousness inquired Bobby was.

Di looked hunted. She could never tell whether her parents were going to tease her about Bobby, or rebuke her for being seen with him. It depended on mood, this mood Di had not the experience to gauge. She now groped for some neutral fact, and mentioned that he was going take her and Jenny for ice cream that night.

Ina's irritation found just expression in her office of motherhood.

"I won't have you downtown in the evening," she said.

"But you let me go last night."

"All the better reason why you should not go tonight."

"I tell you," cried Dwight. "Why not all walk down? Why not all have ice cream . . . " He was all gentleness and propitiation, the reconciling element in his home.

"Me too?" Monona's ardent hope, her terrible fear were in her eyebrows, her parted lips.

"You too, certainly." Dwight could not do enough for every one.

Monona clapped her hands. "Goody! Goody! Last time you wouldn't let me go."

"That's why papa's going to take you this time," Ina said.

These ethical balances having been nicely struck, Ina proposed another:

"But," she said, "but, you must eat more supper or you can *not* go."

"I don't want any more." Monona's look was honest and piteous.

"Makes no difference. You must eat or you'll get sick."

"No!"

"Very well, then. No ice cream soda for such a little girl."

Monona began to cry quietly. But she passed her plate. She ate, chewing high and slowly.

"See? She can eat if she will eat," Ina said to Dwight. "The only trouble is, she will *not* take the time."

"She don't put her mind on her meals," Dwight Herbert diagnosed it. "Oh, bigger bites than that!" he encouraged his little daughter.

Di's mind had been proceeding along its own paths.

"Are you going to take Jenny and Bobby too?" she inquired.

"Certainly. The whole party."

"Bobby'll want to pay for Jenny and I."

"Me, darling," said Ina patiently, punctiliously — and less punctiliously added: "Nonsense. This is going to be papa's little party."

"But we had the engagement with Bobby. It was an engagement."

"Well," said Ina, "I think we'll just set that aside — that important engagement. I think we just will."

"Papa! Bobby'll want to be the one to pay for Jenny and I—"

"Di!" Ina's voice dominated all. "Will you be more careful of your grammar or shall I speak to you again?"

"Well, I'd rather use bad grammar than — than — than—" she looked resentfully at her mother, her father. Their moral defection was evident to her, but it was indefinable. They told her that she ought to be ashamed when papa wanted to give them all a treat. She sat silent, frowning, put-upon.

"Look, mamma!" cried Monona, swallowing a third of an egg at one impulse. Ina saw only the empty plate.

"Mamma's nice little girl!" cried she, shining upon her child.

The rules of the ordinary sports of playground, scrupulously applied, would have clarified the ethical atmosphere of this little family. But there was no one to apply them.

When Di and Monona had been excused, Dwight asked:

"Nothing new from the bride and groom?"

"No. And, Dwight, it's been a week since the last."

"See — where were they then?"

He knew perfectly well that they were in Savannah, Georgia, but Ina played his game, told him, and retold bits that the letter had said.

"I don't understand," she added, "why they should go straight to Oregon without coming here first."

Dwight hazarded that Nin probably had to get back, and shone pleasantly in the reflected importance of a brother filled with affairs.

"I don't know what to make of Lulu's letters," Ina proceeded. "They're so — so —"

"You haven't had but two, have you?"

"That's all — well, of course it's only been a month. But both letters have been so —"

Ina was never really articulate. Whatever corner of her brain had the blood in it at the moment seemed to be operative, and she let the matter go at that.

"I don't think it's fair to mamma — going off that way. Leaving her own mother. Why, she may never see mamma again —" Ina's breath caught. Into her face came something of the lovely tenderness with which she sometimes looked at Monona and Di. She sprang up. She had forgotten to put some supper to warm for mamma. The lovely light was still in her face as she bustled about against the time of mamma's recovery from her tantrim. Dwight's face was like this when he spoke of his foster mother. In both these beings there was something which functioned as pure love.

Mamma had recovered and was eating cold scrambled eggs on the corner of the kitchen table when the ice cream soda party was ready to set out. Dwight threw her a casual "Better come, too, Mother Bett," but she shook her head. She wished to go, wished it with violence, but she contrived to give to her arbitrary refusal a quality of contempt. When Jenny arrived with Bobby, she had brought a sheaf of gladioli for Mrs. Bett, and took them to her in the kitchen, and as she laid the flowers beside her, the young girl stopped and kissed her.

"You little darling!" cried Mrs. Bett, and clung to her, her lifted eyes lit by something intense and living. But when the ice cream party set off at last, Mrs. Bett left her supper, gathered up the flowers, and crossed the lawn to the old cripple, Grandma Gates.

"Inie shan't have 'em," the old woman thought.

And then it was quite beautiful to watch her with Grandma Gates, whom she tended and petted, to whose complaints she listened, and to whom she tried to tell the small events of her day. When her neighbor had gone, Grandma Gates said that it was as good as a dose of medicine to have her come in.

Mrs. Bett sat on the porch restored and pleasant when the family returned. Di and Bobby had walked home with Jenny.

"Look here," said Dwight Herbert, "who is it sits home and has ice cream put in her lap, like a queen?"

"Vanilly or chocolate?" Mrs. Bett demanded.

"Chocolate, mamma!" Ina cried, with the breeze in her voice.

"Vanilly sets better," Mrs. Bett said.

They sat with her on the porch while she ate. Ina rocked on a creaking board. Dwight swung a leg over the railing. Monona sat pulling her skirt over her feet, and humming all on one note. There was no moon, but the warm dusk had a quality of transparency as if it were lit in all its particles.

The gate opened, and someone came up the walk. They looked, and it was Lulu.

"Well, if it ain't Miss Lulu Bett!" Dwight cried involuntarily, and Ina cried out something.

"How did you know?" Lulu asked.

"Know! Know what!"

"That it ain't Lulu Deacon. Hello, mamma."

She passed the others, and kissed her mother.

"Say," said Mrs. Bett placidly. "And I just ate up the last spoonful o' cream."

"Ain't Lulu Deacon!" Ina's voice rose and swelled richly. "What you talking?"

"Didn't he write to you?" Lulu asked.

"Not a word." Dwight answered this. "All we've had we had from you — the last from Savannah, Georgia."

"Savannah, Georgia," said Lulu, and laughed.

They could see that she was dressed well, in dark red cloth, with a little tilting hat and a drooping veil. She did not seem in any way upset, nor, save for that nervous laughter, did she show her excitement.

"Well, but he's here with you, isn't he!" Dwight demanded. "Isn't he here? Where is he?"

"Must be 'most to Oregon by this time," Lulu said.

"Oregon!"

"You see," said Lulu, "he had another wife."

"Why, had not!" exclaimed Dwight absurdly.

"Yes. He hasn't seen her for fifteen years and he thinks she's dead. But he isn't sure."

"Nonsense," said Dwight. "Why, of course she's dead if he thinks so."

"I had to be sure," said Lulu.

At first dumb before this, Ina now cried out: "Monona! Go upstairs to bed at once."

"It's only quarter to," said Monona, with assurance.

"Do as mamma tells you."

"But—"

"Monona!"

She went, kissing them all goodnight and taking her time about it. Everything was suspended while she kissed them and departed, walking slowly backward.

"Married?" said Mrs. Bett with tardy apprehension. "Lulie, was your husband married?"

"Yes," Lulu said, "my husband was married, mother."

"Mercy," said Ina. "Think of anything like that in our family."

"Well, go on — go on!" Dwight cried. "Tell us about it."

Lulu spoke in a monotone, with her old manner of hesitation:

"We were going to Oregon. First down to New Orleans and then out to California and up the coast." On this she paused and sighed. "Well, then at Savannah, Georgia, he said he thought I better know, first. So, he told me."

"Yes — well, what did he *say?*" Dwight demanded irritably.

"Cora Waters," said Lulu. "Cora Waters. She married him down in San Diego, eighteen years ago. She went to South America with him."

"Well, he never let us know of it, if she did," said Dwight.

"No. She married him just before he went. Then in South America, after two years, she ran away again. That's all he knows."

"That's a pretty story," said Dwight contemptuously.

"He says if she'd been alive, she'd been after him for a divorce. And she never been, so he thinks she must be dead. The trouble is," Lulu said again, "he wasn't sure. And I had to be sure."

"Well, but mercy," said Ina, "couldn't he find out now?"

"It might take a long time," said Lulu simply, "and I didn't want to stay and not know."

"Well, then, why didn't he say so here?" Ina's indignation mounted.

"He would have. But you how know sudden everything was. He said he thought about telling us right there in the restaurant, but of course that'd been hard — wouldn't it? And then he felt so sure she was dead."

"Why did he tell you at all, then?" demanded Ina, whose processes were simple.

"Yes. Well! Why indeed?" Dwight Herbert brought out these words with a curious emphasis.

"I thought that, just at first," Lulu said, "but only just at first. Of course that wouldn't have been right. And then, you see, he gave me my choice."

"Gave you your choice?" Dwight echoed.

"Yes. About going on and taking the chances. He gave me my choice when he told me, there in Savannah, Georgia."

"What made him conclude, by then, that you ought to be told?" Dwight asked.

"Why, he'd got to thinking about it," she answered.

A silence fell. Lulu sat looking out toward the street.

"The only thing," she said, "as long as it happened, I kind of wish he hadn't told me till we got to Oregon."

"Lulu!" said Ina. Ina began to cry. "You poor thing!" she said.

Her tears were a signal to Mrs. Bett, who had been striving to understand all. Now she too wept, tossing up her hands and rocking her body. Her saucer and spoon clattered on her knee.

"He felt bad too," Lulu said.

"He!" said Dwight. "He must have."

"It's you," Ina sobbed. "It's you. *My* sister!"

"Well," said Lulu, "but I never thought of it making you both feel bad, or I wouldn't have come home. I knew," she added, "it'd make Dwight feel bad. I mean, it was his brother—"

"Thank goodness," Ina broke in, "nobody need know about it."

Lulu regarded her, without change.

"Oh, yes," she said in her monotone. "People will have to know."

"I do not see the necessity." Dwight's voice was an edge. Then too he said "do not," always with Dwight betokening the finalities.

"Why, what would they think?" Lulu asked, troubled.

"What difference does it make what they think?"

"Why," said Lulu slowly, "I shouldn't like — you see they might — why, Dwight, think we'll have to tell them."

"You do! You think the disgrace of bigamy in this family is something the whole town will have to know about?"

Lulu looked at him with parted lips.

"Say," she said, "I never thought about it being that."

Dwight laughed. "What did you think it was? And whose disgrace is it, pray?"

"Ninian's," said Lulu.

"Ninian's! Well, he's gone. But you're here. And I'm here. Folks'll feel sorry for you. But the disgrace — that'd reflect on me. See?"

"But if we don't tell, what'll they think then?"

Said Dwight: "They'll think what they always think when a wife leaves her husband. They'll think you couldn't get along. That's all."

"I should hate that," said Lulu.

"Well, I should hate the other, let me tell you."

"Dwight, Dwight," said Ina. "Let's go in the house. I'm afraid they'll hear—"

As they rose, Mrs. Bett plucked at her returned daughter's sleeve.

"Lulie," she said, "was his other wife — was she *there?*"

"No, no, mother. She wasn't there."

Mrs. Bett's lips moved, repeating the words. "Then that ain't so bad," she said. "I was afraid maybe she turned you out."

"No," Lulu said, "it wasn't that bad, mother."

Mrs. Bett brightened. In little matters, she quarrelled and resented, but the large issues left her blank.

Through some indeterminate sense of the importance due this crisis, the Deacons entered their parlor. Dwight lighted that high, central burner and faced about, saying: "In fact, I simply will not have it, Lulu! You expect, I take it, to make your home with us in the future, on the old terms."

"Well —"

"I mean, did Ninian give you any money?"

"No. He didn't give me any money — only enough to get home on. And I kept my suit — why!" she flung her head back, "I wouldn't have taken any money!"

"That means," said Dwight, "that you will have to continue to live here — on the old terms, and of course I'm quite willing that you should. Let me tell you, however, that this is on condition — on condition that this disgraceful business is kept to ourselves."

She made no attempt to combat him now. She looked back at him, quivering, and in a great surprise, but she said nothing.

"Truly, Lulu," said Ina, "wouldn't that be best? They'll talk anyway. But this way they'll only talk about you, and the other way it'd be about all of us."

Lulu said only: "But the other way would be the truth."

Dwight's eyes narrowed: "My dear Lulu," he said, "are you *sure* of that?"

"Sure?"

"Yes. Did he give you any proofs?"

"Proofs?"

"Letters — documents of any sort? Any sort of assurance that he was speaking the truth?"

"Why, no," said Lulu. "Proofs — no. He told me."

"He told you!"

"Why, that was hard enough to have to do. It was terrible for him to have to do. What proofs —" She stopped, puzzled.

"Didn't it occur to you," said Dwight, "that he might have told you that because he didn't want to have to go on with it?"

As she met his look, some power seemed to go from Lulu. She sat down, looked weakly at them, and within her closed lips her jaw was slightly fallen. She said nothing. And seeing on her skirt a spot of dust she began to rub at that.

"Why, Dwight!" Ina cried, and moved to her sister's side.

"I may as well tell you," he said, "that I myself have no idea that Ninian told you the truth. He was always imagining things—you saw that. I know him pretty well — have been more or less in touch with him the whole time. In short, I haven't the least idea he was ever married before."

Lulu continued to rub at her skirt.

"I never thought of that," she said.

"Look here," Dwight went on persuasively, "hadn't you and he had some little tiff when he told you?"

"No — no! Why, not once. Why, we weren't a bit like you and Ina." She spoke simply and from her heart without guile.

"Evidently not," Dwight said dryly.

Lulu went on: "He was very good to me. This dress — and my shoes — and my hat. And another dress, too." She found the pins and took off her hat. "He liked the red wing," she said. "I wanted black — oh, Dwight! He did tell me the truth!" It was as if the red wing had abruptly borne mute witness.

Dwight's tone now mounted. His manner, it mounted too.

"Even if it is true," said he, "I desire that you should keep silent and protect my family from this scandal. I merely mention my doubts to you for your own profit."

"My own profit!"

She said no more, but rose and moved to the door.

"Lulu — you see! With Di and all!" Ina begged. "We just couldn't have this known — even if it was so."

"You have it in your hands," said Dwight, "to repay me, Lulu, for anything that you feel I may have done for you in the past. You also have it in your hands to decide whether your home here continues. That is not a pleasant position for me to find myself in. It is distinctly unpleasant, I may say. But you see for yourself."

Lulu went on, into the passage.

"Wasn't she married when she thought she was?" Mrs. Bett cried shrilly.

"Mamma," said Ina. "Do, please, remember Monona. Yes — Dwight thinks she's married all right now — and that it's all right, all the time."

"Well, I hope so, for pity sakes," said Mrs. Bett, and left the room with her daughter.

Hearing the stir, Monona upstairs lifted her voice:

"Mamma! Come on and hear my prayers, why don't you?"

When they came downstairs next morning, Lulu had breakfast ready.

"Well!" cried Ina in her curving tone, "if this isn't like old times?"

Lulu said yes, that it was like old times, and brought the bacon to the table.

"Lulu's the only one in *this* house can cook the bacon so's it'll chew," Mrs. Bett volunteered. She was wholly affable, and held contentedly to Ina's last word that Dwight thought now it was all right.

"Ho!" said Dwight. "The happy family, once more about the festive toaster." He gauged the moment to call for good cheer.

Ina too, became breezy, blithe. Monona caught their spirit and laughed, head thrown well back and gently shaken.

Di came in. She had been told that Auntie Lulu was at home, and that she, Di, wasn't to say anything to her about anything, nor anything to anybody else about Auntie Lulu being back. Under these prohibitions, which loosed a thousand speculations, Di was very nearly paralyzed. She stared at her Aunt Lulu incessantly.

Not one of them had even a talent for the casual, save Lulu herself. Lulu was amazingly herself. She took her old place, assumed her old offices. When Monona declared against bacon, it was Lulu who suggested milk toast and went to make it.

"Mamma," Di whispered then, like escaping steam, "isn't Uncle Ninian coming too?"

"Hush. No. Now don't ask any more questions."

"Well, can't I tell Bobby and Jenny she's here?"

"*No.* Don't say anything at all about her."

"But, mamma. What has she done?"

"Di! Do as mamma tells you. Don't you think mamma knows best?"

Di of course did not think so, had not thought so for a long time. But now Dwight said:

"Daughter! Are you a little girl or are you our grown-up young lady?"

"I don't know," said Di reasonably, "but I think you're treating me like a little girl now."

"Shame, Di," said Ina, unabashed by the accident of reason being on the side of Di.

"I'm eighteen,'" Di reminded them forlornly, "and through high school."

"Then act so," boomed her father.

Baffled, thwarted, bewildered, Di went over to Jenny Plow's and there imparted understanding by the simple process of letting Jenny guess, to questions skillfully shaped.

When Dwight said, "Look at my beautiful handkerchief," displayed a hole, sent his Ina for a better, Lulu, with a manner of haste, addressed him:

"Dwight. It's a funny thing, but I haven't Ninian's Oregon address."

"Well?"

"Well, I wish you'd give it to me."

Dwight tightened and lifted his lips. "It would seem," he said, "that you have no real use for that particular address, Lulu."

"Yes, I have. I want it. You have it, haven't you, Dwight?"

"Certainly I have it."

"Won't you please write it down for me?" She had ready a bit of paper and a pencil stump.

"My dear Lulu, now why revive anything? Why not be sensible and leave this alone? No good can come by —"

"But why shouldn't I have his address?"

"If everything is over between you, why should you?"

"But you say he's still my husband."

Dwight flushed. "If my brother has shown his inclination as plainly as I judge that he has, it is certainly not my place to put you in touch with him again."

"You won't give it to me?"

"My dear Lulu, in all kindness — no."

His Ina came running back, bearing handkerchiefs with different colored borders for him to choose from. He chose the initial that she had embroidered, and had not the good taste not to kiss her.

They were all on the porch that evening, when Lulu came downstairs.

"*Where* are you going?" Ina demanded, sisterly. And on hearing that Lulu had an errand, added still more sisterly: "Well, but mercy, what you so dressed up for?"

Lulu was in a thin black and white gown which they had never seen, and wore the tilting hat with the red wing.

"Ninian bought me this," said Lulu only.

"But, Lulu, don't you think it might be better to keep, well — out of sight for a few days?" Ina's lifted look besought her.

"Why?" Lulu asked.

"Why set people wondering till we have to?"

"They don't have to wonder, far as I'm concerned," said Lulu, and went down the walk.

Ina looked at Dwight. "She never spoke to me like that in her life before," she said.

She watched her sister's black and white figure going erectly down the street.

"That gives me the funniest feeling," said Ina, "as if Lulu had on clothes bought for her by some one that wasn't — that was —"

"By her husband who has left her," said Dwight sadly.

"Is that what it is, papa?" Di asked alertly. For a wonder, she was there; had been there the greater part of the day — most of the time staring, fascinated, at her Aunt Lulu.

"That's what it is, my little girl, " said Dwight, and shook his head.

"Well, I think it's a shame," said Di stoutly. "And I think Uncle Ninian is a sludge."

"Di!"

"I do. And I'd be ashamed to think anything else. I'd like to tell everybody."

"There is," said Dwight, "no need for secrecy — now."

"Dwight!" said Ina — Ina's eyes always remained expressionless, but it must have been her lashes that looked so startled.

"No need whatever for secrecy," he repeated with firmness. "The truth is, Lulu's husband has tired of her and sent her home. We must face it."

"But, Dwight — how awful for Lulu . . ."

"Lulu," said Dwight, "has us to stand by her."

Lulu, walking down the main street, thought:

"Now Mis' Chambers is seeing me. Now Mis' Curtis. There's somebody behind the vines at Mis' Martin's. Here comes Mis' Grove and I've got to speak to her. . ."

One and another and another met her, and every one cried out at her some version of:

"Lulu Bett!" Or, "W-well, it *isn't* Lulu Bett any more, is it? Well, what are doing here? I thought . . ."

"I'm back to stay," she said.

"The idea! Well, where you hiding that handsome husband of yours? Say, but we were surprised! You're the sly one. . ."

"My — Mr. Deacon isn't here."

"Oh."

"No. He's West."

"Oh, I see."

Having no arts, she must needs let the conversation die like this, could invent nothing concealing or gracious on which to move away.

She went to the post office. It was early, there were few at the post office — with only one or two there had she to go through her examination. Then she went to the general delivery window, tense for a new ordeal.

To her relief, the face which was shown there was one strange to her, a slim youth, reading a letter of his own, and smiling.

"Excuse me," said Lulu faintly.

The youth looked up, with eyes warmed by the words on the pink paper which he held.

"Could you give me the address of Ninian Deacon?"

"Let's see — you mean Dwight Deacon, I guess?"

"No. It's his brother. He's been here. From Oregon. I thought he might have given you his address —" she dwindled away.

"Wait a minute," said the youth. "Nope. No address here. Say, why don't you send it to his brother? He'd know. Dwight Deacon, the dentist."

"I'll do that," Lulu said absurdly, and turned away.

She went back up the street, walking fast now to get away from them all. Once or twice she pretended not to see a familiar face. But when she passed the mirror of an insurance office window, she saw her reflection and at its appearance she felt surprise and pleasure.

"Well!" she thought, almost in Ina's own manner.

Abruptly her confidence rose.

Something of this confidence was still upon her when she returned. They were the dining room now, all save Di, who was on the porch with Bobby, and Monona, who was in bed and might be heard extravagantly singing.

Lulu sat down with her hat on. When Dwight inquired playfully, "Don't we look like company?" she did not reply. He looked at her speculatively. Where had she gone, with whom had she talked, what had she told? Ina looked at her rather fearfully. But Mrs. Bett rocked contentedly and ate cardamom seeds.

"Whom did you see?" Ina asked.

Lulu named them.

"See them to talk to?" from Dwight.

Oh, yes. They had all stopped.

"What did they say?" Ins burst out.

They had inquired for Ninian, Lulu said; and said no more.

Dwight mulled this. Lulu might have told every one of these women that cock-and-bull story with which she had come home. It might be all over town. Of course, in that case he could turn Lulu out — should do so, in fact. Still the story would be all over town.

"Dwight," said Lulu, "I want Ninian's address."

"Going to write to him!" Ina cried incredulously.

"I want to ask him for the proofs that Dwight wanted."

"My dear Lulu," Dwight said impatiently, "you are not the one to write. Have you no delicacy?"

Lulu smiled — a strange smile, originating and dying in one corner of her mouth.

"Yes, she said. "So much delicacy that I want to be sure whether I'm married or not."

Dwight cleared his throat with a movement which seemed to use his shoulders for the purpose.

"I myself will take this up with my brother," he said. "I will write to him about it."

Lulu sprang to her feet. "Write to him *now!*" she cried.

"Really," said Dwight, lifting his brows.

"Now — now!" Lulu said. She moved about, collecting writing materials from their casual lodgments, on shelf and table. She set all before him and stood by him. "Write to him now," she said again.

"My dear Lulu, don't be absurd."

She said: "Ina. Help me. If it was Dwight — and they didn't know whether he had another wife, or not, and you wanted to ask him — oh, don't you see? Help me."

Ina was not yet the woman to cry for justice for its own sake, nor even to stand by another woman. She was primitive, and her instinct was to look to her own male merely.

"Well," she said, "of course. But why not let Dwight do it his own way? Wouldn't that be better?

She put it to her sister fairly: Now, no matter what Dwight's way was, wouldn't that be better?

"Mother!" said Lulu. She looked irresolutely toward her mother. But Mrs. Bett was eating cardamom seeds with exceeding gusto, and Lulu looked away. Caught by the gesture, Mrs. Bett voiced her grievance.

"Lulie," she said, "Set down. Take off your hat, why don't you?"

Lulu turned upon Dwight a quiet face which he had never seen before.

"You write that letter to Ninian," she said, "and you make him tell you so you'll understand. I know he spoke the truth. But I want you to know."

"M—m," said Dwight. "And then I suppose you're going to tell it all over town — as soon as you have the proofs."

"I'm going to tell it all over town," said Lulu, "just as it is — unless you write to him now."

"Lulu!" cried Ina. "Oh, you wouldn't."

"I would," said Lulu. "I will."

Dwight was sobered. This unimaginable Lulu looked capable of it. But then he sneered.

"And get turned out of this house, as you would be?"

"Dwight!" cried his Ina. "Oh, you wouldn't!"

"I would," said Dwight. "I will. Lulu knows it."

"I shall tell what I know and then leave your house anyway," said Lulu, "unless you get Ninian's word. And I want you should write him now."

"Leave your mother? And Ina?" he asked.

"Leave everything," said Lulu.

"Oh, Dwight," said Ina, "we can't get along without Lulu." She did not say in what particulars, but Dwight knew.

Dwight looked at Lulu, an upward, sidewise look, with a manner of peering out to see if she meant it. And he saw.

He shrugged, pursed his lips crookedly, rolled his head to signify the inexpressible. "Isn't that like a woman?" he demanded. He rose. "Rather than let you in for a show of temper," he said grandly, "I'd do anything."

He wrote the letter, addressed it, his hand elaborately curved in secrecy about the envelope, pocketed it.

"Ina and I'll walk down with you to mail it," said Lulu.

Dwight hesitated, frowned. His Ina watched him with consulting brows, "I was going," said Dwight, "to propose a little stroll before bedtime." He roved about the room. "Where's my beautiful straw hat? There's nothing like a brisk walk to induce sound, restful sleep," he told them. He hummed a bar.

"You'll be all right, mother?" Lulu asked.

Mrs. Bett did not look up. "These cardamom hev got a little mite too dry," she said.

In their room, Ina and Dwight discussed the incredible actions of Lulu.

"I saw," said Dwight, "I saw she wasn't herself. I'd do anything to avoid having a scene — you know that." His glance swept a little anxiously his Ina. "You know that, don't you?" he sharply inquired.

"But I really think you ought to have written to Ninian about it," she now dared to say. "It's — it's not a nice position for Lulu."

"Nice? Well, but whom has she got to blame for it?"

"Why, Ninian," said Ina.

Dwight threw out his hands. "Herself," he said. "To tell you the truth, I was perfectly amazed at the way she snapped him up in that restaurant."

"Why, but, Dwight —"

"Brazen," he said. "Oh, it was brazen."

"It was just fun, in the first place."

"But no really nice woman —" he shook his head.

"Dwight! Lulu is nice. The idea!"

He regarded her. "Would you have done that?" he would know.

Under his fond look, she softened, took his homage, accepted everything, was silent.

"Certainly not," he said. "Lulu's tastes are not fine like yours. I should never think of you as sisters."

"She's awfully good," Ina said feebly. Fifteen years of married life behind her — but this was sweet and she could not resist.

"She has excellent qualities." He admitted it. "But look at the position she's in — married to a man who tells her he has another wife in order to get free. Now, no really nice woman —"

"No really nice man —" Ina did say that much.

"Ah," said Dwight, "but *you* could never be in such a position. No, no. Lulu is sadly lacking somewhere."

Ina sighed, threw back her head, caught her lower lip with her upper, as might be in a hem. "What if it was Di?" she supposed.

"Di!" Dwight's look rebuked his wife. "Di," he said. "was born with ladylike feelings."

It was not yet ten o'clock. Bobby Larkin was permitted to stay until ten. From the veranda came the indistinguishable murmur of those young voices.

"Bobby," Di was saying within that murmur, "Bobby, you don't kiss me as if you really wanted to kiss me, tonight."

September

The office of Dwight Herbert Deacon, Dentist, Gold Work a Speciality (sic) in black lettering, and Justice of the Peace in gold, was above a store which had been occupied by one unlucky tenant after another, and had suffered long periods of vacancy when ladies' aid societies served lunches there, under great white signs, badly lettered. Some months of disuse were now broken by the news that the store had been let to a music man. A music man, what on earth was that, Warbleton inquired.

The music man arrived, installed three pianos, and filled his window with sheet music, as sung by many ladies who swung in hammocks or kissed their hands on the music covers. While he was still moving in, Dwight Herbert Deacon wandered downstairs and stood informally in the door of the new store. The music man, a pleasant-faced chap of thirty-odd, was rubbing at the face of a piano.

"Hello, there!" he said. "Can I sell you an upright?"

"If I can take it out in pulling your teeth, you can," Dwight replied. "Or," said he, "I might marry you free, either one."

On this their friendship began. Thenceforth, when business was dull, the idle hours of both men were beguiled with idle gossip.

"How the dickens did you think of pianos for a line?" Dwight asked him once. "Now, my father was a dentist, so I came by it natural — never entered my head to be anything else. But *pianos* —"

The music man — his name was Neil Cornish —threw up his chin in a boyish fashion, and said he'd be jiggered if knew. All up and down the Warbleton, street, the chances are that the answer would sound the same. "I'm studying law when I get the chance," said Cornish, as one who makes a bid to be thought of more highly.

"I see," said Dwight, respectfully, dwelling on the verb.

Later on Cornish confided more to Dwight: He was to come by a little inheritance some day — not much, but something. Yes, it made a man feel a certain confidence . . .

"Don't it?" said Dwight heartily, as if he knew.

Everyone liked Cornish. He told funny stories, and he never compared Warbleton save to its advantage. So at last Dwight said tentatively at lunch:

"What if I brought that Neil Cornish up for supper, one of these nights?"

"Oh, Dwightie, do," said Ina. "If there's a man in town, let's know it."

"What if I brought him up tonight?"

Up went Ina's eyebrows. *Tonight?*

"Scalloped potatoes and meat loaf and sauce and bread and butter," Lulu contributed.

Cornish came to supper. He was what is known in Warbleton as dapper. This Ina saw as she emerged on the veranda in response to Dwight's informal *halloo* on his way upstairs. She herself was in white muslin, now much too snug, and a blue ribbon. To her greeting their guest replied in that engaging shyness which is not awkwardness. He moved in some pleasant web of gentleness and friendliness.

They asked him the usual questions, and he replied, rocking all the time with a faint undulating motion of head and shoulders. Warbleton was one of the prettiest little towns that he had ever seen. He liked the people — they seemed different. He was sure to like the place, already liked it. Lulu came to the door in Ninian's thin black-and-white gown. She shook hands with the stranger, not looking at him, and said, "Come to supper, all." Monona was already in her place, singing under-breath. Mrs. Bett, after hovering in the kitchen door, entered; but they forgot to introduce her.

"Where's Di?" asked Ina. "I declare that daughter of mine is never anywhere."

A brief silence ensued as they were seated. There being a guest, grace was to come, and Dwight said unintelligibly and like lightning generic appeal to bless this food, forgive all our sins and finally save us. And there was something tremendous in this ancient form whereby all stages of men bow in some now unrecognized recognition of the ceremonial of taking food to nourish life — and more.

At "Amen" Di flashed in, her offices at the mirror fresh upon her — perfect hair, silk dress turned up at the hem. She met Cornish, crimsoned, fluttered to her seat, joggled the table and, "Oh, dear," she said audibly to her mother, "I forgot my ring."

The talk was saved alive by a frank effort. Dwight served, making jests about everybody coming back for more. They went on with Warbleton happenings, improvements and openings; and the runaway. Cornish tried hard to make himself agreeable, not ingratiatingly but good-naturedly. He wished profoundly that before coming he bad looked up some more stories in the back of the Musical Gazettes. Lulu surreptitiously pinched off an ant that was running at large upon the cloth and thereafter kept her eyes steadfastly on the sugar bowl to see if it could be from *that*. Dwight pretended that those which he was helping a second time were getting more than their share and facetiously landed on Di about eating so much that she would grow up and be married, first thing she knew. At the word "married" Di turned scarlet, laughed heartily and lifted her glass of water.

"And what instruments do you play?" Ina asked Cornish, in an unrelated effect to lift the talk to musical levels.

"Well, do you know," said the music man, "I can't play a thing. Don't know a black note from a white one."

"You don't? Why, Di plays very prettily," said Di's mother. "But then how can you tell what songs to order?" Ina cried.

"Oh, by the music houses. You go by the sales." For the first time it occurred to Cornish that this was ridiculous. "You know, I'm really studying law," he said, shyly and proudly. Law! How very interesting, from Ina. Oh, but won't he bring up some songs for the evening, for them to try over? Her and Di? At this Di laughed and said that she was out of practice and lifted her glass of water. In the presence of adults, Di made one weep, she was so slender, so young, so without defenses, so intolerably sensitive to every contact, so in agony lest she be found wanting. It was amazing how unlike was this Di compared to the Di who had ensnared Bobby Larkin. What was one to think?

Cornish paid very little attention to her. To Lulu he said kindly, "Don't you play, Miss —?" He had not caught her name — no stranger ever did catch it. Dwight now supplied it: "Miss Lulu Bett," he explained with loud emphasis, and Lulu burned her slow red. This question Lulu had usually answered by telling how a felon had interrupted her lessons and she had stopped "taking" — a participle sacred to music, in Warblcton. This vignette had been a kind of epitome of Lulu's biography. But now Lulu was heard to say serenely:

"No, but I'm quite fond of it. I went to a lovely concert —two weeks ago."

They all listened. Strange indeed to think of Lulu as having had experiences of which they did not know.

"Yes," she said. "It was in Savannah, Georgia." She flushed, and lifted her eyes in a manner of faint defiance. "Of course," she said, "I don't know the names of all the different instruments they played, but there were a good many." She laughed pleasantly as a part of her sentence. "They had some lovely tunes," she said. She knew that the subject was not exhausted and she hurried on. "The hall was real large," she super-added, "and there were quite a good many people there. And it was too warm."

"I see," said Cornish, and said what he had been waiting to say: That he too had been in Savannah, Georgia.

Lulu lit with pleasure. "Well!" she said. And her mind worked and she caught at the moment before it had escaped. "Isn't it a pretty city?" she asked. And Cornish assented with the intense heartiness of the provincial. He, too, it seemed, had a conversational appearance to maintain by its own effort. He said that he had enjoyed being in that town and that he was there for two hours.

"I was there for a week," Lulu's superiority was really pretty.

"Have good weather?" Cornish selected next.

Oh, yes. And they saw all the different buildings —but at her "we" she flushed and was silenced. She was coloring and breathing quickly. This was the first bit of conversation of this sort of Lulu's life.

After supper Ina inevitably proposed croquet, Dwight pretended to try to escape and, with his irrepressible mien, talked about Ina, elaborate in his insistence on the third person — "She loves it, we have to humor her, you know how it is. Or no! You don't know. But you will" — and more of the same sort, everybody laughing heartily, save Lulu, who looked uncomfortable and wished that Dwight wouldn't, and Mrs. Bett, who said no attention to anybody that night, not because she had not been introduced, an omission, which she had not even noticed, but merely as another form of "tantrim." A self-indulgence.

They emerged for croquet. And there on the porch sat Jenny Plow and Bobby, waiting for Di to keep an old engagement, which Di pretended to have forgotten, and to be frightfully annoyed to have to keep. She met the objections of her parents with all the batteries of her coquetry, set for both Bobby and Cornish and, bold in the presence of "company," at last went laughing away. And in the minute areas of her consciousness she said to herself that Bobby would be more in love with her than ever because she had risked all to go with him; and that Cornish ought to be distinctly attracted to her because she had not stayed. She was as primitive as pollen.

Ina was vexed. She said so, pouting in a fashion which she should have outgrown with white muslin and blue ribbons, and she had outgrown none of these things.

"That just spoils croquet," she said. "I'm vexed. Now we can't have a real game."

From the side-door, where she must have been lingering among the waterproofs, Lulu stepped forth.

"I'll play a game," she said.

When Cornish actually proposed to bring some music to the Deacons', Ina turned toward Dwight Herbert all the facets of her responsibility. And Ina's sense of responsibility toward Di was enormous, oppressive, primitive, amounting, in fact, toward this daughter of Dwight Herbert's late wife, to an ability to compress the offices of step-motherhood into the functions of the lecture platform. Ina was a fountain of admonition. Her idea of a daughter, step or not, was that of a manufactured product, strictly, which you consistently pinched and molded. She thought that a moral preceptor had the right to secrete precepts. Di got them all. But of course the crest of Ina's responsibility was to marry Di. This verb should be transitive only when lovers are speaking of the other, or the minister or magistrate is speaking of lovers. It should never be transitive when predicated of parents any other third party. But it is. Ina was quite agitated by its transitiveness as she took to her husband her incredible responsibility.

"You know, Herbert," said Ina, "if this Mr. Cornish comes here very much, what we may expect."

"What may we expect?" demanded Dwight Herbert, crisply.

Ina always played his games, answered what he expected her to answer, pretended to be intuitive when she was not so, said "I know" when she didn't know at all. Dwight Herbert, on the other hand, did not even play her games when he knew perfectly what she meant, but pretended not to understand, made her repeat, made her explain. It was as if Ina *had* to please him for, say, a living; but as for that dentist, he had to please nobody. In the conversations of Dwight and Ina you saw the historical home forming in clots in the fluid wash of the community.

"He'll fall in love with Di," said Ina.

"And what of that! Little daughter will have many a man fall in love with her, I should say."

"Yes, but, Dwight, what do you think of him?"

"What do I think of him? My dear Ina, I have other things to think of."

"But we don't know anything about him, Dwight — a stranger so."

"On the other hand," said Dwight with dignity, "I know a good deal about him."

With a great air of having done the fatherly and found out about this stranger before bringing him into the home, Dwight now related a number of stray circumstances dropped by Cornish in their chance talks.

"He has a little inheritance coming to him — shortly," Dwight wound up.

"An inheritance — really? How much Dwight?"

"Now isn't that like a woman. Isn't it?"

"I *thought* he was from a good family," said Ina.

"My mercenary little pussy!"

"Well," she said with a sigh, "I shouldn't be surprised if Di did really accept him. A young girl is awfully flattered when a good-looking older man pays her attention. Haven't you noticed that?"

Dwight informed her, with an air of immense abstraction, that he left all such matters to her. Being married to Dwight was like a perpetual rehearsal, with Dwight's self-importance for audience.

A few evenings later, Cornish brought the music. There was something overpowering in this brown-haired chap against the background of his negligible little shop, his whole capital in his few pianos. For he looked hopefully ahead, woke with plans, regarded the children in the street as if, conceivably, children might come within the confines of his life as he imagined it. A preposterous little man. And a preposterous store, empty, echoing, bare of wall, the three pianos near the front, the remainder of the floor stretching away like the corridors of the lost. He was going to get a dark curtain, he explained, and furnish the back part of the store as his own room. What dignity in phrasing, but how mean that little room would look — cot bed, washbowl and pitcher, and little mirror — almost certainly a mirror with a wavy surface, almost certainly that.

"And then, you know," he always added, "I'm reading law."

The Plows had been asked in that evening. Bobby was there. They were, Dwight Herbert said, going to have a sing.

Di was to play. And Di was now embarked on the most difficult feat of her emotional life, the feat of remaining to Bobby Larkin the lure, the beloved lure, the while to Cornish she instinctively played the role of womanly little girl.

"Up by the festive lamp, everybody!" Dwight Herbert cried.

As they gathered about the upright piano, that startled, Dwightish instrument, standing in its attitude of unrest, Lulu came in with another lamp.

"Do you need this?" she asked.

They did not need it, there was, in fact, no place to set it, and this Lulu must have known. But Dwight found a place. He swept Ninian's photograph from the marble shelf of the mirror, and when Lulu had placed the lamp there, Dwight thrust the photograph into her hands.

"You take care of that," he said, with a droop of the lid discernible only to those who — presumably — loved him. His old attitude toward Lulu had shown a terrible sharpening in these ten days since her return.

She stood uncertainly, in the thin black and white gown which Ninian had bought for her, and held Ninian's photograph and looked helplessly about. She was moving toward the door when Cornish called:

"See here! Aren't *you* going to sing?"

"What?" Dwight used the falsetto. "Lulu sing? *Lulu?*"

She stood awkwardly. She had a piteous recrudescence of her old agony at being spoken to in the presence of others. But Di had opened the

"Album of Old Favourites," which Cornish had elected to bring and now she struck the opening chords of "Bonny Eloise." Lulu stood still, looking rather piteously at Cornish. Dwight offered his arm, absurdly crooked. The Plows and Ina and Di began to sing. Lulu moved forward, and stood a little away from them, and sang, too. She was still holding Ninian's picture. Dwight did not sing. He lifted his shoulders and his eyebrows and watched Lulu.

When they had finished, "Lulu the mockingbird!" Dwight cried. He said "ba-ird."

"Fine!" cried Cornish. "Why, Miss Lulu, you have a good voice!"

"Miss Lulu Bett, the mocking ba-ird," Dwight insisted.

Lulu was excited, and in some ascension of faint power. She turned to him quietly, and with a look of appraisal.

"Lulu the dove," she then surprisingly said, "to put up with you."

It was her first bit of conscious repartee to her brother-in-law.

Cornish was bending over Di.

"What next do you say?" he asked.

She lifted her eyes, met his own, held them. "There's such a lovely, lovely sacred song here," she suggested, and looked down.

"You like sacred music?"

She turned to him her pure profile, eyelids fluttering up, and said: "I love it."

"That's it. So do I. Nothing like a nice sacred piece," Cornish declared.

Bobby Larkin, at the end of the piano, looked directly into Di's face.

"Give *me* ragtime," he said now, with the effect of bursting out of somewhere. "Don't you like ragtime?" he put it to her directly.

Di's eyes danced into his, they sparkled for him, her smile was a smile for him alone, all their store of common memories was in their look.

"Let's try 'My Rock, My Refuge,'" Cornish suggested. "That's got up real attractive."

Di's profile again, and her pleased voice saying that this was the very one she had been hoping to hear him sing.

They gathered for "My Rock, My Refuge."

"Oh," cried Ina, at the conclusion of this number, "I'm having such a perfectly beautiful time. Isn't everybody?" everybody's hostess put it.

"Lulu is," said Dwight, and added softly to Lulu: "She don't have to hear herself sing."

It was incredible. He was like a bad boy with a frog. About that photograph of Ninian he found a dozen ways to torture her, called attention to it, showed it to Cornish, set it on the piano facing them all. Everybody must have understood —excepting the Plows. These two gentle souls sang placidly through the Album of Old Favourites, and at the melodies smiled happily upon each other with an air from another world. Always it was as if the Plows walked some fair, inter-penetrating plane from which they looked out as do other things not quite of earth, say, flowers and fire and music.

Strolling home that night, the Plows were overtaken by some one who ran badly, and as if she were unaccustomed to running.

"Mis' Plow, Mis' Plow!" this one called, and Lulu stood beside them.

"Say!" she said. "Do you know of any job that I could get me? I mean that I'd know how to do? A job for money. . . . I mean a job. . . ."

She burst into passionate crying. They drew her home with them.

Lying awake sometime after midnight, Lulu heard the telephone ring. She heard Dwight's concerned "Is that so?" And his cheerful "Be right there."

Grandma Gates was sick, she heard him tell Ina. In a few moments he ran down the stairs. Next day they told how Dwight had sat for hours that night, holding Grandma Gates so that her back would rest easily and she could fight for her faint breath. The kind fellow had only two hours of sleep the whole night.

Next day there came a message from that woman who had brought up Dwight — "made him what he was," he often complacently accused her. It was a note on a postal card — she had often written a few lines on a postal card to say that she had sent the maple sugar, or could Ina get her some samples. Now she wrote a few lines on a postal card to say that she was going to die with cancer. Could Dwight and Ina come to her while she was still able to visit? If he was not too busy. . . .

Nobody saw the pity and the terror of that postal card. They stuck it up by the kitchen clock to read over from time to time, and before they left, Dwight lifted the griddle of the cooking-stove and burned the postal card.

And before they left Lulu said: "Dwight — you can't tell how long you'll be gone?

"Of course not. How should I tell?"

"No. And that letter might come while you're away."

"Conceivably. Letters do come while a man's away!"

"Dwight — I thought if you wouldn't mind if I opened it —"

"Opened it?"

"Yes. You see, it'll be about me mostly —"

"I should have said that it'll be about my brother mostly."

"But you know what it mean. You wouldn't mind if I did open it?"

"But you say you know what'll be in it."

"So I did know — till you — I've got to see that letter, Dwight."

"And so you shall. But not till I show it to you. My dear Lulu, you know how I hate having my mail interfered with."

She might have said: "Small souls always make a point of that." She said nothing. She watched them set off, and kept her mind on Ina's thousand injunctions.

"Don't let Di see much of Bobby Larkin. And, Lulu — if it occurs to her to have Mr. Cornish come up to sing, of course you ask him. You might ask him to supper. And don't let mother overdo. And, Lulu, now do watch Monona's handkerchief — the child will never take a clean one if I'm not here to tell her. . ."

She breathed injunctions to the very step of the bus.

In the bus Dwight leaned forward:

"See that you play post-office squarely, Lulu!" he called, and threw back his head and lifted his eyebrows.

In the train he turned tragic eyes to his wife. "Ina," he said. "It's *ma*. And she's going to die. It can't be. . . ."

Ina said: "But you're going to help her, Dwight, just being there with her."

It was true that the mere presence of the man would bring a kind of fresh life to that worn frame. Tact and wisdom and love would speak through him and minister.

Toward the end of their week's absence the letter from Ninian came.

Lulu took it from the post-office when she went for the mail that evening, dressed in her dark red gown. There was no other letter, and she carried that one letter in her hand all through the streets. She passed those who were surmising what her story might be, who were telling one another what they had heard. But she knew hardly more than they. She passed Cornish in the of his little music shop, and spoke with him; and there was the letter. It was so that Dwight's foster mother's postal card might have looked on its way to be mailed.

Cornish stepped down and overtook her.

"Oh, Miss Lulu. I've got a new song or two —"

She said abstractedly: "Do. Any night. Tomorrow night — could you—" It was as if Lulu were too preoccupied to remember to be ill at ease.

Cornish flushed with pleasure, said that he could indeed.

"Come for supper," Lulu said.

Oh, could he? Wouldn't that be . . . Well, say! Such was his acceptance.

He came for supper. And Di was not at home. She had gone off in the country with Jenny and Bobby, and they merely did not return.

Mrs. Bett and Lulu and Cornish and Monona supped alone. All were at ease, now that they were alone. Especially Mrs. Bett was at ease. It became one of her young nights, her alive and lucid nights. She was *there*. She sat in Dwight's chair, and Lulu sat in Ina's chair. Lulu had picked flowers for the table — a task coveted by her but usually performed by Ina. Lulu had now picked Sweet William and had filled a vase of silver gilt taken from the parlor. Also, Lulu had made ice cream.

"I don't see what Di can be thinking of," Lulu said. "It seems like asking you under false —"

She was afraid of "pretenses" and ended without it.

Cornish savored his steaming beef pie, with sage. "Oh, well!" he said contentedly.

"Kind of a relief, *I* think, to have her gone," said Mrs. Bett, from the fullness of something or other.

"Mother!" Lulu said, twisting her smile.

"Why, my land, I love her," Mrs. Bett explained, "but she wiggles and chitters."

Cornish never made the slightest effort, at any time, to keep a straight face. The honest fellow now laughed loudly.

"Well!" Lulu thought. "He can't be so *very* much in love." And again she thought: "He doesn't know anything about the letter. He thinks Ninian got tired of me." Deep in her heart there abode her certainty that this was not so.

By some etiquette of consent, Mrs. Bett cleared the table and Lulu and Cornish went into the parlor. There lay the letter on the drop-leaf side-table, among the shells. Lulu had carried it there, where she need not see it at her work. The letter looked no more than the advertisement of dental office furniture beneath it. Monona stood indifferently fingering both.

"Monona," Lulu said sharply, "Leave them be!"

Cornish was displaying his music. "Got up quite attractive," he said — it was his formula of praise for his music.

"But we can't try it over," Lulu said, "if Di doesn't come."

"Well, say," said Cornish shyly, "you know I left that Album of Old Favourites here. Some of them we know by heart."

Lulu looked. "I'll tell you something," she said, "there's some of these I can play with one hand — by ear. Maybe —"

"Why sure!" said Cornish.

Lulu sat at the piano. She had on the wool chally, long sacred to the nights when she must combine her servant's estate with the quality of being Ina's sister. She wore her coral beads and her cameo cross. In her absence she had caught the trick of dressing her hair so that it looked even more abundant — but she had not dared to try it so until tonight, when Dwight was gone. Her long wrist was curved high, her thin hand pressed and fingered awkwardly, and at her mistakes her head dipped and strove to make all right. Her foot continuously touched the loud pedal — the blurred sound seemed to accomplish more. So she played "How Can I Leave Thee," and they managed to sing it. So she played "Long, Long Ago," and "Little Nell of Narragansett Bay." Beyond open doors, Mrs. Bett listened, sang, it may be, with them; for when the singers ceased, her voice might be heard still humming a loud closing bar.

"Well!" Cornish cried to Lulu; and then, in the formal village phrase: "You're quite a musician."

"Oh, no!" Lulu disclaimed it. She looked up, flushed, smiling. "I've never done this in front of anybody," she owned. "I don't know what Dwight and Ina'd say. . . ." She drooped.

They rested, and, miraculously, the air of the place had stirred and quickened, as if the crippled, halting melody had some power of its own, and poured this forth, even thus trampled.

"I guess you could do 'most anything you set your hand to," said Cornish.

"Oh, no," Lulu said again.

"Sing and play and cook —"

"But I can't earn anything. I'd like to earn something." But this she had not meant to say. She stopped, rather frightened.

"You would! Why, you have it fine here, I thought."

"Oh, fine, yes. Dwight gives me what I have. And I do their work."

"I see," said Cornish. "I never thought of that," he added. She caught his speculative look — he had heard a tale or two concerning her return, as who in Warbleton had not heard?

"You're wondering why I didn't stay with him?" Lulu said recklessly. This was no less than wrung from her, but its utterance occasioned in her an unspeakable relief.

"Oh, no," Cornish disclaimed, and colored and rocked.

"Yes, you are," she swept on. "The whole town's wondering. Well, I'd like 'em to know, but Dwight won't let me tell."

Cornish frowned, trying to understand.

"Won't let you?" he repeated. "I should say that was your own affair."

"No. Not when Dwight gives me all I have."

"Oh, that —" said Cornish. "That's not right."

"No. But there it is. It puts me — you see what it does to me. They think — they all think my — husband left me."

It was curious to hear her bring out that word — tentatively, depressingly, like someone daring a foreign phrase without warrant.

Cornish said feebly: "Oh, well. . ."

Before she willed it, she was telling him.

"He didn't. He didn't leave me," she cried with passion. "He had another wife." Incredibly it was as if she were defending both him and herself.

"Lord sakes!" said Cornish.

She poured it out, in her passion to tell someone, to share her news of her state where there would be neither hardness nor censure.

"We were in Savannah, Georgia," she said. "We were going to leave for Oregon — going to go through California. We were in the hotel, and he was going out to get the tickets. He started to go. Then he came back. I was sitting the same as there. He opened the door again — the same as here. I saw he looked different — and he said quick: 'There's something you ought to know before we go.' And of course I said, 'What?' And be said it right out — how he was married eighteen years ago and in two years she ran away and she must be dead but he wasn't sure. He hadn't the proofs. So of course I came home. But it wasn't him left me."

"No, no. Of course he didn't," Cornish said earnestly. "But Lord sakes—" he said again. He rose to walk about, found it impracticable and sat down.

"That's what Dwight don't want me to tell — he thinks it isn't true. He thinks — he didn't have any other wife. He thinks he wanted —" Lulu looked up at him. "You see," she said, "Dwight thinks he didn't want me."

"But why don't you make your — husband — I mean, why doesn't he write to Mr. Deacon here, and tell him the truth—" Cornish burst out.

Under this implied belief, she relaxed and into her face came its rare sweetness.

"He has written," she said. "The letter's there."

He followed her look, scowled at the two letters.

"What'd he say?"

"Dwight don't like me to touch his mail. I'll have to wait till he comes back."

"Lord sakes!" said Cornish.

This time he did rise and walk about. He wanted to say something, wanted it with passion. He paused beside Lulu and stammered:

"You — you — you're too nice a girl to get a deal like this. Darned if you aren't."

To her own complete surprise Lulu's eyes filled with tears, and she could not speak. She was by no means above self-sympathy.

"And there ain't," said Cornish sorrowfully, "there ain't a thing I can do."

And yet he was doing much. He was gentle, he was listening, and on his face a frown of concern. His face continually surprised her, it was so fine and alive and near, by comparison with Ninian's loose-lipped, ruddy, impersonal look and Dwight's thin, high-boned hardness. All the time Cornish gave her something instead of drawing upon her. Above all, he was there, and she could talk to him.

"It's — it's funny," Lulu said. "I'd be awful glad if I just *could* know for sure that the other woman was alive — if I couldn't know she's dead."

This surprising admission Cornish seemed to understand.

"Sure you would," he said briefly.

"Cora Waters," Lulu said. "Cora Waters, of San Diego, California.

And she never heard of me."

"No," Cornish admitted. They stared at each other as across some abyss.

In the doorway Mrs. Bett appeared.

"I scraped up everything," she remarked, "and left the dishes set."

"That's right, mamma," Lulu said. "Come and sit down."

Mrs. Bett entered with a leisurely air of doing the thing next expected of her.

"I don't hear any more playin' and singin'," she remarked. "It sounded real nice."

"We — we sung all I knew how to play, I guess, mamma."

"I use' to play on the melodeon," Mrs. Bett volunteered, and spread and examined her right hand.

"Well!" said Cornish.

She now told them about her log house in a New England clearing, when she was a bride. All her store of drama and life came from her. She rehearsed it with far eyes. She laughed at old delights, drooped at old fears. She told about her little daughter who had died at sixteen — a tragedy such as once would have been renewed in a vital ballad. At the end she yawned frankly as if, in some terrible sophistication, she had been telling the story of someone else.

"Give us one more piece," she said.

"Can we?" Cornish asked.

"I can play 'I Think When I Read That Sweet Story of Old,'" Lulu said.

"That's the ticket!" cried Cornish.

They sang it, to Lulu's right hand.

"That's the one you picked out when you was a little girl, Lulie," cried Mrs. Bett.

Lulu had played it now as she must have played it then. Half after nine and Di had not returned. But nobody thought of Di. Cornish rose to go.

"What's them?" Mrs. Bett demanded.

"Dwight's letters, mamma. You mustn't touch them!" Lulu's voice was sharp.

"Say!" Cornish, at the door, dropped his voice. "If there was anything I could do at any time, you'd let me know, wouldn't you?"

That past tense, those subjunctives, unconsciously called upon her to feel no intrusion.

"Oh, thank you," she said. "You don't know how good it is to feel —"

"Of course it is," said Cornish heartily.

They stood for a moment on the porch. The night was one of low clamor from the grass, tiny voices, insisting.

"Of course," said Lulu, "of course you won't — you wouldn't —"

"Say anything?" he divined. "Not for dollars. Not," he repeated, "for dollars."

"But I knew you wouldn't," she told him.

He took her hand. "Good night," he said. "I've had an awful nice time singing and listening to you talk — well, of course — I mean," he cried, "the supper was just fine. And so was the music."

"Oh, no," she said.

Mrs. Bett came into the hall.

"Lulie," she said, "I guess you didn't notice this one's from Ninian."

"Mother —"

"I opened it — why, of course I did. It's from Ninian."

Mrs. Bett held out the opened envelope, unfolded letter, and a yellowed newspaper clipping.

"See," said the old woman, "says, 'Corrie Waters, music hall singer — married last night to Ninian Deacon —' Say, Lulie, that must be her. . . ."

Lulu threw out her hands.

"There!" she cried triumphantly. "He was married to her, just like he said!"

The Plows were at breakfast next morning when Lulu came in casually at the side door. Yes, she said, she had had breakfast. She merely wanted to see them about something. Then she said nothing, but sat looking with a troubled frown at Jenny. Jenny's hair was about her neck, like the hair of a little girl, a south window poured light upon her, the fruit and honey upon the table seemed her only possible food.

"You look troubled, Lulu," Mrs. Plow said. "Is it about getting work?"

"No," said Lulu, "no. I've been places to ask — quite a lot of places. I guess the bakery is going to let me make cake."

"I knew it would come to you," Mrs. Plow said, and Lulu thought that this was a strange way to speak, when she herself had gone after the cakes. But she kept on looking about the room. It was so bright and quiet. As she came in, Mr. Plow had been reading from a book. Dwight never read from a book at table.

"I wish —" said Lulu, as she looked at them. But she did not know what she wished. Certainly it was for no moral excellence, for she perceived none.

"What is it Lulu?" Mr. Plow asked, and he was bright and quiet too, Lulu thought.

"Well," said Lulu, "it's not much. But I wanted Jenny to tell me about last night."

"Last night?"

"Yes. Would you—" Hesitation was her only way of apology. "Where did you go?" She turned to Jenny.

Jenny looked up in her clear and ardent fashion: "We went across the river and carried supper and then we came home."

"What time did you get home?"

"Oh. It was still light. Long before eight, it was."

Lulu hesitated and flushed, asked how long Di and Bobby had stayed there at Jenny's; whereupon she heard that Di had to be home early on account of Mr. Cornish, so that she and Bobby had not stayed at all. To which Lulu said an "of course," but first she stared at Jenny and so impaired the strength of her assent. Almost at once she rose to go.

"Nothing else?'" said Mrs. Plow, catching that look of hers.

Lulu wanted to say: "My husband was married before, just as he said he was." But she said nothing more, and went home. There she put it to Di, and with her terrible bluntness reviewed to Di the testimony.

"You were not with Jenny after eight o'clock. Where were you?" Lulu spoke formally and her rehearsals were evident.

Di said: "When mamma comes home, I'll tell her."

With this Lulu had no idea how to deal, and merely looked at her helplessly. Mrs. Bett, who was lacing her shoes, said casually:

"No need to wait till then. Her and Bobby were out in the side yard sitting in the hammock till all hours."

Di had no answer save her furious flush and Mrs. Bett went on:

"Didn't I tell you! I knew it before the company left, but I didn't say a word. Thinks I, 'She's wiggles and chitters.' So I left her stay where she was."

"But, mother!" Lulu cried. "You didn't even tell me after he'd gone."

"I forgot it." Mrs. Bett said, "finding Ninian's letter and all —" She talked of Ninian's letter.

Di was bright and alert and firm of flesh and erect before Lulu's softness and laxness.

"I don't know what your mother'll say," said Lulu, "and I don't know what people'll think."

"They won't think Bobby and I are tired of each other, anyway," said Di, and left the room.

Through the day Lulu tried to think what she must do. About Di she was anxious and felt without power. She thought of the indignation of Dwight and Ina that Di had not been more scrupulously guarded. She thought of Di's girlish folly, her irritating independence — "and there," Lulu thought, "just the other day I was teaching her to sew." Her mind dwelt too on Dwight's furious anger at the opening of Ninian's letter. But when all this had spent itself, what was she herself to do? She must leave his house before he ordered her to do so, when she told him that she had confided in Cornish, as tell she must. But what was she to *do?* The bakery cake-making would not give her a roof.

Stepping about the kitchen in her blue cotton gown, her hair tight and flat as seemed proper when one was not dressed, she thought about these things. And it was strange: Lulu bore no physical appearance of one in distress or any anxiety. Her head was erect, her movements were strong and swift, her eyes were interested. She was not drooping Lulu with dragging step. She was more intent, she was somehow more operative than she had ever been.

Mrs. Bett was working contentedly beside her, and now and then humming an air of that music of the night before. The sun surged through the kitchen door and east window, a returned oriole swung and fluted on the elm above the gable. Wagons clattered by over the rattling wooden block pavement.

"Ain't it nice with nobody home?" Mrs. Bett remarked at intervals, like the burden of a comic song.

"Hush, mother," Lulu said, troubled, her ethical refinements conflicting with honesty.

"Speak the truth and shame the devil," Mrs. Bett contended.

When dinner was ready at noon, Di did not appear. A little earlier Lulu had heard her moving about her room, and she served her in expectation that she would join them.

"Di must be having the 'tantrim' this time," she thought, and for a time said nothing. But at length she did say: "Why doesn't Di come? I'd better put her plate in the oven."

Rising to do so, she was arrested by her mother. Mrs. Bett was eating a baked potato, holding her fork close to the tines, and presenting a profile of passionate absorption.

"Why, Di went off," she said.

"Went off!"

"Down the walk. Down the sidewalk."

"She must have gone to Jenny's," said Lulu. "I wish she wouldn't do that without telling me."

Monona laughed out and shook her straight hair. "She'll catch it!" she cried in sisterly enjoyment.

It was when Lulu had come back from the kitchen and was seated at the table that Mrs. Bett observed:

"I didn't think Inie'd want her to take her nice new satchel."

"Her satchel?"

"Yes. Inie wouldn't take it north herself, but Di had it."

"Mother," said Lulu, "when Di went away just now, was she carrying a satchel?"

"Didn't I just tell you?" Mrs. Bett demanded, aggrieved. "I said I didn't think Inie —"

"Mother! Which way did she go?"

Monona pointed with her spoon. "She went that way," she said. "I seen her."

Lulu looked at the clock. For Monona had pointed toward the railway station. The twelve-thirty train, which everyone took to the city for shopping, would be just about leaving.

"Monona," said Lulu, "don't you go out of the yard while I'm gone. Mother, you keep her—"

Lulu ran from the house and up the street. She was in her blue cotton dress, her old shoes, she was hatless and without money. When she was still two or three blocks from the station, she heard the twelve-thirty "pulling out."

She ran badly, her ankles in their low, loose shoes continually turning, her arms held taut at her sides. So she came down the platform, and to the ticket window. The contained ticket man, wonted to lost trains and perturbed faces, yet actually ceased counting when he saw her:

"Lenny! Did Di Deacon take that train?"

"Sure she did," said Lenny.

"And Bobby Larkin?" Lulu cared nothing for appearances now.

"He went in on the Local," said Lenny, and his eyes widened.

"Where?"

"See." Lenny thought it through. "Millton," he said. "Yes, sure. Millton. Both of 'em."

"How long till another train?"

"Well, sir," said the ticket man, "you're in luck, if you was goin' too. Seventeen was late this morning — she'll be along, jerk of a lamb's tail."

"Then," said Lulu, "you got to give me a ticket to Millton, without me paying till after — and you got to lend me two dollars."

"Sure thing," said Lenny, with a manner of laying the entire railway system at her feet.

"Seventeen" would rather not have stopped at Warbleton, but Lenny's signal was law on the time card, and the magnificent yellow express slowed down for Lulu. Hatless and in her blue cotton gown, she climbed aboard.

Then her old inefficiency seized upon her. What was she going to do? Millton! She had been there but once, years ago — how could she ever find anybody? Why had she not stayed in Warbleton and asked the sheriff or somebody — no, not the sheriff. Cornish, perhaps. Oh, and Dwight and Ina were going to be angry now! And Di — little Di. As Lulu thought of her she began to cry. She said to herself that she had taught Di to sew.

In sight of Millton, Lulu was seized with trembling and physical nausea. She had never been alone in any unfamiliar town. She put her hands to her hair and for the first time realized her rolled-up sleeves. She was pulling down these sleeves when the conductor came through the train.

"Could you tell me," she said timidly, "the name of the principal hotel in Millton?"

Ninian had asked this as they neared Savannah, Georgia.

The conductor looked curiously at her.

"Why, the Hess House," he said. "Wasn't you expecting anybody to meet you?" he asked, kindly.

"No," said Lulu, "but I'm going to find my folks —" Her voice trailed away.

"Beats all," thought the conductor, using his utility formula for the universe.

In Millton Lulu's inquiry for the Hess House produced no consternation. No one paid any attention to her. She was almost certainly taken to be a new servant there.

"You stop feeling so!" she said to herself angrily at the lobby entrance. "Ain't you been to that big hotel in Savannah, Georgia?"

The Hess House, Millton, had a tradition of its own to maintain, it seemed, and they sent her to the rear basement door. She obeyed meekly, but she lost a good deal of time before she found herself at the end of the office desk. It was still longer before anyone attended her.

"Please, sir!" she burst out. "See if Di Deacon has put her name on your book."

Her appeal was tremendous, compelling. The young clerk listened to her, showed her where to look in the register. When only strange names and strange writing presented themselves there, he said:

"Tried the parlor?"

And directed her kindly with his thumb, and in the other hand a pen divorced from his ear for the express purpose.

In crossing the lobby in the hotel at Savannah, Georgia, Lulu's most pressing problem had been to know where to look. But now the idlers in the Hess House lobby did not exist. In time she found the door of the intensely rose-colored reception room. There, in a fat, rose-colored chair beside a cataract of lace curtain, sat Di, alone.

Lulu entered. She had no idea what to say. When Di looked up, started up, frowned, Lulu felt as if she herself were the culprit.

"I don't believe mamma'll like your taking her nice satchel."

"Well!" said Di, exactly as if she had been at home. And superadded: "My goodness!" And then cried rudely: "What are you here for?"

"For you," said Lulu.

"You — you — you'd ought not to be here, Di."

"What's that to you?" Di cried.

"Why, Di, you're just a little girl —" Lulu saw that this was all wrong, and stopped miserably. How was she to go on? "Di," she said, "if you and

Bobby want to get married, why not let us get you up a nice wedding at home?"
And she saw that this sounded as if she were talking about a tea-party.

"Who said we wanted to be married?"

"Well, he's here."

"Who said he's here?"

"Isn't he?"

Di sprang up. "Aunt Lulu," she said, "you're a funny person to be telling me what to do."

Lulu said, flushing: "I love you just the same as if I was married happy, in a home."

"Well, you aren't!" cried Di cruelly, "And I'm going to do just as I think best."

Lulu thought this over, her look grave and sad. She tried to find something to say.

"What do people say to people," she wondered, "when it's like this?"

"Getting married is for your whole life," was all that came to her.

"Yours wasn't," Di flashed at her.

Lulu's color deepened, but there seemed to be no resentment in her. She must deal with this right — that was what her manner seemed to say. And how should she deal?

"Di," she cried, "come back with me and wait till mamma and papa get home."

"That's likely. They say I'm not to be married till I'm twenty-one."

"Well, but how young that is!"

"It is to you."

"Di! This is wrong — it is wrong."

"There's nothing wrong about getting married — if you stay married."

"Well, then it can't be wrong to let them know."

"It isn't. But they'd treat me wrong. They'd make me stay at home. And I won't stay at home — I won't stay there. They act as if I was ten years old."

Abruptly in Lulu's face there came a light of understanding.

"Why, Di," she said, "do you feel that way too?"

Di missed this. She went on:

"I'm grown up. I feel just as grown up as they do. And I'm not allowed to do a thing I feel. I want to be away —I will be away!"

"I know about that part," Lulu said.

She now looked at Di with attention. Was it possible that Di was suffering in the air of that home as she herself suffered? She had not thought of that. There Di had seemed so young, so dependent, so — a-squirm. Here, by herself, waiting for Bobby, in the Hess House at Millton, she was curiously adult. Would she be adult if she were let alone?

"You don't know what it's like," Di cried, "to be hushed up and laughed at and paid no attention to, everything you say."

"Don't I?" said Lulu. "Don't I?"

She was breathing quickly and looking at Di. If *this* was why Di was leaving home. . . .

"But, Di," she cried, "do you love Bobby Larkin?"

By this Di was embarrassed. "I've got to marry somebody," she said, "and it might as well be him."

"But is it him?"

"Yes, it is," said Di. "But," she added, "I know I could love almost anybody real nice that was nice to me." And this she said, not in her own right, but either she had picked it up somewhere and adopted it, or else the terrible modernity and honesty of her day somehow spoke through her, for its own. But to Lulu it was as if something familiar turned its face to be recognized.

"Di!" she cried.

"It's true. You ought to know that." She waited for a moment. "You did it," she added. "Mamma said so."

At this onslaught Lulu was stupefied. For she began to perceive its truth.

"I know what I want to do, I guess," Di muttered, as if to try to cover what she had said.

Up to that moment, Lulu had been feeling intensely that she understood Di, but that Di did not know this. Now Lulu felt that she and Di actually shared some unsuspected sisterhood. It was not only that they were both badgered by Dwight. It was more than that. They were two women. And she must make Di know that she understood her.

"Di," Lulu said, breathing hard, "what you just said is true, I guess. Don't think I don't know. And now I'm going to tell you —"

She might have poured it all out, claimed her kinship with Di by virtue of that which had happened in Savannah, Georgia. But Di said:

"Here come some ladies. And goodness, look at the way you look!"

Lulu glanced down. "I know," she said, "but I guess you'll have to put up with me."

The two women entered, looked about with the complaisance of those who examine a hotel property, find criticism incumbent, and have no errand. These two women had outdressed their occasion. In their presence Di kept silence, turned away her head, gave them to know that she had nothing to do with this blue cotton person beside her. When they had gone on, "What do you mean by my having to put up with you?" Di asked sharply.

"I mean I'm going to stay with you."

Di laughed scornfully — she was again the rebellious child. "I guess Bobby'll have something to say about that," she said insolently.

"They left you in my charge."

"But I'm not a baby — the idea, Aunt Lulu!"

"I'm going to stay right with you," said Lulu. She wondered what she should do if Di suddenly marched away from her, through that bright lobby and into the street. She thought miserably that she must follow. And then her whole concern for the ethics of Di's course was lost in her agonized memory of her terrible, broken shoes.

Di did not march away. She turned her back squarely upon Lulu, and looked out of the window. For her life Lulu could think of nothing more to say. She was now feeling miserably on the defensive.

They were sitting in silence when Bobby Larkin came into the room. Four Bobby Larkins there were, in immediate succession.

The Bobby who had just come down the street was distinctly perturbed, came hurrying, now and then turned to the left when he met folk, glanced sidewise here and there, was altogether anxious and ill at ease.

The Bobby who came through the hotel was a Bobby who had on an importance assumed for the crisis of threading the lobby — a Bobby who wished it to be understood that here he was, a man among men, in the Hess House at Millton.

The Bobby who entered the little rose room was the Bobby who was no less than overwhelmed with the stupendous character of the adventure upon which he found himself.

The Bobby who incredibly came face to face with Lulu was the real Bobby into whose eyes leaped instant, unmistakable relief.

Di flew to meet him. She assumed all the pretty agitations of her role, ignored Lulu.

"Bobby! Is it all right?"

Bobby looked over her head.

"Miss Lulu," he said fatuously. "If it ain't Miss Lulu."

He looked from her to Di and did not take in Di's resigned shrug.

"Bobby," said Di, "she's come to stop us getting married, but she can't. I've told her so."

"She don't have to stop us," quoth Bobby gloomily, "we're stopped."

"What do you mean?" Di laid one hand flatly along her cheek, instinctive in her melodrama.

Bobby drew down his brows, set his hand on his leg, elbow out.

"We're minors," said he.

"Well, gracious, you didn't have to tell them that."

"No. They knew I was."

"But, Silly! Why didn't you tell them you're not?"

"But I am."

Di stared. "For pity sakes," she said, "don't you know how to do anything?"

"What would you have me do?" he inquired indignantly, with his head held stiff, and with a boyish, admirable lift of chin.

"Why, tell them we're both twenty-one. We look it. We know we're responsible — that's all they care for. Well, you are a funny . . ."

"You wanted me to lie?" he said.

"Oh, don't make out you never told a fib."

"Well, but this —" he stared at her.

"I never heard of such a thing," Di cried accusingly.

"Anyhow," he said. "There's nothing to do now. The cat's out. I've told our ages. We've got to have our folks in on it."

"Is that all you can think of?" she demanded.

"What else?"

"Why, come on to Bainbridge, or Holt, and tell them we're of age and be married there."

"Di," said Bobby, "why that'd be a rotten go."

Di said, oh very well, if he didn't want to marry her. He replied stonily that of course he wanted to marry her. Di stuck out her little hand. She was at a disadvantage. She could use no arts, with Lulu sitting there, looking on. "Well, then, come on to Bainbridge," Di cried, and rose.

Lulu was thinking: "What shall I say? I don't know what to say. I don't know what I can say." Now she also rose, and laughed awkwardly. "I've told Di," she said to Bobby, "that wherever you two go, I'm going too. Di's folks left her in my care, you know. So you'll have to take me along, I guess." She spoke in a manner of distinct apology.

At this Bobby had no idea what to reply. He looked down miserably at the carpet. His whole manner was a mute testimony to his participation in the eternal query: How did I get into it?

"Bobby," said Di, "are you going to let her lead you home?"

This of course nettled him, but not in the manner on which Di had counted. He said loudly:

"I'm not going to Bainbridge or Holt or any other town and lie, to get you or any other girl."

Di's head lifted, tossed, turned from him.

"You're about as much like a man in a story," she said, "as — as papa is."

The two idly inspecting women again entered the rose room, this time to stay. They inspected Lulu too. And Lulu rose and stood between the lovers.

"Hadn't we all get the four-thirty to Warbleton?" she said, and swallowed.

"Oh, if Bobby wants to back out —" said Di.

"I don't want to back out," Bobby contended furiously. "b-b-but I won't —"

"Come on, Aunt Lulu," said Di grandly.

Bobby led the way through the lobby, Di followed, and Lulu brought up the rear. She walked awkwardly, eyes down, her hands stiffly held. Heads turned to look at her. They passed into the street.

"You two go ahead," said Lulu, "so they won't think —"

They did so, and she followed, and did not know where to look, and thought of her broken shoes.

At the station, Bobby put them on the train and stepped back. He had, he said, something to see to there in Millton. Di did not look at him. And Lulu's good-by spoke her genuine regret for all.

"Aunt Lulu," said Di, "you needn't think I'm going to sit with you. You look as if you're crazy. I'll sit back here."

"All right, Di," said Lulu humbly.

It was nearly six o'clock when they arrived at the Deacons'. Mrs. Bett stood on the porch, her hands rolled in her apron.

"Surprise for you!" she called brightly.

Before they had reached the door, Ina bounded from the hall.

"Darling!"

She seized upon Di, kissed her loudly, drew back from her, saw the travelling bag.

"My new bag!" she cried. "Di! What have you got that for?"

In any embarrassment Di's instinctive defense was hearty laughter. She now laughed heartily, kissed her mother again, and ran up the stairs.

Lulu slipped by her sister, and into the kitchen.

"Well, where have *you* been?" cried Ina. "I declare, I never saw such a family. Mamma don't know anything and neither of you will tell anything."

"Mamma knows a-plenty," snapped Mrs. Bett.

Monona, who was eating a sticky gift, jumped stiffly up and down. "You'll catch it — you'll catch it!" she sent out her shrill general warning.

Mrs. Bett followed Lulu to the kitchen:

"I didn't tell Inie about the new bag and now she says I don't know nothing," she complained. "There I knew about the bag the hull time, but I wasn't going to tell her and spoil her gettin' home." She banged the stove-griddle. "I've a good no notion not to eat a mouthful o' supper," she announced.

"Mother, please!" said Lulu passionately. "Stay here. Help me. I've got enough to get through tonight."

Dwight had come home. Lulu could hear Ina pouring out to him the mysterious circumstance of the bag, could hear the exaggerated air of the casual with which he always received the excitement of another, and especially of his Ina. Then she heard Ina's feet padding up the stairs, after that

Di's shrill, nervous laughter. Lulu felt a pang of pity for Di, as if she herself were about to face them.

There was not time both to prepare supper and to change the blue cotton dress. In that dress Lulu was pouring water when Dwight entered the dining room.

"Ah!" said he. "Our festive ball-gown."

She gave him her hand, with her peculiar sweetness of expression — almost as if she were sorry for him or were bidding him good-bye.

"*That* shows who you dress for!" he cried. "You dress for me. Ina, aren't you jealous? Lulu dresses for me!"

Ina had come in with Di, and both were excited, and Ina's head was moving stiffly, as in all her indignations. Already Monona was singing.

"Lulu," said Dwight, "really? Can't you run up and slip on another dress?"

Lulu sat down in her place. "No," she said. "I'm too tired. I'm sorry, Dwight."

"It seems to me —" he began.

"I don't want any," said Monona.

But no one noticed, and Ina did not defer even to Dwight, who measured delicate, troy occasions by avoirdupois, said brightly:

"Now, Di. You must tell us all about it. Where have you and Aunt Lulu been with mamma's new bag?"

"Aunt Lulu!" cried Dwight. "Aha! So Aunt Lulu went along. Well now, that alters it."

"How does it?" asked his Ina crossly.

"Why, when Aunt Lulu goes on a jaunt," said Dwight Herbert, "events begin to event."

"Come, Di, let's hear," said Ina.

"Ina," said Lulu, "first can't we hear something about your visit? How is —"

Her eyes consulted Dwight. His features dropped, the lines of his face dropped, its muscles seemed to sag. A look of suffering was in his eyes.

"She'll never be any better," he said. "I know we've said good-bye to her for the last time."

"Oh, Dwight!" said Lulu.

"She knew it too," he said. "It — it put me out of business, I can tell you. She gave me my start — she took all the care of me — taught me to read — she's the only mother I ever knew —" He stopped, and opened his eyes wide on account of their dimness.

"They said she was like another person while Dwight was there," said Ina, and entered upon a length of particulars, and details of the journey. These details Dwight interrupted: Couldn't Lulu remember that he liked sage on the chops? He could hardly taste it. He had, he said, told her this thirty-seven times. And when she said that she was sorry, "Perhaps you think I'm sage enough," said the witty fellow.

"Dwightie!" said Ina. "Mercy." She shook her head at him. "Now, Di," she went on, keeping the thread all this time. "Tell us your story. About the bag."

"Oh, mamma," said Di, "let me eat my supper."

"And so you shall, darling. Tell it in your own way. Tell us first what you've done since we've been away. Did Mr. Cornish come to see you?"

"Yes," said Di, and flashed a look at Lulu.

But eventually they were back again before that new black bag. And Di would say nothing. She laughed, squirmed, grew irritable, laughed again.

"Lulu!" Ina demanded. "You were with her — where in the world had you been? Why, but you couldn't have been with her — in that dress. And yet I saw you come in the gate together."

"What!" cried Dwight Herbert, drawing down his brows. "You certainly did not so far forget us, Lulu, as to go on the street in that dress?"

"It's a good dress," Mrs. Bett now said positively. "Of course it's a good dress. Lulie wore it on the street — of course she did. She was gone a long time. I made me a cup o' tea, and *then* she hadn't come."

"Well," said Ina, "I never heard anything like this before. Where were you both?"

One would say that Ina had entered into the family and been born again, identified with each one. Nothing escaped her. Dwight, too, his intimacy was incredible.

"Put an end to this, Lulu," he commanded. "Where were you two — since you make such a mystery?"

Di's look at Lulu was piteous, terrified.

Di's fear of her father was now clear to Lulu. And Lulu feared him too. Abruptly she heard herself temporizing, for the moment making common cause with Di.

"Oh," she said, "we have a little secret. Can't we have a secret if we want one?"

"Upon my word," Dwight commented, "she has a beautiful secret. I don't know about your secrets, Lulu."

Every time that he did this, that fleet, lifted look of Lulu's seemed to bleed.

"I'm glad for my dinner," remarked Monona at last. "Please excuse me." On that they all rose. Lulu stayed in the kitchen and did her best to make her tasks indefinitely last. She had nearly finished when Di burst in.

"Aunt Lulu, Aunt Lulu!" she cried. "Come in there, come. I can't stand it. What am I going to do?"

"Di, dear," said Lulu. "Tell your mother — you must tell her."

"She'll cry," Di sobbed. "Then she'll tell papa — and he'll never stop talking about it. I know him — every day he'll keep it going. After he scolds me it'll be a joke for months. I'll die — I'll die, Aunt Lulu."

Ina's voice sounded in the kitchen. "What are you two whispering about? I declare, mamma's hurt, Di, at the way you're acting. . ."

"Let's go out on the porch," said Lulu, and when Di would have escaped, Ina drew her with them, and handled the situation in the only way that she knew how to handle it, by complaining: Well, but what in this world. . . .

Lulu threw a white shawl about her blue cotton dress.

"A bridal robe," said Dwight. "How's that, Lulu -- what are *you* wearing a bridal robe for — eh?"

She smiled dutifully. There was no need to make him angry, she reflected, before she must. He had not yet gone into the parlor — had not yet asked for his mail.

It was a warm dusk, moonless, windless. The sounds of the village street came in — laughter, a touch at a piano, a chiming clock. Lights starred and quickened in the blurred houses. Footsteps echoed on the board walks. The gate opened. The gloom yielded up Cornish.

Lulu was inordinately glad to see him. To have the strain of the time broken by him was like hearing, on a lonely winter wakening, the clock strike reassuring dawn.

"Lulu," said Dwight low, "your dress. Do go!"

Lulu laughed. "The bridal shawl takes off the curse," she said.

Cornish, in his gentle way, asked about the journey, about the sick woman — and Dwight talked of her again, and this time his voice broke. Di was curiously silent. When Cornish addressed her, she replied simply and directly — the rarest of Di's manners, in fact not Di's manner at all. Lulu spoke not at all — it was enough to have this respite.

After a little while the gate opened again. It was Bobby. In the besetting fear that he was leaving Di to face something alone, Bobby had arrived.

And now Di's spirits rose. To her this presence meant repentance, recapitulation. Her laugh rang out, her replies came archly. But Bobby was plainly not playing up. Bobby was, in fact, hardly less than glum. It was Dwight, the irrepressible fellow, who kept the talk going. And it was no less than deft, his continuously displayed ability playfully to pierce Lulu. Some one had "married at the drop of the hat. You know the bind of girl?" And someone "made up a likely story to soothe her own pride — you know how they do that?"

"Well," said Ina, "my part, I think the most awful thing is to have somebody one loves keep secrets from one. No wonder folks get crabbed and spiteful with such treatment."

"Mamma!" Monona shouted from her room. "Come and hear me

say my prayers!"

Monona entered this request with precision on Ina's nastiest moments, but she always rose, unabashed, and went, motherly and dutiful, to hear devotions, as if that function and the process of living ran their two divided channels.

She had dispatched this errand and was returning when Mrs. Bett crossed the lawn from Grandma Gates's, where the old lady had taken comfort in Mrs.. Bett's ministrations for an hour.

"Don't you help me," Mrs. Bett warned them away sharply. "I guess I can help myself yet awhile."

She gained her chair. And still in her momentary rule of attention, she said clearly:

"I got a joke. Grandma Gates says it's all over town Di and Bobby Larkin eloped off together today. *He!*" The last was a single note of laughter, high and brief.

The silence fell.

"What nonsense!" Dwight Herbert said angrily.

But Ina said tensely: *"Is* it nonsense? Haven't I been trying and trying to find out where the black satchel went? Di!"

Di's laughter rose, but it sounded thin and false.

"Listen to that, Bobby," she said. "Listen!"

"That won't do, Di," said Ina. "You can't deceive mamma and don't you try!"

Her voice trembled, she was frantic with loving and authentic anxiety, but she was without power, she overshadowed the real gravity of the moment by her indignation.

"Mrs. Deacon —" began Bobby, and stood up, very straight and manly before them all.

But Dwight intervened, Dwight, the father, the master of his house. Here was something requiring him to act. So the father set his face like a mask and brought down his hand on the rail of the porch. It was as if the sound shattered a thousand filaments — where?

"Diana!" his voice was terrible, demanded a response, ravened among them.

"Yes, papa," said Di, very small.

"Answer your mother. Answer *me*. Is there anything to this absurd tale?"

"No, papa," said Di, trembling.

"Nothing whatever?"

"Nothing whatever."

"Can you imagine how such a ridiculous report started?"

"No, papa."

"Very well. Now we know where we are. If anyone hears this report repeated, send them to *me*."

"Well, but that satchel —" said Ina, to whom an idea manifested less as a function than as a leech.

"One moment," said Dwight. "Lulu will of course verify what the child has said."

There had never been an adult moment until that day when Lulu had not instinctively taken the part of the parents, of all parents. Now she saw Dwight's cruelty to her as his cruelty to Di; she saw Ina, herself a child in maternity, as ignorant of how to deal with the moment as was Dwight. She saw Di's falseness partly parented by these parents. She burned at the enormity of Dwight's appeal to her for verification. She threw up her head and no one had ever seen Lulu look like this.

"If you cannot settle this with Di," said Lulu, "you cannot settle it with me."

"A shifty answer," said Dwight. "You have a genius at misrepresenting facts, you know, Lulu."

"Bobby wanted to say something," said Ina, still troubled.

"No, Mrs. Deacon," said Bobby, low. "I have nothing — more to say."

In a little while, when Bobby went away, Di walked with him to the gate. It was as if, the worst having happened to her, she dared everything now.

"Bobby," she said, "you hate a lie. But what else could I do?"

He could not see her, could see only the little moon of her face, blurring.

"And anyhow," said Di, "it wasn't a lie. We *didn't* elope, did we?"

"What do you think I came for tonight?" asked Bobby.

The day had aged him; he spoke like a man. His very voice came gruffly. But she saw nothing, softened to him, yielded, was ready to take his regret that they had not gone on.

"Well, I came for one thing," said Bobby, "to tell you that I couldn't stand for your wanting me to lie today. Why, Di— I hate a lie. And now tonight —" He spoke his code almost beautifully. "I'd rather," he said, "they had never let us see each other again than to lose you the way I've lost you now."

"Bobby!"

"It's true. We mustn't talk about it."

"Bobby! I'll go back and tell them all."

"You can't go back," said Bobby. "Not out of a thing like that."

She stood staring after him. She heard someone coming and she turned toward the house, and met Cornish leaving.

"Miss Di," he cried, "if you're going to elope with anybody, remember it's with me!"

Her defense was ready — her laughter rang out so that the departing Bobby might hear.

She came back to the steps and mounted slowly in the lamp light, a little white thing with whom birth had taken exquisite pains.

"If," she said, "if you have any fear that I may ever elope with Bobby Larkin, let it rest. I shall never marry him if he asks me fifty times a day."

"Really, darling?" cried Ina.

"Really and truly," said Di, "and he knows it, too."

Lulu listened and read them all.

"I wondered," said Ina pensively, "I wondered if you wouldn't see that Bobby isn't much beside that nice Mr. Cornish!"

When Di had gone upstairs, Ina said to Lulu in a manner of cajoling confidence:

"Sister —" she rarely called her that, "why did you and Di have the black bag?"

So that after all it was a relief to Lulu to hear Dwight ask casually:

"By the way, Lulu, haven't I got some mail somewhere about?"

"There are two letters on the parlor table," Lulu answered. To Ina she added: "Let's go in the parlor."

As they passed through the hall, Mrs. Bett was going up the stairs to bed — when she mounted stairs she stooped her shoulders, bunched her extremities, and bent her head. Lulu looked after her, as if she were half minded to claim the protection so long lost.

Dwight lighted the gas. "Better turn down the gas jest a little," said he, tirelessly.

Lulu handed him the two letters. He saw Ninian's writing and looked up, said "A-ha!" and held it while he leisurely read the advertisement of dental furniture, Ina reading over his shoulder. "A-ha!" he said again, and with designed deliberation turned to Ninian's letter. "An epistle from my dear brother Ninian." The words failed, as he saw the unsealed flap.

"You opened the letter?" he inquired credulously. Fortunately he had no climaxes of furious calm for high occasions. All had been used on such occasions. "You opened the letter" came in a tone of deeper horror than "You picked the flower" — once put to Lulu.

She said nothing. As it is impossible to continue looking indignantly at someone who is not looking at you, Dwight turned to Ina, who was horror and sympathy, a nice half and half.

"Your sister has been opening my mail," he said.

"But, Dwight, if it's from Ninian —"

"It is *my* mail," he reminded her. "She had asked me if she might open it. Of course I told her no."

"Well," said Ina practically, "what does he say?"

"I shall open the letter in my own time. My present concern is this disregard of my wishes." His self control was perfect, ridiculous, devilish. He was self-controlled because thus he could be more effectively cruel than in temper. "What excuse have you to offer?"

Lulu was not looking at him. "None," she said — not defiantly, or ingratiatingly, or fearfully. Merely, "None."

"Why did you do it?"

She smiled faintly and shook her head.

"Dwight," said Ina, reasonably, "she knows what's in it and we don't. Hurry up."

"She is," said Dwight, after a pause, "an ungrateful woman."

He opened the letter, saw the clipping, the avowal, with its facts.

"A-ha!" said he. "So after having been absent with my brother for a month, you find that you were *not* married to him."

Lulu spoke her exceeding triumph.

"You see, Dwight," she said, "he told the truth. He had another wife. He didn't just leave me."

Dwight instantly cried: "But this seems to me to make you considerably worse than if he had."

"Oh, no," Lulu said serenely. "Why," she said, "you know how it all came about. He — he was used to thinking of his wife as dead. If he hadn't — hadn't liked me, he wouldn't have told me. You see that, don't you?"

Dwight laughed. "That your apology?" he asked.

She said nothing.

"Look here, Lulu," he went on, "this is a bad business. The less you say about it the better, for all our sakes — *you* see that, don't you?"

"See that? Why, no. I wanted you to write to him so I could tell the truth. You said I mustn't tell the truth till I had the proofs —"

"Tell who?"

"Tell everybody. I want them to know."

"Then you care nothing for our feelings in this matter?"

She looked at him now. "Your feelings?"

"It's nothing to you that we have a brother who's a bigamist?"

"But it's me — it's me."

"You! You're completely out of it. Just let it rest as it is and it'll drop."

"I want the people to know the truth," Lulu said.

"But it's nobody's business but our business! I take it you don't intend to sue Ninian?"

"Sue him? Oh no!"

"Then, for all our sakes, let's drop the matter."

Lulu had fallen in one of her old attitudes, tense, awkward, her hands awkwardly placed, her feet twisted. She kept putting a lock back of her ear, she kept swallowing.

"Tell you, Lulu," said Dwight. "Here are three of us. Our interests are the same in this thing — only Ninian is our relative and he's nothing to you now. Is he?"

"Why, no," said Lulu in surprise.

"Very well. Let's have a vote. Your snap judgment is to tell this disgraceful fact broadcast. Mine is, least said, soonest mended. What do you say, Ina — considering Di and all?"

"Oh, goodness," said Ina, "if we get mixed up with bigamy, we'll never get away from it. Why, I wouldn't have it told for worlds."

Still in that twisted position, Lulu looked up at her. Her straying hair, her parted lips, her lifted eyes were singularly pathetic.

"My poor, poor sister!" Ina said. She struck together her little plump hands. "Oh, Dwight — when I think of it: What have I done — what have we done that I should have a good, kind, loving husband — be so protected, so loved, when other women. . . . Darling!" she sobbed, and drew near to Lulu. "You *know* how sorry I am — we all are. . . . "

Lulu stood up. The white shawl slipped to the floor. Her hands were stiffly joined.

"Then," she said, "give me the only thing I've got — that's my pride. My pride — that he didn't want to get rid of me."

They stared at her. "What about my pride?" Dwight called to her, as across great distances. "Do you think I want everybody to know my brother did a thing like that?"

"You can't help that," said Lulu.

"But I want you to help it. I want you to promise me that you won't shame us like this before all our friends."

"You want me to promise what?"

"I want you — I ask you," Dwight said with an effort, "to promise me that you will keep this, with us — a family secret."

"No!" Lulu cried. "No. I won't do it! I won't do it! I won't do it!"

It was like some crude chant, knowing only two tones. She threw out her hands, her wrists long and dark on her blue skirt.

"Can't you understand anything?" she asked. "I've lived here all my life — on your money. I've not been strong enough to work, they say — well, but I've been strong enough to be a hired girl in your house — and I've been glad to pay for my keep. . . . But there wasn't anything about it I liked. Nothing about being here that I liked. . . . Well, then I got a little something, same as other folks. I thought I was married and I went off on the train and he bought me things and I saw the different towns. And then it was all a mistake. I didn't have any of it. I came back here and went into your kitchen again — I don't know why I came back. I s'pose because I'm most thirty-four and new things ain't so easy anymore — but what have I got or what'll I ever have? And now you want to put on to me having folks look at me and think he run off and left me, and having 'em all wonder. . . . I can't stand it. I can't stand it. I can't. . . . "

"You'd rather they'd know he fooled you, when he had another wife?" Dwight sneered.

"Yes! Because he wanted me. How do I know — maybe he wanted me only just because he was lonesome, the way I was. I don't care why! And I won't have folks think he went and left me."

"That," said Dwight, "is a wicked vanity."

"That's the truth. Well, why can't they know the truth?"

"And bring disgrace on us all."

"It's me — it's me —" Lulu's individualism strove against that terrible tribal sense, was shattered by it.

"It's all of us!" Dwight boomed. "It's Di."

"Di?" He had Lulu's eyes now.

"Why, it's chiefly on Di's account that I'm talking," said Dwight.

"How would it hurt Di?"

"To have a thing like that in the family? Well, can't you see how it'd hurt her?"

"Would it, Ina? Would it hurt Di?"

"Why, it would shame her — embarrass her — make people wonder what kind of stock she came from — oh," Ina sobbed, "my pure little girl!"

"Hurt her prospects, of course," said Dwight. "Anybody could see that."

"I s'pose it would." said Lulu. She clasped her arms tightly, awkwardly, and stepped about the floor, her broken shoes showing beneath her cotton skirt.

"When a family once gets talked about for any reason —" said Ina and shuddered.

"I'm talked about now!"

"But nothing that you could help. If he got tired of you, you couldn't help that." This misstep was Dwight's.

"No," Lulu said, "I couldn't help that. And I couldn't help his other wife, either."

"Bigamy," said Dwight, "that's a crime."

"I've done no crime," said Lulu.

"Bigamy," said Dwight, "disgraces everybody it touches."

"Even Di," Lulu said.

"Lulu," said Dwight, "on Di's account will you promise us to let this thing rest with us three?"

"I s'pose so," said Lulu quietly.

"You will?"

"I s'pose so."

Ina sobbed: "Thank you, thank you, Lulu. This makes up for everything."

Lulu was thinking: "Di has a hard enough time as it is." Aloud she said: "I told Mr. Cornish, but he won't tell."

"I'll see to that," Dwight graciously offered.

"Goodness," Ina said, "so he knows. Well, that settles —" She said no more.

"You'll be happy to think you've done this for us, Lulu," said Dwight.

"I s'pose so," said Lulu.

Ina, pink from her little gust of sobbing, went to her, kissed her, her trim tan tailor suit against Lulu's blue cotton.

"My sweet, self-sacrificing sister," she murmured.

"Oh stop that!" Lulu said.

Dwight took her hand, lying limply in his. "I can now," he said, "overlook the matter of the letter."

Lulu drew back. She put her hair behind her ears, swallowed, and cried out. "Don't you go around pitying me! I'll have you know I'm glad the whole thing happened!"

Cornish had ordered six new copies of a popular song. He knew that it was popular because it was called so in a Chicago paper. When the six copies arrived with a danseuse on the covers he read the "words," looked wistfully at the symbols which shut him out, and felt well pleased.

"Got up quite attractive," he thought, and fastened the six copies in the window of his music store.

It was not yet nine o'clock of a vivid morning. Mr. Cornish had his floor and sidewalk sprinkled, his red and blue plush piano spreads dusted. He sat at a folding table well back in the store, and opened a law book.

For half an hour he read. Then he found himself looking off the page, stabbed by a reflection which always stabbed him anew: Was he really getting anywhere with his law? And where did he really hope to get? Of late when he awoke at night this question had stood by the cot, waiting.

The cot had appeared there in the back of the music store, behind a dark sateen curtain with too few rings on the wire. How little else was in there, nobody knew. But those passing in the late evening saw the blur of his kerosene lamp behind that curtain and were smitten by a realistic illusion of personal loneliness.

It was behind that curtain that these unreasoning questions usually attacked him, when his giant, wavering shadow had died upon the wall and the faint smell of the extinguished lamp went with him to his bed; or when he waked before any sign of dawn. In the mornings all was cheerful and wonted — the question had not before attacked him among his red and blue plush spreads, his golden oak and ebony cases, of a sunshiny morning.

A step at his door set him flying. He wanted passionately to sell a piano.

"Well!" he cried, when he saw his visitor.

It was Lulu, in her dark red suit and her tilted hat.

"Well!" she also said, and seemed to have no idea of saying anything else. Her excitement was so obscure that he did not discern it.

"You're out early," said he, participating in the village chorus of this bright challenge at this hour.

"Oh, no," said Lulu.

He looked out the window, pretending to be caught by something passing, leaned to see it the better.

"Oh, how'd you get along last night?" he asked, and wondered why he had not thought to say it before.

"All right, thank you," said Lulu.

"Was he — about the letter, you know?"

"Yes," she said, "but that didn't matter. You'll be sure," she added, "not to say anything about what was in the letter?"

"Why, not till you tell me I can," said Cornish, "but won't everybody know now?"

"No," Lulu said.

At this he had no more to say, and feeling his speculation in his eyes, dropped them to them to a piano scarf from which he began flicking invisible specks.

"I came to tell you good-bye," Lulu said.

"Good-bye!"

"Yes. I'm going off — for a while. My satchel's in the bakery — I had my breakfast in the bakery."

"Say!" Cornish cried warmly, "then everything *wasn't* all right last night?"

"As right as it can ever be with me," she told him. "Oh, yes. Dwight forgave me."

"Forgave you!"

She smiled, and trembled.

"Look here," said Cornish, "you come here and sit down and tell me about this."

He led her to the folding table, as the only social spot in that vast area of his, seated her in the one chair, and for himself brought up a piano stool. But after all she told him nothing. She merely took the comfort of his kindly indignation.

"It came out all right," she said only. "But I won't stay there anymore. I can't do that."

"Then what are you going to do?"

"In Millton yesterday," she said, "I saw an advertisement in the hotel

— they wanted a chambermaid."

"Oh, Miss Bett!" he cried. At that name she flushed. "Why," said Cornish, "you must have been coming from Millton yesterday when I saw you. I noticed Miss Di had her bag —" He stopped, stared. "You brought her back!" he deduced everything.

"Oh!" said Lulu. "Oh, no I mean —"

"I heard about the eloping again this morning," he said. "That's just what you did — you brought her back."

"You mustn't tell that! You won't? You won't!"

"No. 'Course not." He mulled it. "You tell me this: Do they know? I mean about your going after her?"

"No."

"You never told!"

"They don't know she went."

"That's a funny thing," he blurted out, "for you not to tell her folks — I mean, right off. Before last night. . . ."

"You don't know them. Dwight'd never let up on that — he'd *joke* her about it after a while."

"But it seems —"

"Ina'd talk about disgracing *her.* They wouldn't know what to do. There's no sense in telling them. They aren't a mother and father," Lulu said.

Cornish was not accustomed to deal with so much reality. But Lulu's reality he could grasp.

"You're a trump anyhow," he affirmed.

"Oh, no," said Lulu modestly.

Yes, she was. He insisted upon it.

"By George," he exclaimed, "you don't find very many *married* women with as good sense as you've got."

At this, just as he was agonizing because he had seemed to refer to the truth that she was, after all, not married, at this Lulu laughed in some amusement, and said nothing.

"You've been a jewel in their home all right," said Cornish. "I bet they'll miss you if you do go."

"They'll miss my cooking," Lulu said without bitterness.

"They'll miss more than that, I know. I've often watched you there —"

"You have?"

It was not so much pleasure as passionate gratitude which lighted her eyes.

"You made the whole place," said Cornish.

"You don't mean just the cooking?"

"No, no. I mean — well, that first night when you played croquet. I felt at home when you came out."

That look of hers, rarely seen, which was no less than a look of loveliness, came now to Lulu's face. After a pause she said:

"I never had but one compliment before that wasn't for my cooking." She seemed to feel that she must confess to that one. "He told me I done my hair up nice." She added conscientiously: "That was after I took notice how the ladies in Savannah, Georgia, done up theirs."

"Well, well," said Cornish only.

"Well," said Lulu, "I must be going now. I wanted to say good-bye to you — and there's one or two other places. . . ."

"I hate to have you go," said Cornish, and tried to add something. "I hate to have you go," was all that he could find to add.

Lulu rose. "Oh, well," was all that she could find.

They shook hands, Lulu laughing a little. Cornish followed her to the door. He had begun on "Look here, I wish . . . " when Lulu said "good-bye," and paused, wishing intensely to know what he would have said. But all that he said was: "Good-bye. I wish you weren't going."

"So do I," said Lulu, and went, still laughing.

Cornish saw her red dress vanish from his door, flash by his window, her head averted. And there settled upon him a depression out of all proportion to the slow depression of his days. This was more — it assailed him, absorbed him.

He stood staring out the window. Some one passed with a greeting of which he was conscious too late to return. He wandered back down the store and his pianos looked back at him like strangers. Down there was the green curtain which screened his home life. He suddenly hated that green curtain. He hated this whole place. For the first time it occurred to him that he hated Warbleton. He came back to his table, and sat down before his law book. But he sat, chin on chest, regarding it. No . . . no escape that way. . . .

A step at the door and he sprang up. It was Lulu, coming toward him, her face unsmiling but somehow quite lighted. In her hand was a letter.

"See," she said. "At the office was this. . . ."

She thrust in his hand the single sheet. He read:

. . . just wanted you to know you're actually rid of me. I've heard from her, in Brazil. She ran out of money and thought of me, and her lawyer wrote to me. . . . I've never been any good — Dwight would tell you that if his pride would let him tell the truth once in a while. But there ain't anything in my life makes me feel as bad as this. . . . I s'pose you couldn't understand and I don't myself. . . . Only the sixteen years keeping still made me think she was gone sure . . . but you were so downright good, that's what was the worst. . . do you see what I want to say. . . .

Cornish read it all and looked at Lulu. She was grave and in her eyes there was a look of dignity such as he had never seen them wear. Incredible dignity.

"He didn't lie to get rid of me — and she was alive, just as he thought she might be," she said.

"I'm glad," said Cornish.

"Yes," said Lulu. "He isn't quite so bad as Dwight tried to make him out."

It was not of this that Cornish had been thinking.

"Now you're free," he said.

"Oh, that . . . " said Lulu.

She replaced her letter in its envelope. "Now I'm really going," she said. "Good-bye for sure this time. . . . "

Her words trailed away. Cornish had laid his hand on her arm.

"Don't say good-bye," he said.

"It's late," she said. "I —"

"Don't you go," said Cornish.

She looked at him mutely.

"Do you think you could possibly stay here with me?"

"Oh!" said Lulu, like no word.

He went on, not looking at her. "I haven't got anything. I guess maybe you've heard something about a little something I'm supposed to in-herit. Well, it's only five hundred dollars."

His look searched her face, but she hardly heard what he was saying.

"That little Warden house — it don't cost much — you'd be sur-prised. Rent, I mean. I went and looked at it the other day, but then I didn't think—" he caught himself on that. "It don't cost near as much as this store. We could furnish up the parlor with pianos —"

He was startled by that "we," and began again:

"That is, if you could ever think of such a thing as marrying me."

"But," said Lulu. "You *know!* Why don't the disgrace —"

"What disgrace?" asked Cornish.

"Oh," she said, "you — you—"

"There's only this about that," said he. "Of course, if you loved him very much then I'd ought not to be talking this way to you. But I didn't think —"

"You didn't think what?"

"That you did care so very much — about him. I don't know why."

She said: "I wanted somebody of my own. That's the reason I done what I done. I know that now."

"I figured that way," said Cornish.

They dismissed it. But now he brought to bear something which he saw that she should know.

"Look here," he said, "I'd ought to tell you. I'm — I'm awful lone-some myself. This is no place to live. And I guess living so is one reason why I want to get married. I want some kind of a home."

He said it as a confession. She accepted it as a reason.

"Of course," she said.

"I ain't never lived what you might say private," said Cornish.

"I've lived too private," Lulu said.

"Then there's another thing." This was harder to tell her. "I-I don't believe I'm ever going to be able to do a thing with law."

"I don't see," said Lulu, "how anybody does."

"I'm not much good in a business way," he owned, with a faint laugh. "Sometimes I think," he drew down his brows, "that I may never be able to make any money."

She said: "Lots of men don't."

"Could you risk it with me?" Cornish asked her. "There's nobody I've seen," he went on gently, "that I like as much as I do you. I-I was engaged to a girl once, but we didn't get along. I guess if you'd be willing to try me, we would get along."

Lulu said: "I thought it was Di that you —"

"Miss Di? Why," said Cornish, "she's a little kid. And," he added, "she's a little liar."

"But I'm going on thirty-four."

"So am I!"

"Isn't there somebody —"

"Look here. Do you like me?"

"Oh, yes!"

"Well enough —"

"It's you I was thinking of," said Lulu. "I'd be all right."

"Then!" Cornish cried, and he kissed her.

"And now," said Dwight, "nobody must mind if I hurry a little wee bit. I've got something on."

He and Ina and Monona were at dinner. Mrs. Bett was in her room. Di was not there.

"Anything about Lulu?" Ina asked.

"Lulu?" Dwight stared. "Why should I have anything to do about Lulu?"

"Well, but, Dwight -- we've got to do something."

"As I told you this morning," he observed, "we shall do nothing. Your sister is of age — I don't know about the sound mind, but certainly of age. If she chooses to go away, she is free to go where she will."

"Yes, but, Dwight, where has she gone? Where could she go? Where —"

"You are a question-box," said Dwight playfully. "A question-box."

Ina had burned her plump wrist on the oven. She lifted her arm and nursed it.

"I'm certainly going to miss her if she stays away very long," she remarked.

"You should be sufficient unto your little self," said Dwight.

"That's all right," said Ina, "except when you're getting dinner."

"I want some crust coffee," announced Monona firmly.

"You'll have nothing of the sort," said Ina. "Drink your milk."

"As I remarked," Dwight went on, "I'm in a tiny wee bit of a hurry."

"Well, why don't you say what for?" Ina asked.

She knew that he wanted to be asked and she was sufficiently willing to play his games, and besides she wanted to know. But she *was* hot.

"I am going," said Dwight, "to take Grandma Gates out in a wheel-chair, for an hour."

"Where did you get a wheel-chair, for mercy sakes?"

"Borrowed it from the railroad company," said Dwight, with the triumph peculiar to the resourceful man. "Why I never did it before, I can't imagine. There that chair's been in the depot ever since I can remember — saw it every time I took the train — and yet I never once thought of grandma."

"My, Dwight," said Ina, "how good you are!"

"Nonsense!" said he.

"Well, you are. Why don't I send her over a baked apple? Monona, you take Grandma Gates a baked apple — no. You shan't go till you drink your milk."

"I don't want it."

"Drink it or mamma won't let you go."

Monona drank it, made a piteous face, took the baked apple, ran.

"The apple isn't very good," said Ina, "but it shows my good will."

"Also," said Dwight, "it teaches Monona a life of thoughtfulness for others."

"That's what I always think," his Ina said.

"Can't you get mother to come out?" Dwight inquired.

"I had so much to do getting dinner on the table, I didn't try," Ina confessed.

"You didn't have to try," Mrs. Bett's voice sounded. "I was coming when I rested up."

She entered, looking vaguely about. "I want Lulie," she said, and the corners of her mouth drew down. She ate her dinner cold, appeased in vague areas by such martyrdom. They were still at table when the front door opened.

"Monona hadn't ought to use the front door so common," Mrs. Bett complained.

But it was not Monona. It was Lulu and Cornish.

"Well!" said Dwight, tone curving downward.

"Well!" said Ina, in replica.

"Lulie!" said Mrs. Bett, and left her dinner, and went to her daughter and her hands upon her.

"We wanted to tell you first," Cornish said. "We've just got married."

"For*ever*more!" said Ina.

"What's this?" Dwight sprang to his feet. "You're joking!" he cried with hope.

"No," Cornish said soberly. "We're married — just now. Methodist parsonage. We've had our dinner," he added hastily.

"Where'd you have it?" Ina demanded, for no known reason.

"The bakery," Cornish replied, and flushed.

"In the dining room," Lulu added.

"What on earth did you do it for?" he put it to them. "Married in a bakery —"

"No, no," they explained it again. Neither of them, they said, wanted the fuss of a wedding.

Dwight recovered himself in a measure. "I'm not surprised, after all," he said. "Lulu usually marries in this way."

Mrs. Bett patted her daughter's arm. "Lulie," she said, "why, Lulie. You ain't been and got married twice, have you? After waitin' so long?"

"Don't be disturbed, Mother Bett," Dwight cried. "She wasn't married that first time, if you remember. No marriage about it!"

Ina's little shriek sounded.

"Dwight!" she cried. "Now everybody'll have to know that. You'll have to tell about Ninian now — and his other wife!"

Standing between her mother and Cornish, an arm of each about her, Lulu looked across at Ina and Dwight, and they saw in her face a horrified realization.

"Ina!" she said. "Dwight! You will have to tell now, won't you? Why I never thought of that."

At this Dwight sneered, was sneering still as he went to give Grandma Gates her ride in the wheelchair and as he stooped with patient kindness to tuck her in.

The street door was closed. If Mrs. Bett was peeping through the blind, no one saw her. In the pleasant mid-day light under the maples, Mr. and Mrs. Neil Cornish were hurrying toward the railway station.

Birth

Marshall Pitt

1

A day of heat withered Burage. It was the eighth day of such heat. The people had counted, they began to take delight in its continuance. "She's gone up two degrees," they told one another. And: "Looks like this'll go down as the hot summer of eighty-seven." Burage watched the thermometer, observed when the Wisconsin River ice finally blocked and when this ice began to move in spring, kept in vases the list of these dates, and delighted when degrees and dates surpassed themselves. With many, this was no conscious touch with nature, but a substitute for the competition impossible in all town living, and yet not outgrown. However, there were some who kept these tallies for love of them.

At four o'clock on the eighth day of the heat, there came down the Burage main street a youth of six-and-twenty. His hair was flat and glossy-damp on his forehead, a limp handkerchief was tucked in his collar, his cheap, neat suit was dusty. He carried a sample case. His name was Marshall Pitt, and he was "traveling representative" for Hart, Hollow and Orr, Pickle and Fruit Products.

As he went, he glanced at the houses with no appraising eye. Most of these homes he had visited, most had already closed their doors upon him. When he reached Lawyer Granger's iron fence, he opened the gate with doggedness. That morning he had passed this house in the acute belief that it was far too magnificent to be expected to order from his sample case. Now, the worst having happened to him, it was as if he determined to complete his martyrdom.

As he turned to latch the gate, his eye fell on the house across the street. It was a little house, set on an eminence which nobody had the money to cut down, and it was reached by a long flight of wooden steps, absurdly exaggerating the importance of the one-story cottage. Though it was of a size which did not warn him away, Pitt had passed it by that morning, because of the crepe on the door. Now he observed that the crepe was gone, and a woman with huge shoulders and breast was carrying chairs to the next-door neighbor's. He wondered how they got the coffin down the steep steps.

The walk leading to Lawyer Granger's house was swept and sprinkled, and the porch was shaded with vines. There were deck chairs, a long willow long chair, a nest of tables. Pitt had never seen any of these things, and he stared at them as he rang the bell. These and the bright cretonne and the blue and white tea service lay before him as if a curtain had lifted.

Instantly the door was opened by someone who had been on the point of coming out. The house had been closed, and with this lady came a breath of cool air. She was in white, and she had about her neck a long silver chain with a queer blue pendant. This was all that Pitt saw before he began his speech — with the pitiful haste of one whose case depends on emitting as much as possible before he is shut off.

"Madam," he said, "may I have a few moments of your valuable time, not as wishing to take any order direct, you understand, but as representing your local grocer who has agreed to handle the line of superior products that I am carrying—"

The lady had probably not heard a word that he said. His utter physical discomfort, his dripping face, his quite painful eagerness to get something said before she should stop him, were considerably more eloquent than his stereotyped speech.

"Come in," she said; and turned to speak to someone indoors. "Bring tea inside. It's too hot out here. Yes, in the living room."

Pitt followed her into the cool gloom of the hall. He experienced the first lift of victory of the day. Then he caught sight of himself in the hall mirror, snatched the handkerchief from his collar, tried to wipe his face. He set down his sample case, mopped his forehead, seemed to sponge his hands and wrists. He made a wretched figure.

"It's awful hot," said he.

"Isn't it?" said the lady.

He had supposed that she would give him his five minutes or less in the hall. But she was taking her way through a doorway, and he followed her. The room was long and dim and in comforting coolness. Its airs smote him to grateful speech.

"Ain't this elegant?" said he.

"It is," said the lady, " better than the porch."

She came to a chair covered with a slip of rosy canvas, and without invitation he dropped into another, laid his straw hat between his feet, and went on with his drying.

"What we offer," he instantly took up his tale, "is something that guarantees satisfaction, or the empty jars can be returned to your grocer and no questions — "

"Here," said the lady. "Have it here, Ellen," and guided the table to her side. Then she looked across the room. "Come over here and have something cool, Barbara," she said.

Pitt, discomfited, had stopped, with his mouth open, and his scrubbing motion was suspended. For the first time, he perceived that there was someone else in the room. She was a girl of twenty, in thick black gown, and she had been crying. She came quietly and sat near them, and the lady served her and turned to Pitt with a glass of iced tea.

"Won't you have this?" she invited. "You look — melting."

"Thanks," said Pitt, and drained off half the glass. The lady in the act of handing sugar, let her glance dwell on him, set down the sugar without comment.

"Now what is it that you have?" she unbelievably asked.

He spoke with a swallow trembling all through his opening syllables.

"Do you ever use," said he, "tomato soup in the home? I have here a superior brand of the article, purely a sample you understand — only one can to a customer, to get it introduced. Also sweet mustard pickles to use in lunch basket sat the present picnic season. Also a different dessert product than has ever been put on the market — something you can serve when you have company in the home. Also — "

The lady continued to look at him. He had gathered courage and opened his sample case. He looked up at her with eyes like a dog's eyes. He had nothing to recommend him. His singsong, learned speech, his way of leaving his mouth open, his freckled wrists, were all abominable.

"I'll take one of each kind," said the lady, as one who should add: "And now get out."

But she was giving her salesman courage, he brightened, kindled, flung himself upon her.

"Apple butter, now. Have you ever used our apple butter product as a spread for cake?"

"Never," said the lady.

But when at last he had buckled the straps and was poised to rise, her heart smote her. He was trying so hard. . . .

"Sit still for a moment and get cool," she said, and turned her attention to the girl in black.

Pitt, profoundly grateful for his good fortunes, took the fan which the lady extended, and used it with violence. Then he gave himself to looking about the room, turning his head and polishing at his teeth with the tip of his tongue.

"Those things he's got are all good," the girl in black offered abruptly. "Father and I —" and burst into tears and rose.

On her Pitt now concentrated in astonishment, he too rose but involuntarily and not at all as an obligation. He found himself facing this girl. She was not covering her face as she wept without embarrassment, without restraint. She was shaken by her sobs. To Pitt, who was very near her, was communicated something of her surprising emotion. He stared at her.

"I can't stay," she said, "I can't stay —" and went out to the hall. The front door closed.

Mechanically, Pitt picked up his sample case and hat.

"I'm very much obliged to you, I'm sure," he said to the lady, "for your time and attention, and also for your order and — ah — for the tea, both on behalf of myself and my firm, at least — not for the tea. . . ." He dwindled to silence and a great blush.

"Not in the least," said the lady. She was looking toward the door, and was hardly attending.

Then he turned and followed the girl. He might have known that he was following her, when his glance swept the walk on the opening of the door. Already she was mounting the steep steps to the house across the street.

On the veranda of the Halsey House four chairs stood every day, waiting for the public. The public rarely sat there, save the constable, in his idleness; and the host of the hotel. This man, Flo Buckstaff, seemed to have nothing in this world to do but to occupy one of his own chairs.

After supper, on the evening of the eighth day of the heat in Burage, Flo strolled to the veranda and sat down, his feet high on a post. It was this man's tragedy that he had all the social qualities of the host of an inn excepting so to say, the guests, he was gregarious, open-faced, smiling. He would have liked his lobby and not merely his bar to be frequented. He was always wistfully accosting people. Tonight he had it in his mind to waylay the sole guest who had entered the dining room to a doubtful dinner.

Pitt, his coat on his arm, came out and dropped into a chair.

"Hot, ain't it?" said the host, genially. His lip curled engagingly. "I had to start somethin' quick, and I thought o' that."

Pitt assented absently to the heat, stared a bit blankly at the comedian's aside, and looked at Buckstaff as a dog looks when he is questioning. He had known hotel men who thought that the private affairs of their townspeople were none of your business. He risked it.

"Who lives in the white house with the iron fence?" he put in.

"Him? Oh, Lawyer Granger. He's dead, though. His wife's in the house. Her and her daughter. When they 'are' here."

"Nice, easy circumstances," Pitt affirmed.

"You bet," said Buckstaff. "Daughter been east to school. Used to be kind of a high-fly. Come down town in ridin' breeches — 'walkin'.' They said. . ."

Pitt was not listening. Who lived in the brown frame with all those bushes, he wished to know next. A family history which he heard patiently to its end. Who lived in the little bit of a house at the top of those steps, he demanded at last, and blushed.

"The one with the funeral?" said the host. "Sad thing — sad thing." He settled himself. Here was something greatly to his liking. He had known everybody in the village from his youth. In some dim way, he was aware of the poignancy of their sordid, tragic histories. But it was seldom that any one would listen. Everyone else in his world knew these things as well as he.

Lem Ellsworth — Flo first seized on him. He'd had Forty Thousand dollars, had Lem, and had run through it like a deer. Died on his relatives. Left his family without a cent, and worse. They had all gone now, excepting young Lem. Young Lem was sixty, and he it was who had just died and had been buried today. He had been a painter and paperhanger, whenever he was sober enough. None of them left now. Only his girl. Little slip of a thing, and had on her hands the house and the business, both mortgaged. Nice little thing, too — Barbara Ellsworth. Cute walk.

A village election tragedy next claimed Flo, and in the high moment of that recital, to his open disappointment, Pitt rose and stepped down from the veranda. Too late, Flo perceived his error. Some details concerning the first families of Burage, collected at random by Flo and poured out in the hope of delaying this listener, were unavailing. Pitt was off and up the street. Buckstaff was left gloomily surveying his own shoes, pushing at the post at the level of his nose.

On Burage main street, life was faintly stirring. The evening parrot hung before the bakery. The popcorn wagon came creaking to its place. A maid or two, in bright feathers walked tentatively by the post office. The odor of free lunch held the air. It was still intolerably hot. The little buildings gave off heat.

Footing his way through all, abruptly Pitt was smitten with sickening loneliness. Yet his own home held nothing toward which he yearned. Five hundred miles away, he had a father with whom he never had never got on; a step-mother, such as she was; and a younger brother whom he liked well enough to bully. In that town too, there was a girl — but that was all over. She had married the drug clerk and sent him back his ring, all in one night. Pitt had pawned the ring and spent the money, and that was all there was to that. In another town which he "made," there was a soda-fountain girl. He had an engagement to take this girl to a show when next he reached her town. He supposed, in his heart, that he would marry this Bessie. She had a good figure and wore her clothes well. Sometimes she looked pretty. The other boys had asked who she was. What more could you expect, unless you had money? Perhaps if he got a raise —

The little man there on the Burage main street wanted to get on, wanted to be happy. In his undeveloped, inconsiderable person were colossal longings, undirected, indeterminate. And for him the chance of their realization lay solely in the sample case of Pickle and Fruit Products, checked behind the desk in the Halsey House. His life, his manner of death, his descendants, all strapped up there under the desk in the Halsey House. And sometimes he wondered how he came to be selling Pickle and Fruit Products. In a crowded train he had once sat with a man who had that day made a phenomenal sale of apple butter. This man had fired Pitt, shown him his destiny. He had been tossed to this harbor, all the time in the illusion that he was choosing. It was so now, when sick with longing for the unknown, Pitt went up the steep steps of the little house on the eminence.

When he found himself at the top of the steps, and observed, he was terrified. The large woman, with the huge shoulders and breast, whom he had seen with the chairs, was now coming down the walk carrying a hot-water bottle. On a clothesline bed covers were hanging, gratuitous intimacies with the case of the dead, exposed with indecent haste. The woman, on a near view, had a serene and gentle face, now mildly curious. She paused, swinging her hot-water bottle by its neck, and plainly half regretting her leave-taking. He passed her, with no word, and she went her way.

From an unscreened door the house gaped at him. The sitting-room chairs stood about the four walls. He saw a hanging-lamp, a shelf crowded with vases and paper flowers, a spray of fern on the floor. There blew on his face from within a faint, sickly-sweet odor. His knock on the casing made no adequate sound, nothing within was conscious of him, he drew back with a quick distaste, he wanted to run away. He stepped down to the walk, about which unconsidered petunias and four o'clocks presented themselves as if from the little porch, if from anywhere, they might expect the help which had so plainly been denied them. He had taken three steps or four from the house, when a sound of squeaking and nozzling signaled him. Beyond a stretch of garden, plowed but never planted, stood a low red wagon shed. And before this, intent on something on the ground, Pitt saw the girl in the black dress. He went to her.

As he reached her, he saw that she was watching a litter of little pigs. They were running about foolishly, and two or three were feeding at the mother, lying there on her side.

"Good evenin', Miss Ellsworth," Pitt said. He stood, holding his hat. His shoulders were high, and his coat seemed short. He looked little and pinched. But his eyes were clean and level.

She rose and regarded him. She remembered him, and showed her surprise. "Well!" she said.

"I couldn't help coming," said Pitt. "You — seemed to feel so bad this afternoon. I've kept thinking about it."

"I do feel bad," she replied only.

"I found out your name," Pitt went on. "I came to see you. I hope you won't think —"

"Thank you," she said. "I'm used to being pitied."

At this he was taken aback, and tried desperately to explain away what he himself but dimly understood. He imparted name and station, and, " If I could be any help —" he said.

The girl looked at him with attention. She had the air of fitting his words well within some thought of her own, to see if they had a place there.

"But what could you do? " she inquired.

"That's just it " Pitt found to say inadequately. "I — I come to see if there wasn't something."

"Oh," said the girl, "there's everything."

Again she began to cry, not tempestuously, but quietly, and as if this were her habit. Again she did not cover her face. And though this crying was ugly, there was something about the ripe thickness and bloom of her flesh which made of such grief a fascination.

"I guess you better tell me about it," Pitt said finally.

He sat down on the tongue of a wagon standing half without the shed, and the girl began to speak.

"I don't know what to do. I used to think I'd be glad to be alone and get away. I never thought about the debts. I've got them to pay."

"You don't either have to pay them," said Pitt; "not his debts."

"They're folks I know," she said simply. "Aunt Mate let him have a Hundred of Uncle Enos's life insurance money. Aunt Clauson let him have her paisley shawl money. There's others. I've got to pay them up."

"I see," said Pitt, and abstract justice, to whom one may be blind, had utterance through life insurance money and the price of a paisley shawl. "How will you?" he added.

Her look held all the tragedy of her kind.

"I don't know," she answered.

Pitt, profoundly stirred, continued to regard her. He understood surprisingly. In some obscure way, he was felling as if this other situation were his own, as if he, indeed, must solve it.

"Don't you work?" he inquired.

"I clerked in the ten-cent store," she answered. "Till he was sick. They pay four dollars. What's that? When there's debts."

He hesitated. "I s'pose jobs don't lay around loose in Burage," he produced.

"Oh, they don't," she returned, wiping her eyes. "I've got relations," she added. "I could live with them. I'd rather die."

"Oh, sure," Pitt agreed with emphasis. He thought for a space. "You'll be getting married, I expect," he suggested.

She neither bridled nor flushed. "Not now," she said only. "I couldn't saddle anybody with what I got to do. Besides," she added childishly, "I don't know who it'd be. Not in Burage."

"There's as good out of Burage as in," he attempted automatically, then caught himself up in the dim realization of something due to her mourning. He groped to cover that false note, and found nothing.

The girl sat watching the struggle of the little black pigs. Dusk was falling. Below in the street went the desultory thud and tap of feet on the board sidewalk, as now one and another sauntered toward the town, desperately hoping for diversion. These folks had made for themselves errands of mail and yeast and tobacco, to cover the need to be going somewhere. The girls wore little braveries. The married women wheeled crying children, with whom there was no one to leave. They were all dimly aware that something was escaping them, some inheritance of joy which they had meant to share. How was it that they were not sharing it? As soon as work was done, and the lights came on, it was as if this question leaped out on them all and, in some feeble response, they turned themselves "downtown." And as they passed the little house on the eminence, every one of them asked or answered to:

"It must have bothered some, getting his coffin down those steps of theirs." And, "I wonder what Barbara Ellsworth'll do now? What do you s'pose she will do?"

Back of the house stretched vacant lots, grown with weeds, and used as a dump for brush and ashes. Across this waste, the low pink glowing of the west went on, as if minarets and marble were to be silhouetted.

Pitt wanted to say more. The time began touching along his veins. "You've got it pretty rough," he brought forth.

Abruptly the girl seemed to become conscious of him as a fellow being who might, conceivably, have his own situation to face.

"I guess you've had some trouble, too," she said, looking at him.

"Oh, well," Pitt returned, modestly, "some."

"I guess that's how you knew the way I felt," she added, incuriously. She was still in that thin, enveloping shell which is thrown about spirit or body in grief. Nothing seemed greatly to be questioned. The appearance of the stranger was a part of an order of late inverted. It was to her quite natural that he should presently begin to tell her something of his own case:

He sat, continued to regard her. He understood surprisingly. In some obscure way, he was feeling as if this other situation mattered.

"I've had," said Pitt, "a rotten time. My dad and I don't hitch. My step-mother, she's a fright. I lit out on my own six years ago. For a while I knocked around, posting circus bills and like that. Then I traveled — Hart Hollow and Orr, Pickle and Fruit Products, for the last two years. They treat you right. I'm going to get a better territory the first of the year. But," he pathetically added, "I ain't ever liked any of it very well."

He paused, explaining himself to himself.

"I didn't start right," he added, "I never had a chance. A person ought to have a chance — trade, or like that."

She nodded. "It's bad," she said, "getting along."

He fell to telling her incidents of his six years. It was true that it was the whole case had drawn him there, and hers was the imminent problem. But she sat listening. Under this stimulus the little man took on another air. Also, the dusk was setting him at his ease. A narrow escape or two, a clever deal, his best sales flowed from him. He sat erect. He talked with fluency, he drank her monosyllables of comment. In short, momentarily he found that which Burage streamed downtown to seek.

And now the dark was falling. Stars were in a sky which still caught and kept the light. The little pigs had followed their leading to a place remote. Pitt rose.

"Look how I've stayed here, going on," he said, in embarrassment. "I guess you had things to do."

"No," she said, "there's nothing. That's the trouble," she added, and sighed, remembering all.

They stood on the walk before the dark house. Against the darkness with which the black of her gown was mingled, her face showed pale.

"I haven't done you much good, I guess," he said, with a laugh.

"Yes, you have," she assured him. "I'm glad you called. I hate the rest of them. They keep going over it and finding out how he was. I've kind of been forgetting."

"You aren't going to stay alone?" he asked suddenly.

"Yes, I am," she said. "I didn't want anybody."

He looked at the lonely house.

"You leave me go in there with you while you light up," he offered.

She made no objection, but led the way. The rooms were stifling. She fumbled for a match. The oil lamp cast shadows upon the intolerable dreariness: the stiff rows of chairs, definite carpet, high pictures, the multiple cheap ornaments — and all barren of color. In the midst she stood confronting him. He saw again the ripe thickness and bloom of her.

"It seems awful," he said, "you all alone so. But you'll sell, won't you?"

"It'll be sold." she said. "For the mortgage. And the business, too. Unless somebody could come in and carry it on for a while."

"There ought," he said, "to be somebody in this town that'd do that. It ain't a hard business."

"No," she said, "it ain't a hard business. But there ain't anybody in this town that'll go on with it."

Their eyes were meeting. For the first time the same thought leaped definitely to the mind of each. Both colored, and the boy faltered. But the woman continued steadfastly to regard him. The moment's dead silence was filled with the mute crying of voices.

"There's money in it," she went on slowly, "for the right one."

He said nothing, and she took a step or two toward him. Her look measured him, and by the lamp light, with his hat off and his neat, flat, dark hair showing, he looked compact and clean.

"I'm much obliged," she said, "for your call. But I don't see how you came to do it. I didn't think you noticed me there this afternoon."

"Well, I did," he responded. "You can bet I did."

" I don't see why," she developed this. " But I'm glad."

"Only I haven't helped you any," he harked awkwardly back to it.

"Yes, you have," she told him. " Honestly you have. Now you'll go off and I'll never see you again. Well, I shan't forget what you've done." She let the silence fall.

"Look here," he burst out. " I might not have to go tomorrow. There's a fellow or two I didn't see yet. If I'm here, can I see you? "

"Oh, yes," she said. " Oh, yes." Her face was sweet, and it seemed to be in a mist of unshed tears. "I'm awfully alone," she added.

He could think of nothing save: "Well, I'll go along now."

She came to him, and gave him her hand. It was warm thick and deliberate.

"Good night," she said. "And if it's good-by —"

She stood there, quietly breathing, looking at him.

"It won't be good-by," he said, and went.

In the upper sash of Pitt's window at the Halsey House there were four panes. He lay for hours staring at the thin dark of these panes. Occasional bright worlds swung into the squares, crossed glittering, went on into space. The high paper curtain was torn in a triangle. Now and then a world poised there, and passed.

Pitt was not thinking. It was only that within him, atoms over which he had no control appeared to be gathering from the whole area of his being, and approaching one another, singing. His flesh sang, and with it sang his spirit. There had taken place an obscure enhancement of his being. Another level of existence seemed to have presented itself. For this he had in thought no correspondences — he could make no mental calculation whatever. All this had little to do with thought. Only with vitality. He lay awake, and this deepening existence had its way with him.

Occasionally he remembered fragments that she had said. "I'll never see you again. Well, I shan't forget what you've done . . . ." "I don't see why — but I'm glad." "It ain't a hard business. But there ain't anybody in this town that'll go with it" — and then their meeting eyes. Most of all, "Oh, yes — oh, yes. I'm awfully alone." With these, the singing in him mounted.

He had no plan, no decision, almost no speculation. He gave himself up to this slight lessening of the tension of toil, of discouragement, of loneliness. He was happy.

Once Bessie crossed his mind — that remote Bessie, of the soda water fountain: An image of her spareness, her thin lips, her sauciness, her withdrawals. Over against these came no image, but a sense of ripe thickness and bloom. . . .

At dawn he woke to this new consciousness: leaped to it as into receiving arms. Later, he emerged from the Halsey House with no quest, but merely as one going out to see what would befall. But first, he bought a collar and a bright cravat.

The delivery boy of the Burage Grocery, which had "Mark and Arum, Dry Goods" over its door — he had no idea of being a First Cause to anybody. His long wrists, his scattered glances, his slouching gait, his one suspender, all these precluded his entrance on any stage as "god from the machine."

He came driving down Main Street that morning, a loose wheel rattling. His white horse was hanging out its tongue, and not at all because of hard driving, but from preference. As he drove this boy continually looked over his shoulder in an effort to sort out his load mentally, and to route himself. As there was usually nothing else on Burage main street, this habit mattered little, but everybody spoke of it. That Spate boy, look at him, would you. Someday he'd have a collision. You wait. You mark my words.

At the Granger house he had, as usual, a large order to deliver — melons, peppers, rich food which most of Burage passed by till prices succumbed. Then he left his wagon standing before the iron gate, and ran up the Ellsworths' steps and round the house. He was carrying a can of baked beans and a half peck of old potatoes.

On the side of the house toward the wagon shed there was a narrow porch, covered with wild cucumber vines. A pump, a wood-box and a clothes line were background for an old wooden arm-chair, calico-cushioned and minus its rockers. Here Barbara Ellsworth was seated. The thick black waist of the day before she had exchanged for a thin blouse. She was hemming a kitchen towel.

Pitt sat on the step. His hat lay at his feet. The day was another day of heat, and his flat hair was wet at the temples. His shoes had not been blackened, and from time to time, he rubbed at them thoughtfully, with his thumb.

The air was subtly charged. It was like the air of that moment of the evening before when she had said: "But there ain't anybody in this town that'll go on with it ." And then they had looked at each other. That look, it seemed, had grown overnight; had taken unto itself vitality, self-consciousness; had become a living thing; and now it covered them, like a monstrous bean stalk.

Pitt thought: "Why not? What else is there? Why not?"

The woman sewed, and looked down at him.

He said: "I must be at Rickman tonight. I'd ought to sell quite a bill of goods at Rickman."

"What time do you leave?" she asked.

"On the two-ten," said Pitt. " That's the last one," he added. After a moment, he super-added: "I asked for the last one."

"Why?" demanded Barbara Ellsworth, and looked at him over the kitchen towel.

"Why not? " he permitted himself, and let his look take the sting from his challenge.

For answer she met that look, held it, dissolved it within her own — gave everything back to him. "You're awful good to me," she disarmed him.

"I'd like to be a whole lot better," he declared with emphasis. "I'd like to help you. I ain't helping you. I'm just sitting here."

"That's helping," she said.

Thereupon, out of the morning, came this delivery boy. As he walked, he shuffled his feet, probably because they were inordinately heavy feet. And he came whistling, not as one who understands that all motion should be made to music, but as one who wishes that he knew a tune and has never even apprehended one. He whistled laboriously, as a horse might whistle.

"Morn'," said he, at the side porch. "Got somethin' for the p'tats."

"Hello, Jeff," said Barbara, and brought a pan. The potatoes were emptied noisily. Some rolled about the step, and these Pitt recovered. The tin of baked beans topped the potatoes in their pan. The boy, Jeff, his basket dangling, disappeared into eternity, swung out into space as had the stars beyond Pitt's window.

Pitt lifted the pan. "Where do you want these? " he asked, and followed her into the kitchen.

He set the pan on the deal table, and the beans beside the pan. Dishes were in the cupboard at his right. He saw a woodstove, a woodbox, a turkey wing for brushing the ashes. A length of rag-carpet was on the floor. A little clock ticked on its shelf. Barbara Ellsworth took down an earthen bowl and set it on a bench inside the door. "For the milk," she said. Pitt saw her, moving about the kitchen of her house, where no one else lived. He went and stood beside her.

"Let me stay," he said.

Her look searched his, met his level eyes.

"Marry me," he heard himself say. "Let's fix things up — the house, the business — together."

She had worked for this moment instinctively, almost subconsciously. When it came, it genuinely took her aback.

"You don't want to do that!" she breathed.

"Don't I?" said Pitt. "Don't I?"

He went nearer. His mouth found hers. He buried his face in the ripe, thick bloom of her cheek.

Not until he was running for the two-ten to Rickman was he assailed by the obvious: Was it hard, he wondered, to be a wallpaper hanger?

Village girls, ill-adjusted, wistful of the unknown, pretty — Barbara might have been any one of them. She had waked to a measure of consciousness, had gone on with little more. In some richer chamber of nature she might have risen to self-consciousness. But as life offered itself, she moved in little areas. And within her the struggling new functions, brain, spirit, lay budded but never called to bloom. The old inheritances, self-seeking, gregariousness, love of pleasure, passion, laughter, these she bore. She longed for "good times," for laughter. It seemed to be a physical thing which she desired, for talk, as she understood it, was hardly less muscular than laughter — a mere give and take of the discharge of nervous force. A blaring band, flattery, the presence of a strange man, sweets — all these supplied her need. A scarlet wreath in the cemetery filled her with delight. She wanted anything which set in motion anything within her. Of the newer racial gifts, the latest that she knew were the sense of personal liberty — "My head works as good as theirs," you often heard her say — and the kind of passionate honesty about money.

When she was nine her mother had died. Barbara remembered her: A thin woman who cooked, washed, sewed and swept. They were always poor, and this condition had developed in her mother a native austerity. Barbara remembered during her mother's lifetime no lace or ribbon in the house. But they had always bright wallpaper. Paper with borders of blazing fruit. This paper her mother selected, and when she was tired would lie and look at it. It was as if some passionate need for color spoke only here. And then, too, when she died.

"Open the bottom drawer and take out that box with the kitten on the cover," she had bidden Barbara, in that last illness. From the box her mother lifted a pale blue bow. "I want to be buried with that under my chin," she remarked. "Put it where you can find it."

Barbara had never before seen the bow. She kept it, and when they were dressing her mother she went into the room with the bow in her hand, and told. But they drove her back, and agreed that the request was ridiculous; and her Aunt Clauson, stayed on after the funeral, kept both the bow and the box with the kitten on the cover.

As for her father, he had moved for years in a husk. Insensitive, honest, almost without mental processes, he went through the routine of his days and thought of nothing. "Oh, yes, oh, yes," Barbara remembered him saying most frequently. For eleven years these two lived alone in the house at the top of the steep steps, and they never talked about their life. The gossip of the neighborhood, of his business, of the doings at Lawyer Granger's house, these sufficed for communication. Barbara's school, her friends, her work in the ten-cent store, passed before him and were gone and he never tried to penetrate them.

Once, indeed, when his daughter had accepted this good opportunity in the ten-cent store, he had stood in the kitchen door and had said to her abruptly:

"You be careful what you let folks say to you down there."

She had not understood him, and had answered: "I can give them as good as they send."

"I meant —" he said, and stopped. After a time he turned away.

Sometimes he reprimanded her for being late with his supper, or for laughing loudly on the street ("What'll people think of me if you act like that?") or for baking a cake for church. ("You'll have me in the poor house.") These warnings were all with reference to himself. His chief personal attitude might have been expressed in "Don't you bring any disgrace upon me." The one strict discipline which he gave her was in regard to money. No credit! If a statement of account came to the house that was a "dun" and a disgrace. No debts, if they could possibly be avoided.

When he fell ill and was ill for two years, these debts could not be avoided. But his last words had been about them, and when she had promised to pay back the price of the insurance money and the paisley shawl, he had gravely died.

These two beings had left Barbara with her wistfulness, her barren mind, her sense of habitual deprivation. Her little spot of consciousness was hungry for more consciousness. This expressed itself as a hunger for happiness.

One day in Mark and Arum's Dry Goods Store window, she saw a print of a path in a forest, and beyond it a rosy sky. She stood staring at the print. When she looked at it, she felt something which she had not felt before. She often crossed the street to the window, to get back this feeling. "Sometime I'll be somewhere else," she thought. In the woods themselves she had no such stimulus. She liked to be there for a picnic, but it was the picnic, not the woods, that she liked. She looked at a sunset, if it was bright.

However, she was very merry, and she had a little wit, of a sort. She was pleasantly magnetic, the young folk liked her. And she was excessively pretty, with the prettiness which blooms in the streets as in the weeds by the road. But she had no vitality for native growth. She did not think. She did not plan. She was waiting.

If somewhere a great chorus had swelled, she could have joined it. If many feet had been pressing on a resistless errand, her feet would have run. But there was no chorus, no march of feet in unity. The child stood alone on a spot of the world which was as unconscious of the wheel and roll of the world as was the farthest star.

2

Having severed his connection with Hart, Hollow and Orr, in two weeks Pitt returned to Burage to be married. He was taking unto himself a wife whom he had seen but twice, for twice as many hours; and a mortgaged house; and a mortgaged wallpaper business. Also, he had Sixty Four Dollars, and he had never even observantly watched a wallpaper hanger at his job. If society could direct the functioning of courage as efficiently as its agents detect the courses of comets.

He had reached Burage at noon, on his wedding day, and sent his bag to the Halsey House, but he abstracted and took with him a parcel, when he ran up for a glimpse of the girl.

She had walked down the street to meet him, trim in a white shirt-waist which she had made. Happiness had, of course, improved her — happiness, or a kind of assurance for the immediate future. Below a certain income there are the same. The look of anxiety had fallen from her. Beneath this look, much of humanity is beautiful.

"Well!" said Pitt.

"The train *was* on time," said Barbara.

They walked toward the house, immortal little beings, entering upon their future, and very nearly dumb.

Within the house, in the act of taking down a freshly-ironed skirt from the corner of a picture frame, they came on the great-shouldered, deep-bosomed woman whom Pitt had seen carrying the funeral chairs. She was she was known to Burage as Mis' Helmus — Mis' Hellie Copper.

"Forevermore!" said Mis' Copper, when "You meet Mr. Pitt," had been said, "You two little young things! Land, I was ten years older'n either of you when I married Hellie Copper, and so was he, and they didn't neither one of us know enough to spread bread, let enough earn it."

"Is that so?" said Pitt politely.

Mis' Hellie laughed comfortably. "But there." she said, what's the difference? We ain't nothin' to complain of but each other, and we'd do that anyway. Barbara, you want both these white skirts to wear? "

"Yes," said Barbara, and blushed.

Valid etiquette of these villages. They will face the facts, the errors of existence; discuss the details of deaths and births. But at mention of a white starched petticoat they still blush.

Barbara had a surprise for him, she told Pitt, when Mis' Hellie Copper had taken herself to tasks in the little bedroom. This surprise Barbara brought out with an air of happy triumph.

"You know Miss Rachel Arrowsmith?"

No, Pitt could not say that he did.

"Yes — yes you do. Across the street. Where you first saw me."

In her words a bell sounded — but Pitt never heard. Not "where we first saw each other," then? But Pitt never heard. He merely cried out that oh, yes, of course he remembered.

"Well — she's asked us to be married there."

" No." Pitt's interjection masked a world of discomfort. As one would not be miserable enough at one's marriage without being married at the house of a stranger. And such a stranger!

"Yes, she has. And she's invited in a few of my friends — its to be only a few, you know — on account of dad. And she's doing the refreshments — she's an angel." Barbara concluded fervently.

"What — what time are you going to be married? " Pitt inquired.

" At two o'clock - aren't you? " she inquired.

He grinned "Any time you are," he agreed, and produced his parcel.

"I haven't seen my father," he said, "but I wrote to him about — us. And he sent you this."

She took the box. Her hands were so eager at the wrappings that she tangled the string and tore the paper. She would hardly wait to life the cover.

"Oh!" she cried. "Is you father rich?"

"No," he said. "This was my mother's — and hers from her grand-mother. She never wore them. She wasn't — like that."

It was a set of seed pearls, necklace and brooch and old-fashioned earrings. Strange data of some silent and perhaps exquisite ancestress from whom the stock had not come on to robust lives, disdainful of doll's orna-ments; but had dropped to freckled folk, like Pitt, whose mother "wasn't like that."

The girl cried out deliriously, rushed with the pearls to Mis' Copper, sped to the dining room to clasp on the necklace before the mirror there. Last she came back and kissed Pitt.

"I never had anything beautiful before," she told him, "never in my life. You dear — oh, you dear!"

A wave of intense emotion flooded the boy.

"Liberty Ann!" said Mis' Copper, two times or three, and fingered the pearls in her fat pink hands. "Liberty Ann. They's certainly some things that keeps marriage from being a punishment."

Pitt felt himself to have a new importance in her eyes, and in the eyes of his fiancé. He had not looked for this, but he liked it, and under it his manner changed.

"Well," he said importantly, "I expect I must be getting along back to the hotel. Anything you want me to do here?"

" No." Barbara answered. "You go right to Miss Arrowsmith's at a little before two. I got the minister like you said — I wrote you that. Mayme Carbury's going to stand up with me. Who's going to stand up with you?"

He paled. " I never thought — my heavens," he said, "I thought we were just going at it alone." He regarded her anxiously. His importance had left him.

"Oh, you'll have to have a best man." she protested loftily. "Why, I don't know what Miss Arrowsmith'll think."

In some obscure way, this nettled him. He pondered it. "I don't believe," he announced, "that she'll think a thing." He paused, and risked it. "And," he added, "I don't care if she does. I haven't got one, and it can't be helped."

She meditated, with a fashion which she had of catching a corner of her full red lower lip in two small, pretty teeth. She said no more. As he was leaving, she suddenly went to him with a manner of gentleness.

"Sure you don't want to back out?" she asked, and gave him her hands.

His reply was an amazement to them both. He suddenly folded his arms about her and kissed her fiercely.

She gave a little cry. " You love me!" she said.

"Sure," said the little man. "Sure I do!" And was gone.

She stood staring after him. It was as if she had not thought of that possibility.

At ten minutes to two, Pitt once more unlatched the iron gate before Lawyer Granger's house. Two weeks ago he was saving over exultantly — and look at him now! It was almost as if he had attained at a bound to the Grangers' social status. It is true that he was miserable at the immediate ordeal, and saved himself only by reflecting on his grandeur.

Again the hall was cool and dim, but now it was filled with soft stirring and voices. Pitt's eyes began to glaze. Of all that was to follow he would be one-third unconscious — there was that merciful arrangement.

Pitt was aware, as before, of the sweep of a white gown and the fall of a silver chain and a queer blue pendant. This time he managed to lift his eyes to her face. Grave, confident, discerning, she stood to greet him.

"Ah, Mr. Pitt," she said, "we have taken possession of you. Don't be alarmed. You don't have to marry us all."

"That's good," said Pitt easily.

They took him to a little room at the hall's end, and there a boyish clergyman waited, an athletic young clergyman, who wrung Pitt's limp hand. Barbara was there, too, with a ruffled person who wore cherry ribbons about her wrists. Pitt never could remember anything else about Miss Mayme Carbury, at that first meeting. Then, Miss Arrowsmith having gone on, Barbara drew forward a huge, determined-looking youth, with a fiery pompadour and a sheepish grin. He wore his cravat tucked rakishly into his shirt-front, and Pitt, who had perceived this fashion, and had not thought of adopting it, wished that he had adopted it and that he, too, "had some style."

"This is Buck Carbury," said Barbara. "He's going to be your best man — Marshall."

"Oh," said he, blankly, "is he? I'm much obliged," he added earnestly to young Carbury, who grinned yet more and told him not to mention it.

There was a lift of strings, taking the air as if it were theirs, all the time; mingling with the air, so that one breathed music as well as heard. (There is more to be known about this!)

"The orchestra!" cried Barbara. "She never told me. Well, I hope the *Weekly* reporter is out there, hearing that."

This was the thought in Barbara's mind as she entered upon holy matrimony; and as for Pitt, he was wondering whether the bride or the groom ought really to have asked the best man's presence.

In the drawing room were a half dozen of Barbara's young friends and as many more of the neighbors. And the ceremony begin ended, these hesitated, in some imagined delicacy, and then came forward all together.

Mis' Hellie Copper was first. She had found time to retire and to reappear, in a stiff white net, decorated with monstrous medallions.

"My!" she said, "you're a cute couple. I was thinking that right through the ceremony: 'What a cute couple.' Well, may you be as happy as you are cute, I say."

Then little Mis' Matt Barber, who looked away when she smiled, and only looked back at you when she had her gravity, and immediately smiled again and repeated the performance.

"I love a wedding," she confided. "I don't care whose it is. Much obliged for my invite.   You'll hear from me very, very soon in return." She passed on and came hurrying back, interrupting the next well-wisher. "I mean to say," she said breathlessly, "I do congratulate you both upon your future."

Mis' Henry Bates, in a rustling black silk, with a heavy watch chain and broad tight gold bracelets, waited her turn, and after one or two false starts, came forward.   She was of those who take their weddings with tears.

"I was thinking." she said, " the last wedding I was to, the groom was killed in the switch-yards in a month. May you both live long to enjoy your happiness."

Pitt suddenly found tongue. " Oh, I guess we will," he said brightly.

Mis' Nick True, a little woman old at forty, with red eyelids and pale lips, came whispering behind her hand.

"I've got on my wedding dress. I keep it for weddings. I ain't never wore it anywheres except to weddings. This is the ninth. Good luck," she said, still whispering, and for some unknown reason, kept shaking her head.

"The same to you," Pitt earnestly responded.

And then a woman, in a woolen gown, with quiet eyes and a tender mouth: "God bless you," she said, taking a hand of each "and let me give you a piece of advice for a wedding present: Don't both get mad at the same time. Take turns! "

Pitt gazed at her in astonishment, and could find nothing at all to say. Mad . . . say, what did these folks think marriage was, anyway? Mad? At Barbara?

The young people approached in a bevy. One or two exquisitely pretty girls there were, in brave frocks. The others were mediocre, conscious, glib. There was observable in them all an ardent and pathetic wish to speak gayly, wittily, and to laugh. They talked, they laughed, but without the wit, save the wit of cheap slang, of catch expressions, of metaphors unweariedly repeated.

"Well, Babs — walked the plank all right."

"Answered the right places, didn't you?"

"Been me, I'd got giggling. Say, Babs — how'd you keep a straight face anyway?"

"How's you like married life?"

"Believe it. I'll never do it. I'll elope first."

All this with endless laughter, and stiff acknowledgment of their introduction to Pitt.

"Isn't it a swell bunch?" Barbara asked Pitt when they had passed. "Not a stick among them."

"Swell," Pitt agreed, and seeing Miss Arrowsmith making her way toward them, found his handkerchief, fell to rubbing at his hands and wrists, and even at his neck.

In Miss Rachel Arrowsmith's manner there was not a shadow of consciousness that she was other than these. She moved among them fine and, by some inviolable law, remote; but of that they knew nothing. Her triumph was not, however, in their insensibility of the difference. It was in her own. All her life she had known these older women. To her their outer aspect was by no means themselves. She saw them with their backgrounds. And little Mis' Barber, Mis' Henry Bates, Mis' Nick True and Mis' Hellie Copper were respectively in now wise separable Mis' Barber, who had borne seven children and supplemented the salary of her luckless husband; Mis' Nick True, whose melancholia sent her weeping from church, from her table, from parties, and wrought in her strange spells of contentiousness, when everything was an effort and a cause for sharp-tongued attack; Mis' Henry Bates, whose six great brothers were all drunkards and had been known to go roistering home in the night, and batter at her locked chamber door crying for her little savings; and Mis' Hellie Copper, who made the most toothsome desserts in

Burage. To these women Miss Arrowsmith felt very near; and with their giggling, under-bred daughters no less than with the exquisite peach-loom girlhood which some of them had brought forth, she felt an inseparable tie. She was not only developed until she was exquisitely different from these women and these girls; also, she was unfolded to the point of seeing through their transparent differences and falling in her place with the rest, which may be all the democracy of which we are capable until we shall be spiritually regenerate.

"Well, Mrs. Pitt," she said, and took Barbara's hands. Pitt smiled and glowed. "I hope," Miss Arrowsmith pursued, "that you two will be very happy. I hope even more than that, but we'll let that pass. The train leaves at four, doesn't it? Then we'll hurry on the food. How long shall you be away? We want to have the house opened for you."

Pitt blushed. "Two days," he blurted out.

Barbara spoke serenely. "We're just going up in the city to buy a few new things," she said. "I'm crazy to get back and begin going over the house."

"Naturally," said Miss Arrowsmith, and left them.

Pitt turned and looked at Barbara, but she was engaged with Mis' Carbury, who was ostentatiously whispering in her ear.

There were tea and cakes and ices, in the black walnut dining room. There was the bride, extravagantly at her ease, secretly watching Miss Arrowsmith, and imitating her to the last fold of her tea-napkin on her knee. There was the groom, extravagantly miserable, balancing his plate at so perilous an angle that Miss Arrowsmith finally pushed toward him a little table, with a gay comment about honor due. There were the young girls, noisy, determined to keep on laughing. There were the older women, in the respectful silence always induced by the taking of food, every one storing up secret facts as to flavoring — all, that is, save Mis' Henry Bates. She took two "crackers" from her pocket, and asked for a cup of hot water.

"I have," she confided to the servant who brought them, "a very peculiar stomach."

At last the Arrowsmith carriage stood at the door. The bridge had run informally across the street to change her gown; she brought her bag to the door, and the groom went after it before the Arrowsmith coachman could obey his order. Every one was out on the sidewalk before Lawyer Granger's house, and a dozen passers-by lingered. Barbara appeared in a blue lady's-cloth gown which she had made, and a straw hat trimmed with high pink bows. She was forcing on new gray kid gloves, short of thumb and long of finger. From nowhere came a shower of rice bags which filled the carriage and Pitt's hat brim and his neck.

"Go on — get going!" Pitt cried in agony to the coachman.

But the two Carburys, who were to go with them to the station, held the man until the last grain of rice had fallen and an old shoe had landed on the back of Pitt's neck, first knocking his hat over his face and its burden of rice in his eyes. As the carriage started, it was borne in upon him that he had not thanked Miss Arrowsmith for all his misery.

"Much obliged!" he shouted over-shoulder.

Everyone on the sidewalk laughed immoderately. Barbara, at his side, laughed immoderately. Pitt caught a fleeting glimpse of the little house across the street, at the top of the long flight of steps. Was it possible that forlorn girl watching the little of pigs in that garden, was the same as the galvanized little person at his side?

At least they were free of the others. He settled back in his corner with a profound sigh. "That's over," he said fervently. That sigh and this thanksgiving were greeted with laughter from the three. Especially the bridesmaid and the best man seemed to find this relief excessively funny.

At the same moment the reason for this fresh mirth became evident. There dashed alongside another vehicle, a landau, filled with the younger of the wedding-guests who, it seemed, had no intention of being left behind on the sidewalk. And at the corner there bore down upon them a dray which must have been waiting in a side street. On this singularly-chosen instrument rode an old cooking-stove and a baby carriage, the whole decorated with asparagus and green boughs, as was the driver on the high seat. This dray turned methodically and followed the two vehicles up the main street of the village.

The baby carriage was the old-fashioned hooded sort, with high wheels. It came joggling along in good faith, in no way a party to buffoonery. It had been built for a purpose. Here it was, ready to serve that purpose. Serene preface to the little figure who should some day live from the union of those two beings in the Arrowsmith carriage — this stately triumph up the main street of its future village! Here, suddenly, in its non-existence, it was yet abruptly pointed out. The gaping folk in street looked on that perambulator and thought about that one unknown. Fools laughed. A few were disgusted and, having no idea what it was that disgusted them, they inferred that it was the idea of the baby. The baby! As if some day life would not hold for it enough of shame and folly, already they were invading it and holding it up to laughter.

A perambulator and a cooking stove. The two symbols, it seemed, of the state wherein two souls had that day entered. Thousands of years, and the only art form and dramatic representation to suggest themselves were these objects on a dray.

At the Halsey House, where the groom was to alight for his own suitcase, the procession halted, and a crowd gathered. Pitt, emerging from the hotel office, squirming under the friendly slaps and punches of Flo Buckstaff,

caught sight of Barbara's face and was stupefied to discern that she was enjoying all. Pitt plunged for the carriage, buffeted by neighborly hands. "For
cat's sake, go on!" he audibly bade the driver, and the crowd guffawed. Flo
Buckstaff, in his enthusiasm, leaped to the mudguard and rode to the station,
hatless.

The Burage railway station lay burning in the afternoon sun. Supreme
center of the mystery in the tow, it was supreme in ugliness and desolation.
Though one went out from there to new horizons and to far winds, the stage
was set with no properties save a squalid waiting room and freight cars baking on a track.

At this hour three trains left Burage. The two locals awaited the coming of the "Through" to Chicago, and the passengers for all three trains haunted
the platform and the waiting room. These turned as one and regarded these
tempestuous arrivals. And from their midst, with whoops, and by hoops welcomed, descended a half dozen of the Burage youth, freed from toil for barely
time to share in this orgy of leave-taking.

Pitt met them, gave them his limp hand which they wrenched, tried
with dry lips to reply to their sallies, desperately repeated "Sure — sure —
sure" to everything that they said; desperately fought his way to the ticket
window.

"Where's the train?" he demanded, mopping his face.

"Where at?" asked the ticket seller. And the room roared.

They pulled at them, put rice down their necks, plastered their suit-
cases with labels and paper ribbons, sang, ran away with Pitt's hat, and laughed
incessantly. The train was twenty minutes late. When it came, they lifted Pitt
aboard, and shouted to the coach: "Groom! Groom! Groom!" And "Bride!
Bride! Bride!" came the shrill treble of the girls. Barbara was projected into
the car, flushed, radiant, her hat over her eyes. As a parting attention they
opened Pitt's bag and poured in the remaining rice.

The train moved. Barbara, at the closed window, waved and tried to
talk through the glass. Pitt, in all his anguish, was looking at his little bride in
mounting amazement. She liked it!

"Here we go!" she said. "Wave — wave — wave!"

Pitt looked straight ahead.

"I'm darned if I will," he said — but his resentment was not telling.
She did not notice it, or whether or not he waved. Nothing that he did was
telling, poor little man.

3

A t that season there occupied the stage in Chicago one of those hybrid
presentations, half vaudeville, half opera, with which the public appetite, not so much jaded as feeble, sought to excite itself. A "comic opera," advertised exactly as spring styles and sweet-meats are advertised.

The playbills of this amusement, showing a row of pale blue women laughing over-shou1der at a row of scarlet devis — for who can pluralize "Mephistopheles?" — caught Barbara's eye. This play, above all things, filled her desire. She said so.

"Let's go, Marshall. Let's be perfectly happy for once, no matter what."

"Well," said Pitt, "I am. But we can go."

They had dined in the cafe of the hotel which Barbara had named, and had agonized under the eye of the waiter, while they tried to name what they would eat. Perceiving their embarrassment, the waiter, after an interval, had essayed to help, amusing himself by suggesting expensive dishes. Finally Pitt looked up at him.

"I guess you ain't sizing us up right," Pitt said, "we'd just about selected ham and eggs and cold slaw and a couple of lemon pie."

Barbara, divining that something was wrong, grasped at the table. She lifted her eyes from the menu.

"And some celery-on-the-branch," she added with dignity.

They walked to the theater — down Michigan Avenue, where in the hot summer evening, the people, even in the heat and relaxation of the night, were still taking their way in an acquired haste. Open victorias and landaus flooded the beautiful artery. On the lake front already innumerable figures were flat on the earth, in a kind of hot death.

"Nobody knows," said Pitt dreamily, "but what we've got a little place somewheres out, all paid for. And me a job."

"A job!" she cried scornfully. "You know you've got a business."

"Well, but —" Pitt reminded her.

Barbara looked up at the silent buildings.

"I bet," she said, not without acuteness, "that you own your own business just exactly as much as a lot of these big bugs own theirs."

This, Pitt reflected, was doubtless true. Well, then, he had a business and a wife, acquired at one bound. He was a man in the world of men. They were on their way to the theater, like everybody. He squeezed Barbara's hand, thrusting his own through her arm.

"Don't you notice?" she said. "People don't lock arms here."

These two little beings took their places in the theater. Their enjoyment extended from the first moment. They looked about them, anxious to appear accustomed to everything. Neither had ever before sat in the pit of a great theater. Barbara could not keep her eye from the boxes.

"I'll sit in one of them some day," she observed.

Pitt's eyes followed her. "Why, shucks," he said. "Some fellow took a wall where nobody'd sit, and told them it's the stuff and they bit. I bet you can't see a thing from there."

"I'll sit there some day," she repeated.

"Well," said Pitt tenderly, "I'll wait for you in the peanut gallery."

The curtains parted.

A thousand came nightly to share in this amusement. The huge theater, decorated at a period when red was giving place to the universal rose, was obediently done in rose. The splendid stretch of floor, the impressive height of ceiling, the majestic frame of the proscenium became a sort of hospital, where anesthetics and sedatives were administered to the tired and the unhappy.

There was a community forced to ten daily hours of labor, much of it, with a fatal precision, done by those who would rather be doing something else. There were streets of homes, with whose happiness was mingled eating irritation about the inessential and the vital. There was a society, too weary and unimaginative to inaugurate its own diversions, too unaccustomed to great drama to find there that which they sought. And behold every sign board, flaming with pale blue women and red devils, and life could be suspended for one whole evening for two dollars a seat. No one could despise the place. Its value, artistically negligible, was socially enormous.

The adroit excitation of the piece went on. Costumes, rhythm, dancing, innuendo — nothing was lacking. The audience breathed to the measure of the constant vibration from the stage. They dramatized the audience — knew themselves to be the manifestation of the emotion, the memory, the speculation of these people. Stage and pit took one another into confidence, remembered together, ministered to one another's follies. And all to a *repetend,* cunningly devised and varied, so that the whole was threaded on one melody, which began to beat in the blood, that enormous body of common blood flowing and mounting in the veins of people.

"Great!" cried Pitt. "Gr - eat!" And stamped and clapped with the rest. This applause was partly for the sake of pleasure in concerted movement. But no one considered that.

At the fall of the curtain it was as if gigantic and clumsy forces abruptly released their hold. This adventure into other levels, into enhanced life was finished. The people descended.

Barbara was ecstatic, wholly the participant.

"Oh, Marshall," she said, "some day I'm going to live like this. If I thought I wasn't, I'd die now."

His smile was all tenderness, tolerance.

An ice cream soda in a drugstore, the long, slow walk through the dazzling streets to the thronged hotel. Shallow light, wavering shadow, cavernous gloom, mysterious height and the hypnotizing, moving, moving of the people, perpetually thrown out of drawing, diminished, magnified, subject to distance, changing color and line as they incessantly emerged. The city at night became a city on another plane. Nothing was as it is.

In the stream, their hotel formed a whirlpool.

"Let's sit down here a minute and watch," Barbara said. "That don't cost anything." At this they laughed.

They sat in a long lobby where went and came innumerable people. These were methodical in the pursuit of they knew not what, but a few were in a young intoxication with the pursuit itself. Men alone, seeking, weighing, appraising. Women in the evanescent consciousness of being desirable. A few more years and brazenness would supplant coquetry, and down they would go. Meanwhile the Barbaras watched, and copied the flare of their skirts, the tilt of their hat brims, their perfumes.

"These must be the real swells here, aren't they?" Barbara asked.

No man, rustic of the remotest district, unused to every symbol, could have failed in knowledge here. Pitt looked at Barbara with a rush of tenderness. Her ignorance appealed to the dearest of his sensibilities, the vanity in superior knowledge and experience; by vague processes, immemorially active in men, it enhanced his self-respect to know her inferior in anything. He smiled with gentleness.

"They look like it," he admitted.

A woman, boldly lovely, daringly gowned, with heavy lids and disquiet.

Well, she too had a cavalier. Barbara turned and looked at him. Pitt had a way of permitting his head to sink between his shoulders, like a frog. He sat so now, his lean jaw sharply outlined, his tongue meditatively tracing the edge of his upper teeth. His freckled hands were folded upon his hat.

He was still in that momentary crest of tenderness and emotion from her question. His dog-like upward look sought hers.

"Tired *now?*" he said.

"Well, let's get out of this," answered his bride, and frowned.

In Chicago, night is not only the wretchedness, crime, gayety, indulgence, vice, beauty of older cities, but also here it is something else. It is the terror and pathos of the sleep of a giant child, naked by a lake.

One hears this child breathe. One divines its terrible dreams. There go demons and beings in wrath hand in hand with little bright joys and innocent desires, the happy laughter of youth and little lovers of sweetmeat and junketing. There treads the old heaviness, in its ancient dress, woe of failure, of the irrevocable; and there hope plays. But the night streets never hear these breathings. Not the dozing drivers, the roisters with faces out of drawing, watchers of the sick, prowlers, the homeless, the absorbed; not the great hotels, dedicated less to sleep than to waking, to surcease from living; not the homes, small and pathetic backwaters of safety and sweetness or of scum. These are the very figures of the dreams of the child.

Always the substance of place and time and creature goes masked, and the mask is welcomed, but not the substance. Of the actual pageant of every night in the city where a million have gathered in less than a hundred years, nothing is known. The giant child lays asleep.

Only at dawn there comes a moment when the most casual may be conscious of the presence. It is as if the child wakes and regards itself, lies there alone and wonders, catches at fragments of its visions, writhes and bursts into muffled cries.

At dawn, along the lake front, the flat, dead figures on their newspapers gather their sprawled legs, rise, shake themselves and stare at the white east across the white lake.

At dawn, on that July day, Barbara Pitt lay gazing at the gray and green wallpaper, the terrible chandelier, the dusty red lambrequin above the window of a room on the hotel court. And she felt that she detested the little man, sleeping, a freckled hand outspread on the coverlet.

On one errand in the city Pitt had decided. He would seek out a wallpaper hanger and beg to be allowed for an hour to watch him work. He took the address at which such an one was said, at his shop, to be engaged, and announced that he would go there.

"Yes," said Barbara, "you do that."

He hesitated. "I thought maybe," he suggested, "I didn't know but you might go with me. You'd know what points —"

"Oh, I want to go to the shops," she informed him. "I don't get a chance very often to look around."

"Well," he said only.

He put her on a car and took his own. The beat of the traffic, the sun falling through the ties of the Elevated Railway, in incessantly varying patterns, the odor of the sprinkled streets, these excited him and mingled with his sense of hope and adventure. In that little interval, life seemed to him as he had always believed that it might be.

The house at which he found himself was one of those vast dwellings, once formidable and splendid, now isled by encroaching shops, and staring out piteously at they know not what. This house was about to be transformed into a club, and was losing its silver and gilt paper and cumbrous moldings to flowered ingrains. Pitt stood for a space before the sign which bade him keep out, then prowled round the house, entered and tiptoed through the littered rooms, in a pleasant sense of having been sufficiently clever to outwit someone unknown.

A consumptive-looking man, with veins on his bare arms, was at work at the top of a step-ladder in one of the enormous parlors. Pitt stood at the foot of the ladder and put his ridiculous question.

"Say," said he, " could you give me some pointers on the wallpapering business?"

The man, who was scraping away old paper, laid down his tool.

"What? " said he, and peered over at Pitt, and on his repetition, burst into dry laughter. "Gosh," said the workman, "There's an order. What are you going to do? Paper the flat?"

Pitt leaned against the casement of a door, and looked up with innocence.

"No," he said, "I got a little wallpaper business of my own. I — I just took a hold of it. I'd like to find out how to run it."

The man descended his ladder, and had a thorough look at Pitt, and spat on the wooden floor.

"You got your nerve," he said, "and it's a good thing *for* you. How many men you goin' to hev workin' for ye? Get in some that knows the business and you don't got to know it. That's the way they mostly does. I'm workin' for one that's like that now."

Pitt flushed. "I expect," he said, "I won't have any men, to start with. That," he added with simplicity, " is why I've got to get some pointers."

The workman rubbed the edge of his jaw, began to speak, broke down with a hunching of shoulders and a lifting of eyebrows, and laughed.

"Well," he said. "What do you want to know?"

Pitt had no idea what he wanted to know. But the man was kindly, and he was working by the day. Also, he liked his work and was proud of his knowledge.

"I don't know nothin' about the commercial end of it, y'understand," he warned Pitt. "But when it comes to gettin' the stuff on, or gettin' the stuff off, that's me."

Pitt stayed on, listening, watching, while the good-natured fellow held forth to him. Pitt took notes, feeling important, using the back of the hotel dinner menu which, at Barbara's whisper, he had managed to get into his pocket. When he met her at their hotel at noon, he was buoyant.

"It's a cinch — it's a cinch," he told her. "There's nothing to it. I could do it now."

Barbara listened.

"That's nice,' she observed. "Look what I bought. And, Marshall, I'm going to put it on now, for dinner."

It was a suit of blue linen, and became her charmingly. She unwrapped a hug, soft rose and pinned it to her hat. Then she produced white canvas shoes.

"I haven't had anything new in ages, except my wedding dress," she observed and slipped on the shoes. "Now let's go down to dinner. How do I look?"

Pitt had thought that they would find "some little place" for lunch. He had even inquired of an idle and approachable policeman. "Some place in this town where you can eat on the cheap," was the way Pitt had put it. His own bachelor experience at the city cafes had confined itself to the lunch counters. Now he saw at once that Barbara in blue linen, in which shoes, with a huge soft rose on her hat, must be ushered back into the hotel cafe. Already her eyes were bright at the prospect.

"You look great. You look just great," Pitt told her, and followed to the elevator.

"This is the kind of thing Miss Arrowsmith could have all the time, if she wanted," Barbara observed with a sigh and a far look. "I wouldn't stick there in Burage, if I didn't have to."

Pitt's fancy mounted. "Maybe we can come up to the city some day and have a little flat," he said, "if we should sell out."

Barbara's eyes had a look not of stars but of fire.

"I'd like to live nice!" she cried.

"We will live nice," Pitt promised, and his eyes were like a little boy's eyes.

4

They reached Burage toward six o'clock the next afternoon. The station "hack," commonly known as the "rig," received them. Both would rather have walked down the village street, in the late gold, with its leaf and cloud shade. But this, they indeterminately felt, "wouldn't do." So to this new home which they were founding they jolted in a moth-eaten, closed vehicle, and drew back in the corners to avoid observation. It was not only that thus they lost the idyll of that return; they lost too the savor of a sacrament. A ritual should have been written for the moment. Instead, these two went into hiding. And they could not even have told you why.

The house was opened. Pitt dreaded the explosives of somebody's greeting. They saw no one. The sitting room was in exquisite order, and centered in a jar of hollyhocks. In the dining room the table was laid, and there were a few dishes covered with fringed napkins. A penciled sign directed them: "See Ice Box," and below two figures, dancing about a huge laden dish.

"That's Miss Hellie," Barbara cried. "She draws on everything. She's a born artist. But this," she deducted at the refrigerator, "is Miss Arrowsmith, I tell you."

A platter of jellied chicken, a bowl of salad, a cream cheese, melons — oh, yes, this "was Miss Arrowsmith" without a doubt. Fresh flowers on the table, a tiny pitcher of raspberry sherbet — all, all Miss Arrowsmith. When everything was ready, and Barbara and Pitt looked at each other across that table, his face held a satisfaction which was almost reverent, but hers was shining with happy pride alone.

"Haven't I got some swell friends?" she put it.

Over this first breaking of bread, alone together, in their home, there was a spell to which neither could be insensible. It filled Barbara with an excitement which all but excluded Pitt; it filled Pitt with a sensation which intensified Barbara.

And yet they were almost inarticulate.

"Isn't this chicken the grandest, Marshall?"

"I should say."

"Can you make out what's in the salad?"

"Not me. But it suits, you bet."

"This is the first melon I had this year."

"Me too. Must be like eating money."

"Oh, we can't have things like this, though. Get ready for the pancakes and syrup."

The well-being of the moment filled Pitt with valor.

"Oh. I don't know! " he observed, and glowed under her approval.

It was evident that both were using all the elegancies which they knew. Both were behaving as if they were under the scrutiny of their late waiters themselves. And this was not only in deference to each other, but in unconscious homage to the delicate factors at the feast and, dimly, to the occasion.

Afterward, they strolled out to the garden, keeping circumspectly in the rear of the house. The tread of feet which had set in toward the town, toward the cheap theaters, revealed no shrinking from indelicacies, which might be about to claim those who hastened. But Barbara Pitt stayed in the back of the garden.

In the little kitchen, they washed the dishes at the deal table. Pitt, with an air of proprietorship, built a fire to heat the water and, later, with the same air, climbed the wind and set the clock. Once he brushed at the ashes with that turkey wing. Inexplicable circumstance, that where before he had not been and where he could have claimed no rights, now he moved a free being, with authorities. He wondered if Barbara welcomed this.

"Don't you wish I wasn't here? " he asked her.

As a matter of fact, she had just been thinking of the equally inexplicable circumstance of her burden having been shifted to other shoulders, almost without her stir. She looked at him, over-shoulder, as she washed the dishes, and her eyes were gentle.

"I'm dead glad you're here," she said, simply.

His not to reason why. Still standing behind her, he clasped her waist and rested his chin on her shoulder. She went on with the dishes. Soon he found a towel and dried them. He whistled and recalled a funny story or two to tell. Dark fell, he lighted the bracket lamp, together they put the dishes on their shelves. He was in the seventh heaven. He was giving everything.

For an hour they sat in the parlor. Vaguely conscious of something due to the situation, they instinctively tried to deepen the time by recalling the events of the last two days. But, these events were virtually unknown to them. They had as little idea of the significance of all that they had encountered as if they had not been even spectators.

"Wasn't that funny man great, to the show? "

"Oh, Marshall — and I'll never forget her dress — the one he was sweet on. It must have cost a hundred dollars."

"Remember that lemon pie?"

"Sure I do. And that stuck-up waiter?"

"Isn't the city dirty, though?"

"Something terrible."

"I don't care. I got some ideas that'll make Mayme Carbury sit up."

And so on. It was not only that they had functioned merely in externals. Even the externals had been veiled to them.

At ten o'clock they lighted the little bedroom off the parlor. The wallpaper was stained and peeled, the matting was discolored, the yellow oak furniture filled the room save for a little aisle before the bed. The one window's Nottingham curtain was starched and white. The room was exquisitely clean, and there was a vase of Sweet William on the bureau.

The bureau was worthy of attention. It consisted of a rectangular mirror at the left, a lower block of drawers at the right and two drawers below all. Its mirror was thickly filled with a fringe of Christmas cards, valentines, mottoes, illustrations from advertisements, a decorated blotter, a prescription. The two flat horizontal surfaces of the bureau were burdened with sundries: Ink, a thermometer in a plush case, a glass box bound with ribbon, a mirror in a curled celluloid frame, a wire brush. Near the matches was a sheet of cardboard ornamented with a frog of sandpaper represented as saying: "Scratch my back." On the wall above the wash stand was a " splasher," etched in red cotton, a design of cattails and of more frogs, jumping with "Splash!" below their red-cotton splatterings. The red-glass hand lamp smoked a little. The room was intolerably dreary and stuffy — a place where some poor, broken person might be lying ill.

But Pitt saw Barbara in that delicate haze which, in love, is poured upon all, as if then alone the creature sees true, in light which would always lie over all if he but knew how to perceive.

"Is this," he asked, "where you stayed alone that night I first saw you?"

"Yes, here," she said.

He laid the back of his hand on her cheek, with a gesture beautifully tender.

"Barbara . . ." he said, " I'm so afraid — s'posing you don't get to like to be with me as much as I like to be with you?"

She said nothing, but stood fingering the woolen fringe of the bureau cover.

"If I thought you wasn't going to be happy with me, I'd — I'd croak." His earnestness was out of all proportion to his ridiculous words. Realizing this, he laughed foolishly. He caught sight of himself in the glass, colorless, muddy, sharp. His eyes, which were really beautiful in their depth and directness few to her face. "But I don't see how you can," he added, in a kind of terror.

She was on the verge of speech. Something silent, difficult of life, was struggling its way to her lips. A shade of his solemnity communicated itself to her. Instead, an abrupt change came to her face. She lifted her head in an attitude of listening.

"Hush . . ." she said.

There was no need. At once, in a hideous dissonance, there rose from beneath their window the shrieking of innumerable instruments, devilishly contrived. Horns, pipes, whistles, mouth organs breathed upon with violence, Jew's harps, combs covered with tissue, and the horrible beat and grate of that instrument known as a "horse-fiddle." Voices mingled and groaned. The night was rent by them. All this possessed the world.

"They're cha'rivariing us! " cried Barbara. "I thought of that."

Pitt gazed about him. Something of the unspeakable desecretion penetrated to his soul. "Thought of it! " he shouted. "Then why didn't we have the sheriff up? We'll have him now —"

"Marshall! The idea. It's the bunch. They want to come in. They'll want some root beer. You'll have to give them a couple dollars to go and get some root beer —"

"I'll never do it! " said Pitt with firmness.

She wheeled toward him.

"Don't be a stingy!" she flashed. "Don't leave them say I've married a stick."

Her accent stung, her look shook him. He stared at her stupidly. Outside the awful clamor mounted intolerably. Without a word to her, he walked to the front door, unlocked and opened it.

"Come along, you fellows!" he cried, and fumbled for his purse.

Miss Rachel Arrowsmith dropped in next morning.

She happened, for her arrival, on a pretty moment. But then Miss Arrowsmith had never arrived anywhere unseasonably. She had a genius for the opportune, and such faculties and their failures are almost as real as the operations of the five senses.

Barbara and Pitt were in the little wallpaper house near the wagon-shed. Barbara was in a pink linen, prettily faded, and so short that she looked like a little girl. About her head she had twisted a length of pink ribbon in conformity with the evening coiffure of the ingenue in that musical comedy of blue women and red devils. She and Pitt were absorbedly bending to the rolls of paper which they were sorting.

Miss Arrowsmith stood in the doorway, entered, and at a breath delicately absorbed the place and those within it. Immediately nothing there was of the slightest consequence beside her. And this through no claim of her own, but merely in the fortuitous tribute of the lesser to something exquisite, fire-fibered, gentle, inclusive. It was a sign of the new dispensation — this unconscious quality of her. Miss Arrowsmith had no condescension. But she lost none of the homage due to innate exquisiteness of spirit, of body, of inner fire. This is the only caste distinction there is.

Barbara fell upon her with : "Angel! That supper. We don't know how we can return it, do we Marshall?"

"It certainly was a swell outlay," Pitt replied fervently.

"Don't thank me," Miss Arrowsmith observed. "Mrs. Copper did all the work. And how is business?"

"That's what we're wondering," Pitt admitted, with his doglike upward glance.

"Barbara tells me," said the lady, "that you are an expert paper hanger."

Pitt continued to regard her with his dog-like look, and now his lips slightly parted.

"Dear me, come on in," the hostess observed precipitantly. "What in the world are we hanging around here for?"

"Yes, let's — let's go in," Pitt stammered.

The eyes of Miss Arrowsmith dwelt speculatively on the little man, there in the midst of his domain: The weed-grown lot, unplanted garden, the empty wagon-shed, the poor house, and that little wallpaper place whence must issue the nourishment of his pathetic hopes. With that look in his eyes at her own innocent reference to Barbara's casual comment on his expertness, Pitt stood before her as naked as souls can be — Pitt and his future and Barbara and her future, all naked and piteous. Miss Arrowsmith accepted the situation as simply as she would have accepted the need to fill any other awkward gap in her surroundings.

"Because I wondered — *do* you think that I could have you at once — tomorrow? I want my own two rooms done over, walls and ceiling."

"Oh, my God!" said Pitt. " I couldn't do that."

She wanted to put her arms about him.

"Marshall — the idea! Yes, you can. Of course you can!" Barbara's voice landed on the moment like an admonishing slap.

"You won't find me so hard to please, " Miss Arrowsmith covered it. "Come — I must have you. I'll be in this afternoon to look over your samples. You will?"

Barbara had moved to a place at his side. There was no such thing as an inobvious nudge, and even if there were, Barbara was hardly the one to have achieved it.

Pitt swallowed. "I'll — I'll try. I'll — I'll see. Much obliged. I'm sure," he contrived to answer.

With that the lady was gone, and he turned to meet Barbara's eyes.

"Where's your nerve?" she demanded shortly.

Pitt spoke softly, almost reverently. "She's an angel," he said. "How can I risk spoiling her rooms for her?"

"You got to do it, somehow," returned Barbara positively and ambiguously withal.

Mis' Hellie Copper, with the perfect authority of long custom, had entered and was rattling dishes in the kitchen. This woman went about among her neighbors, doing their work for them as another might have carried them flowers. She was as definitely beyond payment as one in the offices of consolation or the pouring of tea. Something of her quality came to Pitt as he stood there by the side porch where Miss Arrowsmith had left him. For all his anxiety, he felt a kind of sweetness and a faint joyousness. He smiled down at Barbara, and touched her. Life looked to him with an unsuspected fate.

5

It was this face of kindness which now continually turned toward him. Within two days, Mis' Matt Barber, true to her intimation on their wedding day, notified Barbara that she meant to give a "company" for her and her husband.

"Don't expect much," she warned them. "I can't do the work I used to do. Twenty years ago I could kill myself, easy, getting up a spread. I can't do it any more. Don't you look for it."

About twelve were to be bidden, Mis' Barber imparted, for six o'clock supper. The women could come "any time they were a mind to," and bring their work. The men could come when they got around to it. "And I do hope it'll keep cool," she added. " It's like pulling a cough medicine cork to get our men out when it's hot weather. They like the victuals, but they *will* not dress up. And of course I let it be known that this is dress-up."

Mis' Matt Barber's house had a little porch of such a width that two rows of chairs, facing each other, almost touched. The house stood close to the street and had no fence and the porch was not six feet from the side-walk. There she placed the chairs, rocking-chairs, and dining-room chairs, for the women who would spend the afternoon.

"I'll hev to be in the kitchen most of the time," she said, "but the party's the supper, I always think, and they won't mind."

There was a little side yard, and here her supper table was laid. ("In this way I can keep all the dirt out of the house.")

Barbara timed her arrival so that the women should have reached there before her. She was wearing her wedding dress. The front of the white lace had not been put in quite its appointed place, and this lace she constantly adjusted, with a little glance to see if she was observed.

As she approached the house, the women burst into greeting and laughter. Mis' Nick True held open the door, and kissed Barbara roundly. Then the other women rose and kissed her — none of them quite knew why. Mis' Henry Bates gazed into Barbara's eyes, her own eyes reddening.

"Sweet girl," she said, with a little sad shake of her head. "Sweet girl."

Mis' Arthur Miles was the third to greet her. Mis' Miles was called Mis' "Monument" Miles because her husband had the monument works and must be distinguished from Mis' Pickle Miles, of the Burage Pickle Factory. She was a spare, white-skinned woman of middle-age, wearing a button picture of a little boy with no clothes on. This little boy, her oldest son, was now a miner in Arizona, and when he had come home to visit, he had taken his mother to the theater, and she had worn the button.

"Barbara," she said, "I had a recipe book all wrapped up ready to bring you, but at the last minute I forgot and left it on the window sill. No, I guess it was on the machine. I wouldn't have forgot it, only the vegetables came, and I'd ordered eggs too. And if I'm not right there in the kitchen when they come, the boy puts them loose in the sink, and he usually cracks one or two. I've told him and told him about it, but I might as well be birds in the trees. Of course, Mr. Miles is very fond of eggs, and nothing upsets him like wasting fresh ones when. . . "

Mis' Nick True broke in with determination to discuss Barbara's wedding, still fresh though every detail had been many times reviewed. Mis' Miles dwindled away without resentment. Somebody always had to do that to her. Sometimes they had let her go on to see how long it would last, but nobody had ever had the patience to see her through.

"Well now tell us," said Mis' True, "about the city. What was the sights?"

Barbara, her eyes sparkling, straightened her lace front and told about the play. She attempted the plot, such as it was, and was early lost in the bewilderment of "he says" and "she says" and "then the other fellow that he took him for," until the thread was indiscernible. Then she gave the "cute speeches" of the heroine, and the funny man, laughing heartily herself. It is well known that a comic stage piece cannot be related. But everyone continued not the less to smile, and waited with patience to say something herself.

"See here," said Mis' Henry Bates, working forward to the edge of her low chair. "Here we are now, by ourselves. I wonder if we can't give Barbara some advice? I know I've wished, often and often, that I could have had some advice when I was her age and starting life."

The others, understanding *I* in place of her metaphorical *we*, kept respectful silence.

The tide of the return home from the Burage business world had now set in, and this advice was broken by the continued passing on the sidewalk of acquaintances, who tried to say something pleasant. ("'Have-a-kind-word-for-everybody' is a business bringer." Or "You want to smile. Nobody knows when you'll be running for office, and folks remember back.") So Mis' Henry Bates's monologue was troubled.

"Washings, now," she said " Once in two weeks is often enough. Take off the lower sheet every time and use the uppers for lowers — that saves one sheet a week. Evening, Mr. Brock. Yes, ain't it? Rinse out your wiping towels, and they won't need to be laundered. If you find you've got a little time on your hands, wash out a few. Evening, Mr. Pennybad. Yes, consider'ble. I have a little line in my shed, and I usually keep something out there, drying. Evening, Mr. Isberner. Pretty good, thank you — better than most. And boil out your dishcloth often in the skillet — with ends of soap. Nothing is slacker than to neglect that. Keep your dishcloth delicate, Barbara — remember what I say."

She hesitated and glanced over-shoulder. Her voice fell. The other two women drew nearer. The advice dropped to intimate details. And still it was punctuated by one and another greeting the passers. The voices became whispers. The sun slanted up the street and struck full and hot upon the little porch. Barbara, intensely uncomfortable by the free-masonry into which she abruptly found herself admitted, listened with eyes downcast. "Being you haven't any mother," they threw in occasionally. Yet it was not only what they said that troubled her, but their gentle, evil manner of secrecy. Sound of dishes came from the kitchen where the hostess, who had not yet appeared, prepared the supper, assisted by Mis' Hellie Copper. Fragments of what the two were saying came down the passage, and odors of the cooking — coffee and baked meat and sage.

At a little after six o'clock the men began to arrive. The host, Matt Barber, was first, and he cut through the yard to the back door, postponing his greeting of the women until he should have made his preparations. Nick True and Arthur Miles arrived together — Nick a little brightly smiling man who always said "Well, ladies!" and waited — thus throwing on them the burden of speech and himself escaping without having uttered a word. And "Monument" Miles, incredibly huge, with four distinct facades and domed by something huge and bald and pink and moist. The men stood about in the yard and on the sidewalk, and talked of shade trees.

Poor Pitt came alone, in acute anguish. He adroitly pretended not to see the women at all, and joined the men, and colored furiously, and said "Sure. Sure. Sure, I *should* say. . ." *ad infinitum.* He held thought long of having an evening engagement with a wallpaper sample man. But he had not had the courage. No deceit would have staggered him, in his extremity. But deceit takes courage, and the poor little man had none.

At length Mis' Hellie Copper appeared among them, her blue apron over the white dress with the medallions. She saw no one, but fixed her eyes up the street.

"I never saw anything like Hellie in my life," she observed acidly "He'll be late to my funeral. He'll be late to his own funeral. It isn't as if I hadn't laid out all his things. He's just late — that's all, the way some folks are blind, or halt. Everything's ready and spoiling — there he comes, taking his time. I declare, I'd get a divorce now if it wasn't for keeping the supper waiting."

Mr. Hellie Copper crossed the street, narrowly escaping a sprinkling cart.

"For land sakes," began his wife blankly, and as he mingled with the men and gave his good evening, she burst out upon him. "What have you got *that* coat on for? " she demanded. "What was the matter with your other one?"

He was, in fact, wearing striped gray trousers, and waistcoat, and a light linen coat. He stood at the foot of the steps and looked up at her.

"I had," he said, in the manner of one super justified, "a good many things in the pocket of this coat that I wanted to bring along."

He was saved from her by the appearance of the hostess, round the house. Her directness was magnificent.

"Good evening, folks," she said "It's all ready. Bring the chairs you're setting in."

They filed down from the little veranda. The chairs, including the rockers, were placed about the table. The men, circumvented in a flank movement to seat themselves together at one end of the table, were seized upon and suitably distributed.

As they all took their places, there arose a spirited debate between the hostess and Mis' Hellie Copper.

"Nonsense," said Mis' Copper. "You've been on your feet this whole day till you're ready to drop. You set down and let me bring it on."

"The idea," protested Mis' Barber. "I never heard of such a thing. You don't know where things are."

"I can find them," Mis' Hellie promised capably. "Sit down, I say."

Mis' Barber turned on her sharply: "Am I giving this supper or are you, Kate Copper?" she demanded. "I guess I'm going to serve it, like any hostess would."

Mis' Copper, worsted, sat down in the remaining chair. No place has been laid for the hostess. Throughout the supper, she went and came tirelessly, serving her guests; hardly once did she enter the conversation.

Hellie Copper, put out of conceit by the public criticism of his wife, had a store of bitterness which had to be disgorged on somebody. His ill nature was further nourished by the slices of watermelon at each plate. Hellie could not eat watermelon, and he realized that he would therefore eat nothing for good five minutes more. He looked about for a suitable victim, caught sight of the minister a few chairs away, and landed on him.

"Well," he said clearly, " have you fellows got rid of hell yet? Or ain't you?"

The minister's polite avoidance availed him nothing. Mr. Copper went on — "giving out to the minister that they wasn't any hell," his wife related it, next day. It was she who saved the moment from disaster.

"Get him a roll — get him a roll," her agonized whisper penetrated to her hostess. "He'll be all right if we can only get some bread and butter in him."

Supper was served. Scrupulous nicety of linen and fine flowered china; solid silver forks and spoons. A centerpiece exquisitely embroidered and edged by intricate crochet; a vase of glorious rose phlox. Never was meat so roasted and so seasoned with the unexpected, with sauce and dressing so savored; and vegetables so delicately done in cream and brown butter, and served in pastry cups of indescribable lightness, spiced bread, steaming hot; jellies and preserves and pickles, with unknown dainties lending strange and delicious flavors; odorous coffee, served with cream, in huge cups with the meat; thick creamy, frozen dessert and lemon layer cake, with its largess of "filling." Here was a thing as perfectly done of its kind as in any chamber of the world. The very perfection was the despair. For it made up the feast, and there was nothing else to talk about.

"You don't say! You must let me have that recipe. It beats mine to a froth. Little mite more I use — but I dunno but I like yours better. Mis' Emmet says she only uses one, but I don't think she's a real true judge when it comes to meat. Dessert is hers. *Could* I have some more without anybody putting it in the paper?"

Once, to be sure, Mis' Monument Miles did her unconscious best to create a diversion.

"What mustard pickles, Mis' Barber!" she ejaculated. "What mustard pickles. I never tasted their like. The nearest I ever come to it was when Mis' Bates's brother was sick, and we were down there for two weeks. Fifteen days we were gone in all. They had a neighbor — a Mrs. Capwell — no! No! What am I thinking of? Mrs. Farwell. She lived next door but two — or was it three? She asked us over there one night and he got a little better so's it didn't look queer to leave him that long. I remember it was a nasty, drizzly night and I wouldn't put on my black silk to go out in it, and I wished afterwards I had, she had everything so nice. I must say, her mustard pickles come pretty close — "

"Mis' Barber!" cried Mis' Hellie Copper. " Bring me some hot water when you bring Mis' Bates's, will you? Can't I come and get it myself? I shouldn't ever go to sleep again if I drank my coffee this way, dearly as I'd love it — Does your stomach let you drink coffee more than once a day, Mis' Bates?" she inquired, with determination.

Mis' Miles looked up mildly, waited to see if there was going to be a pause, discerned none, gave everything up, and returned to her occupation without resisting.

("Honestly, she makes me think of a puppy hanging onto a root," Mis' Hellie Copper once confided. "I get so nervous waiting for her to leave go that I can't keep my mind on what she's saying.")

Mis' Henry Bates, with folded hands, sat waiting for her hot water. "My stomach," she replied to a question, "won't let me take coffee *at all*. No. Yes, it was a great cross. And what I shall give up for Lent now, I can't imagine."

She always spoke as if her stomach stood back of her chair.

The men were virtually silent. Infinitely content, they saw no reason for infringing upon that commitment. "Well, now say: I don't know but I will. Better not have asked me." "I can't refuse the ladies." "Yes, you might fill it up" — this comprised conversation among them, until the first edge was gone. After that a flight revival of comment on Burage politics, Burage business. And by the women, speculation on a coming bazaar, the new porch on the manse, a newly decorated Burage store window.

The single note from the outside world was sounded when the minister produced from his wallet a cutting of a sermon of the Reverend T. DeWitt Talmadge, preached some weeks before.

"I hope," said the host, "I hope that my life will be spared until I have heard that man. I would go to Chicago to hear him preach — I should feel warranted in spending the money for the fare, and I could stay with relatives."

"Give me Henry Ward Beecher," said Mis' Hellie Copper. "You could have knocked me down with a feather when that man died. I was set on hearing him, and now I can't do it."

The minister lifted his hand, held flat, with the fingers together.

"Don't speak of him," said he.

Hellie chuckled. "He put hell where it belonged," said he. "Hell — they ain't none."

"You may be repudiatin' your dwelling-place to come, as well as your given name, Hellie Copper," said Nick True, with a wink.

"I don't care anything about hell or Beecher or any of them," said Mis' Copper, "compared to Jenny Lind. If she ever gets within a hundred miles of me, I'm going to hear her sing if I never get a new parlor set."

"Land," said Mis' Henry Bates, " the only new thing I ever expect to set on my parlor is my coffin. You know, honestly, it seems a terrible waste, all that nice black-broadcloth covered article, just lasting the two days, when my red rep has set in there for fifteen years. I tell 'em I've a good notion to buy my casket now, and fix it up nice with cushions, like a sofa, and get some good out of the money."

In the midst of the laughter, Pitt stole a glance at Barbara, and felt a thrust of dismay. She was looking at him with a displeasure as marked as words. Her brows went up in a question, down in a comment, and she held his eyes. He knew. He ought to be saying more. His silence had been virtually unbroken. Of this he had been for some time uncomfortably aware, had tried to make up by joining ardently in the laughter, and in warm, promiscuous endorsement and assents. He understood swiftly that she was ashamed of him. So he turned to his host, on whose right he was seated, and burst his way into the talk with:

"Well, it's awful nice to be here with all you folks, this way. I haven't been used to anything like this, I can tell you."

There was a hush. Barbara's eyes were on her plate. Everyone looked at Pitt, and then at her. What had he been used to then? . . .

"Marshall means," said Barbara, with a little laugh, " that he ain't ever really what you might say, lived private. He's been around to hotels, more."

This they accepted, and glanced at Pitt with a new respect. Hotels! He must know how to do things. . . .

"I expect our food don't seem like much side of hotel dainties," observed Mis' Barber, pouring coffee, as she walked behind her guests.

"Oh," said Pitt, "it wasn't hotels as much as it was lunch counters. Fried egg sandwich and a doughnut was most of mine —"

Even Barbara could not cover this. She began talking to Nick True, beside her, but first Pitt had seen her face, and he was troubled. What was the matter? Everybody ate at lunch counters. . . .

Walking home in the starlight, Pitt waited for Barbara to speak. He was wretched in the knowledge that he had made her ashamed of him. She wasted no time, no words, no delicacy.

"Why don't you talk more, Marshall?" she said.

"Barbara," he cried eagerly. "I thought of that. I wanted to. But you — but you got to give me a little time. I —"

"Surely you aren't afraid of folks like that?"

He was not sure he understood.

"If it was folks like you see in the city — but these folks are so different —"

She cried out petulantly: " You're so funny, Marshall! Kind of — I don't know. Old fashioned. And stiff."

"I know," he said humbly, "I can't help it. It'll be better when I get acquainted. I'll try, Barbara — I'll think up things to say. . . ."

"Well," she said cruelly, "when you do it, don't feel that you have to tell about everything — lunch counter and all."

This puzzled him.

"I can't see —" he said, and stopped. "I've got to talk what I am if I talk," he said, and laughed in apology.

She thought: "That's the trouble." Aloud, she said: "Well, it was a nice party, anyway."

"I had a grand time," he fervently declared. "They did something great for you, all right."

"I've got nice friends," she admitted.

It seemed to occur to neither that the party was given for Pitt, too.

From the heart of his intention to live up to Barbara's certainties concerning him, Pitt telephoned to his new friend Strain, the paper hanger, in Chicago. Strain had said that he would do him a good turn, if he could. Well, would he send a man to Burage, immediate, to help out on an unexpected job, a job which must be done, Pitt stressed it, particular. Strain could do that, certainly; but there would be the man's expenses. Pitt accepted everything. Only the job must be done. For it was most particular.

And when the man presented himself, to Pitt's great joy it was Strain himself. He explained that he was glad of a peep at the country, that he was, in fact, looking out for a little place in the country where his wife wanted to bring up their boy. Pitt hardly heard him. He had on new white overalls and a white cap; he boldly marched into Lawyer Granger's house, ascended to Miss Arrowsmith's rooms, faced those expanses of wall and ceiling, reflecting on what would have been his feelings had he not been flanked by Strain. When the doors were closed upon them, little Pitt, the employer, took his lessons in the arts scraping and applying.

"Gritty little devil," thought Strain, as they worked.

And no airs — Pitt had no airs. In the presence of Miss Arrowsmith, he did no less than address his authoritative helper as "Mr. Strain." Pitt was pure gold; and so universal is that material that Strain, not less clearly than Miss Arrowsmith, might read.

"Phone me up when you need me," Strain said heartily when he left him. "If I ain't workin', I'll be glad to go out o' town."

Pitt glowed. Already he was a business man, making business connections.

Miss Arrowsmith owned a Burage house or two, and a store building; and these, it appeared, simultaneously needed paper. Other walls paled and flowered at Pitt's touch. He was getting so that he dare take a job on his own account. When the day came that he could put in the bank Fifty Dollars toward the debts, he sang and whistled about the house, hugged Barbara, surreptitiously chased the little pigs — now "growing to size," Miss Hellie said — and to his friends shed greetings that were as light.

Barbara said to him: "Marshall! You're grand about that money. Don't you think I don't know you're grand."

But she said it with an air of compunction. Always now, in her rare moments of melting, she melted with that air of compunction. This the little man never noticed. It was enough for him that the days were his.

For the first time in his life, Pitt was living a life of relationships. No more lonely evenings in Halsey Houses, no strolling the streets of strange towns, wistfully peering here and there, wondering how a man could "get to meet a nice girl," no such paucity of interests that Bessie, of a soda-water fountain, could fill imagination.

Pitt had become a member of that which called itself "the bunch." Mayme Carbury, Buck, the whole bevy who had been present at the wedding, had attended the bride and groom to the train and, on their return, had chanted and groaned under their window that terrible epithalamium. "The bunch" welcomed Pitt to fellowship. They called themselves lively, "up and coming," said they, always ready for a good time, inaugurating, devising, going "Dutch treat." In their humble way they were prototypes of the young world of country clubs and yacht clubs and luxurious summer camps. "Something doing all the time," was the way Burage put it. Inexpensive pleasures, but involving endless trouble, to row to Government Bend and take supper in baskets; to go to Loon Lake to spend a day; to charter the little steamboat for an evening; to walk to Midgeville to the Wild West show; to haunt the county fair; to get up a party to go to the Glen; to have a picnic out at the Point; to camp for a week at Buck's shack up the Inlet. Never had Pitt found himself included in anything like this. To be sure, none of the day excursions were his. If he was not working, he was in his hot shop, rearranging, writing for samples, waiting for a possible call. But here, or at work, it was soothing to know that at Glen or Point or Bend, there were folk of his own kind who actually wanted him to be with them.

"Barbara's got grand friends," he often thought.

One day when she had been going to the country berrying, Pitt came home to find her yawning on the porch.

"Oh," she said, in answer to his question, "I can't *stand* a hay-rack. They came on a hay-rack."

She followed him into the house and began her preparations for supper. "I always thought," she said, "that when I was married, I was going to see different folks and do new things. It looks like I'd go right along all my life, this same way."

"What — what would you want?" asked Pitt blankly.

"Oh, folks and — show windows — I don't know. Folks that do different. Like the city."

Pitt hung his white overalls and cap on a nail behind the kitchen door. "You wait," said he, "maybe we got a future in front of us!"

He came to her, slapped his arm about her waist, would have laid his face against hers. She shrank away and shut her eyes, and her shrinking lived in her face which she turned from him. Pitt looked up, and on the little looking-glass over the wash basin, he saw her face, and read it.

"Pitt!" she cried. "My head aches. Leave me be."

He went to the door and stood staring out at the yard. But if her head ached, that must be it, he reflected. Yes, certainly that must be it.

Then came the day at Dorset Wood. The others went in the morning. Pitt was to follow in time for supper. He found them on the bank of a little stream — a spot of heaven, floored, roofed, hung in vivid green, cupping a water of gold and silver. Unknown flowers yellowed the hollows.

And there they were, scattered on the moss — these jolly folk who had so suddenly become integers in his life. They greeted him with pleasant faces and little howls. He approached them, bringing the heavy basket which Barbara had made ready. Its weight brought a long wrist to view. Pitt's idea of outing clothes was a coat of seer-sucker, which Barbara especially detested. His straw hat was well back on his head and pressed forward his ears. He was very warm. He tried to answer with a cheery, off-hand shout — that, as he had thought about it, was the tone which he wanted to try to assume — cheery and off-hand. He tried it. Somehow, his efforts at ease with Barbara's friends never struck him as convincing. He always hoped that the others failed to notice anything wrong. When he spoke, he usually followed his words by a quick, questioning look at everybody, to see if it had sounded right. Sometimes a short silence followed his observation, and then he was wretched. Once or twice, quite inadvertently, he had made them all laugh, and then he glowed warm, and kept remembering with little shivers. He felt no sense of unity with them. But he was vastly content to be taken as one of them. Like many another in certain societies, he had his satisfaction not in actual experience, but in the consciousness that the experience was his.

"Where's the pop?" Barbara demanded.

Pitt's face fell. He had forgotten the pop.

Barbara's look darkened. There was a momentary silence. Pitt was conscious that they believed him to have forgotten the pop purposely, because of the cost. He was miserable. He always did something wrong. No matter what care he took, he always either omitted or introduced something which ruined all.

He felt himself discredited and did his best to get back in favor. He ran for wood, opened cans, offered eagerly to make the coffee. Not that he had ever made coffee, but it was simple enough, he thought, to put the stuff in. He put the stuff in, and served them a weak, tan liquid, thick with grounds and smelling like grain.

Barbara, who had been looking over berries and had not witnessed his service, cried: "What frightful dish water. Who made it?" The company burst into laughter. Pitt looked helplessly from one to another, his lips parted. "I'll make some more," he offered eagerly, and the laughter doubled. The stock joke of the evening now became pop and coffee. Having nothing to talk about, they seized on this. Pitt laughed, joined in their jokes and even referred to pop and coffee once or twice himself. But he felt a slight physical sickness, and a great longing somehow to make up. If one of the girls' dresses would only catch fire so that he might rescue her, beating out the flames with his bare hands. . . .

Supper done, the other men drew out cigarettes. Pitt could not smoke. He had owned to this, and it had become fuel for them. An anti-cigarette measure was a part of the Woman's Christian Temperance Union propaganda, and his friends accused him of being "good." He always denied this hotly, and carefully explained that tobacco made him ill. Every time they made him explain this, and took delight. The girls laughed too.

He felt their disfavor and, too, a certain kindliness. They were making an effort, on Barbara's account. He must try — he must make them see that he wasn't such a bad fellow. Barbara's scornful emphasis on the night of the charivari came back to him: "Don't let them see I've married a stick." If he could only make himself seem to them the way he really knew himself to be, he thought desperately.

He tried to think of a story to tell. At last he remembered one that had made him laugh — oh, yes: That one about phosphorous. He delightedly called their attention, launched in the story, floundered, repeated and, by one word, missed the point. Blank silence. Then a kind little giggle from Mayme Carbury, and the talk went on. He was left with bent brows. What was the matter with that story?

The ease with which the others made light and laughing comments filled him with longing. If he could but do that, all would be well. This he essayed, and more than once. Usually his own comment was drowned. If it lived and lifted, it sounded flat and forced. The only observations in which he felt real confidence were his "Sure. Sure. Sure." Or, "I should say."

He looked about on them. A young drug clerk, handsome, brown, compact. A clerk in the express office, huge, magnetic. The choral club director, with curly hair and a way of laughter that was contagious. A teacher of mathematics from a neighboring town, raw-boned, white-lashed, but with a fund of good anecdotes. And Buck — good old Buck, who somehow always seemed to stand by him, though he could not help very much. Then the girls — Mayme, ripe, in the noon of development, with her darting eyes; the Hart girls, who laughed unceasingly; a lovely blonde, the inevitable visitor ("Miss Minnie Hatfield, of Skillet Creek, is sojourning with her friend, Miss Mayme Carbury"). And Barbara! Lovely, appealing, with her loose hair and great eyes. How in the world had Barbara ever married him, he wondered wistfully. Why was it he could not learn to talk like the others, be one of them? They weren't so grand, taken one by one.

So then he would try again. There is often this ineffectual voice, piping at the edges of a company. The one at whom others never look while they are talking. No one ever looked at Pitt when something was being related. Usually his comments were unheard. Once he succeeded in saying: "Well, wouldn't that beat you to a froth? " as he had heard some one else say, and he was heard. Whereupon they all shouted: "Pitt, pass the pop!" many times, and made a sort of yell of it, with a yodel.

On the way home he made them all go in the drugstore. They stood at the counter, with its uncovered fruit-juices and cloying odors and swinging, fly-specked signs. Pitt was aware that three or four of a lower estate were having milk-shake and enviously watching the gay group. He ordered something all round, and felt the magnanimous, dispensing host. Buddy Winchell, the young drug-clerk himself, was serving them. When Pitt tried to pay, Buddy winked at the others and said:

"My treat, old man. Bring yours with you next time."

So that, too, was poisoned. Pitt laughed it off, swore he'd had a fine time and that they must do it again soon; said "Sure, sure, sure" times innumerable, and went off with Barbara, the empty basket on his arm, his long, thin wrist, cuffless, pressed at the basket's edge.

❧

At the bend in the road, the maples made a green dusk for their treasure of silver light. The little houses, withdrawn in their lawns, looked always out instead of in, and waited for the house holders. These little villages at night have the aspect of tryst places for gods, wistful of green seclusions.

"For heaven's sake," said Barbara, " why couldn't you have remembered that pop? They all think you forgot it on purpose."

"I know," said Pitt humbly. "I'm sick about it."

Barbara said more. And then: "And that coffee. What*ever* made you think you could make coffee?"

"I don't know," Pitt answered miserably. "I thought anybody could make coffee — you just put it in."

Barbara said yet more. And she wound up. As they mounted the steep steps: "Marshall, why on earth didn't you talk? You hardly opened your mouth."

"I tried to — I tried to! " Pitt cried. " I thought of things to say. But every time I got a chance to get one in, you was four miles past what you'd been talking about."

Barbara made a vicious little click with her tongue, and mounted the porch. Pitt felt for the key on the nail among the vines, and turned to her.

"Bobs," he said, "I guess you'll be ashamed of me, and I don't blame you. Your friends are awful good to me — and I know it."

Back somewhere in Barbara's little soul her compunction clamored, trying to get her attention. She would not listen. There was, she thought furiously, such a thing as too much.

"You certainly were a stick tonight," she said coldly.

Pitt opened the door, lighted a lamp, and cried:

"Barbara! You don't think I'm one?"

She looked at him, seer-sucker coat and all, and answered:

"I'm thinking of what my friends think."

He stood miserably before her. He saw it all. He had made her unhappy — he had shamed her — she wished that she had never seen him! When, in a little while, he tried to have her hands, she pushed him from her, with a jerk of shoulders.

"This isn't because she has a headache," Pitt thought, in mortal terror now.

The moonlight shone full on the little houses. Here and there was Love, the solvent. Here and there was tragedy. Seldom, though, a tragedy of love or hate or grief. Instead, there were tragedies of pop, and the like. As if the gods, wistful of green seclusions, had fallen in a trap.

Compunctions are social graces. They have little to do with regret, still less with the processes of regeneration. They are a kind of physical correspondence to something which, far later, will function as love. Love is wrung for what another may have suffered. Compunction is concerned with what itself may have said to cause suffering.

The morning after the picnic at Dorset Wood, Barbara felt compunction. This she exhibited by her gentleness, by a taint of coquetry, by saying little, by looking at Pitt . . . by making waffles.

To these faint signals the little man leaped joyously. His wretched night, his wakefulness, his sad dreams became as though they never were. She had been tired, that was all. She was trying to tell him so. By every means in his power, he strove to meet her, to show her that she need not apologize. Barbara had no idea of apology. She thoroughly meant what she had said. That she had shown this and hurt Pitt — poor Pitt, who was paying off those debts as fast as he could — this was her compunction.

Not a word fell from either about the evening. In Barbara a delicacy, rising from her compunction, aped the very manner of the breathless bowers; in Pitt, this was delicacy itself, rising from his heart.

"Where today, Marshall?"

"Halsey House. Flo Buckstaff has up-and-concluded to calcimine the bar."

"The only room in the house that's ever used."

"Sure. Sure. I should say." And laughter at the well-known jest.

"Can he pay?"

"*I* d'no', But I owe him one. He's the first person I talked to about you."

"Wouldn't anybody else listen?"

"Nobody else got the chance. I headed for you myself."

"Silly!"

This was decidedly better. Conversation like this had not of late been prevalent. Pitt went, whistling, to his work. The little houses in the street, still looking outward, were as regardless of that which went on within as if all were merely their digestion. Strong sun on the leaves, a martin's laughter, a cart rattling by — and Pitt was glad again.

The village day went on. Everywhere the invisible ruled. The sign for the Angelus was given from the steeple, and the memorial to a moment — mystic and imperishable — beat in many hearts. The little shops were opened, and out came the humble symbols — cakes, fruit, fabrics. Awnings were lowered, watering cans made cool the old boards, anemic little boys drew large mops across the windows. A faint odor of browned crust began to steal from the bakery. The photographer set out on the little " cobbled " shelf before an upper window, his negatives — a bride and groom, an old man who "sat" for the last time and to please the children; a naked baby. The doors of the *Burage Weekly* were open, and the smell of wet ink and paper hung in the air. In the cramped Post Office the contents of a lean bag were distributed by the old post-master, as slowly as if the mail were the mills of God; dusty, fly-specked little hole, where the state functioned as precisely as under hard wood and marble; and, in their tiny glass coffins, marked with worn red letters, were popped missives of death, of life, of love, of unspeakable commonplace.

Epps, the undertaker, ran round the corner. He was going to make ready for the burial of Lee Asche. His body lay at the house of a friend across the alley, and there his funeral would be held, because his own parlor had never been furnished. A freckled, hairy man, this Ashe, who had a way of button-holing folk and talking close to their faces. When one saw him coming, one crossed the street. He had liked others and no one had liked him. Now there went the undertaker. Men saw the crepe and thought: "Well, it would have been easy to talk to him sometimes, after all," and they wondered why Epps didn't get his wife to press out the old crepe.

A farm wagon was hitched at the bank-corner, and three angular women crossed to the lawyer's office. " Batten, Attorney-at-Law," the sign said, and their hearts beat as they went up the sunken stair. A square man of their family, a man with lips and eyeballs like puffy plums, sat waiting for them. They all talked at once to Batten, who listened with his eyes shut and had occasional twinges of rheumatism and twisted in his chair, held his breath, and emitted it in a whisper. All this was about a line fence which had been discovered to be two feet farther east on the surface of the world than was thought to he true righteouness. The man of puffy plums smashed down his fist. One of the angular women sat tense, with thin lips and tossing head. Outside the earth stretched twelve thousand miles each way from Batten's office, and no one was thinking about it.

All down the little Main Street men came to their work. They thought about the orders they must fill that day, the amounts due them; a train whistled and they knew that it was ten minutes late; so-and-so's grass needed cutting, they noted; and there was his brother visiting him from Seattle, why didn't he do it? Fat geese waddled about a back yard. Somebody had a little tree of crab apples, and the family was gathering them for a jar of marmalade. Locusts sang. It was going to be a hot day. Cans of cream were driven to the creamery. A bill poster put up a terrible warning, calculated to lure: " The Candy Ladies. Come and See." Old Mrs. Jellsie fed the white rooster which her son had sent her a week ago. Little Curt Whitman went by with his red cart. The Messers' baby cried.

Once an excitement was caused by Aden Older, whose mind was queer, appearing on his front veranda and screaming about the protective tariff. His daughter, with her embroidery in one hand, came and led him away, successfully diverting his attention from national politics by telling him that his custard was ready. Once Aden Older had been the boss of the county. Now he almost ran to his custard.

This was the day on which Jenny Berry let her mother go to the poor house. By scrubbing and cleaning, Jenny had been able to support both, but she had no one with whom to leave her mother. Alone, the old woman cut off her hair, burned the bed clothes, chased chickens, emptied a pot of pickles on the front steps. And no one would care for her. So Jenny stayed at home, and they both came near to starvation. "Take her then," said Jenny at last. "One hell more won't burn nobody. Me? No, I don't care. And ma don't know enough to care. But if anybody invites me to the missionary circle again, I'll knock the top of their head off."

At the Carters', Josephine Carter had just brought home her young husband to the shabby yellow frame house and the sloping-roofed room where she had slept since she was a girl. A great occasion. And yet the low windows of the sloping-roofed home looked no different. Next door the Bennets' new house was going up. Only the two of them, and all that room! They say there'll be windows in the closets. What do they want of a fireplace — can't they afford a furnace? Both! Say, where did Sim Bennet get his ideas?

About noon a loose horse appears. She gallops on the brick walks and on the sidewalk boards. Everybody who has oats comes running with a hatful of oats. She dodges down an alley. Everybody remembers the Johnsons' baby in that block. Whose horse is it? Barnay's again. Funny he can't keep his barnyard shut up. There she goes! Her master comes running, the horse takes the bridle, and everybody turns indoors, secretly disappointed.

The summer afternoon slips through the little village and is gone. It seems to have touched nothing. A few women water the plants. Ministers go patiently about making expected calls and entering them in their little books. A load of hay comes creaking under the elms. Tillie Paul strolls by with a cake which her mother has baked for somebody. The Youngers are carrying their father's supper down to the shop. Poor Jeff Cribb is out walking up and down the bricks — waiting. Everybody knows for what he waits, walking there every day, coughing. A group of girls in pink and blue and yellow, as yielding as thistledown, go footing home from some errand, manufactured for its own delight. Children pass, singing or quarreling. Garments are gathered in from lines and from grass, and sprinkled. Bennie Jedd drives home his mother's cow.

Six o'clock. Over the golden aisles of the streets, mysterious with maple boughs, once more the Angelus, the bass of the round house whistle, the treble of the brickyard whistle. Burage breathes deep, all the tension of the day dissolves. A new air permeates the village. It relaxes, expects. It is as if some great brooding, wistful face, so close to all, changes expression; and every one replies. A creative moment, spiritual, tender, human. All Burage either goes home or welcomes home. Meetings, supper, complaints, tenderness, irritations, control. An impressive and spectacular and glorious moment, and a terrible moment. The expansion of human beings in centers carefully contrived. Or the crushing of human beings into centers benumbing, crippling. Beings seldom thrilling from creative work, but leaden from toil of rote. The cry of all the world in the throat of the people from Burage at six o'clock.

At six o'clock Pitt left the Halsey House and flew along the main street. He walked always with rapid steps and stiff knees, lowered head. Usually he whistled in a limited and piercing register.

He ran up the steep steps of his home, cleared the porch with a swelling sense of proprietorship, and sped to the kitchen. He meant to take Barbara in his arms and make her know (he said) how much he thought of her.

In the kitchen door he stopped. By the deal table — of late she had spread their food — she sat, her head bowed on her arms. Before her was a pan of half-pared potatoes. She was shaken by sobs.

"Bobs! Bobby! What is it? Did you cut you? "

She lifted her face, and it frightened Pitt.

"You're sick, Barbara! "

She held her voice and told him, sobs breaking through

"They've gone and got up a party to Cuff's Farm without us. We aren't invited. They've left us out. That's what you did for us in Dorset Woods! "

Mis' Hellie Copper, having three visitors, called in a passing little boy and sent him to the bakery for a pint of ice cream. He brought it in a paper pail. Mis' Copper sent him off with his nickel, apportioned the delicacy in four of her china saucers, and served it on the front porch.

Her front porch was close to the sidewalk. The four ladies were all large, with rolled gold wedding rings which cut fat fingers. They rocked gently as they ate, with little elegancies of fingering and of deliberation. The creak of a board mingled in their talk.

And, as they ate and rocked, the events of their world moved about them in fantasy, strangely contorted, strangely guised, and by that guise, all judged them.

"I declare," said Mis' Copper, "I don't believe a word of it."

"Nor I," said Mis' Bates.

"Nor I," said Mis' Miles.

"Nor I," said Mis' Barber.

"How did you hear it, just exactly? " Mis' Bates inquired.

"Well, I got it like this," Mis' Copper answered, nothing loath. "Of course Mr. Pitt took over the business *and* the debts *and* the mortgage and that was quite a good deal to marry. But to be married *and* mortgaged *and* snubbed in company is more than any man could bargain for. I heard that when they was invited to Cuff's Farm, Pitt just naturally said he wouldn't go and neither should Barbara. But now that ain't like him. She wipes her shoes on his hair and that man don't even notice when it pulls."

"W - hy," said Mis' Bates, long drawn. "I heard Barbara did go alone, last minute, and with only a pie to take for lunch."

"Oh, no, she didn't!" Mis' Miles spoke with decision. "They didn't either of 'em go. I heard neither of 'em had an invite. That strange girl visiting to Carbury's made fun of Pitt, I heard, and they left him out. I donno who got that from where, but I guess it's true."

Mis' Barber drew her breath deep, lifted a spoonful of ice cream, balanced it, and spoke with deep feeling.

"Well, sir," she said — the "sir" being purely a figurative apostrophe, "he's a nice little man, but I declare I can't bear him. I don't know what's the matter with him. But the way he *smiles,* and *steps off,* and *looks* and *is* and *speaks,* I could slap him."

Mis' Hellie Copper looked troubled.

"Ladies," she said, "I guess you'll laugh at me, but first time I see him, I felt that and plus that. And I says to myself, 'They's only one way to get over that, Kate Copper, and that's to just play I was him whenever I see him around.' So to the church supper, when he set down in the minister's chair at the head of the table, and never knew it, and got to eating, and wouldn't nobody tell him, I set there playing how miserable I'd be if I was him *and knew* what I'd done. And while I was doing that with my eyes shut, he says: 'Mis' Copper, I s'pose you ladies have been pretty busy today, ain't you?' And before I knew it, I snapped him up something cruel and says, 'Oh, no. We been laying in hammocks,' and they all laughed, just like they always like to do to him. I could've kicked myself. But that's what he does to me.

"Henry says," said Mis' Bates, "that the men say he can no more pay that mortgage off than he can fly in the air. They say he prob'ly thought he could get hold of the property somehow. They say he'd never snapped Barbara up so quick if he hadn't."

Mis' Hellie Copper flicked her head, sidewise and back and up all at once, eloquently, forcefully.

"The men make me sick," she said, "and we make me and I make myself sickest of all — But I donno what to do to my spirit towards him unless I get down on my knees the minute he comes in sight and stay there till his back's turned. Did you ever hear of *praying* that you might like somebody? "

"Oh, my, yes," said Mis' Miles, "I had a cousin that married to please her folks. All her married life she prayed to like her husband. l guess she done it, too. Anyway, she put 'Erected by his loving wife' on his grave-stone."

"Well," said Mis' Copper, " that's nothing but a decoration. That goes on instead of a weeper."

She gathered up her china, Mis' Henry Bates hurrying to include the last mouthful.

"My stomach will not let me eat hasty," she explained in apology.

"Anybody want a damp towel for their fingers? " Mis' Hellie inquired, poised in the doorway.

"It isn't as if," Mis' Miles resumed, when attention had been restored, "Barbara and him had known each other longer. As it is, I'd believe almost anything might come of it."

"Do you think she can love him? " Mis' Barber inquired flatly.

"I'm sure I don't know," returned Mis' Miles, considering this with a manner of great fairness. "I often wonder. Often," she repeated, her look slanting.

"I believe I could have liked a man sole because nobody else did," advanced Mis' Hellie. "I like to fight for somebody. It's kind of like a virtue and yet you get all the fun of the fight."

"I don't know but *I* could have," Mis' Miles agreed. "I used to be very, very popular in my time of beaux," she volunteered.

"Were you?" said Mis' Barber. "Why, so was I. There was always somebody waiting outside the church to take *me* home. Dear, dear!" She laughed softly.

"Well, I had my little triumphs, too," Mis' Henry Bates took it up "My waist measured just eighteen inches, and my curls met it."

She gazed round, remembering. This woman was fifty, heavy, shapeless. But her face seemed to gleam and soften, as if the girl spoke in her. Mis' Bates had had seven children and two husbands. The solemnities, the humanities, the realities, had pressed her round. She knew all the externals of middle-class life, which is life close to the naked structure of events. Health, malady, religion, sin, childhood, had stirred where she walked. But through it all strove and was perpetuated this old value that had been set upon her: Waist and curls.

"Well," said Mis' Hellie, "nobody much liked me. I used to think it was because I let 'em all know what I really thought of 'em. But now I think it was because I was so mortal hombley. I never had any very pretty clothes, either," she pathetically added.

"You drew Hellie," remarked Mis' Barber, brightly. There was a silence. Mis' Barber was a newcomer of ten years. Somehow there had escaped her the fact which the rest knew and which Mis' Hellie knew: That Helmus Copper had married her when her sister jilted him. It was one of the secrets which a whole community cruelly shares.

"You've made him an awful good wife," Mis' Miles hastened to say, and Mis' Hellie's cheeks burned. Twenty years ago it had happened, but the wife's cheeks burned.

"Barbara was popular enough," Mis' Bates grasped at their thread of talk. "She could have married here, seems to me. Couldn't she?"

"Who?" demanded Mis' Copper. "I never knew of her having a beau! She's in luck enough to get that little man slaving for her, and I hope she appreciates him. *I* never saw her treat him anything but decent."

"She does try to like him, I s'pose," Mis' Barber admitted indulgently.

"If she'd just be patient, all that would come in time," Mis' Copper advanced.

There was a moment's silence.

"Yes," Mis' Barber admitted. "It would."

"After a little," said Mis' Miles, nodding.

Mis' Henry Bates sighed. "If it didn't, I don't know what would become of a lot of the marriages," she said.

The four women stood on the brink of that pit and looked in, and withdrew their eyes, and went on rocking. Mis' Hellie remained silent. She had loved Helmus even before her sister had left him.

"It ain't as if a girl could pick and choose," Mis' Hellie explained. "She takes the best thing she sees that loves her. And generally I guess she makes out to love him."

They passed over it. About them, in block after block, their words would be dramatized that night when dusk fell and the lamps burned and light gowns came down toward the gates.

"Oh, those two'll come out all right," Mis' Hellie prophesied. "The first year of marriage and the second summer for a baby — pass them and you swim. Speaking of a baby, that'd settle the little scraps of them two — same as an egg in the coffee."

The women's eyes consulted. Their voices fell. Of spiritual mysteries they could speak with uplifted faces. At the mystic in human life they veiled the voice. They failed of that mysticism, grew confused by its physiology, missed the creative word beneath all.

Their vast collected store of experience, these village women brought, tale by tale. The birth records of Burage were bared. Great physical victories, evasions, excesses, disappointments, shames — these passed their lips as lightly as ice cream. A hundred tragedies they knew, and all from the secret history of Burage. None of it in the newspapers, all of it kept alive in this wise by whispering groups on idle afternoons. Burage was bare before them, its women, its men, its relationships. And there was only one of them who could now and again step back and throw the whole on a great screen and bid them look.

"Well said! " she cried at length. "See where we get to, just talking about Barbara. We're all poor suffering human critters, I say — and mebbe with it all, God's got something in the back of His head saved out for us."

"True for you, Mis' Copper." they said, but they did not think of it intimately.

"Good afternoon, everybody," said Barbara's voice, and Barbara herself was at the foot of the steps.

They started, laughed a great deal, spoke involuntarily. Barbara, trim in her bride's blue traveling gown — Burage had never heard of a " going-away gown," having no society column to teach it the pure English of our period of the undefiled — Barbara sat in the chair which Mis' Copper produced, and told them that now she should "call on" all four.

"I've been making gingerbread," she owned. They noted this. Gingerbread sounds substantial, settled, domestic. Nobody should make gingerbread with a crisis in the house.

The welcome subject of cookery being introduced, they plunged in, wanton. Gingerbread suggested asparagus. Some one had scalloped the white tips. Plenty of toast crumbs, mind — in a tone of warning as of actual moralities. And of brown butter — "we use a great deal of brown butter in our house, anyway."

The visit went on smoothly, as if the viands themselves were being absorbed. One passing might have heard "— but don't try it without using a double boiler." Or, "and you beat it and beat it and beat it --" that favorite morality of Burage society.

Then a little pause and Barbara let it fall serenely:

"Mr. Pitt's going away in the morning."

The hush was electric. *So!*

"For long?" inquired Mis' Henry Bates, leaning forward.

"Oh, we don't know how long," Barbara gave out airily.

So!

She was, in fact, storing for her effect and this she yielded up at length, as if she and Pitt were no more than one and the honors hers.

"Yes, he has a job in Chicago. One of those big houses out on Michigan Avenue that they're doing over. They telephoned for him last night."

It was true. One of Strain's men having fallen from a scaffolding precisely on a collarbone, Strain had bethought himself of the gritty little devil.

"Oh, good! How well he's doing!" Mis' Hellie Copper cast, with her words, a glance of definite triumph at three of her guests. This glance of triumph distinctly nettled the three. Had not they, too, insisted that they believed nothing? They vied with one another.

"My dear, I'm delighted," Mis' Henry Bates cried. "We all think your husband is doing marvelous. Marvelous."

"He's just old business, that's what he is," Mis' Miles assured her.

Miss' Barber was not to be outdone.

"The men admire his practical ability so," she said, and gazed across the street.

Barbara faintly glowed. Not for Pitt. But she felt herself somehow salved.

"You must all come and see me while I'm alone," she said. "Mr. Pitt will come home for Sundays, but that's all. It will be a month anyway."

She did not know that it would be a month. But why not a month? It had to be some time.

She walked with the three visitors down the street. At the corner they left her, buying blueberries for supper, her little gloved finger pointing here and there for the best box, her forehead puckered, housewifely. And the three told one another that of course there was nothing in all this. Blueberries and gingerbread. . . .

Pitt was in the bedroom packing his bag when Barbara came home. He looked older. Three days and nights of acute anguish had drained the little man of any boyishness. His was no droop of wings for he had no wings, seen or unseen; it was a droop of being.

She was light enough in manner. The praise of him by these women was in her veins. It gave her back a sense of his value. Indeed, from the moment of the receipt of Strain's telephone call, Pitt's value to her had begun to return.

When the message had come the evening before, the third since the day of the party at Cuff's Farm, Pitt and Barbara had been at the depths. From deep to deep they had gone in the three days. She had spared him nothing — tears, recrimination, her inability to eat and the resulting attacks of nerves. They were sitting silent at the supper table. And everything hung in the balance. For Pitt's contrition was at last being ridden hard by his neat sense of justice. Indignation, self-pity, so far held in leash by his over-mastering conviction that he was a bounder, began to be assertive in his heart, and to claim a voice. Three times or four, over the dish of baked beans which made their supper, he had gone through in his mind what he could say. In another five minutes he would have said it.

When came the message that he was wanted by Central for long distance. He put on his cap and essayed to stalk. Poor little man, he had never stalked in his life. He merely walked fast and stiff-kneed, and slammed the screen door, which was comic.

He came back as another presence. He took his seat in silence, an approach to dignity which anyone can maintain. Barbara sat gazing into her empty plate. Pitt threw out his news carelessly — but in spite of all that he could do, a little catch of breath belied him: Strain wanted him to run down to Chicago and help him out on a Michigan Avenue job.

Barbara's eyes brightened.

"Well!" she said.

He read his advantage in her eyes. He flushed, assumed indifference, said that he could put off some Burage jobs, he thought, and that he was "glad to help Strain out." Last he mentioned what Strain would pay.

"Oh, Marshall," Barbara said. "That's fine."

His response to her words was instant. To hide it, he strolled to the door. For the remainder of the evening he kept a dignified silence. He heard her tell Miss Arrowsmith the news. He tried to think how he could let Buck Carbury and the rest hear it.

The swing of the pendulum of Barbara was full and frank. She became almost cheerful. One would have said that she had believed in him all the time and was now quietly enjoying her justification.

"Got everything?" she inquired, when she entered the bedroom that afternoon and saw his things strewn about.

He looked up, kept his distance, spoke without looking at her.

"Barbara," he said. " I — want to ask you about something."

She held up a hand-mirror, burdened by an immense cut and curled band of celluloid, and regarded the back of her head.

"I'm going to be there a while with Strain — and I'll have my evenings off," he said.

"Yes?" She looked at him over the hand-glass. Did he want her to go down to Chicago for a theater some night? . . . .

"I've been thinking," he went on, "I could do something with what time I have there."

He hesitated.

"What could you do? " she asked curiously.

"If I knew how to go at it," he said, and seemed not to know how to go on.

She took off her hat and drew her hands through her hair critically.

"If I knew what you were talking about —" she suggested.

It came with a rush.

"Barbara! Something's the matter with me. I don't know what it is. And I thought if I could find an evening school or something —"

He stopped, his eyes searching her face. With unwonted vision, she read there his fear lest she should laugh at him. She sat down abruptly on the edge of the bed.

"Why, Marshall!" she said.

"I don't know who'd know where to go," he went on. "Strain wouldn't, I don't think. But I could find out. Only I was thinking: What would I ask 'em to teach me? Barbara! What's the matter with me?"

At that she was wrung and gave a little cry and put out her hand. She found his, but it was inert. He was breathing fast, his eyes anxiously on hers.

"Don't you be afraid to tell me," he said. "I'd ought to know, so's to ask right."

"Oh, Marshall," she said. "Why, there's nothing. Why, you couldn't do that!"

"Why couldn't I?" He was dogged for his martyrdom. "There must be places where they teach folks how to be. Barbara — nobody ever told me. I've just acted the best I could. And I don't seem to be the way these folks are used to. If I could get 'em to polish me off some, somewheres in the city — "He smiled weakly. "They do those things," he added defensively.

She began to cry, softly, her face buried in his pillow. He stood beside her, awkwardly, and amazed at her tears.

"I hate like the devil to have you ashamed of me," cried the little man. "Not for me — I don't mean that. For you. And there must be something to do!"

With all this, she was utterly inadequate to deal. She continued to cry helplessly.

"Look here," he said. "Once I wondered something else. Maybe you notice things and don't like to tell me. Maybe you could tell me what I do? "

"Oh, Marshall!" she cried, then. "It isn't that. It isn't anything —"

"That I *could* help?" he supplied quietly. "I thought that, too. I mean — I thought, that if I was just a dub, and nobody could teach me." He stared at the wall. "I thought I was a dub," he said. " I don't feel like a dub!" he cried, passionately.

"Marshall — Marshall!" she poured out his name. "Don't — why, don't! It wasn't that — it wasn't anything, Things just went wrong — and then I guess Mayme's company filled up the rig so there wasn't room. I'm sure it was that. I was horrible, Marshall — I was horrible. It was all my fault making you feel so —"

Her abasement was complete. In her pity and her penitence, she believed what she was saying.

"Do you think it wasn't all me?" he cried tensely. "Do you?"

She sat up and put out her arms. He fell on his knees, buried his face in her lap, clasped her.

She put her hands on his head. His cravat was over his collar at the back, but this time she did not chide him, or see.

"Dear Marshall!" she said.

And heaven was within the little man.

7

S ome rumor of the party at Cuff's reached Miss Rachel Arrowsmith.

"They left out the Pitts," she said. "Yes, I can see how they have never had a glimpse of the inside of that man of Barbara's. They've never had a glimpse of their own inside either, bless them."

The heart and the head of Miss Arrowsmith usually acted together -- a coordination not hackneyed. Early in the week of Pitt's absence, she was having six friends at luncheon. She invited Barbara to be the seventh.

And now Barbara skipped and sparkled. A luncheon at Miss Arrowsmith's! Miss Arrowsmith had always been kind but Barbara had known no closer association than kindness. Between kindness and a luncheon of eight there stretches a desert.

She decided to wear her wedding gown. This was her grandest costume and this her occasion of greatest grandeur. She would bind her hair like the ingenue in the Chicago play. She must have silk hose. A fashion department in a Chicago daily had said that you could define a woman if she wore cotton hose. The department had not defined her.

Barbara arrived first at luncheon, carrying an offering of salvia from her garden. She looked almost beautiful, glowing with the delight of being there, of bringing her gift. Barbara loved to make little gifts. She loved the moment when the gift was made by her in person.

While the guests were arriving, Barbara sat tense with satisfaction: Stubbs, Brewster, Hudson, Ames! She swam to the dining room, feeling that she was one of them. They were all young married women like herself. They were of her own age or slightly older. They were of the elect of Burage.

The elect of Burage consisted of the dozen families who — a hasty generalization would almost certainly put it crudely — had been to Europe, kept a carriage, went to Florida or Mississippi in winter and lived in the "residence part." Strictly, they belonged not to Burage. Habit, business, property, parents, these held them there. They were not dependent on the town for recreation — they kept in touch with Chicago theater announcements, the horse shows. They were familiar with Chicago and New York hotels. They did their buying in absentia — rugs, curtains, bedroom suites, clocks, sideboards. "This came from Field's. This is from Chapman's. This is a Tiffany chair," they told you. They were continually going to Chicago to have a gown made, a suit fitted. When, on rare occasions, they went to the Burage Opera House, they wore evening coats. They traveled in the drawing room and mentioned it. They patronized Mame Selby, who did manicuring and shampooing over the bank. They carried their picnic lunches in hampers.

Miss Arrowsmith's luncheon table was charming with frail dishes on the black walnut. Barbara, whose eyes instantly had frank account of the details and silver and china, felt dimly that the others were taking these things for granted, and that she must remember not to watch the maids. How easily these women talked. . . . Not even the usual little pause at seating themselves at table.

These ladies had lost none of their emphasis. In the long process which they were undergoing, emphasis departs last, and there remained to them many an artless custom which their progeny would discard—unless, as was always happening, one of their progeny abruptly reverted, and might be seen on a porch in shirtsleeves and waistcoat, on two legs of his chair, at seven.

Mrs. Malcolm Brewster was reading. It was she who always had something extraordinary to tell — an occurrence of her own or to her own, but not necessarily recent; a neighborhood disclosure; or, these failing, an article of the press. A matronly hand was outspread on her chest as she spoke now right, now left.

" — with kerosene, as we had told her repeatedly not to do. She knows quite well that she had been told not to do that. But she did. the kitchen stove blew up — yes, ours! One morning at six a.m., under the sleeping family. Burned two walls and *destroyed* the store-room with a lot of Mr. Brewster's old ledgers. We thought we were good not to sue her for the damage. What was the use? She didn't have anything. My dear, here she turns around and sues *us,* if you please. And in the complaint says we have a defective stove that wouldn't light *without* the use of kerosene, dangerous to her life and —"

Laughter drowned the tale. And the one crime, by osmosis perhaps, spread to all immigrants.

"That's the way with them. You needn't talk to me about not restricting immigration. Why, my husband had a man working for him. . . ."

At the conclusion of this tale, "The whole immigration question, though," Miss Arrowsmith suggested, "isn't bound up in these two cases."

Mrs. Hugh Ames bent from the waist in one of her pretty bows — like a blue jay's bow, on a branch, in spring.

"Pretty much," she insisted. "*All* immigration laws are framed for" — with a little nod toward the kitchen — "the lower classes."

The talk slipped along the surface of a town scandal. Here Mrs. Jack Stubbs began to shine.

"But that's nothing," she declared, "to some of the things that go on in Burage. I was told something a while ago — folks you all know. You'd be surprised to death if I was to tell you. It may come out any minute. I've known about it all along, but I can't speak yet."

A moment's general pause for speculation. A pause which Mrs. Jack Stubb's enjoyed in its fullness. She had matured early, a thick woman, busy, ends of her veil always a-fly; her eyes quick-moving, upon externals. She had a fathomless fund of secret detail in allusions to which she wantoned. "There isn't much goes on in this town that somebody doesn't find out about," she was wont to say; and social references abounded in her.

"Are you going to Florida this winter? " Mrs.. Hugh Ames asked, and instantly added: "I think we shall. We have relatives we can visit all the way down to Jacksonville."

Beside Barbara was Mrs. George Hudson, a silent, darling woman, with the reputation of "being literary." "She reads a great deal," they said of her. She now made an unrelated effort to lift the talk.

"Have any of you read *Excursions of an Evolutionist?*"

No one had read it. "Let me see, though," Mrs. Brewster recollected. "Isn't that by Darwin?"

"Mercy, no. I'm not quite that had. This one is by Professor John Fisk, the historian. I enjoy reading him because he's American."

"Oh, then I must get it. I love travel. What country is it in?" Mrs. Ames inquired.

"I'm only over to the seventeenth page," Mrs. Hudson confessed. "As far as I've got, it strikes me as quite an unusual book. And so well written. He certainly has a bright mind."

"I know what I was thinking of," Mrs. Brewster triumphantly reinstated herself. "I knew I knew him. I had a paper on him last winter at the William Shakespeare club. I was thinking of Herbert Spencer. He uses the word 'evolution' quite a good deal too."

"What did you say this book is?" Mrs. Ames asked. She had out a shopping memorandum-book, and wrote the name. "My husband likes to hear of such books," she explained. "I always get him at least one deep book for Christmas."

The memorandum-book was in a blue bag. Bags seized upon literature and choked it. Mrs. Hudson turned to Barbara and asked pleasantly: "Do you do much reading?"

So far Barbara had merely listened, looking from one to other, noting their clothes, their ornaments, laughing when they laughed, and sipping a good deal of water.

"Quite a little," she now answered complacently. " I'm very fond of reading," she confessed.

"What have you been reading lately? " Mrs.. Hudson pressed her kindly. Barbara could not remember. What had she read? She struck out desperately. "I read *David Copperfield* a while ago."

Mrs. Hudson raised her eyebrows. " Dickens. I read all Dickens before I was fourteen," she said.

Barbara became miserable. She should have read Dickens long ago, it seemed. . . .

"I always read *all* the late magazines," she amended eagerly.

Bags having been exhausted, someone caught this. It was Mrs. Stubbs.

"Magazines!" she exclaimed. "My, my! I just wish you could see our house. We take seven magazines. Seven."

"We take eight," said Mrs. Ames. "I'm reading three continued stories. I just have mental indigestion every minute."

"I see by *Demorest's* some kind of Greek dress is coming in," said Mrs. Brewster. "Won't they be dowdy, after bustles?"

Mrs. Hudson still hoped to keep the conversation in the right channels.

"I've started in reading Waverly novels all through again," she observed. "Then I've been reading my Eggleston." No one met this. Someone said that mosquitoes were prevalent. "Do you read Eggleston?" Mrs. Hudson asked Barbara, not to be submerged.

"No," said Barbara humbly. "But I've heard of him."

The fruit-pudding provoking comment by an unfamiliar combination, a new avenue opened. "My Ellen makes very good puddings." Ellen. Emma. Lena. 'Melia. How well they did this. How impossibly that. Talk of cookery this, but delegated, vicarious. No one knew much about the process, it seemed. Everyone professed to be judge of the result.

"'Melia feeds us like a hotel," Mrs. Ames complacently owned.

"It's as hard to get help here as in a factory town. Don't you find it so? " Mrs. Hudson asked Barbara.

"Yes, indeed," said Barbara, and crimsoned. This crimson she felt that Mrs. Hudson saw, and fathomed; and wretchedness increased.

For Barbara perceived them to be living in another world from her world: Maids, Florida, excursions. . . .

To her misery the final touch was given when Mrs. Brewster mentioned Europe.

"Have you aspirations that way?" Barbara asked her across the table, and took a pleasant pride in the word.

Mrs. Brewster's look questioned.

"To go abroad?" Barbara explained, and faltered. Of course Mrs. Brewster would have been abroad. All these women must have been abroad.

"Oh, my dear," said Mrs. Brewster. "I've been abroad twice. When I was nine, and again when I was eleven."

"Oh." said Barbara respectfully. "I might have known."

She hardly heard the others speaking. "London is intensely interesting," she might have caught. And again, "Yes, Rome is full of associations."

Minor and attendant miseries pursued her. She poured cream in her coffee before she perceived that the others were taking their black. She folded the napkin carefully, crease for crease, and then observed that the rest, by some freemasonry of understanding, were leaving theirs on the table without folding. Her bonbon had been popped whole between her lips, before she noted the pretty nibblings.

She went in silence back to the living room, and sat by a window. What was the use? She had never had anything, she was never going to have anything. These women must know, every one of them, that she was different from them. She saw now that her wedding dress looked like a wedding dress, there among their trim summer silks and simple challie gowns. She ought never to have come there. She was — why, she was the way Pitt was with her own friends. Her eyes filled with tears. She felt a dizziness and a physical nausea. This she had often felt of late, and now her anxiety to do her best brought it back upon her.

On the table lay a volume of Wordsworth. Mrs. Hudson fell upon it and turned eagerly to Miss Arrowsmith.

"Been studying poetry?" she demanded brightly.

"No," said Miss Arrowsmith. "No."

Mention of poetry was instant suggestion to Mrs. Ames.

"Recite us something, Bird, do," she said to Mrs. Hudson.

Mrs. Hudson demurred: Her voice, her memory, the heat. She then recited — "a thing I've just been learning." It was *Pauline Pavlovna*. They smote soft hands. How could she ever remember by heart like that? "I haven't worked my gestures up very well yet," Mrs. Hudson confided. Then from everyone, "You ought to have gone on the stage; that's what you *ought* to have done." And from Mrs. Hudson a sigh, a meditative look, a momentary catching of the lower lip in white teeth, and "George Hudson," uttered in four tones, — oh, so wifely!

Wouldn't someone play? Mrs. Ames? "Oh, but so out of practice." Mrs. Stubbs?

"I haven't kept up my music one bit since I was married." Mrs.

Brewster? "If I'd known! I haven't my notes." Mrs. Hudson? "Well, what was there on piano? *Schubert's Serenade?*" She used to play that. She would try. . . .

Barbara listened. To her this was the height of accomplishment, of versatility. And, as remote from her as Chicago, as Europe, as the stage.

Miss Arrowsmith came to sit by her. Barbara smiled weakly, tried to answer. She was longing to leave, to be at home, to anywhere. Miss Arrowsmith saw her tense hands, her twisted handkerchief. She looked in Barbara's face and saw her pale and her lips pale. Some one rose to leave and Miss Arrowsmith turned. There were cries and dashes. Barbara had fainted.

In the room across the hall, she was attended by the old doctor; everyone's old doctor he was. The eyebrows of the young married women consulted one another significantly. And at the possibility thus incarnate among them, they became all solicitation, even tenderness. Poor little thing! She had looked pale. She had been so still, too. They would send her things. She might like to take the carriage some forenoon. Yes, but she looked strong. She'd pull through. They turned to Miss Arrowsmith with the same genuine anxiety and alarm. Couldn't they do something? A world of human sympathy for illness, and one-tenth of this sympathy, at luncheon, would have given Barbara her innocent and expected joy.

Reluctantly the guests left before the doctor did. They had word of her. She was right now, and sent good-bys. When the doctor had gone, Miss Arrowsmith sat beside Barbara. Barbara said nothing. But she kept looking in Miss Arrowsmith's face in a kind of terror.

"Don't you like Mrs. Ames?" Miss Arrowsmith suggested once.

Barbara nodded.

"Would you care to dine here some night with them — the Hudsons — you and Mr. Pitt?"

Barbara sobbed.

"Oh, no," she said. "Oh, no. Oh, no."

Saturday night, when Pitt came home, he found Barbara with that same look of abject terror. She went swiftly to him and looked at him like that as he kissed her.

"Well, well!" he began. "If it don't seem just grand —"

She cut him off.

"Marshall!" she said. "The doctor says I'm going to have a baby."

Pitt stared with parted lips.

"You are!" he exclaimed.

Again the bell which so often sounded. One would have said that the baby was all Barbara's.

"Marshall," she cried. "I'm afraid of it! I hate it! I wish I was dead."

The glory of November sunsets falls full and glows on the exposed walls among the trees and on an open bridge over the little river at Burage. Teams cross, and the drivers do not turn their heads to look. They go oblivious, sodden, black against the yellow west, as if they were cartoons called "The Sunset." Carriages drive onto the bridge, and pause; and the occupants tell one another that it is "too heavenly." Usually, a few pedestrians linger there, caught by some call, obscurely divined. Little boys gather and skip stones on the red water.

Burage numbers her trees by thousands. In the morning, the sun comes in strong gold, lavished upon the grass, save where the leaves lay their veils. All the narrow green strips outside the walks turn bright.

In rain, the town, like any other, lying folded in a visible medium, becomes an enclosure cut off from something. Rooms become more intimate. Something ceases, and something is present instead. An influence is withdrawn, a substitution, as of the less definite, is made. Pedestrians greet one another differently.

For a week of each month, the people of Burage fall under a spell at night. Then the moon, in some unguessed potentiality of fecundity, utters herself in brightness. She becomes a besettling presence. Everything is briefly reciprocal — enchanted streets, enchanted door-yards. On the river there is an air of heaven. The people stare at it *and know* that they have nothing to say.

Within all this are signs of creative spirit, but these seldom break through into the field of consciousness. These signs the soul recognizes. She is old. For immeasurable centuries she has watched and absorbed such signs. Now she communicates these to her strange new mechanism of mind. In vain! Its instruments have not the delicacy. Her old tools of the flesh quiver and yearn along old paths, while the new paths of the brain are but faintly marked — in a thousand years more they will function and report. Meanwhile, only the soul knows what she sees. And here and there she finds the means of utterance: A child crossing the market-square in starlight; a homeless man swept by his isolation; lovers. To these comes that sudden enhancement of being which intimates new channels into the unknown. The unknown is the creative. The creative motivates all.

When at last on these same paths folk tread in deepened consciousness, they will look backward to our intimidations as we look on flint and steel. For them sunsets will flame, rain will fall, sun and moon resume; and deep within all, their eyes being lightened, creation will burn, as with a countenance. As might be now, even in Burage, save that eyes sleep the sleep of the dead. Also, the meaning of such word will be heightened that they will be quick with an essence now withheld.

Among such potentialities was Barbara. But her days were bitterness, her nights were a kind of death. If this natural expectation of hers had ever occurred to her, manifestly it had occurred as a far-off possibility, sometime to be faced, like death. But as remotely. Met by the certainty, her attitude was of exasperation, of outrage, of stupefaction. She dreamed that it was not true, and woke happy, and plunged again to despair. She was confounded by the impossibility of escape. Hope, it seemed, was cut off. The event was absolute.

The women of the village knew her attitude. She isolated herself, and when they went to seek her out, they found her face discolored with weeping. "After a while, I shouldn't have minded," was the way she put it.

Mis' Hellie Copper, who was with her a great deal, strove in vain to infuse her with a saving sense of the casual.

"Dear, dear," Mis' Hellie cried, "Anybody'd think nobody was ever born before. Others! Why not you?"

Vaguely, too, this good woman sought to impress on her some dim sense of dignity.

"Why, Barbara," she said, "God expects this. Can't you expect as much as He does?"

The attitude of Mayme Carbury and her friends was frankly sympathetic. "A perfect shame," they characterized the circumstance. Why? Because she should have had two or three years of "her own."

The older women, regretting Barbara's attitude, yet by their chance phraseology, gave it their understanding. "Barbara is in trouble," they communicated the news.

"Oh, never mind," said the doctor. "It'll soon be over."

And happy young mothers, who themselves had welcomed the consummation, said merely that it was too bad Barbara took it that way — as if it were like music lessons, to which some respond gracefully and some do not, and there is no accounting for tastes.

In all the little town there could be found nobody to help Barbara discern what was occurring. There never had been anybody to help her to discern relationship. To her no one had ever mentioned marriage as an art, daughterhood and neighborliness as roles requiring pains; that to take one's place as a member of a town is even more delicate a business than to take one's place behind a counter. Recipes, fancy-work, the care of a house, with details about taking smoke from isin-glass and fruit stains from table-linen, and much concerning bodily decoration, these had been offered to her indiscriminately. She might have breathed them in. But she had breathed in nothing about the nature of being. And this whole area upon which she now entered belonged to the limbo of things whispered about, commiserated upon, avoided; and associated with the risque. If she had chosen to be a bookkeeper, she would have gone to a school for a period of weeks, paying in return her dollars. But motherhood was the gulf to be crossed by amateurs. Here the apprenticeship system sufficed.

The Great Mother tried to tell her. Nature, conscious of this mite, and of a blind reflection of her own fertility, spoke to Barbara with delicate urgency. Sometimes, when her mind had been momentarily absorbed by something alien to her own state, Barbara would be conscious of a dim sense of pleasure, as if she had been thinking of some delight which she now strove in vain to recall. Often, on taking in the morning, or in the darkness, there would he present some tremendous sense of happiness, which fled with her lifted lids. When the mind was engaged, or was blank, some other means of intelligence was opened to her, and hinted at glories. These were always dispelled by her thought, as if the mind were an outsider, and as if something finer tried to prevail.

The only voice which might have reached her was that of Miss Rachel Arrowsmith. And Miss Arrowsmith, in such a case, would have nothing to do with words. She disliked them as a medium. And she was infinitely delicate in touching at the mysteries of converting anybody.

Miss Arrowsmith took Barbara to drive, and sat beside her, silent. She brought her flowers. She ordered for her a great Madonna. She employed nothing but beauty. Often she sat looking at Barbara without words, as if she were giving to her the sweetness of her soul. At such times there was about the two a breath that was like perfume. Upon them may have converged rains of influence, as if that creative spirit of sunset and soft air might speak likewise in some gentle presence. After such an hour, Barbara would turn home with consciousness untouched; but in some seat beyond consciousness, little wings moved — as if her child were being nourished from without, by means which her body was powerless either to create or to intercept.

Also, Miss Arrowsmith understood the springs of laughter. Her familiar spirit did not go gravely, but explored with her the sources of humor, a spiritual bestowal. Sometimes, in her companionship, Barbara had fleet glimpses of that which living might be. But she never thought of this as possible to her, or as conditioned by anything save vague physical preferments and escapes.

When his child was born, Pitt was calcimining the parlor of the little house on the edge of town. By its emptiness and its silence the room seemed to ally itself with the open fields. A bee drifted in, inquired, and its buzz died along the warm air. Below on the road a hidden farm-wagon creaked and passed. The simple presence of early summer was in exquisite evidence, and all the emanations of the time offered some inheritance.

Pitt's brush was approaching the window. On the wall, giants and huge animals were bodied forth by stain and crack. Pitt's brush made its clean progress. Before its sharp slap there retreated the exquisite gentleness of the wind's sound. He touched away at a spider, demolished its careful web, and felt sharp compunction. Where were the little spiders? They might be hidden and waiting. He held up his brush, waited for the fat, alarmed little life to spin itself clear, swing over the abyss, catch and cling safe to the casement. Beyond the pendant body stretched a long, slope, bright with short grain. On the road the sun fell in ocher pools, so that the shadows became positives. Along this road came running Nicky True.

Pitt got to the door and met Nicky. The child's absurdly high eyebrows were disappearing beneath his blown hair. His head tipped side-wise as he talked, with loose lips. He spoke with the breath of a runner. "M-m-m-my ma says you should come home. You got a n-n-new baby."

"I have!" shouted Pitt. "Why, I can't have!"

He had the general impression that all children are born by night.

"M-m-my ma seen it," said Nicky. " You - you - you should come home," he added, in the manner of one saying something which might not have occurred to Pitt. Nicky dropped from the step to run back, arrested himself by a sharp gyration. "Comin'?" he called, conceiving his errand to be unfinished until he had wrung from Pitt a promise to return.

There was no answer. Pitt was off through the house to the dooryard, shouting to the mistress of the place. Running, he passed Nicky on the road and did not see him. Bare-headed, his long wrists flying, Pitt ran. His trousers flapped about his thin ankles above his white splashed shoes. The fields swam to meet him. They did not exist. Only the miracle.

A dog ran barking into the road before him. Behind the dog came a child, dirty, eating a muddy apple. The child stumbled, fell, lost his prize. Pitt stopped to raise him, brushed his apron, found his apple, sought to free it of earth. He touched the child's wrist, of an incredible softness. The child roared and darted away. Pitt ran on, with an added sense of some nearness.

At the top of the hill, across the smoke of engines, Burage sprang into view. He shuddered as if here he faced all his thought, and it overwhelmed him. It was the sight of a woman, beating a carpet, in her commonplace yard, as if nothing had happened, which gave him his rush of certainty that all was well.

Across the tracks and into the village. Down the main street, and his pace did not lessen. By the Halsey House where Flo Buckstaff, heels on post, called out something of which Pitt knew nothing. Through town where once another man in his own guise had supposed that the sale of pickles and apple-butter was the center of his absorption. On up the street where, on a day, a dray had driven holding household goods and a baby carriage. The little figure had been without reality, and lo, now it was real. And the father running.

One or two whom he passed knew why he ran. A leap of understanding was in their hearts. In their passionate sympathy, which flashed to him, was all the fire to warm a world. If the mystery of birth might flame in the faces of us all, no one could wrong another. There he went, that white-faced chap, running to his wife and their new-born child. Not a shop, not a conversation, not a movement of traffic which would not have subordinated its business to that awkward, flying figure.

The sitting-room in an unearthly silence. Pitt shrank into the dining-room, and stood alone. He mopped his face and rubbed diligently at his wrists. There, sometime after, he was found and told. A boy. And everything was well with Barbara. Would he come now and see her? Oh, no, no. She would not want him yet. But, man, she had asked for him. Asked for him? *Had she asked for him?*

He pushed open the door and stood there, half expecting the peevish voice to which he had now grown used. She heard, looked, saw him; and she smiled. He stood beside her, choking, inarticulate. She put out her hand and it closed about his own. He kissed her and she kissed him.

"Have you seen him?" he heard her say.

Afterward, he went into his little wallpaper shop and closed the door. He stood there, swept clean of everything save love and awe. It was as if strong currents were blowing through him, and a new orb lighted his sky. Sweetness, emptiness, the dominion of love within him. He was in the exhaustion of a great spiritual experience. Something had taken him. He would never be the same. He had laid hold upon a guarantee of life. He was face to face with a great light and re-made by it. He felt infinitely able — he felt tall.

W hen the baby was six months old, there took place the advent of Barbara's Uncle Phoenix and Aunt Clauson, come to collect the money loaned from the paisley shawl. With them, as they had not thought to announce, came Bonniebell.

Uncle Phoenix, who always conducted the social correspondence of all three, wrote to say that Aunt Clauson found herself "a tiny wee mite run down," and a change seemed advisable. They therefore proposed a visit to their niece. By coincidence (he said) this was the end of the third year of the note given by Barbara's father for the paisley shawl money. Perhaps it would be convenient. Uncle Phoenix did not say perhaps what might be convenient but ended tactfully with a neat cross for period.

They came. It was a night of sleet; and Flo Buckstaff, who drove them from the station, ordered them to stay where they were till he could tie and give them an arm.

"I need no arm, my good man," said Uncle Phoenix, alighted and perceived that he needed all available arms and legs for the progress.

"As you please," said Flo, " I'll take care of the leddies, then. *You'll* want all your own faculties."

Uncle Phoenix demurred no more and, in the utter blackness, mounted the steep steps on feet and hands. Flo gave his attention to Aunt Clauson and Bonniebell. By Aunt Clauson's heavy breathing and sharp warnings, and by the faint squeaks of the other lady, Flo made his deductions:

"Heavy old party. Sickly little thing. And the old gentleman crisp as sandpaper."

The three entered; Barbara and Pitt supplied that movement and exclamation implicit in welcomes, and akin to the barking and wagging of dogs.

Aunt Clauson sat down without greeting, without taking off her wraps.

"Those steps," she said, "are crimes. Crimes. I shall go up them in my dreams. Like Jacob. No. Jacob left the steps to the angels, didn't he? Barbara!"

She put up her cheek. Barbara fumbled at her thousand buttons. Aunt Clauson lifted her hands. Barbara pulled off her gloves. Her feet, and Barbara removed her galoshes.

"Four hat pins," said Aunt Clauson. " Jet. Bead. Rhinestone. Milkagate. Got them all? No? I'll hold my front and you lift the bonnet. So. I took them both off together on the train. People don't like it."

Pitt was seeking to minister to Uncle Phoenix. The little host, obsessed by his host-ship, danced like a shadow, questions pouring from him.

"On time, were you? Good train, ain't it? Too bad you couldn't have told us when so's I could have met you. Pretty slippe'y, isn't it? Bad weather like this in the city? Let me take your coat. Are your feet wet?"

To all of this which Uncle Phoenix responded for a time absolutely nothing. Deliberately he removed his garments, sat down by the fire, made use of a clean pocket-handkerchief without in any way unfolding it, eyed Pitt sternly and answered everything at once and with great distinctness:

"We were on time. It is a good train. It was not necessary to meet us. It is slippery — obviously slippery, I should have said. The weather in the city was villainous. My feet are dry. Are you Pitt?"

"Sure. Sure. Sure. I should say," replied Pitt, laughing heartily.

"How do you do, Pitt?" said Uncle Phoenix. "I shall glad of two tumblers of water, each half filled, for my powders."

Meanwhile, Barbara became conscious of the little person who had entered with the others, and who stood back of the stove, her mittened hands on the pipe. Aunt Clauson and Uncle Phoenix so pervaded consciousness that this third guest almost escaped observation. There was something psychic about this. Also, no third guest had been expected.

"Aunt Clauson," said Barbara, with a start, "who is this?"

"Oh, Bonniebell," exclaimed Aunt Clauson. "Come here, child. This is P. W.'s sister. She is making her home with us. Miss Clauson, you know."

P. W. was Uncle Phoenix, whose Christian name his wife regarded as heathen and refused to employ. The "child" must have been forty.

She came forward, with bright, appealing eyes — a little colorless thing, flat-chested, wrinkled, with the patient manner of the social inferior to everybody.

"It's real nice to be here," she said. Her handshake was without a current. Her hand might have been a blotting pad. She took off her wraps and revealed a figure without hips, breast, or shoulders, and a head with only a wisp of tight brown hair. She followed Barbara to the kitchen where some supper was to be prepared, and looked up with luminous eyes, luminous smile, and the air of a bird.

"You just let me take right hold," she said.

For this process she had, it developed, a kind of genius. She went by instinct to the right water pitcher, and the right blue cups. She knew where the bread plate was kept. When she sat at table, it was Bonniebell who, un-instructed, went for the tea-strainer, and found it.

"Wait," said Aunt Clauson impressively, "until I tell you about my breakfast. My breakfast is my best meal. I can get along without much else, but give me my breakfast. This morning at that hotel I had a piece of corn bread and an apple. Positively. Nothing else fit for me. And with such a hard day and all."

"Isn't there something else I can get you now, Aunt Clauson? " Barbara inquired anxiously. Aunt Clauson surveyed the table, point by point. "I don't eat cheese or ham or cake or pickles," she checked off what she saw. "I can make out very well on my tea and my bread and butter and my sauce. I like toast — but *don't* you bother. I'm very sensitive about making bother. Oh, now, Barbara, that's too bad."

"What," demanded Uncle Phoenix, fiercely, "is the population of this town?" And having ascertained, he turned, with a free mind, to food and silence.

In the midst of supper, the baby cried. Barbara went to him, and on her return Aunt Clauson was claiming compunction.

"To think that I hadn't asked for the blessed-wessed lamb, him just born and all. How old is he? Is he well? What does he look like?" and on, to no end.

"What kind of soil have you got here? " Uncle Phoenix injected in the midst of this.

As the cake was handed, the kerosene light began to waver, Barbara knew it first, remembered that the lamp had not been filled that day, and hoped in agony that the cake and canned peaches might be dispatched before the catastrophe. Vain hope. The failing light became as evident as the sun in heaven. Before she could rise, Bonniebell had snatched the lamp.

"The can's in the cupboard under the pump, isn't it?" she said. "I saw it there. I'd love to fill this."

In the darkness, Aunt Clauson and Uncle Phoenix sat in unrelieved silence. Barbara tried to talk. Pitt laughed uproariously. Never was such a joke, it seemed, as to have that lamp go out. At last the silence had its way until Bonniebell came back.

"It's a chore to be a good housekeeper," Aunt Clauson remarked then.

When the others had gone back to the sitting room, Bonniebell looked up at Barbara as they cleared the table.

"I didn't know you had a baby," she said. " You must let me take all the care of him. Will you?"

Something of her eagerness reached Barbara. It seemed to her that the little thing was trembling slightly.

"He's a great big boy," his mother answered.

"That don't matter," Bonniebell said, and unaccountably blushed, and said no more. As they were leaving the kitchen, she whispered:

"I don't believe they told you I was coming, did they?"

"I'm so glad you did come," Barbara said.

"They never think of it," added P. W.'s sister. "I don't mind that — only it makes it bad about the beds. You just let me bunk on the floor or anywheres."

After supper came the ceremony as Pitt had planned it for many a night. He brought in the tin dispatch box from the office, and from it took a packet. This packet contained two envelopes of bank notes. These he laid on Uncle Phoenix's knee. Uncle Phoenix counted the bills with the fearful deliberation and regard with which some men handle money. It was all there. Pitt could not forbear a side glance at Barbara. It was a surprise — she had not known that the money was all saved. She sent Pitt a look that left him tingling, refreshed as from a draught. The whole paisley shawl debt paid! And the last interest.

"Commendable. Commendable," said Uncle Phoenix, and hunted through his three wallets for the note. At this note, Barbara looked and wept. It was signed by her father — a cramped, open-lettered hand in which was revealed the poor man's pathetic history. Of this she saw nothing, but she wept for the hand that had signed. "Commendable!" insisted Uncle Phoenix at intervals. Aunt Clauson was nodding. She had slipped off her shoes and she held them in her hand and occasionally let them fall, roused, picked them up, and observed conservatively that it was beginning to be bedtime. Bonniebell was tatting. Pitt glowed; agonized for Barbara's grief; but he glowed.

Being relatives and reunited, there was a certain etiquette to be observed about not going to bed too early. Everyone got very sleepy. Uncle Phoenix, reeking with fresh information regarding the number of trains that ran through Burage daily, the price of Burage real estate, and the tax percentage, at last frankly slept, chin well down and sidewise. Pitt yawned and stifled each yawn irrevocably too late. At last Uncle Phoenix awoke, looked about him in a pretty defiance, and inquired: "Was it Hamlet who said 'To bed, to bed, to bed?' William Shakespeare always hit the nail on the head, didn't he."

When they were alone, Barbara went to Pitt, put her arms around him, kissed him. And as she kissed him she was weeping. It was as if she had said, as plain as words: " If I could love you. If only I could love you! " Pitt took the kiss, knew her gratitude, was repaid for everything.

Aunt Clauson had lived in Burage in her girlhood. Next day she fared forth to pick up certain threads. In Burage there is no sending of cards, no time wasted on notifications. He is the visitor who goes about calling on old friends, and must slight no one. Uncle Phoenix, in the abject discipleship of the man who goes a-visiting, accompanied her, with the unjustified hope of finding diversion. At every visit, he annoyed Aunt Clauson rising prematurely with "Well hadn't we better be getting on?"

When they were alone, Bonniebell turned eagerly to Barbara. "Let me bathe the baby!" she cried. Barbara, in the vivid importance of young motherhood, proud of her recently achieved technique, demurred, and had the baby taken summarily from her arms. She fell silent. P. W.'s sister was one of the women who have the right to children. Her hands caressed, her arms, her heart possessed. It was as if she had brought over from another way of life her skill and her accustomedness. Only there was also eagerness. Barbara bathed her child as if already the process were routine. This woman moved as if the ceremony had a ritual. A spiritual motherhood came forth in her, and shone.

When the baby slept, the little dun-colored Bonniebell, in her flapping, bodiless print skirt and starched white sacque, came to the kitchen where Barbara was ironing. In the guest's hand was an illustrated weekly.

"Look," she said, shyly. "I bought this, when they weren't noticing. Just now I kind of thought you'd like to see."

Barbara let her iron cool, and the two women stooped to the pages. Colored prints of mincing figures, in bright gowns whose making was mystery. Ladies leaving white porticoes, ladies stepping into victorias, ladies with greyhounds walking in gardens, ladies on glossy mounts cantering along smooth bridle paths, with flowers in the trees. Ladies at tea, with bending cavaliers, and in the distance tennis. Ladies boating on lilied inlets. Ladies in negligée.

Bonniebell looked and lingered.

"Ain't they ridiculous? " she said wistfully.

Barbara looked and lingered.

"Ain't they?" she agreed. "My! Some folks live that way?"

They turned the pages, commenting, returning, laughing, in a tacit pretense at light scorn. Bonniebell slipped the magazine in the newspaper rack on the kitchen wall. "I looked at them last night," she owned.

Barbara said nothing. An old wound had been opened.

Her own attitude toward her child was fond, tolerant, tender. She had felt the initial thrill, the growing wonder. But these had not filled her. Her spirit was satisfied, but she was not yet sufficiently identified with her spirit to be aware of this satisfaction. Barbara' flesh was her true identity, and it was still seeking.

In a week Uncle Phoenix announced that they were going on. He was bound to get out of this country. The climate was fit for Injuns. Injuns. As for him, he had been reading the Florida folders. They could board themselves and keep warm. Cool nights, daylight temperature of eighty degrees, warm gulf waters — he detailed those folders.

"I think, with his kidneys and all," said Aunt Clauson, judicially, "we'd better go. We might as well use up what we've got. I did dread the spiders for a while, but I'm reconciled. I've got a great deal of faith in Eucalyptus oil."

"Will you go too? " Barbara asked Bonniebell.

She smiled, shook her head slightly, framed, "I don't know."

"Who? Bonniebell? Why," said Aunt Clauson, "we shall board ourselves. We couldn't get along without her."

P. W.'s sister flushed with pleasure. So she was going!

Barbara looked at her enviously. Florida. Warmth and palms and *people*. Walks along the beach, boating, pavilions with dancing, and always the people. Then there was something they called the esplanade. She sighed. Was it possible that she was going to die after all, and see nothing?

There descends upon the house the furious turmoil of departure. Uncle Phoenix, at the last moment, is discovered not to have on his chamois-skin waistcoat. This is corrected, with concerted help. At another last moment, his powders are remembered to be in the bottom of his bag. Further correction, all in panting haste. Aunt Clauson's milk-agate hat pin is nowhere. One of her rubbers leaks and should have had newspaper folded over the aperture. Everyone ready, wrapped up, wound up, ten minutes before time for the 'bus to come. Anxiety profound and intensely communicable. Pitt out on the thin ice of the walk, his hair blowing, peering down the street for Flo Buckstaff.

"If we don't get that train, we stay in the city all night, on expense," Uncle Phoenix booms.

"We might see a theater," Aunt Clauson suggests.

"Theater! Theater! All you think of is theater," retorts Uncle Phoenix with manifest injustice.

"Ain't that just like a man?" Aunt Clauson appeals to the women, seeking solace in their freemasonry.

"You think the train's going to sit on the track and wait for us, do you?" Uncle Phoenix sneers, glaring.

Aunt Clauson falls silent. Lifted eyebrows signify unplumbed depths.

"Very well, we'll stay," says Uncle Phoenix. "*I* don't care whether we get to Florida, I'm sure. It was for you womenfolks *I* was planning." He begins the deliberate removal of his overshoes.

"Here she comes!" Pitt explodes, having barely heard an invisible vehicle. It proves indeed to be Flo Buckstaff on the Halsey House 'bus. Anxiety disappears. Thanks and blessings and kisses. Uncle Phoenix and Aunt Clauson depart down the walk with Pitt between. They have not thought of Bonniebell. Here she comes from the bedroom where the baby lies asleep.

"Good-by, Barbara," she says, and kisses her with surprising passion. "Good-by. Oh, love what you've got. Love what you've got!"

The little bird-like thing clings to Barbara. For a moment she has spoken free, with no bonds, no veils. She is gone. High time, too, for Flo Buckstaff is just closing the 'bus door, having forgotten all about her.

Following a departure, a house must be tuned to the pitch of those left behind. There is a general disturbance, a new orientation. It was evening before the sitting room resumed its wonted air.

Evening, and such an evening as had settled upon the house since the coming of the child. The baby having been put to bed, Barbara lay on the couch behind the sitting room stove. Pitt read to her. Pitt's idea of reading aloud was to sit with a newspaper before him, and from intervals of silence, while he skimmed or digested, to emerge with occasional plums conceivably interesting to Barbara. She, whose vitality was not yet at its highest, lay quietly, half dozing, first speculating what on earth he thought would interest her about So-and-So having installed a new gas engine; last, slipping away in thought with her guests. Florida! What did Pitt think? That she never wanted to do anything or be anything but just this?

The price and the interest of the paisley shawl money. Now the insurance money — one hundred and ten. That would take longer to save, but then there would not be the expense incurred by the birth of the baby. Say that they were able put that aside by spring. Then they might begin to plan a little trip. There would be the fare. And they could board themselves somewhere. . . .

There swept upon her the picture of white porticoes, smooth bridle paths. She thought of the gowns, the brightness. One gown was hard to achieve, even when she made it herself. And the baby must graduate from long dresses. Then she thought of Pitt, Pitt in his seer-sucker coat and his one best suit.

Pitt, reading placidly of the virtues of the new gas engine, was startled by a sob. Barbara had buried her face in the baby's pillow on the lounge.

"Barbara! Are you sick?" Always to a physical ill went Pitt's first search for explanation.

She sat up and smote the baby's pillow.

"Marshall! All my life I thought that when I got married I could have things different. And they aren't different!"

The horror and the terror of the old days came flooding back to Pitt as he saw her face. For these six months he had almost forgotten. Almost he had believed in his security. He let fall the newspaper, his hands. The strength went from him.

"Why couldn't they take us to Florida?" she cried. " They'd never know the difference."

Florida! Pitt would never have dreamed of Florida.

"I thought," he said, "we'd save up for a little trip as soon as we got paid up —"

"A little trip," Barbara repeated cruelly. "What good are all the little trips we could afford to take?"

She lay silent, thinking of Bonniebell, envying her. But no one would look at Bonniebell. There she would be, and no one would dream of giving her a good time. While she, Barbara, if she had the clothes —

Pitt did not speak. He was face to face with he knew not what. A kind of death was in the room.

As for Bonniebell of the anomalous name, she was watching her own pinched face against the flying night beyond a car window. She had no envy, almost no wonder. She was the colorless sister of her benefactor. She was trained to no work, she had no hope. Perpetually she lived the lives of others without the radiance of self-sacrifice. She accepted all, she died to her physical possibility, her social relationships — but she grew luminous. A thousand filaments bound her. Of these she fashioned her garments. Incalculable waste — incalculable victory. There was a kind of silence in her, where pure influences found entrance. Virgin, she was a mother. In Barbara, the mother, a brood of desires ravaged, unmothering her.

Miss Mayme Carbury, in a rose broadcloth, white velvet toque and flowing veil, came down Burage main street on an afternoon an early spring.

She had no errand, yet she walked as one having an errand. This was part of Miss Carbury's air. On Spring afternoons, she dressed in the best that she owned, and fared forth into the open, like a robin and for a robin's reasons, lacking their dignity.

Mark and Arum's store, with its was ladies and pampas grass in the windows, she entered, traversed its length, priced lace, returned the salute of the junior proprietor.

"Hello, Miss Mayme. No trouble travelin' with you, I hope?"

"Nothing but the trouble I meet in the aisles," she returned, with a lift of eye that defined it.

At the desk, Miss Carbury halted her progress. Lounging there was a blond young woman who had scattered her gold rings on the open ledger and was engaged in rubbing them up. She wore a low blue band about her head and court-plaster on her throat.

"Well, the Mamie!" this young woman greeted her. "All dressed — up."

Miss Carbury smiled languidly.

"Not much place to go in this burg," she disdained it. "I've got a call or two to make for Mamma. Mamma's limb is troubling her again."

"Nothing to do but gad around," said the young woman in the desk. "I wish I had your dad. Going to the show tonight?"

"I guess so." Mayme Carbury admitted. "Not so much else to do and you got to do something. Seen anybody that belongs to it? "

"No. They got their private car. They're a swell troupe, I heard. Who you going with?"

"Nobody," said Miss Carbury. "What do you think I am? Engaged? Why not us girls go together?"

"Sure, I got the thirty-five."

"I guess I'll see the bunch then. We'd ought to start something. So long!"

Miss Carbury's circuit included the dental office over the bakery. Here another of "the bunch" was employed, yawning over a magazine while she awaited patients.

"Hello, Ella!" said Miss Carbury. "Are you in for out, tonight?"

This young woman was as round and pink as a peeled radish. While she talked, she polished her nails on her skirt, on her palm, inspecting each effect.

Her suggestion accepted, Miss Carbury had something to confide.

"Where do you s'pose I'm going? I'm going up to see Barbara Pitt. I think it's a shame the way the bunch treat her."

At this, Ella opened her eyes.

"I haven't seen you around her neck." she suggested with direction.

"And so," Miss Carbury serenely continued, "I thought I'd up and go to see her. Supposing I ask her to go out with us tonight?"

The young woman named Ella assented. She had always liked Barbara, she was sure.

"She hasn't been anywhere," said Mayme. "I can swallow her little man, rather than be mean to her. The baby and everything have kept her home. But I bet she'd be glad to get out, now. Seen any of the show folks yet?"

"Me? Who can I see up here?" inquired the dentist's young woman, gloomily, and polished and polished. "I might as well be the Goddess of Liberty. Say, what a swell rig!"

"This old thing! " Miss Carbury shrugged and was gone.

Barbara was cutting a little petticoat on the dining room table. She wore a blue calico skirt, a flannel dressing sacque and an apron. The baby rolled at her feet. When the bell rang, and rose broadcloth and white velvet filled the house, Barbara grimly ushered her guest to the dining room, strewn with her work. If Mayme Carbury wanted to pity she should pity.

By right of her father's position as health officer, by right of her mother's money, and by right of their square brick home at the end of Main Street, Miss Carbury should have belonged to the group of the Stubbs, the Brewsters, the Hudsons and the others But Miss Carbury, it appeared, was common. A drive or two with a traveling salesman picked up by means far from circuitous, a pronounced taste for color in street-clothes, a penchant for expressions "not used," these had gradually barred her. She had slipped down to the next estate, and there she ruled discreetly. She had a large heartedness, an unconscious democracy and a really fine independence. "I won't be miserable just to be grand," she dismissed her dismissal from the self-constituted *élite*. The story of her gradual descent is a chronicle. And of course at large social affairs, Miss Carbury and friends were always included. They need hardly have observed the difference, had not the accounts of the small affairs from time to time reached them. But then a reversal of some standards exists in Burage. To be bidden not to the small affairs but to the large ones is the compliment. "Oh, no. It wasn't much of a party. Only eight." And "It was a wonderful success. The house was crowded. Everybody was there," mark the relative desirableness. In like manner, the front seats in the Burage Opera House, far from being sought, are at discount. "Side seats and first six rows and last ten rows, thirty-five cents. House fifty cents," it is advertised. The choice seats are "back where you can see somebody."

Partly by this sovereignty of hers and partly by her magnetism, Miss Carbury's influence was unique. Barbara succumbed to her first friendly word. Where *had* she kept herself? Because she was smart enough to have a baby, was that a reason why she should cut all her friends?

"I didn't think anybody missed me," said Barbara.

"You didn't think anything about us — that's what you didn't think," Miss Carbury accused her. It was a delicate flattery, a veiled approach. Did they really think that she was the one who had been neglecting them, Barbara wondered? She became more than ready to forget old slights. After all they had not been unkind to her — only to Pitt.

She held the baby as they gossiped. Barbara had grown lovelier. Her ripeness was now perfect, and sufficiently unconscious. Her smooth, colored cheek and white throat had that peculiar quality which is no less than warmth. Her lovely bosom was warm. Her arms, round, filling her sleeve, were arms to hold her child, to clasp and pillow. Shoulder and thigh confessed her fine vigor. But her face was empty, like a beautiful fabric touched by flat line. She quivered with the energy of the flesh, while brain and nerve lay veiled.

"Look here," said Miss Carbury, at last. "I'm forgetting what I wanted. Isn't the baby almost old enough to leave? You leave him and come on with us tonight. Dove-party — just the bunch. To the show."

Barbara glowed and lighted.

"The show?"

"The Milt Pepper Players," she reminded her. "Don't you read the papers? A whole week in the Opera House. Come along tonight. I'll see about the tickets. You can leave, can't you?"

Oh, yes, Barbara could leave. Mis' Hellie Copper, who had constituted herself prime minister of this small court, had repeatedly assured her of her availability in mixed capacities. An acceptance trembled on Barbara's lips, when she thought of the rose broadcloth. If she went, what would she wear?

"I can't," she said decisively.

Oh, come now, yes, she could.

"I can't do it, not this week," Barbara insisted. "Marshall's in Chicago helping Strain. I tell you what I'll do, though. The next thing that comes along, I'll go, sure."

"It'll be next month before anything good comes," said Mayme. "That's the tent show."

"The tent show?" Barbara repeated. A thrill ran through her. Nights in the Market Square, with pine torches and a band. "I'll go then," she promised. "Whether Marshall's here or not."

With this Miss Carbury was at last content. She went away shining good humor and friendliness.

And now Barbara sat by the dining room window, the baby her lap, and the baby's little petticoat forgotten. Certainly she must have a new dress. She had meant to "get along," but she should have known that this was impossible. She thought blue — pale blue, with white broadcloth . . . she saw herself so. The baby had an adorable way of thrusting his hand in her bosom, and looking in her face. For the first time, now, he did this unregarded. She looked down at last to see his lip quivering.

"Want to see mother in pale blue? " inquired Barbara.

Next day she put the baby in his cart and went to look at cloth. Before she returned, she had engaged a seamstress. "It's time I had something," she defended.

That night Mis' Hellie Copper came in, an apron folded and thrown about her shoulders.

"Law, what a night!" she cried. "Why ain't you out enjoying it? It's spring on the gallop."

"My child's asleep," said Barbara gayly. "What'll I do with him?"

Mis' Copper looked at her sharply.

"I declare," she cried, "you seem 'most like your old self. Get out some, and you'd be her. If you'd dilly-nip around a little, you'd look like a girl."

"Maybe I'll ask you to stay with the baby a night or two before long," said Barbara. "Would you?"

"That white lamb?" Mis' Copper wished to know. "Try me. Don't say another word," — with an incomparable gesture and briefly closed lids — "try me."

When Pitt came home on Saturday night, he heard Barbara singing in the kitchen. At his step, she ran through the house, clasped his neck.

"Wait'll you see what I've got," she cried, like a little girl.

Pitt held her hungrily. He kissed her and she kissed him tempestuously. Who here to tell the little man that it was not he whom she saluted, but some effigy of life itself?

The tent show was in the Market Square. There were huge dirty canvas, with three flaps raised, and rows of rickety seats, without backs, facing a stage whose curtain was painted with dancing figures, neither of yesterday nor of tomorrow. Outside the door, a band, dressed for no reason as common sailors, played brief, frequent, assailing tunes. On the sidewalk, a crowd was gathering. The tide from downtown turned idly up the main street toward the music. These folk were peculiarly a part of the picture — their laughter, their bold gestures, their emphasis. But the great elms of the square and the lemon and rose in the sky were as alien as if they had been superimposed in the vain hope of obscuring the ruck of folk and their noises.

Barbara and her friends came, laughing. It seemed essential to laugh — a kind of *faux pas* not to laugh, or a lack of good faith. There were six or eight young married women and girls. All continually looked about them. They were like cats in the time of young birds. Husbands and sweethearts were to join them at large in the street. But Pitt was in Chicago, helping Strain.

These girls were all splendid in strength and development, with glossy, abundant hair and long bodies and red mouths. But their faces had stopped. That was it — some years back their faces had ceased. Now the girls could only wait for the faces of the next generation to take on whatever it was that their own features had been intending to express. It was strange to see these countenances arrested. A violence had somewhere been done. Where?

They waited, idling about the tent. The man at the door understood that he could speak to them. This was unmistakable.

"Come on in, girls," said he. "What's a quarter?" He spat to show how little he thought of a quarter.

"It's nothing at all, is it? — a quarter?" Mayme Carbury beguiled him.

"Sure, it ain't," he dropped into the trap.

"Then leave us in free!" she cried triumphantly. The girls and the idle band registered their hilarious delight at this touch.

The leader of the hand was watching Barbara. This man was beautifully built, but he carried himself loosely and his handsome face was quite pitifully marred by his living. His eyes however had escaped — in that miraculous hunted fashion which some eyes escape the life of the body, and forever wait their own. It was as if this man were now lost, and his eyes were the anxious description of what he had once been. Barbara saw his look. In the aimless moving of the group, she contrived to find herself near him.

"You'd better see the show tonight," he said. "I think you'd like it."

It was a strange method to use. He merely dropped his voice and spoke quite seriously. The one method, to do her justice, which she would have responded. "How do you know what I'd like?" she asked in the same tone.

He lifted his eyebrows.

"Don't you think I can see you're different from your bunch?" he suggested.

Her eyes lightened, in that piteous and revealing thirst of the human spirit to have its distinction divined. This instinct for difference leads men to monarchy, to titles, to university degrees, to money getting, to appalling architecture, to beards. And there it was, operative between Barbara and Max Bayard, the band leader. She met his look and gave her own, in a rush of crude and pathetic gratitude. She forgot her coquetry. The man watched her. Never yet had he known this scheme to fail.

"Do you know," he said, and stooped a little to her. "I'd like awfully to get your idea on the play, after you've seen it."

At this she drew back, as he had known that she would. He shrugged.

"Oh, I see you are like the rest," he said, " looking for the wrong thing. I tell you, though, I get pretty sick for somebody to talk to. Do you s'pose," again his voice went down, "that I can talk to *this* bunch any more than you can to yours? They wouldn't understand me. You would. It's all right, though — I don't blame you."

He turned, lifted his chin to his men, set his cornet to his lips and treated it as a missile, entering upon *The Blue Danube*.

Immediately Barbara was flooded with a sharp reproach. She was vulgar. What was the matter with her, she wondered? Couldn't she tell a gentleman when she saw one?

Then came Buck Carbury and the other men, shouldering through the crowd. They had bought little red whistles, which became balloons, and then either collapsed to a wail, or exploded, as fancy swayed. By common consent these were now exploded in the girls' faces.

"Telephone call!" shouted Buck.

They laughed uproariously. ("Isn't Buckie killing?" they asked one another.)

Buck went for the tickets. Barbara waited desperately. *The Blue Danube* dragged on, all its treasure of memory and emotion prostituted, rifled, hung naked and crippled into Burage Main Street. But the blind, deformed thing gave out its imperishable rhythm, and to it there answered the hearts of the crude, the gross, the wistful.

"Fine! Grand! Play it again!" shouted those nearest when it was done. Barbara cried "Fine!" to the band master. "I didn't mean to take it like that," she added tremulously. "I didn't misunderstand." He looked at her skeptically.

"Then will you drop outside here after the third act?" he demanded. "I can have somebody take my place."

Buck was beside them, his tickets ready in a crimson string.

"Nine times," he counted them. "Fall in. Come along. Catch hold of father's apron string!" They moved toward the tent door. Barbara looked over-shoulder. The man stood there gravely watching her. She nodded.

Two hours later she stood once more in the doorway of the tent.

"Here." she heard him say. She followed him into the dusk of the square. The Burage Ladies' Improvement Association had bought seats on the square. On the farthest seat, under an old elm, they sat down together.

"You're here!" he said. "I didn't hardly dare hope for it."

"Why not?" she asked. "You saw me nod."

"Well," he told her, "you see I know the kind of a girl you are — first families and all that. And you don't know what kind of a chap I am. How can you?"

"I do, though," she ventured.

"You do?" incredulously.

"I saw you march from the depot, playing," she confessed. "I said to the one that was with me: 'There's somebody different!'"

"You thought I was different too?" — very low.

"I knew it."

"And I knew it about you. I guess we —" and then a pause, "understand each other all right, don't you think?"

"I guess we do." And this from Barbara with a little fall of happy laughter.

"I tell you what," he said. "I haven't had a very easy time in my life. I'm — I'm getting discouraged. . . ."

"Oh, no. Don't do that."

"Yes, I am. What's the use? Would you like this rotten going around all the time?"

"Oh, *yes!*"

"You would?" He leaned never so little closer. For this question was skillfully contrived. And he never yet had never yet found a young girl in a little village who had not answered him the way Barbara had answered.

"I mean —" she said, and drew hack. His return to the impersonal was instant.

"Not one of the fellows'll risk it," he declared recklessly. "Not one of them is married. It's too hard on the woman."

"The different towns — and the travel — and the crowds," said Barbara, lamely.

"It ain't only that," he said. "A man wants a home. A little place to go back to. And that's where he wants a woman. . . ."

All the primal strings. One after another he plucked at them. In a moment he told of the child in the company, and of what pals the two had become on the road. He sighed. "Cute kid," he said. "It makes a man wish —"

But after all it was not what he said. It was that he bore a gift of the gods, and continually flaunted and bartered it. That vital thing which comes from afar, and flows through the human body and beats out in pulses and rhythms to join with other pulses in like rhythms, this thing was his, as truly as if he had been already immortal as a lover. In some obscure fashion, he knew of this. He sat quietly and very near. He bent his head. He lowered his voice. He was grave. He let his intangible power flow through him and meet with the intangible power of her.

"Can't we have a little walk?" he said.

"You have to go back?" she cried.

"No," he said. "No. I told the second cornet to lead for *if* I didn't come back. If I didn't come back. You see I thought maybe I'd want to go back." A pause. "Well — I don't."

They walked up the long main street. A train was passing, and they stood while it passed, his hand on her arm. Then they went across the track, and along the quiet country road. The enormous night received them. They were motes, crawling on the bottom of the black bowl. They thought nothing about the bowl. It was alien, remote, inarticulate. Between these little figures of dust and the giant spaces which had given them birth, there was no more conscious correspondence than between two beetles and the stars. There amazing intervals are incident to life. Times when men and women cease to exist as they existed before, times when they cut the current between themselves and infinity. It is almost as if they might be forgotten, as if the titan thing might sweep on and omit them as they have chosen to go. But the tender adjustment does not fail. There is that which remembers, regards, returns. One forgets the universe, but the universe does not forget. There is something which is incredibly intimate with one.

Across the casual, on to the turn, and along the road toward old fort. And Bayard scrupulously remote. But by every unconscious power of his and thwarted mind, by every instinctive power to control the forces between men and women, Bayard was weaving, weaving.

It was twelve o'clock when they reached the flight of steep steps before her house and Pitt's.

"No — don't come any farther," she said.

"Tomorrow? " Bayard asked gently. "Or don't you want to see me?"

She answered as if some one else were speaking for her.

"Yes. Oh, yes, I do."

"In the daytime? Can you risk it? Or —"

"No. Not the daytime."

"At night, then. Just before the second act. It's dark by then. And that'll give me longer. Give us longer," he corrected, very softly.

She gave him her hand.

"You'll be there?" He kept her hand until she heard herself answer: "I will — yes — I'll be there."

He released her hand, gravely bowed, and was gone. Barbara went up the steps, a soft current threading through her, or through this one who spoke and moved in her place.

10

Pitt was in the city for four days. For four nights Barbara walked until midnight with Max Bayard.

Those days saw in her a process almost atomic. However the process went on, it concerned itself not at all with her thought. It was as if a great area of the old Barbara were inhibited and as if, across areas now first unsealed, were flowing unguessed forces with which she could not cope. But none of these forces were of the mind. What forces were they? She knew. But she found her refuge in the form which they took. They were not as one would have supposed. One would have supposed that they were evil, but they were good. This was not in the least like all that she had learned to fear. Here was nothing save the tenderest understanding. So she herself spoke and answered. Then:

"Well, but what about Marshall?"

Dim chambers, sounding to a dim thought. Marshall would not

understand. He would think this was evil. It was not in the least as he thought. Marshall could not understand.

"Well, but where would it end?"

End? Max Bayard would go away. She put that from her. And even the impulse to put that thought away told her nothing which she could hear.

From Bayard there was not one shadow, one direction which would disquiet her. Barbara could deal with that which she was doing so long as no word made him articulate, definite. He walked with her, talked with her, was silent with her. He tasted every inch of his progress of delight. He was a sportsman. The joy was in the race as much as in the goal. He was immensely expert. And above all, he was sure.

On Saturday noon, Pitt came home. He had finished his work. He had Twelve Dollars clear to put in the dispatch box. All but Twenty-eight of the insurance money.

"All but what?" she said sharply when he told her. "Why, Marshall! I thought it was Sixty."

"I haven't been telling you right," he confessed. "I wanted to surprise you. I was going to wait till I got it all, but I couldn't."

"Why, Marshall," she said. "Marshall!"

She sat staring at him. She had reached the point of promising herself that she would stay where she was until all the insurance money was earned. This she made not as a real promise but as if she were playing at promising, seeing herself in some fascinating role, which she might or might not step in and fill.

She had reached this point on Friday night, when Bayard left her at her door.

"One night more," he said. "One night more. See here. Can't you meet me for the afternoon tomorrow?"

She knew that she would go, but she stood for a moment trying to think out how to go.

"Couldn't you?" he repeated. "I've got something to tell you. We — may have things to talk over. Give me that time."

She answered: "I will. I'll come somehow." And, from that moment, there blazed upon her brain that, no matter what he said, the money, the money must all be raised before — It was as far as she had come. Her hold upon the moral life was her understanding of money obligation.

Now Pitt sat looking at her, his soul in his eyes.

"You poor little thing," he said. "How it must have worried you." And when she burst into tears and drew away from him, he said: "To think it makes you glad like that!"

On Saturday for the first time in the day she made use of Mis' Hellie Copper's offer to stay with the baby. She had shrunk from doing this, but it was one thing to leave the baby asleep at night with a faithful little girl, and another to leave the baby awake for half a day.

Pitt would be busy in his shop. At Mis' Copper's wholehearted consent to come, something pierced Barbara's breast. She went, however, but dressed in a little worn muslin which she had had when she was married. Since that first night, she never once wore anything that Pitt had bought for her, when she had gone with Bayard. These compunctions were a part of Barbara.

She met Bayard that afternoon in the little grove on Prospect Hill. Before them lay a treasure of hills and water poured out by great powers in a continuous riot of giving. A roof of thin leaves and blue sky, the odor of smoke, the creak of an occasional wagon from the road below. The great presence of spring and of the year — innumerable other presences yearning for relationships with the incarnated. Whether they are the next stage or whether man is their next stage, there remains the pressing summons to relationship. But Bayard and Barbara saw only each other.

Through four hours their talk went on. Now came the breakdown of the old scrupulous reticence, the tearing away of masks; questions, recollections, coincidences, a great play of the functioning of feeling through into areas of speech, of interchange of eyes; a total readjustment of two beings from separation to a kind of unity. It is a triumph of being. Peculiar manifestations foster it; the clock stands still as the recognition of sacraments. Birth, death, meeting, parting, marriage, are like the moment when this new relationship begins, within infinite trembling. But Bayard was of those who drag it to that mid-ground where it has no real being. To be sure he was genuinely moved, he had found Barbara adorable. But he had nothing to bring to a sacrament. He did his best, but she was celebrating the hour alone. Only this she did not suspect. She mistook his manner for his spiritual presence.

When the six o'clock whistles blew, she sprang up in terror. He drew her down beside him.

"Tonight?" he said.

She said: "I'll meet you tonight to say good-by."

She explained at home that she had been after wildflowers, and had gone farther than she intended. The wildflowers were not manifest. She said that they had withered.

"What do you say?" said Pitt, after supper, "let's go to the tent show tonight."

"No. No. No!" she cried.

"Why not?" asked Pitt in amazement.

"You go," she said. "My head aches too much."

"You didn't say you had the headache!" he exclaimed.

It was true that she had not said so. She did not know what she was saying. When he refused to go without her, she wept. She *would* be alone, she cried, angrily. Couldn't she ever be alone when she felt like it? Pitt, bewildered, went away. She ran after him to the steps, and made him promise that he would go to the tent show without her. And he promised.

He went, and heard Bayard conduct the overture. Pitt liked music and knew not good from bad. At the first *entr'-acte* he wondered where the good-looking chap with the straight back had gone.

The good-looking chap with the straight back had gone to the little grove where Barbara sat waiting. And now he spoke plain, and now Barbara listened. She cried:

"I've never had anything! I've never seen anything! I'll never be anything — I know that. But I couldn't do it — I couldn't go away with you. You don't know what you're asking."

It was as if the words were projected onto the dark like beings, and she stared at them. Had it come to this? . . .

Why not, why not? — he pressed it. It did not occur to her that in her unwillingness to mention Pitt, Bayard was misunderstanding. He, who knew nothing of Barbara save her name, thought that he had perceived her to be of no social importance, and had inquired nothing about her. Also, this was a part of his caution. He supposed her hesitation to be because he said nothing of marriage. He played on all the strings to which he knew that she would respond — travel, cities, people, fun, *life.* . . . The personal note for once Bayard was not stressing, save to dwell on that good influence which she had been to him, would be. . . . As clearly as he read her, he had never seen anyone like her, and he saw that he did not read all.

He was obliged to be content with that which he had. There would be no letters. He told her that he should come back, that he should think of nothing but her, that he should never have the pleasure without longing for her to share it — the dances, the shows. . . . One would have said that Bayard's life was a revel of color and light.

All this had gone swiftly. She reached home before Pitt and was mixing bread sponge in the kitchen when he came in. As her spoon stirred, something within her was laughing and crying: Bread sponge.

Pitt sat reading, moving his lips with a whispering sound. This did not disturb her — it was so that she herself read. But he had slipped off his shoes, and this did disturb her, not because it disturbed her, but because she divined that it is not done.

She went into the dark bedroom and leaned above the baby. He followed her there, stood by her side. It is as if the soul discerns the ruin of its own, and can seize upon last moments to prolong and to remember. He said nothing, and she felt the silence like an evil. In the darkness they could not see the baby or each other. They merely stood there, hearing the breathing of the child. Pitt did not touch her. She felt as if he knew all. Life seemed to have stopped about them, and they to be rushing on. She went weeping from the room. He came and said a thousand stupid things, as "Now then! "

"There, sir!" "Well, well, well!"

"Barbara," he said at breakfast, "I've got something to ask you."

She rose, and turned her face from him, cutting a bit of apple for the baby.

"Would you want to sell the house? " he asked.

She sank down in her chair and stared at him, weakened by the swift turn in the current of her feeling.

"Sell the house. *Sell the house?*" she repeated.

"Strain wants to buy it," Pitt said. "I thought I better not bother you, last night. Would you want to? You're the one to say."

"Oh, yes," she said. "Oh, yes. Oh, yes."

His disappointment was in his face. He went on quickly.

"Strain says that his wife thinks she'd like to bring their little boy up in the country. She thinks it's a good place — for a little boy."

He watched her wistfully. She said nothing. He wondered of what she was thinking. He felt left out, and suddenly in an extremity of wretchedness.

"He would pay Twelve Hundred for it," he said. "That would pay off the mortgage and the interest, and leave Three Hundred for you."

She amazed him by bursting into tears, with "I'll never touch a penny of it!"

He could make nothing of this, and at last he asked: "If we did sell, what would we do then?"

"The city!" she cried passionately. "Couldn't we go to the city, Marshall?"

He said: "I've talked with Strain. The flats we could afford, they're up three flights. There wouldn't be any place for the little fellow to play but the hall — and the street." His voice rose sharply. "Barbara! You wouldn't want that?"

She answered with relief. No, she wouldn't want that. That was by no means what she meant by the city. What she meant by the city was Bayard's revel of color and light. She looked at Pitt, stooping above his plate. She had always disliked him at table. He chewed so absurdly. How much would he miss her? She counted on his anger to cure him of his love. But the baby — she knew how Pitt would miss the baby. However, the other person who was doing her thinking now, while she was feeding the baby, was not to think about that.

"Then you don't want to sell?" he said.

"You do as you like with the place," she said. "But one thing you must do: If it is sold, you must keep whatever is left after paying the mortgage. You must promise that."

She said to herself that this would partly repay him, and from that hour she insisted that the house should be put in Pitt's name. He protested, but her point was won. In any case, she must stand by Pitt until the debts were paid; then, if he had the house, he would have lost nothing. To the one scrupulous nicety of her upbringing she was true.

Within a fortnight, Miss Rachel Arrowsmith desired a floor waxed and certain walls hung. Pitt's bill was Twenty-eight Dollars. It had amounted to slightly more than that, but he had a fancy to keep it at Twenty-eight, the sum that he coveted.

He threw the check in Barbara's lap. She was feeding the baby. With her free hand she spread the check on the baby's shoulder, read, raised understanding eyes. He was profoundly affected by the change which the movement wrought. Listless, brooded, relaxed, she had been sitting. At sight of the check, her cheek colored, her eyes filled with light.

"Marshall!" she cried. "It's it!"

She sank back in quiet weeping.

The little man knelt at her side, tried awkwardly to clasp her. His hat fell off, and he put his finger in the baby's eye. Barbara comforted the child, herself wept on, and she held stiffly away from Pitt. It was as if he were hardly a factor in her moment. But he thought that he was sharing her relief and her delight. To show her how deeply he understood, he did little things: laid the supper table, sliced the cold boiled potatoes, tumbled the tins tempestuously about to find the toaster.

When the baby slept and she had made ready the supper, she went to her bedroom and lay down. He came to the door, chewing, red cotton napkin in hand, and coaxed her. She shouldn't feel so bad on account of feeling so glad, he told her earnestly.

"Go on, Marshall — please go, your toast'll be cold," was her response to this; and then a flurry of irritation.

She was thinking: "I shall never go. He's good — he's wonderful. He has earned this money. It's true that the house will pay him back — but I see that I can't go. That's finished."

For a week she was sane again, but this was because she still nourished some sense of expectation, knowledge of a secret peak which might at any moment catch highlight.

One hot night Barbara and Pitt went to the Bakery for ice cream. The Bakery of the parrot had lately opened an "ice cream saloon " in the back room, and there at four tables with white cloths, Burage might be seated for its ice-cream instead of standing before a soda fountain.

The room had one window, covered with mosquito netting. The walls were unpapered. There was a shelf of shells, and there were crayons of the parents of the baker's wife. On the hanging lamp was a net bag filled with something known as pom-poms — from the milk-weed, a favorite bit of home decoration. The ice cream was shaped in high pyramids and was served in saucers.

At one of the tables sat Mis' Monument Miles, Mis' Matt Barber and Mis' Nick True. They were dressed in challie, made without collars, and they wore no hats. All carried palm-leaf fans and plush hand-bags. Bits of their talk came to Pitt and Barbara who sat in silence.

". . . always wanted some solid spoons," said Mis' Barber, "but plated I was born, and plated I've et all my day, and I s'pose I'll die taking my medicine plated."

"Plated eats just as good," Mis' Miles offered.

"I donno whether it does or not," Mis' Barber countered. "I can quirk my finger a good deal grander if I know it's solid."

"I've got a dozen solid," Mis' Nick True observed with complacence. "They were my grandmother's and thin as a wafer. I haven't had them out of the box for years."

Laughter was heard in the Bakery, and the lift and touch of skirts. At the door of the "saloon" appeared Mrs. Jack Stubbs and Mrs. Hugh Ames. These ladies nodded to the others, friendly, unrestrained greetings; but as they gave their orders, and waited, the speech of the three women was unconsciously dropped a key. And Barbara could hear Mrs. Ames and Mrs. Stubbs, in their smiling toleration of this strange place of refreshment.

". . . I shall give a dinner here. It is the town's only private dining-room."

"When Elizabeth and Marcus come, we must bring them."

"Will you look on the hanging-lamp!"

"Elizabeth and Marcus gave us the most delicious dinner at the Palmer House — quail, fresh oysters on the half shell . . . I can't begin to tell you."

"Where is Elizabeth now?"

"New York — with Aunt Sally. Having the loveliest time . . ."

"Oh, say!" said Pitt to Barbara. "I got a letter and a paper — looks like — from New York. Here in my pocket. On my way home. I forgot."

Barbara took the letter and the paper and recognized the light, uneven writing of Bonniebell Clauson.

"New York!" said Barbara. "How did she get there?"

Having the impression that it was bad form to open a letter at table, she forbore, for the sake of Mrs. Ames and Mrs. Stubbs, who presently left their ice cream unfinished and went away, still laughing. Barbara kept every detail of their costumes — wine red silk skirts, looped over huge bustles; and a longish white basque, made of embroidery. They wore bangle bracelets and gold beads. On the right hand of Mrs. Jack Stubbs was a ring having a gold bangle attached by a tiny chain of unusual length; this bangle had flirted engagingly whenever she lifted her spoon.

Barbara now opened Bonniebell's letter. It set forth in childish delight that they had come to Hoboken, New Jersey, to visit distant relatives of Uncle Phoenix's; that they had been there for two weeks; and that Bonniebell had been twice to New York.

I was never so happy in my life as when I had two hours to spend alone in Lord and Taylor's store. Barbara, I didn't know there were such lovely things in the world. Dresses trimmed with fur —can you imagine? Velvet dresses, with panels embroidered in colors. Brocaded dolmans. Damask curtains . . . a magnificent set of garnets . . . enormous swan's down fans . . . and a pink dress **with no sleeves at all.** *. . . . Everyone here drives about in open carriages. We went to the Grand Opera House, and I heard Patti — I took the money I had for a hat, because I got some ideas free here and can trim my own. I saw one. . . .*

"Bonniebell! " said Barbara. "Think of her having all that! "

"Look what she's sent," said Pitt.

It was her Patti concert program, and a Lord and Taylor catalogue. Barbara turned the pages, looked, longed. It was Bonniebell in her flapping woolen skirts who sent Barbara this news — Bonniebell, the lover of home, with a genius for its mere machinery.

". . . shake my rugs twice every week, and that's enough for anybody. We eat in the kitchen in the summer, because I use the summer kitchen and it's cool. And we eat there in the winter, because the range makes it warm. So the dining-room rugs don't *need* — " Mis' Nick True went on explaining.

"Oh, let's go!" Barbara said.

She went, with no good-night for the three at the table. They were symbols of a life which she hated with passion.

She spent the days in waiting, for something which she could not name. She was emptied of herself, whatever that reality of self had been And now nothing guarded her. She was subject to wild, random forces. Within the week they came knocking for their entrance.

One night she went for the mail, as she often did when Pitt was busy. There was no mail, and she kept on, without destination, up the main street. She went the length of the single block of shops and idlers. She went looking, as one who has no ties.

Before the Burage Opera House a band was playing; and she sought and passed this spot where clamor centered and excitement looked out.

She glanced idly at the men who played — tawdry uniforms, tawdry instruments, tawdry glances flung among the people — but some there were who played for the sake of the playing, and the bread.

And she was smitten with delight and with terror to meet the eyes of Bayard. He was standing at the edge of the sidewalk, before the men of the band. But he had turned, had already seen her, had ceased playing, and leaned forward, groping for her eyes.

She stood still; and he made his way toward her, passed her.

"Round the corner, by the blacksmith's shop," she heard him say.

She went there and waited, trembling, in the memory of his hand that had just brushed her own. She did not speculate, or question, or think at all. She was empty of fear, and of warning. When he came his bigness, his violence left her no room. The sweep of his will was like a flight of wings.

"Have you missed me?"

"Yes — oh, yes!"

"Did you want me back?"

"I don't know — I was afraid — I —"

"Did you — did you want me back?"

"Yes! How did you come in Burage?"

"Changed places with a chap for two days — when I knew they were coming here. I've passed your house a dozen times."

"Our house!"

"You beauty — think of your living in that little — look here! I've something to tell you."

She trembled. She looked about as if she would have slipped away. He took her hands.

"In two weeks I leave for the Coast."

Oh, the Coast!

"California — San Francisco — everywhere. You must come with us."

"No, no!"

"Yes!"

The old skill, the clever painting of their ways, the opening of a door beyond which she thought that she saw color. And withal, that indefinable possessing magic. He broke off in his plans for their meeting in Chicago.

"See here," he said, "I've got to be in the orchestra tonight. We leave before twelve. Promise me — promise me now."

"How can I — how can I promise now. . . ."

"You'll meet me after?"

"No, no. I can't do that."

"Barbara — you're coming with me?"

But he seemed at last to understand that Barbara would do that which she would not put into words — again her compunction, plus her inarticulateness. Then, too, there was her starved romanticism. And her emptiness. Understanding none of these things, Bayard yet understood how to treat all.

"Put a light for me tonight then," he whispered. "Near your front window. To say you'll go. You'll hear me answer — I'll whistle back some tune. And that's our promise. You'll go! Don't fail me, dearest. . . ."

All the evening Pitt worked at his sample books in the little shop. Barbara sat in the parlor, in the darkness. It would be the red glass lamp which she had filled that morning and set on its shelf in the kitchen. If she had known that to light that lamp tonight would open the door for her. . . .

Her mind was clear and occupied with matters of no importance, or with the tasks which she had in hand for the morrow — to wash her hair, to turn the mattresses, to pin a clean cover on the ironing-board. She had promised Mrs. Nick True ten cents for the missionary society and had forgotten to take it to her.

Pitt came in and said: "All in the dark? Why don't you have a light in here?"

"No, no, no!" she cried, as if it were time for Bayard to be waiting outside.

She went into the dining room, and Pitt followed. He yawned aloud, so that every room in the house heard.

"Marshall, good heavens," she said.

"You stop finding fault with me," he retorted irritably.

He rarely spoke like this, and she looked at him in surprise. His words made a channel down which her own obscure irritation found its way.

"I don't find fault with you when you act like other folks," she said.

He looked up at her quickly. This was his old wound that she had touched. She knew it, and was silent.

They sat in the dining room where a bracket lamp burned. Barbara closed the door into the parlor, so that no light should shine through the windows. Pitt read the paper. Barbara did nothing. Ten o'clock came. Half past ten. Pitt yawned aloud again, remembered, and looked at her swiftly. She appeared not to have heard. He took off his shoes, went to lock the side door, his stockinged feet striking hard on the floor.

"I wish you wouldn't do that! " she cried.

He made no comment. But presently he came out of the bedroom, leaned over the back of her chair, and said:

" Barbara."

She caught the faint odor which he bore, an odor of caramom seeds and dye and warmth. She sat silent.

"Would you be any happier," said Pitt, "if I was to go off again? And leave you here — with the boy? And only come back once in a while, to see both of you?"

Her heart beat. "Would you be any happier?" she said.

At her answer his face wore a look of death.

"I want to do what you want," he said. "I — I don't belong here, I guess. I — I want —" He stopped.

She laughed. "What would you leave me here for? It's the last place I want to be. It's the last place I've ever wanted to be."

"You could be the way you were," said Pitt. "And it wouldn't be my fault."

She leaned her head against her chair and closed her eyes. In a few minutes he turned away. He left ajar the door into the parlor.

"Shut the door! " she cried sharply. And "What in time do you want this door shut for?" he asked shortly, and closed it. She heard the tread of his stockinged feet as he moved about that room.

Veil upon veil fell about the essence of her, of her sense of Pitt, of relationship, home, homely routines. She saw them all encased in their matter, regarded matter alone, died to her spirit and to their spirit. She saw the physical fact of a new distance, and Bayard's voice she felt in her flesh. And now Pitt had proposed going. She must not let him go. It would be less selfish to go herself.

Eleven o'clock. She had decided nothing. Into her mind had come some fragment of her intention to have Pitt shorten the legs of the ironing board. She was in the kitchen lighting the red glass lamp. She was suffused with an obscure excitement, pleasant, terrible, and having a taint of the sickish, as she felt after long wakefulness. She set the lamp in the parlor window.

Pitt's voice came from the bedroom.

"Don't set it there. It shines in my face."

"I'll take it away in a minute or two," said Barbara.

She stood in such wise that her body should shield Pitt's face from the lamp's rays. For a long time she stood there. From the little hot bedroom came the sound of the creak of the springs. Then she heard a gay tune. whistled in the street. It was a cheap, popular tune of the time — "Two Little Maids in Blue."

11

In her preparation she was detached and without thought, as if her mind hung somewhere in solution.

All that last day, Pitt was at home. She did her packing almost before his eyes. She pressed her laces, ironed the baby's best white dress, blackened shoes, took stray stitches, all in Pitt's presence. He noticed nothing. Pitt never noticed anything.

The weight which lay upon her whenever, for a flash thought did come, was not the burden of her choice, but the burden of Pitt's loss of the baby. In her confusion, it had not once presented itself to her that she could do other than take the baby. She had never been anything but a physical mother, and the bond of the body held. She could measure Pitt's loneliness for the child, and about it there formed her inevitable compunction.

As the hours went by she became frantically anxious to have him spend them all with the child.

"Marshall," she said, "take him off somewhere, will you? Put him in his buggy."

But Pitt for some reason demurred. "I want to make a sort of inventory for Strain," he objected.

"Yes, but take the baby off for just a little while," she persisted. " You don't have to make that thing today, do you?"

He looked at her in surprise.

"Why, yes," he said. " I told you I was going to meet him in Chicago tomorrow."

She had not heard this. So he too would be in Chicago on that morrow of hers. . . . And would he look for her when he found that she had — she caught herself from the words "run away."

"Well," she said, " take the baby for half an hour."

"I'm going to finish this now," said Pitt. "Then I will."

She knew that he would remember this incident. She had only succeeded in adding to his bitterness.

Toward noon he finished his list, and took the baby while she was preparing dinner. He slipped on the seersucker coat which she hated, and went out by the back way, where the street was level. She came to the door and looked after them, a cooking fork in her hand.

"Daddy, daddy, daddy!" the baby was persisting foolishly, twisting in his seat. Pitt was not looking at him. He had an appraising eye on the broken four-board fence at the back of the lot.

"Hush, son," he said, absently.

And she knew that this would be one of the things that he would remember.

Abruptly Pitt turned and looked at the house. He saw her watching him and momentarily stopped, with a sense that she wanted something or something was wrong, since she was looking after him. She smiled and waved the fork. He waved back with his sudden high-eyebrowed grin. And this, she thought, he would remember.

She was cooking the dishes that he liked best. And when he came back, she went through the dinner quite serenely. "The big thing is afterward — not yet," she thought childishly.

Pitt was at home when she dressed and when she left the house. When she wrote her note to him, he was in the next room, hammering at a broken catch on a door.

— that I could never keep this up all my life, Marshall. . . . It's nobody's fault — not yours, not mine. It just is this way. . . . I waited till the money was earned — the house is yours. Strain's buying it makes it that much easier. . . .

Pitt was singing:
It won't be a stylish marriage,
We can't afford a carriage—
She wished that he would not sing the words — they bothered her as she wrote.

"Good as new," said Pitt "Ain't it, baby?"

Save for the gown that she wore and the baby's clothes, she was taking nothing that Pitt had bought. It gave her some trouble to slip her bag into the baby's carriage, when Pitt was out of the room.

"I'm not going to have him tell the baby good-by," she thought. She felt obscurely that this she could not bear,

"I'm going out for a while," she said, at last. "I'm going out," she corrected conscientiously. She tried to glance back at Pitt casually. He was examining the latches on the other doors.; but he came toward her, executed an insane and favorite noise of his to make the baby laugh, and stooped and kissed him.

"Good-by, Marshall," she said, before she knew that she was going to say it, and put up her face. That look of passionate and dog-like devotion flamed in his eyes with the quick surprise of what she had done. As usual, he was speechless. He watched them down the street. Barbara did not look back.

The Chicago train left at six o'clock. For an hour she walked about the Burage streets, making little purchases, chatting with a friend or two. Toward six she asked Mis' Nick True's little boy if he would take the baby carriage home for her and be sure to give that note to Mr. Pitt. She did not know that it was by chance, Nicky True who had gone to the farmhouse to announce to Pitt the birth of their child. Then she walked to the station with the baby in her arms, boarded the train without buying a ticket, and gave herself up to her new singing.

🍄

These were the days of the beginnings of cycling. All Burage cycled on high wheels, and on the installment plan. Buck Carbury did little but cycle — he wore goggles and a visor and knickerbockers and leggings and bent over the handlebars like a monstrous monkey.

He came coasting down a hill at Packard just as the afternoon train for Chicago drew in. He swung off on one foot at the crossing, and waited for the intruder to pass. He looked up at the car windows. He saw the still profile of Barbara, holding her sleeping baby in her arms. She did not see him.

"She and Pitt must be going to Chicago," he thought, and shot on toward home and supper.

Home and supper lay at the extreme end of the main street, in Burage. As he wheeled past Pitt's house, he saw Pitt mending an eaves-spout. And Buck dropped in to say "hello."

"Hello," he said.

"Well, well, well," returned Pitt pleasantly, and could think of nothing to add to this, according to his custom.

"Danged hot," said Buck. "I could have made ten miles farther only it was so danged hot."

"Dear me," Pitt said, discarded two or three other available remarks, and said nothing.

"I see the Missus has gone to town," observed Buck, to bridge the gap.

"Who?" Pitt asked, regarding the eaves-spout.

"Oh, no," said Pitt. "No."

"Why, I certainly saw her at Packard, on No. 5," Buck insisted, and for some reason, stopped short.

"Nonsense," Pitt said "Why, there's the baby carriage."

The lack of conclusiveness in this seemed to smite him.

"She went out an hour ago with the baby," said he. "Nicky True brought the carriage back for her —"

Then Pitt stopped. Until that moment it had not struck him as extraordinary that Barbara should have sent the carriage back. Now he moved toward it uncertainly. Buck followed him. There, on the cushions, they saw the letter which Nicky True had not found it necessary to mention.

"What's this?" said Pitt, without alarm, and broke the seal.

But, as for Buck Carbury, he stopped breathing. Something that Mayme had been saying since that first night of the tent show recurred to him.

Pitt raised his eyes.

"What is this, Buck?" he said. " She's playing off. Was Mayme with her . . ."

Buck stepped to his side. Together they read the letter through, and stood staring at each other.

"Glory," said Buck. "That was the last train out."

"She — she don't say anything about the Chicago train," Pitt found to say. He stood with the back of his hand on his mouth, the picture of the incomprehensible and the ineffectual.

"But I tell you, man. I saw her — at Packard — headed toward Chicago," shouted Buck.

"I'll take the first train in the morning," said Pitt dazedly. "She'll come back with me. Oh, I know she'll come back with me."

Buck took him by the shoulders.

"Pitt, old man — pipe this," he said. "You don't suppose for a minute she's gone alone, do you?"

"No, no," said Pitt. "She's got the baby. My God, the baby," Pitt said and began weakly to cry.

Buck led him to the side porch, and as they stood there tried to think how to intimate to him that in all probability — but then suppose this wasn't so!

If only he could remember what Mayme had said. Hot as it was, he shivered.

"Pitt," said Buck, "was there any man that Barbara — that might -"

"No, no, no," said Pitt, and gave this not even a passing thought.

Buck saw that he wanted to be alone, and moved away. Then he came back and poured out his intention.

"I'll go up with you in the morning," Buck said. "On the six-twenty — you'll take that, of course."

Pitt looked at him perplexedly.

"I was going in on that anyway," he said. " And now look at..." The little man's ineffectualness was tragic.

"I don't know that I ought to leave him," Buck thought. But he went. And what is more, he kept silence. Only, as he met his sister Mayme in the upper hallway of their home, he inquired of her what it was that she had said to him about Barbara Pitt, lately. Something — queer?

Mayme replied that his face was dirty, and as for Barbara, she had been seen walking with Max Bayard, that tent-show bandmaster. But that Buck was not to feel compelled to repeat this fact. To which her brother replied crossly and ungratefully that to his knowledge no one had repeated it excepting herself. And he kept thinking of Pitt as he had last seen him, with his face all awry and ugly.

At midnight Pitt had moved only from his empty porch to his empty kitchen, and there he sat, seeing nothing. Once he rose and looked out, and brought in the baby carriage.

"In case it should rain," he explained aloud.

The baby was sleeping.

Barbara had laid him on the bed in the room Bayard had engaged. When she had made her trembling inquiries at the desk, the clerk, recalling Bayard, had lifted inquiring eyes, noted the baby, and dismissed the whole matter.

Bayard had been unable to meet her when the train arrived at half past seven. He had always to be at the tent for the opening concert. Secretly he had thought it just as well that she should find her way to that tryst without him.

She made herself as pretty as she could, put her toilet articles back in her bag, and sat down by the window to wait, wearing her hat.

Still she was in that area in which there is no consecutive thinking.

She sat recalling Bayard as he had been in the grove; his size, his nearness, his good looks, his warm, close clasp of her hands — all the things which Pitt did not have. And she remembered, with a physical pang, that she had not left the missionary money for Mrs. True. This kept recurring to her — the missionary money for Mrs. True.

A telegram came for her. "Will be with you before nine, bless your little heart," and there was no signature. She had never dreamed of a telegram sent without necessity, or sent to one in the same town. She had never dreamed of endearments and intimacies in a telegram. She kissed the yellow paper.

The messenger had wakened the baby who laughed and lifted his arms to be taken. She had brought his bottle, filled and ready. She sat with him in her arms, feeding him, and reading over and over the telegram. He fell asleep again, and she laid him on the bed but she did not undress him. "I'd better wait," she thought. She turned off the light and stood by the window.

She was standing there when Bayard came. He swung open the door without rapping, and stared into the darkness. She saw him outlined against the brightness of the passage and ran to him.

"Sweetheart!" he cried. "How you scared me. There isn't any light — I thought —"

He covered her face with kisses. They moved to the window and stood quiet, in each other's arms. There flashed through Barbara's mind the picture of that other little room in the hotel of her choosing, where, a year an a half ago, she had found herself shut in with Pitt. She trembled at the difference. She remembered her tears. Without the power to shape her understanding, she thought of the wrong that had been done then. She was conscious of some old quest satisfied now. But the little thing had no conception of any of this. She merely wished this moment would last forever.

It did not last forever. Bayard wanted to look at her.

He fumbled for the gas, stood staring at her with delight. She was even prettier than he thought, he cried out. He drew out her hat-pins, laid her hat on the bed, and saw the baby.

"Good God," said Bayard. "What's that?"

Barbara answered: "He isn't the least trouble — I knew you wouldn't mind him."

"Married?" said Bayard. "You're married?"

Barbara stared at him. "Didn't you know that?" she said. "Why, everybody knows it."

Bayard searched her face. It was as open as a flower.

"My fair child," he said "I didn't know everybody. I only knew you."

He walked to the window and stood silent.

"Maybe I ought to have left the baby —" she faltered, miserably. "But I couldn't. . . ."

"Leave him!" he threw back, surprisingly. "I should think not."

"And then I thought, if he was yours, how I'd love him — If there'd been more time — oh, did I do it wrong?" she cried. "You said you liked that little kid with the show —"

"Why, it isn't the baby so much," said Bayard. "It's the man. What am I going to do with *him*."

This man's processes were simple: A lark with a village girl was one thing. A mix-up with a husband was another. For this he had no mind, and he did not see the necessity. This necessity, however, he reflected, was now thrust upon him. Whatever they might say or do, the die had been cast.

He swung round and leaned on the sill, looking at Barbara. She was very lovely, very desirable. What he had intended for the future he could not have told. He had been drifting, according to his custom. And this now was no fault of his. In fine, he might as well hang for a sheep as for a lamb.

He held out his arms.

"You scared me, that's all," he said. "You never done anything but surprise me — but this is the worst. You see, I thought you were mine — and you aren't."

She went to him. "Yes, I am. Yes, I am!"

He now said to himself that nothing should come in his way. As for the future — well, that was usually ahead of one.

"I'll send down for my grip," he said presently. "It's checked. I forgot it, I was so crazy to get up here."

She asked, "Don't you want to look at the baby?"

He looked, laughed, turned away.

"This," he said, "is the funniest I ever saw. Look here, were you goin' to leave your husband, anyway?"

"I — I wanted to get away," she answered. "I've never been happy. He was good. Only —"

"Only you didn't love him," Bayard supplied.

She nodded.

He threw out his arms. "Well, let's forget it," he said.

"I better undress the baby," said Barbara.

Bayard smoked and watched her, as she made ready the baby's things. This act and her tenderness, her motherhood, there, moved him vaguely, but he thought that what moved him was the humor of the time; and now and then he laughed.

"Honest to Mike," he kept saying, "ain't this domestic?"

He watched her gentle, expert hands, heard the baby's sleepy gruntings as she lifted him. It was a queer world, he reflected, but, say, this was the queerest —

Barbara was searching for something in her bag. He saw her take out her toilet articles, each wrapped in a bit of newspaper, save a broken wire brush. A little piece of soap dropped from its newspaper wrapping — the soap, in fact, that had been in the kitchen sink at Burage. The ladies with whom Bayard was familiar spent money for toilet luxuries whether they had money or not. Even to him, in these things which Barbara had brought her whole life lay clear.

He rose, and went back to the window. When he turned, after a time, she was unbuttoning the baby's frock, supporting with her hand the little nodding head.

"Wait a minute," said Bayard.

He threw away his cigar and folded his arms.

"Barbara," he said, "my life's been pretty rotten. I've been wanting for quite some time to clean my soul. I don't know whether you'll see it — but I guess this is the time."

Swift maturity is one of the possibilities of its universe to which the human animal is unused. Ripening is expected to be gradual. When some forcing process is operative, he falls to the inarticulateness to which he is subject in all extremes — grief, fear, love.

In this stupor, Barbara sat through the night. She had wept, sat quiet, wept again. But all the time her understanding was hardly functioning. She was beaten upon by that of which she had no knowledge. She was like primitive man, shocked by electricity. She had nothing to which to gauge her experience. It was notable that the whole effect was as much physical as spiritual. Because her body was accustomed to function more responsively than her mind, her reaction was an aching, a smarting, a physical nausea, dizziness.

She went over what Bayard had said. Bayard was not delicate. He had no gift of words. What he had to say he brought out naked as well as newborn. But this was precisely the treatment suited to this woman's comprehension. Pitt's gentle way of stating his qualms would merely have irritated her. Bayard's sledge hammers shocked her into a response as exact and as terrific as if these had been his passion.

"By the Lord Harry, I'm going to do the decent thing. Go home to your husband — you and the kid. I'll get one star in my crown if I never get another."

This was the sum of his attitude. The words were no infection from others. They were no glib repetition. Here was a positive spring of action, a little tongue of vital fire.

"What about me?" were Barbara's first gasping words.

Bayard stared. "You!" he said. "Why, you'll be a long sight better off. You and the kid."

She burst into tears, laid the baby down, then clung to him, weeping and trying to talk. Her nearness, and that same ripe, thick bloom of her might, after all, have been his undoing, but the balance was struck by her habit of weeping with uncovered face. Those delicate distortions infinitely repelled him.

"What's the use?" he protested. "I'm going to be square with myself, I tell you. I been doing dirt enough. I'm going to get right."

"Why don't you think of me a little!" Barbara cried.

"Think!" he cried. "What's thinking? You do something or you don't. Well, I don't — see? Why didn't you let me see you walking down towards the tent wheeling a kid?"

"You said you loved me. . . ."

"I do — I do love you like anything," he declared, and fondled her arm, breathed deeply, frowned, shook himself free. "Damn it all," he said, "I'm trying to be decent, Barbara, leave me alone."

More of this, her tears and passion, his kiss on her mouth, and she was alone.

Then the night to get through; blank hours of misery, frantic clasping of the unconscious child, despair. At last fragments, unrelated glimpses of persons and events: Mayme Carbury, the Burage main street, the broken board fence, the little porch, Pitt.

What was Pitt doing? By now, he knew. Had he told Miss Arrowsmith? *Oh, Miss Arrowsmith. . . .* What had he said when he read the note? And now — oh, no, oh, no! She could never go back. She hoped that he had taken in the baby carriage at night. There kept recurring to her that hope, that he had remembered to take in the baby carriage.

Last, the sweeping sense of baseness, of self-recrimination. Pitt had given everything, he had never spared himself, had worked, earned, saved, paid off her father's debts. Her old strong sense of money obligation and its fulfillment accused her. But the money from the sale of the house would repay him. And what of that? For the first time her sense of money value was transcended. What would the house be to Pitt, or the money for the house?

At dawn the idea was there, waiting for her. It was as if it had been somewhere near, expecting her, in some progress of hers, to come upon it.

She came upon it, found it full formed. The baby must go back to Marshall.

She was incapable of reasoning. As Bayard had said: "What's thinking? You either do a thing or you don't." She seized on this plan, passionately. It was as if she had thought of something for immediate expiation. Old, savage instincts of sacrifice stirred her flesh. Superstition, laceration, every madness . . . But safe within all, motive. A little tongue from vital fires.

Such a reparation was tempered. Barbara loved the child, but she had never been aware of spiritual filaments or able to sustain them. And then she was unimaginative, and such a course presented itself as involving no finality of separation from the baby. The suggestion once given, her cloudy mental processes were wholly usurped. She held only to the fact that Marshall would be in the city on the next day and that she herself might take the baby home. There followed the physical relief of planning.

It was early when she came down stairs and, in the lobby, asked her direction of a young girl. This girl, ruddy, laughing and carrying a gold-mesh bag, was entering the cafe with her parents, substantial and preoccupied. The girl directed Barbara kindly, and with a pretty air of importance at knowing her way. To Barbara, seeing her so safe, with her braided gray gown and her gold-mesh bag, she represented another period, another order of being, like Helen or Titania.

Into the Chicago train-shed Pitt came with an air of death. He had not slept or eaten or shaved. He had on the seersucker coat and his hat was too large. He looked as men look about whom young, giggling girls cruelly remark: "Somebody loves him."

Buck Carbury silently walked beside him.

"Where do they inquire for — for folks that go off like that? " Pitt asked.

Buck groaned. "Oh, Lord. Oh, Lord." He kept on with his meditations. He could not tell Pitt what he suspected. He must tell Pitt what he suspected. Buck suffered, trod upon the feet of those who glared at him in consequence and were not even observed. Finally, in the station, Buck managed to intimate what he feared. Pitt merely shook his head, and absently. Oh, no. Buck was mistaken. Why, he, Pitt, had never heard Barbara even mention a Mr. Bayard.

13

As she alighted from her train, Barbara stared about the Burage platform. For an instant she thought that it was not Burage.

The trainmaster, passing, pointed to his hat with his thumb. Barbara nodded, crimsoned, her eyes shifting. Did he know?

"Why, say," the man cried in concern, " you just missed your husband. He went in on Number 8."

"I know," she said, and in her double relief, she smiled at him radiantly. "It's too bad," she added lamely, and signaled the hotel "rig." Flo Buckstaff himself was driving. She was alone in the vehicle, and he flung one leg over the arm of the seat and discoursed to her.

"Gosh," he said, " if it hadn't been for your dime this mornin', I might as well have been dead as drivin'. That's all the public cares about you. Do you s'pose they'll ride so's to patronize you? Not them lubbers. They'll hoof it and leave you starve to death."

So *he* did not know either!

He drove through the main street, and every blind seemed to Barbara to shield accusing eyes. Mis' Miles was painting her fence a sharp green. Barbara looked straight ahead, but Mis' Miles's voice called to her gayly, and Flo pulled up.

"Land, Barbara, been gaddin'? Look at us. Ain't we scrumptious?"

She came outside and Barbara knew at once that she, too, knew nothing. Mis' Miles made dabs at the baby, and would have exchanged a few words with Barbara save that Flo, his leg still over the side of the seat, plunged into talk about the proper paint for fences. Mis' Miles winked at Barbara and retired. And as they drove on, Barbara's eyes blurred: Mis' Miles had winked at her, and everything was just as if —

One or two waved at her, their hands bending at the wrists, as in the Eighties, and not lifted stiffly and held motionless, as later. The grocery man ran out to ask her if she would take her watermelon home — why, didn't she remember she had ordered one when he got some good ones? Well, some corkers had just come in. The corker was brought out and put on the seat beside her. Mis' Nick True, whom Barbara supposed with a bound of the heart, must surely know, since it was Nicky True who carried the note, came running our and asked for the missionary dime. Barbara gave it, and in her dumbness looked out so strangely that Mis' True asked her anxiously if her head ached.

At Barbara's door Flo carried in her bag, and lifted one shoulder high as he turned away.

"This here ride is my treat today," he said. "I might want to borrow fif' cents of you some day, and now you dassant refuse me."

On the nail, beneath the vines, hung the key.

The strangeness which had overhung the Burage station persisted in the house. Everything was in order, but it appeared to be another place. The baby, however, recognized upon the floor his red flannel dog with shoe-button eyes, and with cries fell upon it.

Barbara went through the rooms to the kitchen. The table was not set. There were no remains of food. "He didn't eat," she thought, with a pang. There was the baby carriage — he had brought it in. Mechanically she went to the ice chest and pulled out the pan of waste water; the pan was brimming full. Pitt always forgot that. She knelt and dipped out with a cup a part of the water. It was a good thing that she had come home, she was thinking.

Half past eleven o'clock. Pitt could not get home until six. Before she left yesterday she had set the house in superficial order. Now she plunged into work. And first she put on her blue calico work-dress and old shoes. She stared at herself in mirror. "I look just the same," she thought.

She swept the rooms. shook the rugs, rearranged, dusted. The baby lay in his carriage on the side porch and slept. Occasionally she stepped out to look at him, and to adjust his mosquito netting. The milkman came, and she asked for cream. "I'll bake up a big batch of cream cookies," she thought. "He likes them."

While she was scrubbing the kitchen floor, there was a knock at the front door. A youth presented himself carrying a sample case. It was a youth having what he denominated a "line of can' goods." He spoke with anxious rapidity.

"No, no, no!" cried Barbara in a terrible voice.

The youth stopped, abashed.

"No, no!" she cried again, shaking her head. She was frowning and her eyes were strange. The youth, terrified, retreated down the walk. She heard his feet on the long steps. She laid her head on the table by the red glass lamp. The smell of kerosene assailed her from the felt mat. "I mustn't forget to fill the lamps," she thought, and went back to the kitchen.

Still in her blue work-dress, she took the baby and ran over to Mis' Hellie Copper's. She was making apple butter on a wood stove, and the temperature of her kitchen was of frightful heat.

"Hello, Barbara," she cried. "Taste this, will you? I've tasted till my tongue couldn't tell pickles. Best set on the stoop. It's fire in here. I donno's I'm ever going to get through."

Barbara sat down. Mis' Copper, then, did not know either. Had Pitt told no one?

It chanced that Mis' Copper was filled with pleasant gossip. There was a row over the new cork for the church floor, and she had all the particulars. Ingrain or cork carpeting was tearing them asunder. "Mis' Henry Bates was set firm on having Ingrain. 'Ingrain nothin',' says Mis' Miles, 'unless you want moths to breathe.' 'Well,' says Mis' Bates, 'I'm very good friends with my Heavenly Father, but I cannot worship Him on cork.' 'Since when,' Mis' Miles says. 'Mis' Bates, does the Bible stick out for three-ply Ingrain?' So they had it, back and forth. Ain't it queer how the simple gospel gets all mussed up with cork carpeting?"

Mis' Copper came outside and sat down on the porch.

"And land, the air in that church." she added. "It's September, but I bet we could still hear the Christmas carols, if we listened."

She leaned forward, her broad face shining with perspiration and broadened still more by smiles.

"Well, sir." she said, "and what do you think? You know the rummage sale last week? Well, I give 'em one of Hellie's vests — it was pretty good yet, but I had to give 'em something. And Hellie went in and saw it, and bought it for a quarter. And I don't dare tell him. Ain't that what it is to have husbands?"

She went on recounting this and that about the folk whom they knew.

Barbara thought: "Now I'm here and everything is the way it was. She doesn't know. I could almost think it was yesterday. . . . Supposing it was yesterday?"

"And Matsey Fider is going to have a baby," said Mis' Hellie. "Why don't you go to work and have another one, Barbara? A little girl'd be nice, just that much younger —"

"I must go now," said Barbara.

Mis' Hellie laughed pleasantly.

"Oh no harm," she said comfortably. "That was easy to think of. I could of thought of that with my elbows."

Barbara wanted to kiss her. "It won't do," she reflected. "She'd wonder."

"Well, good-by," Mis' Copper returned. "Drop in again when the work's light."

"If I could just die now," Barbara thought, on her way home. "Why don't God let folks say when?"

She changed her dress and hung her blue work-dress in her closet. "Who'll take that dress down?" she thought. As she came from the bedroom, the exquisite familiarity of the old things just momentarily assailed her, rather than the aspect of their strangeness. "Oh, oh, oh," she whispered, and smote the door post. "Even the clock," she thought, and stared at it. These things could not keep her.

"Yesterday at this time," she kept saying over. "Only just yesterday. And now I can never get back. I want it to be yesterday!" she said aloud.

She turned to the worthless articles in her top drawer, and every one wounded her. A card was caught in the crack. She drew it out. It was the hotel menu of the dinner in the city on their wedding day: Ham and eggs, lemon pie, celery-on-the-branch. . . .

Three o'clock. She took the baby to put him in his buggy. He smiled at her, and breathed with little gruntings as she lifted him. Her arm fell across her shoulder in the old way, she felt his strong little body straighten and move, and his leg pounded her side. And now she remembered how she had felt his strong stirrings there in her side before he was born.

"God, make it all stop being true!" she said, and held the little baby, and shook with sobs that came hurrying and broken like a little child's unreasoning grief.

The thought that after all to stay might be possible came to her only once, and it was at that moment. She put the thought away. "I couldn't tell Marshall," she thought, "and I couldn't not tell him."

She went out with the baby and locked the door.

She had meant to ask Mis' Hellie Copper if she might leave the baby in his carriage on the porch by her open kitchen door. Sooner or later, then,

Mis' Copper would come bring child home, and Pitt would be there. But as Barbara emerged from the side gate and came down the hill, she saw Miss Arrowsmith alone on her veranda. Barbara crossed and went there. On a margin no wider than this, the future strove to form itself.

"Well, Barbara!" said Miss Arrowsmith. "Come and have some tea. And let me hold the baby!"

She took the baby in her arms. In her delicacy and fineness she was to Barbara as some quickening spirit to but half quickened clay. Rachel was of the daughters of God and Barbara was of the sons of men. And yet the baby was rather of Rachel's spirit than of Barbara's clay. Rachel and the baby were, in a way, naked spirit, never yet entirely enclosed. Barbara's temple was closed, and it was the temple which one regarded.

"Whatever you do, Barbara," abruptly said Miss Arrowsmith as she poured tea, "don't lie to that baby. Even in fun. Even absent-mindedly. Or to keep him still — or to make him laugh. I have no patience with the mothers who lie to their children — between prayers for their children's souls. I wish I had a baby."

"You do?" said Barbara.

It was true that she had said this repeatedly, but it had seemed one of those things which people say and forget.

"I want a baby," Miss Arrowsmith continued, "but everyone would make such a fuss. Maybe I can put up with a husband yet. I'll see. You couldn't spare me this baby?"

"I came over to ask if I might leave him here — for a while," said Barbara.

"Oh — but a while? Out of a lifetime?"

Barbara said no more. When she took her tea, she realized that she had eaten nothing that day. She drank thirstily, staring at Miss Arrowsmith. What if she meant what she had said? What would Marshall say when she proposed it?

When she rose, she shook hands with Miss Arrowsmith, and said good-by, and was not recalled to that which she had done until she saw the lady's eyes question. Barbara crimsoned and looked at the baby. She did not touch him. She said nothing. As she went down the walk she saw nothing. At the gate she looked back. Miss Arrowsmith's fine head was bent above the child on her knee.

It is necessary to understand these things before one is equipped to live justly. Everything is different from that which one supposes. In the beginning, nobody visualizes himself as a criminal, a wife-beater, a creature of unfaith. This means no less than that the race dreams of itself as going upright. These children whom we summon arrive and see themselves in futures of honor, respect, happiness. But the little chameleons become like us. That is their only crime.

Bayard had dreamed of himself as a great bandmaster and composer. There was no one to teach him music. He played by ear in music halls. At thirty, there was Bayard, never once visualizing himself as a seducer of women. Merely as a man who had not had his chance and who longed pathetically to strike the balance, somehow to find something to take the place of that which was lost to him.

Barbara had dreamed of love and beauty, and she had missed both. She sought them. This is the epitaph for every woman who fails.

Where is the medium which will preserve the racial hope of decent, distinctive living? Some day, we shall move there — "or else we are mocked." But in the meantime, one ceases to judge, ceases to classify, ceases to feign an understanding. Nobody understands who does not understand that sin is nothing and righteousness is all.

14

At four o'clock, Pitt came to Burage alone. He came against the advice of his friend, who remained in town.

That they had left at the central police office descriptions of Barbara and the baby and had visited dozens of hotels, were as nothing to Buck.

"I'm going to do more," he said, and stayed. He had no plan, but he was bent on retrieving.

As for Pitt, when he had done all that he could think to do, he wanted to stand on street corners and watch the passers.

"She might come past," he said. "Such lots of 'em do."

He did this for two hours. Buck would go away and leave him and return to find him still loitering up and down State Street, searching among the faces. Then Pitt would catch at Buck, and speak to him softly, lest the State Street crowd should hear and know.

"I know why she went, Buck," he would say. "She feels so bad about me paying the mortgage. She wants I should have all the money for the house. I know what's why she went. And I've got to find her."

Of his appointment with Strain, Pitt did not once think. Toward three o'clock, he announced his intention of going back to Burage. "If she comes, I've got to be there. I left the key — but she might not understand. Yes. Yes. I've got to go back."

At Burage, he swung from the train and ran through the streets. On the nail under the vines at his door hung the key.

The exquisite order of the rooms escaped him. To him, everything looked as he had left it. He went in every room, returned to the front porch, sat down and held his head in his hands. So this was what he had done. All this was his own doing.

He reviewed their life together, and blamed himself for everything. Why had he not insisted on selling the house, paying the mortgage, and taking her to the city? Then she could have had some of the things that she wanted — people, little trips to the parks, the zoo, the store windows. Why had he been so mad? She would have been with him now. Just yesterday — if only he could have thought of this yesterday. It seemed such a little thing, to have thought of this yesterday, instead of today; and he had not done it.

He slipped down in his chair and stared across the street. There was Miss Arrowsmith, moving about, knowing nothing of it. If only he could keep it from every one until Barbara came back. Miss Arrowsmith, how it would grieve her! There she was, looking just as she had looked on the day of their wedding. He continued to watch her, fascinated, as if by being there just the same, she could bring back that day.

Miss Arrowsmith rose and came down the veranda steps. Someone was with her — a child. Tenderly she was guiding its steps. She lifted it to its carriage on the walk, and the child laughed out.

At the sound of that laugh, Pitt sprang to his feet, and stood gaping at those figures. Miss Arrowsmith moved between him and the child, but he could see the hood of the carriage. He ran through the house to his kitchen. No! The carriage was not there. Fool, not to have noticed that. The carriage was there!

He was across the street, running crazily. As he entered the gate, his child saw him and laughed again, and stretched out his arms. He ran to it. He laid his hands fiercely upon the child, leaned across the carriage to Miss Arrowsmith, and gasped out his question:

"Barbara? Where is she?"

"She left here an hour ago," said Miss Arrowsmith.

"An hour ago? Today? You mean today?"

"Certainly, today."

"But my God where did she go?"

"Down that way. I don't know where. She asked to leave the baby here."

"But where did she come from? Which way did she come?"

"Why, from home. She'd been there at home all day."

"All day!" Pitt shouted the words, whirled and looked at his house, then reeled and trembled.

"She must be dead," he thought. "They let her come back to fetch the baby."

"My friend," said Miss Arrowsmith, " what is the matter?"

He told it. The naked briefness of his words was terrible. Meanwhile, the baby rubbed at his hand with the red flannel dog with shoe-button eyes.

"She may be to somebody's house," he said piteously. "Oh, mebbe she's to Mis' Copper's. I'll see." He ran a few steps and turned. "If she comes back while I'm gone, you'll keep her?"

He ran. Miss Arrowsmith stood quiet for a moment, remembered that Barbara had said good-by, had crimsoned. After a moment, Miss Arrowsmith took the baby, and went to the telephone. The baby leaned and tried to bite the cool nickel of the instrument, and pulled at the cord. No'm, the agent at the station had sold no ticket to Mis' Pitt, but he had seen her take the five o'clock train.

Pitt ran from house to house. To Mis' Hellie Copper's, and Barbara had been there for half an hour about noon. To Mis' Miles, and she had talked with her that morning on the street. To Mis' Nick True, and Barbara had given her a dime, missionary money. He raced back to Miss Arrowsmith's, his face pitiful with his hope. She told him her news. He dropped to the step like something broken.

She let him talk, listened to his self-reproaches. Barbara wanted folks, and little trips to the park, and the zoo, and the store windows. She'd ought to have had them. What a fool he had been. It was too late. Where did people go, when they went away like that? Where did Miss Arrowsmith think that he could look for her? And, oh, my God, if only he had stayed to home that day!

At last, when the baby cried, Miss Arrowsmith went across to his house with him. She wisely did not offer to help him with the child. All this would be something for him to do. She peeped in the refrigerator and the pantry and understood what Barbara had been doing that day. She left him mixing the baby's milk and talking.

Alone, he fed the child, and undressed him. He took the little night things from their accustomed place in the closet. There he saw Barbara's work dress, he gathered it in his arms, buried his face in it, caught the odor of it, and so holding it sand on the edge of the bed and fell to sobbing.

"Barbara! " he called, as if she were somewhere that his lifted voice might reach.

The baby came creeping toward him, his eyes fixed on his father's shoes, but was diverted by the fringe of the rug and lay pulling at it.

Barbara: We'll sell and move to the city where you can have it like you said. We both want you back. P.

In the "Personal" column of the Chicago papers this notice appeared, week after week.

"If I take it out," said Pitt, "that might be just the day she'd buy a paper."

Six weeks and no response. On the day when he ordered the notices discontinued at last, Pitt was like a man a part of whom is dying.

"Look at the theaters and little trips that money would have bought her," he said to everyone, over and over again.

He talked with everyone in the village. With Clem Austin, who ran the gasoline wood cutter. "Why, Clem," he said, "I never thought of it. I never once thought of it. I give you my word, I didn't." With Peter Meyer, his milkman, "You saw how she was — singing around the kitchen here. That was only a week ago. And now look." With the men in the shops: "Going and coming just like these other women, she was. Don't it seem like she must come in the door there?" It was the surprise of it which he kept on emphasizing, piteously. "I give you my word I never thought of such a thing." And when they sympathized with him and said that it was sad, this business, Pitt would say, "Sure. Sure. I should say."

They were very good to him. Here was grief naked and stunned, and about this they understood. There were not many words. These were not the way of Burage. Food was set inside the screen; or the key was taken from its nail in the and the offerings left naively in the refrigerator. Once a week in his absence, Mis' Hellie Copper slipped in with broom and duster, and ordered the lonely chaos. This Pitt probably never noticed at all, or ever knew. They tried to invite him to their homes, but he would talk about nothing but Barbara, and his wistful asking for advice in tracing her was more than they could hear. "You ain't had any word? I thought maybe —" he would say, when he met Barbara's friends.

One day, wearing his working clothes, he walked into Mis' Hellie Copper's house.

"You know," he said, "that piece Barbara used to hum so much?"

Mis' Hellie did not know. Pitt tried to make her remember. "That one that sort of went up, right from the very beginning?" She could not recall it. Nor could he. "But," he said, "if I could only get a-hold of it, it'd kind of bring her back for me to hum it."

About this tune he asked every one. No one knew what it could be. At last he rushed to Mayme Carbury, with an air of a man on tip-toe lest something he frightened away. "I got it!" he cried. "You play it off." He sang it to her, with gesticulation, with eager eyes, with utterly unbridled tones. Again and again he did this, and it sounded like nothing at all. No one could play it. He went sorrowfully away.

One day someone stepped to his kitchen door, and Pitt had a crust of bread laid on the grate of the open oven. When he found himself detected:

"Smells like baking day," he said, with a foolish laugh.

Gradually the people began to smile at him. It was sad and all that, but he ought to be more of a man. So, to his grief was added the bitterness of a glance, a shrug, a word aside. His sorrow had its own dignity. But his talk, his ceaseless repetitions, his shy foolish laughter wore upon his friends. And to his dog-like eyes, forever straying and seeking, they grew cruelly accustomed.

The one ray of life in this his death was the child. This child was exquisite. He was now a year old, the mind miraculously lighting. He was sturdy, but delicately fashioned. Although he looked normal, solid, rosy, he had all the air of spirit which may shine through a child. And already there came darting through the flesh those arrows of another being dwelling within, speaking in flashes. You touched the child, and you touched a creature unknown to you, but known to a thousand influences transcending you.

The little man Pitt adored. In Barbara's presence the child had been absorbed by her, devoured by her. Pitt had then approached on sufferance. He knew nothing, so to say, of the technique of his baby. He adored from afar, and without comprehension. He never had said: "What are we goin' to do with the baby?" He had said: "What are you going to do with the baby?" Veils had been between the two. In those ecstatic intervals during which he had been left alone in the room holding the baby, he had felt suddenly naked. On these occasions, when Barbara returned to the room, she had always found him trying to talk to the child, but acting shamefaced.

And now suddenly the two rushed together. Pitt turned to his child with a passion which was the cry of his own flesh to his own flesh. He clung hungrily to this thing that he could call his. All in him that had been Barbara's went seeking after Barbara and found instead the child. It was the passion of family, of possession. This primitive passion became the driving force of his days. He lived only in the child and the hope that his wife would come back to them. For Pitt in his essential life, the governments, dreams, ideals, sciences of the world did not exist. In his essential life existed only the powerful, primal race hunger for wife and offspring. This was the flower which Pitt had put forth from his being. It had bloomed upon a twin stalk. When one shoot perished, the other became his sole hold upon the eternal.

At first his work was utterly disregarded and he went nowhere.

"She might come back and go away again, like she done," he would say.

Later he would take the baby in his cart and tramp free of the streets and along country roads. On these days, he never met a farm wagon or passed a woman working in her door yard without his piercing scrutiny.

At last, when a job or two clamored to be finished, everybody asked to take the baby. Not offered. Asked. Mis' Nick True, Miss Matt Barber, Mis' Miles, — they all asked. And Mis' Copper swept up time royally with: "Mr. Pitt, any time you go away and can cheat anybody else out of keepin' the baby a spell, just you bring him over to me."

But Miss Arrowsmith simply crossed the street and took possession of the baby. She said to herself that this poor little man must be helped out. In her heart she understood that what she desired was the physical presence of the child, looking in her face. Sitting with the child on her knee, sometimes her senses swam with the wonder of this little being who breathed, turned its eyes, knew simple words, could occasionally speak. On these occasions, she would look about on her sewing basket, her mirror, her flowers, as if these commonplace objects too were motived by unsuspected spirit, like this feeble thing.

"Mr. Pitt," she said one day, "if ever you can think of it and will let me have this baby — you know what I want."

Pitt smiled, gratefully, negatively.

"I couldn't, though," he said, his eyes seeking down the street as if someone might at any moment appear. "He's all I've got."

If may have been that to herself she said: "My dear man, you haven't got him. This is the great parental delusion." But to Pitt, she merely smiled and understood. He had a torn heart and the business of the baby was to provide balm. The baby did it. Lately, on his father's approach, he had learned to throw up both hands and shout: "Mine! Mine! Mine!" In this gesture Pitt sank as within cherishing arms.

At last, Strain, in Chicago, tired of writing and receiving no answer, came down to Burage to see Pitt about the sale of his house. With him came his wife and their little boy.

"Hello," said Strain, appearing on the porch one morning. "Great Josie, what's the matter with you? I thought you was dead."

Pitt laughed. "Did you?" was his way of meeting this.

"What's the matter with you? " Strain continued. "Do you want to sell the house, or don't you? This is my wife. I've brought her to see the place."

"Come in," said Pitt, and looked at Mrs. Strain with attention. His wife! Yes, there were people who went about in this way, still.

In the kitchen was the baby. Mrs. Strain fell upon him. She was a woman of positiveness, and a magnificence exceeding her due. She wore a great plume, walked from the shoulders, and her eyes went everywhere.

"The darling! He's not like you, Mr. Pitt. Is he like his mother?"

Pitt said: "His mother's gone away."

Something in his manner told everything. This was no announcement of a visit. It was the news of a kind of death. Pitt could say no more. The sight of this man and his wife choked him.

Mrs. Strain was subdued. "Who takes care of the little angel?"

No one? What, he himself? Mrs. Strain was scandalized. She poured out to Pitt a volume of undigested facts of which he had never dreamed. His child, it seemed, had been walking the ledge of death, was well purely by accident, was in no fit hands.

"I'll tell you," was her inspiration, " if we buy the place, you can board with us and I'll look out for the baby — to earn my pin money."

Pitt felt a sick distaste. Live there, with this woman and Strain in Barbara's place and his, and this woman's hands on the baby?

He could have shouted " No!" and rushed from the room. He felt savage, violent. But he merely rubbed his wrists and said he'd have to think this over. He ended by promising to let Strain know in twenty-four hours whether he could buy the place. Strain's wife's voice gradually receded. Pitt looked after her and hated her. This was because he feared that she was right.

You might have seen Pitt that evening with his baby cart, questioning Mis' Hellie Copper, while she watered her sweet peas.

No, since he asked her, it wasn't any way to bring up a child. It was only the mercy of Providence that everything had been the way everything had been, so far. Yes, the others thought so, too. They had talked about it. Yes, when cold weather came, they *were* going to speak to him about it. Well, she didn't know what to do. That was the trouble. But no baby could get hisself into boy with nothing but a father for parent. It wasn't nature.

Pitt listened. He was even thinner now and his seersucker coat fell in deep folds. His straw hat was down to his ears. He bore no visible relation to the radiant child. Another flesh, another spirit, another level of the race, spoke from the little cart, cried aloud against poor Pitt's ever dreaming that these were his own, save by the faint bond of the body.

Mis' Hellie Copper looked at the two, and set down her watering can and went close to Pitt.

"There's some way out," she said. "I don't know what it is. But when you can quit pitying yourself long enough to think about your boy, that way'll bob up before you."

At that moment, the sword entered. At that moment, by a pang of spirit and flesh in separation, Pitt knew that she was right.

The lagging intellect tried to argue it, went through the dreary formalities of reason and common sense. Beneath all, like a burning soul illuminating a countenance, flamed Pitt's certainty.

That night he undressed the child and sat with him on his knee. There was some affair of a button in a bottle which was absorbing the child, who regarded these things with intentness, lifted his eyes and syllabled some indistinguishable question, came near to his father's face, in a great earnestness, and at last broke into an irrelevant and angelic smile. Like most fathers, Pitt could not caress his child. He played with him and rolled with him, tossed him, tickled him, all in the fury of his great affection. For these offices he always chose the half hour before bedtime, and marveled that the child could not afterward go to sleep. That night he held him in his arms until sleep came.

Asleep, his child seemed nearer to Pitt. In the littered sitting room, beside he open window, he sat quiet with no lamp. What if this was the end? What if he was to sell the place to Strain for a price which would pay off the mortgage and leave Three Hundred Dollars? This he could deposit in the bank to Barbara's account. The furniture he could store for her. For the little wallpaper stock which he himself had bought, Strain would give him a few dollars. With these he could go away. Where? This was a matter of entire indifference. But the child, the child. . . .

He thought of that day on which he had gone to the Lawyer Granger house, after leaving once passed it. Suppose he had not entered. But he had entered, and now here lay this exquisite life. Some dim sense of his own iso-lation from the event came upon him. Had he been a tool in some colossal hand? Having brought to being this inexplicable tender thing, were the two destined to leave him now? Was Barbara's going also destiny? All this he did not know how to think. These ideas flitted through his mind like ghosts. They were ghosts.

But the physical presence of the child besieged him. This little angel was sweet and warm, was tender, was filled with a thousand graces; he alone of all humanity was near to Pitt, was uncritical, was fervently glad to see him, loved him. How was it possible to live without him? To cut away the years of his growth, to take that future — precarious, niggardly, accidental, with-out wife, without home.

But she would not come back. Naked, implacable, there was in Pitt the gaunt head of the certainty which, for all his poor attempts, had never left him. She would not come back. From the first, that which dwelt within had told him that.

With the child so near to him, he had no armor. Pitt laid the child on the bed, then wandered through the dark house. He wanted something. He struck a light in the kitchen, irresolutely opened the cupboard door. There were the remains of a cold roast which Mis' Hellie had baked for him. He carried it to the refrigerator, and nibbled at it as he went. Then he took a slice and stood in the kitchen door, eating; man the small beast feeding on the flesh of a big beast. The old wooden rocker was on the porch. He sat there in the shadow, light from the bracket lamp in the kitchen falling in a rectangle upon the blackness of the yard.

He ceased to think. He sat quiet, not even conscious of the soft chorus of the night. Everything in him seemed to be silenced. He sat staring out at that rectangle of light, or down at the braided rug and the old broom. The sharp hurt of that which he must do was stilled, the sound of his old loss was closed. He was suddenly emptied of all these. It was as if every energy suf-fered a cessation. For a long time he sat there.

Quite without preparation, there lay upon him something else. He was penetrated by a new sensation. It was as if he had taken a deep breath after suffocation. As if a hard edge against which he had been pressing were fallen away. At this he wondered and looked about in a mild surprise. He felt as if there was something immediate urging itself upon his attention. He stood up uncertainly, looked into the dark, and at last turned and went into the kitchen. There he wound the clock, and remembered that by eight o'clock next morning he must telephone to Strain about the house.

"He'll be glad," he thought.

He wondered if it was too late to speak to Miss Arrowsmith about taking the baby, saw from his front door that there were lights behind the vines on her veranda. He started to cross the street.

"She'll be glad, too," he thought.

Then he felt a shock of wonder. When had he made up his mind what he must do?

Outside the screen, within the vines, Pitt appeared before Rachel Arrowsmith.

"If I could speak to you a minute? " he said.

He entered the veranda, sat down instantly, hunched his head low between his shoulders. He did not see the table with its shining coffee service, or note her movement toward the urn.

"I guess I'll let you have the boy — if you meant it," he said.

He did not know how much easier she made it for him by her level lack of surprise.

"Oh, I do mean it," she said simply. "Just, you know, until you want him back. Or until —"

"Sure," said Pitt, "sure. Or till his mother wants him. Sure."

"You know what good care I'll try to take of him?"

"That's what I figger," said Pitt.

She bent her look upon him, no more deceived by his exterior than an angel would have been deceived.

"You are going away?" she asked.

"I guess I'll sell. That'll put Three Hundred in the bank clear for —"

He stopped because he must, but he smiled weakly.

"Yes, of course," said Miss Arrowsmith. "And where will you go — do you mind?"

"I don't just know where I'll locate," Pitt said. "I'll look around. I don't just know where I'll locate."

He rose, and fumbled at the chair-back.

"I guess that's — that's all," he said, with his wild look about him.

She went to him, put out her hand, and saw herself standing with his hand in both her own.

"You must let me write to you — oh, often! — how he is getting on?"

"Sure," said Pitt, as one bestowing a favor.

She felt that she did not speak through to him, and she tried.

"You know," she said, " how deeply I appreciate and understand — the trust you give me? And how I love him?"

At this Pitt could not speak for an instant. He nodded, lips parted, and he detached his hand.

"Sure. Sure. Sure," he said at last, and went. He heard in agony that he had let the screen door slam with violence.

Pitt packed and was besieged by tender things. There was an old plush album, in which some one had saved photographs of Barbara as a little girl. He stared at these for a long time. In these pictures her life was before her. Here also was fastened a newspaper notice:

Miss Barbara Ellsworth entertained six of her little friends yesterday on the occasion of her eighth birthday. The occasion was greatly enjoyed by the little ladies.

He read this many times. It hurt him intolerably, that birthday party. There were Sunday School diplomas of hers, and a book with her name in childish letters. Far back in a bureau drawer, a little box of soft hair, like a baby's, marked, "Barbara, five years old." In the attic some dresses which she must have worn as a little girl. And her school books penciled with trivial jests. What had he done? Here was some one who had been living a continuous life orderly, arranged. He had entered, and everything was other.

The furniture he refused to sell. Barbara would want that when she came back. He accepted the use of the Coppers' loft, and there were piled the familiars of his house.

On the day on which he was to give possession, he longed to be left alone, with the baby staggering about, delighted at the changed aspect. But every one came. He was raw and sore, and he turned surly.

At noon, when he was making bread and milk on the pantry shelf, Mis' Hellie Copper pushed in brightly.

"Irish stew today," she said. "You come along and have some."

"No sir! " said Pitt fiercely. "I'm going to stay here."

"Get along," she said goodnaturedly. "There's plenty of it, and a big fat pie."

Pitt waved his spoon.

"I don't want any of your Irish stew, thank you! "

"Well, do let me take the baby over and —"

"You leave the baby be!" cried Pitt. Then he laughed. "We're all right," he said. "We don't want anything else!" he added testily.

"Mercy," observed Mis' Hellie on her way home, "sometimes I donno as I blame Barbara."

Pitt was suffering intense emotion. But he was inarticulate, and his only way of excess in expression was irritability. At last he drove everyone away with something like savagery.

In the late afternoon he put the baby in his cart out in the yard, and brought out the huge old valise, containing the child's clothes. With these he went out the side gate and down the hill to Miss Arrowsmith's.

She was not at home, the maid thought. This seemed to give him a respite. While the servant went to determine, he stood in the hall, where he had stood on his first day in Burage, and again on his wedding day. But neither of these days came back to him. Nor was he fully conscious of today. He was thinking what a rusty old satchel that was for Miss Arrowsmith to see.

The servant came back. Miss Arrowsmith would not return till dinner time. He felt strong relief. So he need not leave the baby now. Perhaps he might even miss the six o'clock and have to stay until the next day. He heard the maid speaking. Miss Arrowsmith had left word that, if he came, he was to leave the baby.

Pitt looked down. The child was leaning sidewise in his cart, rubbing at the wheel. A ruffle of his cap had fallen forward and hid his face. Pitt dare not stoop.

"All right." he muttered. "Tell her, all right."

He went toward the door. He did not meet the servant's eyes or hear what else she said. An instant and the door had closed behind him. He went blindly to the gate. A voice hailed him. A dray was before his gate. Was the rest of them things to go to Mis' Copper's?

"Round the back door," Pitt said. "I'll lend a hand."

The last things were loaded. Pitt brought his bag and stood on the dray and rode down the street. It was the dray that had followed to the station on his wedding day, bearing some household goods and a baby carriage.

At the corner of the main street, he paid the man and continued on foot to the station. Flo Buckstaff and his 'bus were there. He called out to know if Pitt had anything to check. Pitt had nothing, but he smiled and lifted his hand. Buckstaff, he reflected, was a good fellow. If only he would not smoke such fine cigars. His cigars must cost him more than he had.

In the ticket office, the usual crowd from the branch road waited for the Through. Women traveling in dresses which they believed too good for the train, and taking great care; children begging for the lunch which they were told it was not yet time to eat; red faced men who departed, and lounged back again. The station boy had chosen this moment to sweep up fruit peelings and papers. Pitt waited for his turn at the window. He was glad that the ticket agent did not lift his eyes. To him the world was an endless procession of hands laying down money, taking up money. Whether anyone got anywhere with the tickets which he handed out gave him no concern. Pitt took his ticket, and it was no more to this man than Nicky True, next in line and off for a ten-mile ride and hop-picking.

Pitt waited inside till the train came in — a through train from the coast. He walked down the platform past the glossy Pullmans, whose inmates looked out on Burage as if it were remote from life, an interest, a lapse; and on its loungers and watchers at the station as if they too were lapses; and on Pitt in hurrying by in his seersucker coat.

The conductor of the branch road came up the platform and saw him.

"Seems to me you're gadding pretty frequent," said the man.

"Sure, sure. I should say," Pitt replied and laughed, and climbed aboard.

He was obliged to share the seat of an old gentleman studying a time card. When the train started, and crossed the main street, Pitt leaned forward and looked. He joggled the elbow of the old gentleman who glared, and wondered why a man would want to do a thing like that.

It was in this manner that the child was born. There he was, sentient. A rift in experience, the crossing of the street by Barbara at one moment rather than the next; the opening of a gate by Pitt in the afternoon instead of the morning. Then joy, ill, the depths, madness, flowing about the two. These passed. But there remained the child — living, exquisite, sturdy, sensitive, a new microcosm, experiencing within himself the act of God.

Jeffrey Pitt

1

The destiny of Pitt's child seemed to move at the touch of a lady who had never spoken to Pitt and was never to speak to his child.

Observing the influence of Mrs. Granger, in invalidism, upon her household, one speculated on the potential effect of her in health. Influence? Hers was rather preponderance. She had not influence. She had clutches. No, poor lady, she was guilty of neither. Merely, she was compounding more violent vibrations than emanated from other members of her household. These vibrations had their way with her as well as with family, the despot always achieving one victim on whom he has not counted: Himself.

Mrs. Granger always occupied a high-backed, upholstered rocking chair, packed with pillows. The only piece of comfortable furniture in the room — a green long-chair of Rachel's selection, the mother could never bring herself to use. "It feels affected," she said. All that she said was spoken in a low-pitched voice. She was an invalid, but she used only chest tones. It was as if a granite cliff should languish.

There was about Mrs. Granger's physical frame something of the cliff. She was vast, gaunt, angled. It was as if she had been begun on some colossal pattern and then abandoned by the genius who projected her. Great ears, knuckles, facial bones, and powerful thighs — you saw them move. Left thus alone, she had suffered some nameless caving-in. There she was structurally. But the substance had departed. This absence she knew as her invalidism, and accepted it as her role. Nothing was omitted. She wore her hair in two braids. Usually she sat with her eyes closed. Her face was habitually contracted as if in expectation of some imminent pain. One's pity mounted to an intolerable longing to shout: Where are your chains?

In that household nothing was ever mentioned late in the day which might encroach upon the night's rest of Mrs. Granger. Therefore no one had mentioned to her the baby's advent. Woven in was a darker strand: Rachel, not having thought Pitt's departure imminent, had not mentioned the baby to her mother at all, or any hope of his adoption. Now in her mother's presence Rachel felt like a little girl who has informally accepted a puppy no longer to be withdrawn in the coat-closet from the interrogations of the family.

"Is the sun shining?" Eyes closed Mrs. Granger inquired as Rachel entered.

Rachel replied cheerfully that the sun shone, asked her mother if she thought she might not drive a little, and even as she asked repented the question. It always irritated her mother to meet a suggestion. She was herself essentially the suggestor, the positive. At the idea of a drive her forehead was now still more contracted. She closed her lips in a thin line and kept her silence. Whereupon Rachel remembered in haste to say that the vines were turning, and all the time she was thinking: "I am certainly not I, when I enter this room. I feel like a little girl. I feel indefinite, fluid. . . ."

But she faced her mother, produced her intention with her own fine directness, quite lacking in the approach due to invalidism.

"Mother, Pitt, over there, has gone away. He wants me to take his baby. And, mother, I want to take him."

Mrs. Granger did not open her eyes. A faint smile invaded her mouth, departed. What Rachel had said survived somewhere in the air of the room, but not in this lady's consciousness.

"I told him," said Rachel, "that I would take him."

Mrs. Granger opened her eyes. "My dear child, what a preposterous idea."

"He has gone," Rachel concluded. "He went last night. And he left the baby here."

"Here? What impudence."

"But, mother, I said that he might. I've consented — I really asked it, mother. I ought," Rachel said, "to have talked it over with you before. But it all came about suddenly — I didn't realize that he was to go so soon. And," with a rush, "anyway, if I want the baby, you don't mind, do you, dear?"

Mrs. Granger did not change her position or move her hands or raise her voice.

"I mind exceedingly. You mustn't think of it, Rachel."

"But I have thought of it . . . mother, he will be downstairs. You need never see him. I'll pay for him out of my own money. You see, dear, I've done it. The baby is here in the house."

"Then you must send it away. I wouldn't think of assuming such a responsibility at my age."

Rachel pointed out earnestly that it would be she herself who assumed. Mrs. Granger said "You?" in indulgent amusement. It went on: Certainly. No end of women have babies at twenty. Rachel is twenty-six. "But, my dear child — you, to bring up a baby!" And to this the trenchant impertinence of: "You were twenty-four when I was born." On which without a hint of humor Mrs.

Granger replied that at twenty-four she was much older than are most women of thirty now.

Watching, one wondered whether, when we multiplied by breaking off and swimming away, the parent plasma tried to retain the scuttling progeny within her own side. Whether by vague gestures the pieces, as they swam clear of her, made it known through the ooze that they were themselves. Separate. If so then Rachel, remote kinswoman of those broken bits, had somehow lost the trick of the emphasis, and biologically it seemed important that morning. Yet why should we go back and learn of plasma? Have we not love?

"Mother! It isn't for you. *I* want that baby. I have wanted a baby for along time. Don't you understand? I want a child. I want that baby to care for and bring up."

The parent plasma looked sidewise at the rug, for a silence.

"I thought that we two were a great deal to each other. . . ."

Compunction. Protestation. That primitive antagonism between mother and daughter which, in our tedious development, is as common as antagonism between the sexes, had kept this woman from glimpsing the first abyss of her daughter's soul. It is proper that abysses of the soul should be private. At least no one should be obliged to exhibit an abyss as an argument. But now Rachel drew back a veil. Simple enough in its revelation; loneliness, delayed motherhood, lack of creative expression — that which lies in silence she voiced haltingly. And to all this: "Dear child, I know — of course I know. You will marry some nice boy—but what would he want of this child? Trust my counsel. You will thank me some day. 'Mother,' you will say, 'how right you were.' Try to see it now, my dear little girl." Again the inarticulate cry of the piece that has been broken off. "Mother! Let me decide for myself. It isn't as if it need burden you. . . ."

There was no discussion, because Mrs. Granger admitted no points. She was merely maternal, patient, sure. "This child should be sent to some excellent institution. Why, Rachel, what if you should take it and it should die?"

And Rachel: "What if he should go to some institution and should live?"

"You are unreasonable, Rachel. I am sorry, but this is a thing that I cannot allow."

It was at "allow" that Rachel made a passionate gesture.

And now Mrs. Granger summed up: "Let us not discuss it, Rachel. You are making my head ache."

Little devilish forces, set loose in any air by hot discussion now contrive to act, as usual, through the inessential. As Rachel rises her mother becomes fretfully aware of the uncurtained window. "That shade," she says, "do lower it." Its string snaps, and Rachel swings her strong body to the sill. The white paint, the white paint — "How many times," Mrs. Granger cries, "must I tell every one not to mar that enamel?" The enamel is not harmed, and this is established. The tension snaps. Mrs. Granger affirms that no one pays the slightest heed to her wishes. It is true that she will not be here long to trouble anybody, but in the little while that she has, it does seem. . . . She weeps, utters accusations having no bearing on the moment. Rachel is betrayed into self-defense, least admirable of the petty immoralities.

"Go, go," Mrs. Granger beseeches, "leave me alone. I know that I'm a burden. I know how much I'm in the way. . . ."

The sun, surging upon the window, is cut from the room. The room, sufficiently modern with its white paint and oak floors, yet conforms to the shell boxes and velvet frames on the mantel; and the photographs are of those who are almost certainly dead.

Early the next morning Mis' Hellie Copper went down to her cellar to see if she had any of that raspberry cordial left. She rather thought there was one bottle, behind the jelly. She held her breath, closed her eyes, reached a bare, capable arm. There it was! She brought up the bottle, dusted it with her apron, observed that she should have to have some new rubber rings before it came time for the pears. Only rubber rings were not what they used to be, by any means. One season and they were flabby.

"What? Ros'berry cordial for breakfast?" her so-called lord inquired.

He was finishing the last griddle cake in the dish and drowning it in syrup, because the last griddle cake was always too moist. He was unshaven — it was toward the end of the week — and his feet were about the legs of his chair.

"Never you mind," said Mis' Hellie. "I told you I thought I heard the doctor rattle up to Mis' Granger's, long toward morning," she added.

Hellie pushed back his chair. In the process he always wrinkled the carpet under which straw had been freshly laid that spring, too late to be really "stomped down." He pushed at the wrinkle with his great boot.

"Good souls," said he, "if I could get down sick and miserable, mebbe my wife'd look after me some instead of feeding the neighbors."

"Hellie," said his wife irrelevantly, "wouldn't it have been grand if Pitt had asked us to take his baby?"

"Well," said Hellie, "he didn't."

"Would you have?" Mis' Hellie pressed it.

"Why, sure I would," said Hellie soberly, "if you would."

She stood polishing thoughtfully at the bottle — a brown, drunken-looking bottle, with "Rosberry," in her best hand, on the label.

"Things go queer," she remarked, and sighed. "I'll run over to the back door with this, so's to find out about the doctor," she added, and had off her apron. She walked as far as the gate with her husband, and they parted amicably and without a word.

Rachel was in the kitchen, giving the order for her mother's breakfast. She welcomed Mis' Hellie who, vowing that she couldn't stop a minute, leaned comfortably against the side of the house.

"How's your ma seem?" she asked.

Rachel stepped out on the little porch. It was a lavish morning — a ripe-baked earth, all-possessing air, a blue that claimed the eye, and a thin wash of gold over all. In that light it was to be seen that Rachel looked less exquisitely transparent, as if something had obscured her spirit, clogged its motions.

"Mrs. Copper," she said, "I've got to give up having the baby here. He worries her."

"You ain't!" Mis' Copper poured herself into the word as if she were fluid.

Rachel nodded. The mute misery of her hurt the other woman.

"Say!" Mis' Copper cried helplessly. "Say!"

Rachel set the raspberry cordial in the refrigerator, caught the faint odor, as of crumbs and suet, from the food, noted that there was only one melon. . . .

"I've got to plan something," she said.

"You was thinking of taking him away with you?" Mis' Hellie thought that she comprehended.

This was just the thought which through the night had besieged Rachel. She had money. Her mother had no physical need of her. Why not go away and take this child? But she was not honest, and she knew that she was not honest, in believing that she considered this alternative. Rachel was of a fine independence in inessentials; in essentials she had been seized upon and netted round, airily walled in by the physical vibrations of a personality stronger than her own.

"No," she answered, "I couldn't do that. I—"

On that hesitation stood Pitt's child, as at a threshold.

Miss Hellie asked no details. Even if she had not divined all, she would have asked no questions. Her reticence with Rachel approximated delicacy. Moreover, she was assailed by the one aspect.

"Whatever under the dickens'll you do without him?" she mourned, "now that you've planned, and all." She was drooping, every atom of her the participant.

"That will come," said Rachel. She was not at all sure of this, but she wished to relieve Mis' Hellie's genuine distress as much as to avoid sympathy. "I meant," Rachel added, "I must plan now what to do with him."

"What to do with him?" Mis' Hellie repeated, and searched Rachel's face.

"I should like," Rachel continued, "to try to find somebody in Burage who will take him. If ever Pitt or Barbara come back—"

Mis' Hellie struck out with her hand.

"What you talking about?" she said. "Why, my land, we'll take him."

Pitt accepted with his terrible quiet the change from Rachel's roof to that of the Coppers. Four times a year he wrote to Hellie Copper enclosing a money order for his son's care and lodging. But he did not come to see him. When Mis' Hellie suggested it, as she did more than once, his reply was always the same. He would write:

I believe not. I'd have to get used to it all over again, and I couldn't stand that. You make him a good boy.

This he wrote in every letter: *You make him a good boy.*

. . . Have you the patience to look in on little Jeffrey Pitt, to understand what sort of creature Marshall Pitt and Barbara had compounded? Here was Jeffrey, born of a chance pity in Rachel Arrowsmith for a wretched little salesman of pickle and fruit products. What sort of creature can nature produce on a margin such as that?

The child was not pretty. His forehead was prominent, the mouth too large, the neck too slender. But the whole face was made luminous and lovable by the eyes. They were already the eyes of a person alive and thinking. In them was to be seen a look of pure contemplation. Later they would become misted over with deductions concerning action. At the beginning they exercised merely the divine right to examine the outside world and to select from it stuffs for the weaving of an inner vesture.

Look in on this child, for a flash, as he mounted to four and five years. Remembering all, explain if you can the sources of such moments as these— for he generally had the better of Mis' Hellie when she offered him ethical concepts:

"God wants you to be a nice little boy, Jeffrey," she said to him once, after some sounding rebellion.

"I know that," Jeffrey replied with superiority.

"Well, don't you want to please Him?" Mis' Hellie pursued.

"I do please Him," the child returned, "an'—an'—an'— He pleases me. We play together."

"Why, why, *why!*" cried poor Mis' Hellie.

"He don't spank me," returned Jeffrey pointedly. "He loves me, nice."

Her good sense betraying to her that her theology was here being superseded, she said no more — not knowing what to say.

Then Hellie Copper took the child walking and began on a line to which he had given thought.

"Kid," said Hellie, "why do you reckon that everybody keeps at you to be a good boy?"

"I do' know," said Jeffrey, and looked up with some idea that this was actually going to be solved.

"Why do you want to be a good boy?"

"I don't know."

"You do want to, don't you?"

A nod — the tongue exploring the depths of the mouth, the eyes on the distance.

"That's right. Everybody wants you to, I reckon. So you always try, won't you?"

Jeffrey kicked the gravel. He was ill at ease when folk did this to him. "There goes a dog," he observed in an effort to turn the talk. This was vain.

"That's what God wants too — that you should try to be good," Hellie proceeded.

"How do you know?" Jeffrey demanded, turning.

"Why, that's what God always wants," answered Hellie, considerably confused and unable, off-hand like this, to produce his proofs. Of course he had them.

"Did he tell you?"

"Why, no. But—"

"Well," said Jeffrey, "He told me. I was talking with Him."

"Look here, kid," said Hellie severely, "you mind what you're a-saying."

So that theological discussion also terminated.

Jeffrey's sense of God did not begin. It was. No one remote, all-objective, but someone both within and without. "I shut my eyes and play I'm God. Now I'm breathing for God." And once, "God in, God out, God in, God out," he chanted with his breath. He announced further: "I'm going out in the garden to keep house with God." Out there, as he played, he talked with God, as he had said: "And, God, you must tell me all about yourself, so I'll know." His invocations were constant. He built a house of blocks and petitioned: "God, don't let it fall down yet." He walked the fence and prayed not to fall off. He shocked Mis' Hellie by refusing jam with "God says more will make me sick" — his hand laid on some center near the breath. He put on his hat after breakfast and stepped from the threshold with "Come on, God." Once, when he was laughing and playing at his prayers, Mis' Hellie shook him and said angrily "How can God listen?" — on which he turned his head from her and murmured: "Please excuse me, God" — a lyric utterance. As he grew older this sense did not diminish but rather sharpened. He said less of it, but it obsessed him, beset him. When he had done "wrong" he wept, not because he had offended Mis' Hellie, but because he had somehow hurt God. He had a sense of something withdrawn, an intolerable nostalgia.

. . .

There was a night when he had disobeyed — it matters little what the command was; the heinous part was that he had disobeyed, and he was put to bed at six o'clock. He lay looking at the sun on the bright green of the June leafage, and there was upon him some terrible burden of anguish. It was not that he had not done what was commanded — that he hardly remembered. It was something else, nameless, oppressive, overwhelming. His throat ached with it. He wept in his pillow, ignorant of what he suffered, ignorant of the remedy. He was acutely wretched at some sense of immeasurable wrong done, not to him, but by him to something else.

"Please forgive me, please forgive me, please forgive me," he said over deeply within himself.

He went to sleep, repeating these words, as if they made for him a presence and a comforting.

Gradually, he located God in a corner of every room in the house. And he looked there, knowing well who was there, though no one else knew. But when he fell into a rage, these corners disappeared and were not. Over his rages he seemed to suffer remorse no more than for having had measles. His passions of regret were likely to seize on him when he had offended in some trifle.

When he was seven, Rachel sent him a volume of the King Arthur stories. He was always to remember those evenings: In the dining room, the wood-fire hot in the sheet-iron stove, the canary covered with Mis' Hellie's apron, a newspaper protecting the geraniums from the frosty window. The engine-house bell ringing for the firemen's meeting. Feet squeaking by on the trodden snow. Mis' Hellie in her alpaca afternoon dress, covered by a white apron, and she bending above the book, protected by a brown-paper cover, carefully fitted. Then Guinevere and Camelot. Hellie listening too, but with a pencil stump and an envelope, that he might figure in case King Arthur's court palled. Perhaps Jeffrey was never to have keener mental delight. By eight o'clock he was in agony lest it would sometime become nine o'clock and bedtime. But nine o'clock falling in the midst of a tournament, so keen was Mis' Hellie's sense of the unities that she went seven minutes beyond, to leave no lance ignominiously suspended. In those evenings Jeffrey's inner life was readjusted for him, as is the outer world adjusted for children when they learn some facts of physical life.

"Is that stuff true?" demanded Hellie, when Jeffrey had gone to bed.

"That's what I been wondering," said his wife. "It reads true but it rings foolish."

"I don't believe any of it," Hellie concluded, "but it's got a nice sound to it."

A night or two later when his wife had "clothes" to sprinkle, Hellie essayed to read in her stead. When Jeffrey had gone and she had come back, Hellie looked up with eyes pointed in thought.

"It hain't all moral," he burst out.

"I thought o' that," said Mis' Hellie, "but then *Guinevery* got come up with."

"So did that Miss Elaine one," said Hellie gloomily, "and she never done a thing."

At Hellie's elbow lay the *Burage Weekly,* and all was no less mysterious in the secrets of their township — in Rocky Run and Maiden Rock and Skillet Creek.

Toward spring of that year Jeffrey began to wear his cap inside out, and he mentioned that he was Galahad. In sending the book, Rachel had reflected that every child wished to be Galahad, and she wondered who it was that was thwarting the general wish. There were such multitudes of Galahads in knickerbockers and so few with gray hair. Whose fault was that?

One morning he was playing in the yard when Rachel drove by, and stopped to beg to take him home with her. While she waited, she reflected that if he had been hers, as she had dreamed, she would certainly have liked him only when he was clean and in good-humor, and that after all it might be best—she never saw him without trying to marshal reasons why all was best.

He went with Rachel, as he loved to do. The Granger house enthralled him. The size, the silence, the rooms beyond rooms, the unknown objects. All children love space and height — all children should be brought up in some Vatican.

In Rachel's room a miracle happened. He was happily investigating all things when she opened her bag and took out a beautiful, shining cup, curved like a vase, with double handles and a standard. It was a tennis trophy. He flung himself upon it.

"Look! Look! You've found the Holy Grail."

Rachel had that rarest of gifts — the recognition of the essential. She saw here an essential.

"I want you to have it," she said, and laid it in the child's hands, as the bishop gave the candlesticks.

Jeffrey held it in his arms. He would not set it down. He lunched with the beautiful thing beside his place. When she took him he begged to carry it, and they went through the streets, in the sweet airs of spring, the child clasping this treasure. Of those who passed him no one noticed what he had save Mis' Matt Barber, who thought that a child should never be trusted to carry a thing like that. He took the cup to his room and set it among the cheap china ornaments in his cupboard. He made a little tuneless song, which he called the Holy Grail tune, and chanted it at dressing and undressing.

One night when Mis' Hellie went to look for him before he slept he was not in his bed. The window was open and the air, still keen, rushed in, mingled with moonlight. This light fell in a flood upon Jeffrey. He was kneeling at the window in his white night drawers. On his outstretched hands was laying his little wooden sword. He did not hear Mis' Hellie enter.

She swooped down on him, with a clatter of words. "Don't! Don't!" he begged. "I'm waiting for the blessing." Blessing indeed! She lifted him, kissed him, shook him a little, and tucked him up warmly "where he belonged."

Next day Mis' Hellie related all this to Rachel in the presence of the child. Rachel could not meet this shame-faced look, or Mis' Hellie's tender and humorous indignation. At home Rachel wept, wondering why she had no courage to take the child and permit him to grow. The humor of this seized her. What guarantee could she give that in the end she would not muddle things for the child still more hopelessly? Already everything was confused. Jeffrey was in the care of these kind Coppers, and kindness was not enough. She faced the lacerations and bludgeoning to which the sensibilities of the child had been a thousand times subject, would be subject innumerable times to come. Later she tried to talk with the Coppers about Jeffrey.

"We must stand aside," she said more than once. "You see, he is wonderful. The best thing that we can do is to keep out of his way."

The Coppers listened. The first blossom had come on the apple-tree that day — not that they knew this, but Jeffrey knew. In the yard the boy was galloping like a colt, he was shouting, he was making guttural noises in his throat. He was an animal. Unconsciously he was dramatizing spring.

Hellie went to the side door.

"Jeff!" he shouted. "Jeff! Don't you be so wild."

He came officially to life at the gift of a box of water-colors which Rachel brought from New York. He fell feverishly at work to paint everything that he had ever seen. He first attempted the Winter scene from a window, and toiled gallantly. When the picture was finished, he tore it across and threw it in the cooking-stove before any one had seen it.

"It wasn't it," was his critical analysis.

He tried again and again, and was manifestly puzzled when that which he saw outside was not transferred to the paper. At last he ceased to try to reproduce and took refuge in dabs of clear color. One day he went to church with Bennie Bierce, and that afternoon he painted steadily, elaborating figures in cream and black and yellow.

"See! See!" he cried, running to them with his sheet. "There's the church. There's the door. There's the organ. And there's where Bennie sits."

"What's this?" demanded Mis' Copper, pointing to a dark brown mass at one end of the paper.

"That," said Jeffrey, "is the noise the minister was making."

Later he drew a picture of God. It was a wash of pure blue.

2

The town forgot Pitt, and the years closed over his head.

If he were to have returned to Burage at all in those days, then by all the laws he should have returned with some faint stress, or at the least with a gesture. But nothing in Pitt's life was done with an appearance of effect. For him events seemed never to move with reference to values or selections. And on the one occasion on which he did come to Burage to see his boy, he came, so to say, parenthetically. Everything that he did seemed parenthetical — his love, his marriage, his work, all had been parenthetical; and yet these made his life. Pitt himself was a parenthesis!

Hellie Copper was tying blackberry bushes to the picket fence, one evening in early summer. Mis' Hellie was digging grass from the bricks of the narrow walk which ran round the house. Jeffrey was swinging on the front gate, thrilling to the shock of the closing. This sound, coming regularly to Mis' Hellie in the side yard, told her that he was "behaving." In Burage the verb "to behave" is always used in a good sense.

The sound ceased. Mis' Hellie working on, waited for it.

"I don't believe he'd go out of the yard without asking me," she thought. "More like he's knocked the rope down and spilled the stone." A pail of small stones hung upon a rope made the gate-spring.

The silence continued to assail her until at length she laid down the black-handled cooking-knife, which was her tool, and went round the house.

"Good, heavy dew tonight," Hellie called. "Better not stay out too long." Always the dews were a source of anxiety to Hellie, and he eluded them as others elude rain.

Mis' Hellie found Jeffrey sitting on the grass inside the gate. By his side sat a man whom, in the dusk, she did not recognize until on her approach he saw her and got awkwardly to his feet.

"Say!" he said, in his bright helpless way. "Say!"

"Forevermore!" Mis' Hellie greeted him.

Pitt stood before her, his head drooping a bit sidewise, his eyes on hers, one of Jeffrey's hands in both his own — a detail which was causing Jeffrey to twist.

"I'd ought not to come," Pitt said. "But I'm going back on the midnight."

"Well, you're not!" Mis' Hellie told him flatly. "And you needn't think you are."

Pitt laughed heartily. "Yes, I am," he insisted. "My soul, ain't he big?"

"Well, he's eight years old," said Mis' Hellie. "It's time he was big.

You come right straight in and have some supper. Hellie!" she informally announced, "Look at!"

They received him with gracious bustle — Hellie came running and laid his pipe on the door-sill according to the law of the house. Jeffrey ran for kindling to "bring fresh life" to the coals. Mis' Hellie sliced potatoes and filled the room with the odor of browned butter and made toast on a short fork before the red front grate of the stove. A cloth was spread double across one corner of the kitchen table, and Hellie sociably partook of a cold boiled potato, held in his fingers, salt in his palm, and a jack-knife to cut and to serve.

Pitt neither heard what any one said to him, nor took great account of the food which was spread for him. He was conscious of Jeffrey alone.

He moved the lamp aside so that he could see him. He wanted passionately to talk to him, but he was almost as inarticulate as the boy.

"Say!" he said. "I can't get over what a big boy you are."

Jeffrey twisted.

"Go to school?" the father asked the son.

"He's going this fall," Mis' Hellie put in.

"What you going to study?"

Jeffrey had no idea.

"Oh, I s'pose 'rithmetic and reading," Hellie hazarded. "Spelling like enough. He's a big boy, ain't you, Jeff?"

This sort of talk Jeffrey, of course, loathed, and he glowered.

"What do you do all day?" Pitt pursued. His only idea of talk with a child was, it seemed, a thunder of questions.

Jeffrey tried to think. To save his life, he could not remember a thing that he did, from morning till night.

"Marbles, mostly," Mis' Hellie contributed.

Pitt's face fell. "Say, now," he said in distress, "why didn't I think to bring you some marbles?" He produced what he had brought, and it was a camel, which being wound up would walk.

Pressed to know why he must go back on the midnight, it developed that Pitt did not have to go until Monday morning — but profession of haste was the old Burage manner of covering embarrassment.

They sat by the fire. For a time Jeffrey was interested and even excited, listened to the talk, and was very well off save when his father turned to him, as he did incessantly, with another of those streaming questions. But then toward ten o'clock the boy began to grow sleepy. At this signal Mis' Hellie, who usually welcomed it, suffered acute distress. She brought a string, and started cat's cradle. She recalled the rabbit and goose shadows which she used to make on the wall, hands technically twisted, and they all tried that. She manufactured errands, sent Jeffrey to bring the album, sent him to get his new shoes to show. At length all was exhausted, and he was nodding.

"Jeffrey," she said, "I know you don't want to go to bed — but, Pitt, don't you think. . . ."

"Oh, leave him get his sleep," cried Pitt. "I thought of that. Sure. Sure."

Mis' Hellie gave Jeffrey a match. "Want to go up and see his room?" she asked Pitt.

"Yes. Let's all go up," Hellie proposed, and had one great foot almost publicly stepped on by his wife. This woman, who had few conjugal delicacies, abounded in those of maternity.

Pitt went with Jeffrey to his room. The little unshaded lamp on the wash stand being lit, a slight smell of kerosene and lamp-smoke took the air. Pitt gazed on the small bare chamber — the plump bed with low head-board and "pieced" quilt; the length of matting; the kitchen chair with the bright calico seat, the sloping ceiling, the green paper shade and tassel.

"Say!" he said.

He was invaded by the sense of being with Jeffrey. And he could think of no way to use the precious moment.

"Quite a nice room," he observed, and took a tour about its few square feet. He came before the shelf where stood Rachel's tennis trophy. "What's that?" he demanded.

"I call that the Holy Grail," Jeffrey explained.

"The what?"

"The Holy Grail, you know."

"Oh," said Pitt blankly. "I guess I don't know that story."

Jeffrey looked with widening eyes at his father.

"It helps you to—to be—why, they saw it when they were good enough," Jeffrey reminded him. "Galahad and some of 'em."

Pitt compressed his lips and nodded his head a great many times, with lifted brows.

"You don't say," he met the moment.

He came to Jeffrey and took him awkwardly by the elbows. It was a terrific moment. Here was Barbara's boy . . . his boy. . . .

"Jeffrey," he said, "I think an awful lot of you."

Jeffrey colored.

"I s'pose," said Pitt wistfully, "you don't feel like you knew me at all, do you?"

"Not exactly," said Jeffrey, swinging on the bed-post.

"You—you kind of try to remember me some, will you?"

"I'll try," said Jeffrey dutifully.

"You don't remember me at all, I s'pose?"

Jeffrey shook his head with terrible positiveness.

Pitt sighed profoundly, remained staring at the boy until he shifted.

"Well," said Pitt, "might as well say good night, I s'pose."

"Good night," said Jeffrey.

Pitt hurriedly stooped. The boy lifted his face with a funny little twist and was pecked at. Then Pitt went. But to his inexpressible delight Jeffrey followed him to the top of the stair, kicked at the baseboard, jumped up and down a time or two, throwing out a leg and said:

"You ain't goin' tonight, are you?"

From the foot of the stair Pitt lifted a face altered by its leaping response.

"You bet I ain't, sonny!" he shouted.

The look was still on his face when he returned to the kitchen. Pitt's face was thinner than of old. His cheek bones showed, his eyes looked larger. His hair was still combed straight back, and was slightly rough at the back. His cravat came over his collar, his trousers caught on his shoe tops, his hands felt vaguely for his pockets. Pitt had an air of being chronically detached from his background. As he grew older, he was going to look like a little gnome who had been left out of the enchantment by mistake and wasn't supposed to show.

Hellie and his wife had been having a conference, and its results were in Mis' Hellie's brisk voice.

"Why under the canopy don't you come back to Burage and live?" she demanded.

It appeared now that Pitt was in some strong excitement which in the presence of the boy he had been disguising. He sat down at the end of the table, his figure humped and fallen.

"I got a chance to go out West," he said. "I'm goin' to leave next week."

"What's that for?" Hellie demanded.

"It's big money," Pitt explained. "They all say so. Yes—the mines. If I go for a matter of three-four years, I can come back here with enough to do grand by him."

"All-fired risky, *I* think," opined Hellie.

Pitt looked at them in his clear and ardent fashion.

"Well, this of mine is a pretty sure thing," he imparted. "I'm pretty lucky to be in on it."

He talked about it, told how he would come back and make a home for the boy.

"You think he'd be old enough in two-three years so's I could do for him all right without—without hurting him. . . ."

"Oh, land," said Mis' Hellie miserably, "I didn't ever meant you'd hurt him, Pitt."

"Well—" said Pitt, apologizing.

"Sometimes I think I was all wrong anyway," Mis' Hellie burst out. "Just because he didn't have a mother, we all seemed to think a father was kind of risky—all alone. I dunno's it was. I dunno but we was all meddling with something we hadn't ought to 've touched. But we done it for the best. . . ."

Mis' Hellie wiped her eyes. In these years the thought of Pitt had always wrung her heart. Now that she saw him, heard him speak, watched him with his boy, she was dimly conscious of the motions of destiny, and of how stupendous a thing she had touched.

"I wouldn't have done things good," said Pitt earnestly, comforting her. "It's all for the best. When I went I thought mebbe. . . ."

By his look they knew what was coming.

"I s'pose you ain't never heard—"

"Not a word," Hellie and his wife spoke together. "Nor you?"

Pitt shook his head. "Ain't it the funniest thing?" he put it to them, "the *funniest* thing—"

He leaned forward, thrust his clasped hands between his knees till the pale, veined wrists showed. "One thing," he said, "why I couldn't have stayed here — I wanted to be where I could kind of look for her. I know she's in some city somewhere — she wanted city, you know. I had to be there. But city ain't the place for a little boy—" He meditated briefly, turned his beautiful eyes upon them. "You mustn't ever think you didn't do for the best."

Hellie was looking troubled. "But now," he said, "you're going to leave there anyways. Why not come back here, and earn what you can, and take the boy? We'd hate to lose him like sin, but seems though — why don't you do that?"

"I thought o' that," said Pitt gravely, "but I want him to have some chance. I never had one — and if I can get some money ahead — and give him some school — I think if I'd ever had some school it would have been different with Barbara. . . ."

He sat thinking, and seemed to forget them. Hellie leaned forward with an air of confidence.

"Look a-here," he said, "Miss Arrowsmith, now. You know she was set on having the boy, if 'twa'n't for that ma of hers — I wrote you and so did she, I expect. . . ."

"A grand letter," Pitt cried, "I'll never forget the letter she sent me. She thought an awful lot of Jeffrey."

"You see!" said Hellie, as if he himself had made this statement. "Well, now: Little things she's said, we calc'late *she's* calc'lating to give the boy his education. What's the use of you—"

Pitt looked at Hellie in astonishment. "Why in the world," said Pitt, "should I lay back on Miss Arrowsmith for somethin' that I can do for the boy myself?"

"But this mine business — they ain't no certainty. . . ."

"But they's a chance," said Pitt, "a grand chance. I'm pretty lucky to be in on it. Mebbe I can build Jeffrey and me a nice home here—and send him off to school like anybody. I—I'd like to do somethin' like that," said Pitt.

Mis' Hellie took it up. "Miss Arrowsmith's got more than she knows

what to do with," she said. "Goes traipsing off to New York, spending it on
a sleeping car, like it was water. Well, why not leave her do this for Jeffrey
when the time comes? Too bad she ain't here now, so's you could talk it up.
And why not you come here now and take a little comfort with the boy yourself?"

Pitt shook his head. "I'd like that awful well," he said, "but I couldn't
let her do what I can do myself." He straightened. "He's my boy," he said.
Then he was afraid the he had said too much. "Colorado's a grand state," he
added. "It'll be big money out there."

He brought out some folders, showed the picture of Colorado, read
aloud accounts of the mines and other natural resources, told about the men
with whom he would make the trip. "Bartlett, now, you can tell he's made a
good thing. He's got a diamond that he wears worth Nine Hundred Dollars.
That's Forty-five Dollars a year interest. And yet he can afford to throw away
that Forty-five, just to wear that diamond. You see?" In the end, Hellie himself was faintly fired, and went to bed telling his wife that this was no climate
to live in, anyway.

🦐

The next afternoon, Sunday, there was to be in one of the churches
an illustrated lecture on "Ober-Ammergau." Mis' Hellie had intended to take
Jeffrey to see the pictures, and now they all went, Hellie remarking that he
might as well, as his clothes were changed anyway. It developed that the trust-
ees had vetoed having the pictures shown on the Sabbath, and the lecture was
to be given unadorned. "What was there wicked about showing pictures of
Christ and the disciples and the crucifixion, I'd like to know?" Mis' Hellie
demanded aloud in the pew, and was suppressed by a nudge from Hellie,
embarrassed by such rationalism. After the lecture began Mis' Hellie leaned
and whispered: "I know what the trouble was. The pictures was colored!"

The lecturer dwelt too long on the topography and then made everything worse by reading a great deal of poetry. But Pitt listened with a
manner of absorption, head well on one side. At the end, he asked the others
to wait for him, and went down to speak to the lecturer. Mrs. Malcolm
Brewster and Mrs. Hugh Ames were already there, to speak with this man,
and Pitt waited while they informed the lecturer that they had been at Ober-
Ammergau — Mrs. Brewster when she was eleven.

When Pitt's turn came: "That was real nice you told about the man
that played Christ," said he.

The lecturer, a superior youth, regarded with secret amusement this
frail man whose cravat was over his collar.

"Glad you approved," said the youth. "Rather a smaller auditorium
that I'm accustomed to speaking in."

"I was wondering," Pitt pursued, "if they was some way I could get a hold of whatever it was they learnt that man."

The youth stared. "The lines of the Christ in the play?" he hazarded. "Well, I should think not."

"I meant—" Pitt was flushing now, because Mrs. Jack Stubbs had come up to tell the lecturer that she too had been at Ober-Ammergau and had been entertained at the house of one of the players. "I meant," Pitt continued when he could do so, "you said that man was an awful good man, all the while he was getting around to play in it. Well, I was wondering what they learnt him all that time."

"Oh, that," said the lecturer. "Why, it would be impossible to find out anything like that."

"I s'posed it would," said Pitt humbly, dimly defending himself by the past tense.

"Very poor acoustics you've got here," observed the youth as Pitt retreated.

"What on earth did you want to see *him* for?" demanded Mis' Hellie, "I don't think he knows much." Every thought in her head was regarded by this woman as fit to come out.

The truth was that Pitt had been obscurely troubled by his discovery that Jeffrey was having no "outside" religious training. Not that Pitt had ever had any himself, but the boy, it seemed, was different. They all went for a walk that afternoon, as did the majority of the people of Burage, and Pitt, lagging a bit behind with his son, attempted to talk with him on the whole subject of ethics. Thus:

"I guess you're a pretty good boy, ain't you, Jeff?"

"*I* don't know."

"Well-a, what do you think?"

Grave silence.

"I know a fellow, and he's got a son that's no good on earth. No good on earth."

Grave silence.

"You wouldn't want me to be like him, would you?"

Silent writhing.

"Well, I thought not. Now, I'll tell you what you do. You be a good boy."

Here Pitt himself fell silent, pressed upon by the fear that he was getting nowhere. They were passing through the familiar streets, there was Matt Barber's, Nick True's, Monument Miles's. Pitt looked, recalled, caught remembered bits of talk which he had held with Barbara, on this street corner, that crossing. There was the Grangers' house, where he had left Jeffrey that night, where he had driven away on his wedding day, where. . . . He thought of the dray faring down the street, with the baby carriage which represented Jeffrey. Now here *was* Jeffrey.

"It beats all," Pitt thought. "It certainly beats all. . . ."

And the little house at the top of the steep steps. . . .

"There," he thought, "there. *There.*" He felt a kind of faintness.

Hellie turned to ask him how much they paid for a cord of dry wood in the city.

Later Pitt said privately to Mis' Hellie: "Does he say his prayers?" jerking his thumb toward Jeffrey.

Mis' Hellie looked troubled.

"He use' to," she said, "but he give me the creeps doing it. He use' to look right into the room, as if he could see — something."

"And don't he any more?"

"Well, you see," Miss Hellie explained, "now he says his own prayers and takes his own baths. And I sort of leave him run the both of them."

Toward evening Pitt went down town, found a drug store open and brought home a dozen illuminated texts, with pictures of men in eastern dress and of many lambs, the whole tied with tassels, for the wall. This he hung in Jeffrey's room, at the foot of the bed, below Jeffrey's Holy Grail.

"You can read them over," he said, "and it'll—it'll help you remember me." He found that he was abashed and wanted to excuse the texts.

That night he lay for a long time awake, trying to think what he could say to Jeffrey on the way to the station in the morning. Pitt collected all his store of spiritual wisdom. And on the station platform, as the train was pulling in, he spoke, having put it off all the way down the street.

"Jeffrey," said Pitt, "don't you let anybody make you ashamed of God, will you?"

From the heights and depths of his reverence for the unknown, the boy looked at this father.

"No, sir," Jeffrey said.

3

Over the son of Barbara and Marshall Pitt the years bore, casually continuing the work on the creature casually begun. By a thousand influences and negations outside himself he moved until, after seven such years, Hellie Copper abruptly rearranged all by dying.

On a day of incomparable beauty toward the close of the spring term of school, Jeffrey came home to rake the grass which Hellie had risen early that morning to cut with a scythe.

Jeffrey was now a slight, under-developed lad, with neck still too slim and head too large; and rough, dark hair, having two cow-licks. His hands were strong, the skin chipped and scraped, his feet looked too large and his ankles too finely drawn. He was decently dressed, with not more than three shoe-buttons missing, and with iron rust on his coat from too tender association with a broken rail which he had somehow acquired and cherished. When

Bennie Bierce came by, Jeffrey stopped raking and hung over the fence for speculation on the plausibility of the suggestion gathered somewhere by Bennie that a string bean made just as good bait as anything.

In short, on this day Jeffrey was a school-boy, with presumable years of institutional education before him.

He had interrupted his raking to stand in the wood shed and engage in the entertaining effort to fasten a broken window catch in a clapperless bell. He heard Mis' Hellie moving about the kitchen —she was preserving "pie-plant," and the sweet acid of the odor was on the air. The sun slanted across the two-board walk which ran down to the shed, a wren was singing in the box-alder over the well; doves wooed on a low roof next door, and a tortoise cat was delicately walking the boundary fence.

Jeffrey heard hurrying feet. A man came running down the road— twice notable, for a man seldom ran and seldom ran in the road. Dimly Jeffrey divined that these two circumstances portended danger, or evil news, and he watched the man with boding.

The man leaped the Coppers' fence. It was Axel Golithar, and Jeffrey took a few steps to meet him and stared at him in some inquiry which could not be formed. Axel arrested his running, making an awkward, floundering step, and he craned his neck and moved his arms as he spoke — for some reason lowering his voice to a throaty whisper. Long ago something had struck Axel on the eyeball and broken a blood-vessel, and Jeffrey saw this red blotch on the widened eye.

"Kid," said Axel, "it's Copper. His delivery horse kicked 'im."

"In the stummick," said Axel. "It's goin' hard with him. We thought best bring 'im home." . . . Axel looked back down the street. "There they come," he said, and motioned with his thumb to Mis' Hellie, at the kitchen stove, her back toward the doorway. "Tell her," said Axel, and bolted.

Jeffrey saw heads coming above the pickets. These heads were coming slowly. He ran into the kitchen, and in his hands were still the clapperless bell and the broken window catch. These Mis' Hellie saw before she saw his face. With the elbow of the arm with which she was dipping the fruit, she shoved him a little away.

"What's that you've got?" she asked, and saw his face. "What—" she cried, whirled to the door and saw the bearers coming. Before Jeffrey could tell her, she knew. While he was still trying to tell her, she sent him to unlock the front door. She set her preserving kettle back on the reservoir — but this she could not afterward remember — stripped the bed in their bedroom off the dining room, and stood in the front room when they came up to the door. Hellie was on a green blind. He was in his shirt-sleeves, as he had entered the stall, but they had thrown over him his coat, a coat thick with spots and grease which Mis' Hellie had meant to sponge.

All the neighbors said that Mis' Hellie was wonderful. But Jeffrey was more or less in everyone's way until three o'clock in the morning, when he fell asleep and was waked by the undertaker's squeaking boots.

His boy said his last words were "Take that pesky harness out o' my way." It seemed strange that a man should abruptly end his career on no more than that. He had said so many things, for so many years, and then those few words were all that were left for him to say, and when he had said them, everything was done. Jeffrey wondered if it could be possible that Hellie knew that he was dead at all, dying so alive, with words about a harness.

All next day Burage poured into the house. As a matter of course Mis' Hellie received everyone. If she had not done so, it would not have been understood. In the afternoon, she lay down for a little while, but those who came in that time sat and waited until she woke. Jeffrey wandered, outcast, hearing snatches of their talk, a potpourri of Burage accidents for generations.

In the evening the doors of the house stood open, and all the rooms were lamp-lit. As the people came and wished to look at Hellie, Mis' Monument Miles rose. She, as the neighbors said, "was the one." She had her hat off, and knew where everything was. She took everyone to the parlor where Hellie lay in his best clothes, as they had seen him look for years. They all tiptoed out saying that he looked very, very natural.

Mis' Hellie sat in her alpaca afternoon dress, to which she was accustomed to change every day as soon as the dinner dishes were washed. To every newcomer she was obliged to relate all that had occurred in the night. And as she talked, she rocked a little, and ran a pin in and out of the folds of her skirt.

"It was at nine minutes to two that I noticed the change. I saw the change, and looked, and it was nine minutes to two. I never took my eyes off him after that. At twenty minutes past, it was time for his medicine, and I give it. At half past, or mebbe a little mite more, the doctor come. He see the change, and he said he'd fix some different medicine. He went out in the kitchen, and he said he didn't have something or other he wanted, and he stepped down to Hoey's, himself, to get it. Right after he went out, Hellie begun to get gray. I see what was coming. I raised him up, and I was in there all alone, raising him up, when he stopped breathing. And I laid him down, and stepped to the door, and I saw Mis' Barber asleep in *that* chair, and him in *that* one. 'Mis' Barber,' I says, 'have your husband catch up with the doctor. Tell him the medicine will not be needed.'"

This recital she repeated more than a dozen times, as new visitors arrived. She was tearless and so tense that the effect was that of quiet. Other details were asked, and she gave them with the same clam. Only once did her voice break.

"He ask' for buckwheat cakes for breakfast yesterday morning," she said, "and I forgot to set 'em, and he had to have graham." On "graham" her voice broke.

Quantities of garden flowers were sent the next morning. Two or three of the young women of the neighborhood took charge, borrowing many jars and earthen crocks. The flowers were packed tightly about the coffin. There was a "set piece" from Hellie's lodge, and everyone knew that it cost Five Dollars. When the party had left the house for the cemetery, all the flowers were tumbled into a wicker clothes basket, hurried to the side gate where a horse and buggy were waiting; and two young women drove at breakneck speed, by back streets, to the cemetery. Everyone hoped that they would reach Wisconsin Street ahead of the procession, and those in the forward carriage peeped out to see if they could sight them, and were relieved to discern buggy and basket bouncing over the cross-walk just ahead of the bearers' carriage. By the time the cortege reached the grave, the flowers were all neatly arranged on the mound of fresh earth, the basket tipped up behind a handy monument, and the two young women fanned with their handkerchiefs all through the prayer.

When Mis' Hellie and Jeffrey returned to the house, Mis' Barber and Mis' Bates, who had stayed behind, had piled all the undertakers' chairs in the yard, had placed Mis' Hellie's furniture as nearly in its accustomed position as conference could recall, and had ready tea and bread-and-butter and strawberries. They were not averse to talking it all over.

"I must say," said Mis' Bates, "the Rever'nt done a good thing in his remarks."

"Didn't he?" said Mis' Barber, pausing in her dusting. It was not clear why all must be dusted, but the neighbors had swept and dusted continually since the accident. "I didn't know what he could scrape up to say and Hellie not a believer," she added, *sotto voce*. "Didn't you think Rever'nt What's Name spoke real feeling?" she added to Mis' Hellie, who came from the bedroom.

"I didn't sense it much," Mis' Hellie owned. "But I guess he spoke up so's everybody could hear him." Her best cloth dress, new shoes which squeaked a little, and an elaborate drawn-work handkerchief gave her as much aloofness as did her grief.

"They don't make you cry to funerals the way they use' to, ministers don't," said Mis' Bates, serving strawberries. "Why, I remember to Nort Sandford's funeral how the minister went on. 'Nevermore,' he says, 'nevermore shall you hear his voice to the foot of the stairs crying "Huldy! Huldy! *Get* up. *Get* breakfast. *He's* gone."' The whole room cried like a child."

She stopped. Mis' Hellie was wiping away a tear. "I keep thinking about the buckwheat cakes," she said. Mis' Hellie being the only one who ever observed a *faux pas* and kicked the perpetrator, Mis' Bates went unrebuked.

"Land," said Mis' Barber comfortably, "Hellie's got all the buckwheat cakes he wants, by now. Don't you worry."

Jeffrey listened and was oppressed at the difference from it everyday appearance now presented by this room. Soon he devoted himself to his tea.

He had been fond of Hellie, but these were the first strawberries that he had had that year. And the strangeness of the time was upon him, the detail, the importance, the surprise. Above all, he was engaged in the realization that he must stand to Mis' Hellie in Hellie's place. He looked at her with new eyes, tried to anticipate her wishes, and helped her down steps — an act which obscurely irritated Mis' Hellie.

When Hellie's affairs were settled, it was found that he had died solvent, but with no estate save his small insurance. Mis' Hellie wept when she found that she could not keep the hardware business — she had held the secret conviction that she could conduct this business considerably better than had her husband.

"Jeffrey," she said, "I shall go to the poor-house. My old age will be spent in the poor-house."

This fear was always somewhere in her mind, and had lurked in Hellie's mind. And it found place in many of those snug little Burage homes, with lace curtains and a piano and upholstered furniture assembled on the edge of the abyss.

Jeffrey scoffed at this poor-house fancy.

"Why, of course you won't!" he cried with spirit. "There's me."

"Yes, you lamb," she said, and wept and did not observe how the boy loathed being called a lamb — "But you must go to school, as your father wants."

"I shall not go to school," announced Jeffrey.

At that point he stuck. As Mis' Hellie's total source of income would be the interest on her little insurance, her egg money, and Pitt's payments for Jeffrey, his point seemed reasonably maintained.

During these last years Pitt's inadequate letters had withheld information which the irregular receipt of his money orders had supplied. He wrote cheerfully, vaguely, rarely. Almost every letter bore a new postmark. From New Mexico and Arizona, his trail had crossed Nevada, and then his letters came from Washington and named Vancouver. He had a chance up there, he wrote, that looked like a pretty good thing. Folks seemed to think it would be a good thing. He was really "right down lucky" to be in on it. The last letter had come from Alaska.

Jeffrey's memory had changed his father's aspect. His tendency to idealize all was blurring his picture of Pitt into one of dignity and fine proportion. Jeffrey dreamed of the time when his father should come home, when they should have a home together, when he could say "my dad says," like other boys. However, there was a certain romance about a father in the gold fields. When Pitt had sent home a nugget, Jeffrey had enjoyed a definite popularity — here was a form of distinction which entailed no disapprobation.

The boy had now grown eager to see his father. The nugget had sharpened that eagerness, defined the remote, thrown up a background. Pitt, however, had never proposed a return to Burage. Mis' Hellie had regularly written suggesting this, but she had no faith in the post-office department ever delivering a letter in Alaska. And this doubt she felt to be borne out by the evasiveness of Pitt's replies.

"My land," she had said once to Hellie, "I begin to think he's married up there."

She now wrote to Pitt of all that had occurred, detailed her financial outlook, warned him that Jeffrey insisted on leaving school. To point the importance of her letters, she affixed a special delivery stamp. What they thought of this stamp in Alaska, when the letter began its sledge journey across the ice, can never be told.

Mis' Hellie wished helplessly that Rachel were at home — More than once Rachel had spoken of sending Jeffrey to college. If some such vague intention might be carried out now, Mis' Hellie herself would "do somehow" — the gallant Burage phrase. But Rachel and her mother had gone to Marienbad for an indefinite stay. Mis' Hellie wrote to Rachel of all that had taken place and of Jeffrey's purpose — but Mis' Hellie waited to hear as those who wait without hope. Alaska and Marienbad — certainly neither letter would ever arrive.

With the fate of these letters Jeffrey himself was not concerned. He had passed from a position auxiliary, incidental into importance, not to say freedom, as the family burden-bearer. The fact that Mis' Hellie was quite as able to work as he, he discounted. He was seized with a sense of responsibility joyous, tonic.

"Oh, dear me, you was going to be a great artist," Mis' Hellie reminded him casually.

That was true. All this time had deepened his formless intention to be an artist. Through his school life he had been drawing at random when they had directed him to study instead. The boys laughed at him — Bennie Bierce called him "artist" as a term of scorn. Gradually Jeffrey hid his purpose as it he had thought to be a corsair. He still messed about with colors, but rather more indefatigably than spontaneously, one would say. He informed Mis' Hellie that there were oceans of time to be an artist — oceans, and went into the street, walking with the first faint rhythm of a swagger.

There came a cable from Rachel at Marienbad. Mis' Hellie had never had a cable message in her life, and she was in a delicate spasm. The little lad without uniform who delivered the message was a good deal excited himself, and knew all about it.

"It's from the old country," he said.

"My land," Mis' Hellie decided, signing in zig-zags, "Mis' Granger's dead and they want me to see to it—" as if, in that case, all that remained of

Mrs. Granger would be arriving neck-and-neck with the cable.

The message itself still further upset Mis' Hellie.

"What do you think of that?" she demanded of Jeffrey. He read, dazzled: "Recommend preparatory school for Jeffrey. Will finance gladly. Writing. Rachel."

"What's a preparatory school?" Mis' Hellie cried. "Preparatory for what? Sounds like for a minister."

"Oh, she means prep," returned Jeffrey, with superiority.

"Prep?" cried Mis' Hellie blankly. "Who's he?"

When she understood, Mis' Hellie was clamorous. He must go to this place which Rachel recommended. Where was it? What — there were more than one? All with the same name? Well, what one did she mean, then? In any case, he must go.

"If anybody sends me to school," Jeffrey said with dignity, "my father'll do it. Let's wait till we hear from him. But anyway, I'm not going."

In his heart he said: "After I've bragged on going to work, I'm not going to prep — like an old baby."

Rachel's letter, urgent, accompanied by a draft, did not change him. Leave Mis' Hellie when she needed him? Never. This was his argument.

In Marienbad, Rachel opened Jeffrey's letter, and the draft told her all. For years she had said to herself that when he finished the high school, she would make all up to Jeffrey — all that she might have given him and had withheld. He should have school, travel, and the foundation of that wholesome upbringing of his, she analyzed it, would perhaps prove best for this admirable superstructure, which should be her care.

Now she read:

I want to go to work. And I think I shall like work. And when she has been so good to me I can't go and leave her just to go to school. And I have decided to go to work.

The letter closed with his awkward thanks, and an assurance of the fine weather of Burage.

Rachel read, and pictured Jeffrey behind some Burage counter or in some dingy work-room.

"What have I done to him?" she thought. And added: "What have I done to myself?"

4

Jeffrey went forth in Burage to find a "living" — courageous and pathetic word. There he was, suddenly detached from the chorus, flung out upon the main street as one of the principals.

Old Mrs. Albert, walking stiffly about among her petunia beds, did she know that there was passing her house not merely the boy who had chased her chickens, but a creature in the act of learning to walk on its own legs.

The Widow Galloway, had she any idea that to have treed her cat with frequency clung to this Jeffrey Pitt but as his yesterdays, while today was over him like a banner? These two women gave no sign of divining anything of this, and no shop recognized his advance upon it. Yet this being was in the act of setting his shoulder under a great and terrible wheel, and the time might very well have been attended by some ceremony.

The creature himself was acutely conscious of the difference. He was looking out in a new way. Instead of Myer's for fishhooks, Morrison's for molasses candy, Graham's for school supplies and baseball paraphernalia, here was Myer's who might want a boy, Morrison's who might want a boy, Graham's who might want a boy. The very buildings looked different.

Craney Staples was standing in the door of his little clothing store, and abruptly Jeffrey saw what a tremendous thing this man had done: *He had got himself a shop*, with his name over the door. What triumph, what mastery. Jeffrey walked backward and stared at the black letters of this man's name on his cheap sign. Should he ask Craney Staples himself for a job? Impossible. Jeffrey had seen what a great man he was.

Jeffrey walked through the business district and on to the residences. He was overwhelmed by the greatness of this whole machine which had been operating quietly down here in this little area. He dragged a stick along the fence pickets, stopped to watch a child sailing chips in the gutter and to frighten the child into thinking that he meant to sink his navy. In that moment Jeffrey was both boy and man.

He went back downtown, entered Mark and Arums's (could this be the place at which he had so often carelessly bought spools of white thread Number Sixty, for Mis' Hellie?) and asked to see Mr. Mark. Spectacles on the top of his head, another pair low on his nose, a pencil back of one ear and a pen behind the other, so that his head looked like a rack, Mr. Mark told Jeffrey kindly that they were letting people go for the slack season. (The slack season which, it seemed, they had all known about and faced in that marvelous downtown which Jeffrey was discovering.) At Arthur Hoey's Drug Store it was the same. There Jeffrey lingered, sniffing the grateful air, examining sponges of which he had never had enough. Arthur Hoey would like to take him on and said so, skillfully hanging hot-water bottles in the windows for the July trade.

"Bet you'd like to be head soda squirt," said Arthur.

Jeffrey looked reverently at the fountain, with its mysterious ceremonial apparatus of nickel and marble.

"When I'm a man," he assented respectfully.

Davies at the White Market was not in need of a delivery boy, but there Jeffrey acquired a handful of peanuts and felt encouraged. Lawyer Skinner, whom Jeffrey knew "by sight," met his request by patting him absently and asking him indulgently what a boy was *for* in a law office. (Was this all

that a successful Burage lawyer had to offer to a boy who was making his trans-
formation?) Mrs. Wyland, at the five- and ten-cent store, inquired of him
where would her profit be if she hired delivery and, mercy, how he was letting in the flies! She was kindly. They were all kindly. Only they did not recognize that he was undergoing a kind of commencement. Into his new world
there was no rite of entrance. It was merely a lad, marching stiffly in and out
at doorways, with a look of fear in his eyes.

He said to Mis' Hellie that he should never get a job, never. She was
inclined to assent. She was much changed by her widowhood. She had lost
her bright, clamorous way of speech, and though she still had humor, she had
ceased to enjoy it herself, and one began to suspect that it never had been
intellectual, but that she merely secreted it like a juice. Once she would have
laughed at Jeffrey's fear, but now she was inclined to assent — as if the very
economic adjustment of the world altered at the death of Hellie.

In the evenings the boy wandered about Burage, and now the iron
was in him, that first touch of the lack of self-respect of him who would serve
and can find no master. It was corroding, paralyzing. He tasted the bitter bread
of the millions who have nothing to offer.

The complacent little town showed its lights, took its amusements,
bore its sorrows, locked its doors, went to sleep planning for breakfast, for
school, for laundry, for "deals" to be consummated, flowers to be carried, skirts
to be turned, streets paved. . . . In all its passion of activity, the boy perceived
himself to be useless.

He was hanging about the magazine rack at Hoey's one morning.
At Mis' Hellie's, a farm weekly, a monthly fashion magazine and *Cooking* were
all that visited. Jeffrey loved the look of the popular magazines, their sense of
promise, their improbable ladies, their advertisements of necessities which he
had never seen. And he loved to tell himself comfortably that he should be
painting better illustrations than those, some day.

A great voice filled the place and demanded tobacco. Fine cut. "Good
deal of a hurry, my boy. Could you—"

Arthur Hoey left the children whom he was attending and came up
from behind the cigar counter with a handful of what he called "a nice article." This nice article the great voice repudiated.

"Nonsense! Mean to say this is the best thing you can trot out to your
sufferin' customers?"

Jeffrey looked up. From the spot where he stood, he saw Arthur Hoey
return the nice article to its pail, pick another handful from the same paid,
and extend it.

"You pay twice as much for this here," said Arthur, "but it's velvet.
Just velvet."

"Do it up," commanded the great voice, and as its owner received its velvet, the voice persuadingly added: "What's my bill doin'? What—growin'? Beats all, don't it? Well say, send it around some day."

"Sure," said Arthur Hoey, with alacrity.

"Not too soon!" He held up a big hand. "But, on the quiet, I'll tell you, I've got some money owin' to me that's goin' to set me on my feet before long. Settle up then like a prince or two!"

When he had gone, Arthur grinned pleasantly at Jeffrey.

"You saw that," Arthur observed.

"You gave him the same thing, didn't you?"

"Same identical."

Jeffrey laughed, not at the trick, but because he was flattered by the confidence.

"You have to do that to Beck," Arthur defended.

"Was that Beck?"

"Yes. Why not strike him for a job?"

"Does he want somebody?"

"No. But he's awful easy-going. Maybe you can make him think he does." Arthur reflected. "He has times," he added, "when he drinks like a fish. My dad says he spends better'n he pays. But *I* like him fine."

Jeffrey would not have thought of Beck, who had an obscure cleaning and dyeing establishment on a triangular lot in a side street. Jeffrey wandered down that way, found Beck not returned, and waited in a disorderly room cut by a counter, with more disorder revealed in this room beyond. In there a blond boy, named Platt, whom Jeffrey knew, was working, elbows bare, and appearing extremely technical. The place smelled like Mis' Hellie's skirt when she had been out in the rain. The cleaning and dyeing plant was completely unattractive, but it is characteristic of a search for a master that choice becomes gradually eliminated. It did not occur to Jeffrey to hope that he could not get a job there. Indeed, he was actually hoping to stay in that place.

But as he waited, Jeffrey was gradually aware of a soft clamor of voice, of impression within him. Something was pulling at him, trying to urge him out of the place. This inhibition had frequently beset him. It was as if the sense of right and wrong, which he obscurely knew as conscience, had extended its function, had broken through into the immoral domain. As if there were an inward monitor of the commonplace. Sometimes it reached consciousness merely, did not touch its way through to volition. But there were many times when it had influenced him, acted for him in a fashion which he accepted half-superstitiously. Now, however, he argued it away. Nonsense. Mis' Hellie had sat through dinner making figures on the back of a calendar. He wanted passionately to be able to tell her that he had a job. Jeffrey waited until Mr. Beck arrived. The voice ceased.

Mr. Beck presented the pathetic spectacle of the man who is seeking to make a living at a service of which his community wants little. Few cared to be dyed; almost nobody cared to be professionally cleaned; or, if one did, a quart of gasoline on the back steps was sufficient solution. Mr. Beck ought to have known that no town will be dry-cleaned very often when it is still making its soap in kettles in the shady door-yard, on spring mornings. The odor of that soft soap should have warned Mr. Beck that he was expecting too much of Burage. But he had rushed on headlong, invested his capital, and now strove all day on that wretched little triangle of his. He had a wife, who looked brave and sweet and blemished in her one delaine; and a baby whose gurglings were as yet aristocratic. Mrs. Beck had some things to be dyed for herself and the baby, and dreamed of looking quite trim, but it was difficult to get these things colored, her husband being in the business.

Mr. Beck came in. He was large, high-templed, thin-bearded. He moved quickly, was preoccupied, was grave, and affected a manner. In Burage few were grave, no one else among the men affected a manner. All this had its results, took the place of capital. On very little money, he held his place among the business men. Beck was one of those men of small towns who look and act like men of large affairs. Beck looked so many parts and played so few.

"Mr. Beck," said Jeffrey, "I wondered if I could get a job here."

You would have said that Mr. Beck would shout: "Job! I wish I had one." But no — Mr. Beck was sanguine.

"Let us see. A job. Now it's singular you should come in at just this time. Very singular."

Jeffrey's heart began to beat.

"If," said Beck, "business continues to look up, as it *may*, I shall have to have another assistant. Who are you?"

They went through the preliminaries, Mr. Beck with the air of the large employer, accidentally acting as his own agent. Secretly, Mr. Beck collected and returned most of the garments which passed through his hands, saying each time that he just happened to be passing, and then presenting his bill with such a hopeful, upward glance that one took from the corner of the drawer the money meant for the butter man, who had a big farm and could wait.

"Not much of a salary at first," Mr. Beck said.

Oh, no, indeed.

"But a chance to rise — a chance to rise," said Mr. Beck, looking about his mean little establishment. "Platt!" he called.

The blond helper with bare elbows appeared in the doorway.

"Any out-of-town orders in the last hour?"

"No, sir," said Platt.

"Ah," said Mr. Beck, "that's good. Little difficulty in rushing through, *some* days. But I think we shall get along here till fall very nicely.

And *then....*"

He asked Jeffrey more questions, with a manner of keen appraisal. While he talked, Mr. Beck continually combed his thin beard with the fingers of a large veined hand, whose cameo ring on the little finger was turned sidewise. It was true that he had no need of a boy now, but he felt that in the fall all Burage was going to rush upon him to be cleaned and dyed. To say nothing of the county trade. In the fever of his certainty, he definitely engaged Jeffrey for September 1, at Five Dollars a week.

"Don't mention it," said he, lifting the hand with the cameo ring. "Fact is, you've saved me the annoyance of advertising."

He dismissed Jeffrey kindly, not on his own account, for Mr. Beck had never heard of him; not on Marshall Pitt's account, who came and went long before the dyer's day; but because granting this application for employment gave to Mr. Beck an indeterminate self-respect, put him in good humor, made him feel "a man among men."

Jeffrey had never been so happy in his life.

Now! What had Burage to say to him? He walked it streets and regarded the store fronts differently — again. Not the old Myers and Morrisons and Grahams providing casual supplies; but also not the indifferent spots which he had lately sought, suppliant; instead, here were business houses, shouldering, afar off to be sure, the colleague business house to which he too belonged. Oh, if the *Burage Weekly* would set it in the Supper Table Jottings!

Nobody paid the slightest attention to his new dignity save Mis' Hellie, who folded him in her arms and named him her lamb. By then he was so in need of some art form to express his condition that it was a second or two before he wriggled away. No ceremony was instituted. One would say that folk get jobs every day. It is possible that miracles are common, but this did not occur to him.

He met Bennie Bierce and clumsily led the talk to the next year. What was Bennie going to do next year? Going to school, Bennie admitted in disgust. "I'm goin' to work," Jeffrey threw out carelessly, choking with pride. "To work?" said Bennie in awe. Jeffrey nodded, but the yawn which he essayed was too much for him and changed to a grin. "Gee," said Bennie, "and me slavin' for Tweezers." Tweezers was the school principal, but for the name they could give no reason. It was arbitrary, like Marquis or Duke.

There was a summer of odd jobs, and on September first, at eight o'clock in the morning, Jeffrey presented himself at the Beck Cleaning and Dyeing Establishment, and found Mr. Beck not yet down and the blond Platt astonished that any one should have expected him.

"Not for an hour yet," said Little Platt. Little Platt breathed through his mouth, talked through his nose, walked with his shoulders and upper body;

and this miscellaneous distribution of function covered a personality of power and charm. But it was inarticulate, save for his boisterous smile, whose incidence, however, always seemed to embarrass Little Platt so that he instantly looked away and down. Jeffrey knew him as the son of a woman whose husband had devoted his life to collecting old rubbers, rags, tin and the like; and on his laying down his pursuit with his life, she — the widow-woman, as Burage said, with a fine ear for the pathos inhering in alliteration — continued the business. But Burage wore its old rubbers and made over its rags and mended its tin to such an extent that Little Platt had been obliged to leave school. Jeffrey had often seen him on the street, too absorbed to have much to say to the older boys who bullied him. Seeing him now, so authoritative and responsible and expert in vague techniques, old standards began to totter.

"Say," said Little Platt abruptly, "was you thinking of coming here to work?"

"Why, yes, I was," said Jeffrey, divided between his diffidence in this new business world and his desire to patronize Little Platt. "Why?"

"Oh, nothing, I guess," said Little Platt, slowly.

"You willing I should come?" Jeffrey asked sarcastically.

Little Platt flushed. "Maybe you wouldn't be so willing, if—" he said, and stopped. Something more waited beyond his lips.

"See here," said Jeffrey haughtily, "I'm not after your job."

"Oh, my job!" Little Platt laughed good-naturedly. "It was you I was thinking of," he said, and returned to the back room with his intention, whatever it was, sealed within.

After nine o'clock Beck arrived, greasy but somehow magnificent, with his manner of the capitals and the centers.

"Pitt? Who — Jeffrey Pitt? Told you to come in September, did I? Well, that had completely slipped my mind. . . ."

And while Jeffrey's universe trembled,

". . . I can't keep track of everything, can I? Oh, I guess we can make room for you — always plenty to do about a place of this sort, you know. Let me see — Four a week, didn't I say? What, five? Well, make if Four-fifty to start on, m—m? All right, all right. Ready, are they, Platt? Here — what's you name? Jeffrey, is it? Jeffrey, take this box to Brewster's *and* collect the money. Don't neglect that, you know. And on your way back, get the mail. By the way, you might stop in for the mail every time you come by the office. I haven't got a lock box — avoid useless expense when you can, my boy. Now run along. Show me how spry your legs are. . . ."

Tremendous instant. On that little side street, down by the canal and the lumber yard, emerged all the joyous forces of a creature concentrated on its first step in the long role. Nothing like that ardor had ever filled him. The zest of it transformed the streets, sent him flying down bright ways, caused him to neglect his instant, consuming dislike of Beck. Mrs. Malcolm Brewster, receiving that box at the front door — side doors had no place in Jeffrey's order that morning — and hoping that they had not taken all the body out of her flesh-colored waist, and looking critically, and counting out the money, how could she know to what she was ministering in the person of that youth on her threshold? "Who was that boy? I don't know the young people in Burage any more, anyway — they grow up so fast . . ." she merely thought, while Jeffrey trailed his radiant route to the post office. And Zeri Wing, the old post-master, caged in the stuffiest room in town, did he know that in handing out to this youth the modest announcement of a wholesale dye house, he himself was taking part in a ceremony for which — again we have failed — there should be march music?

When Jeffrey returned to the office, luminous with pride in the quick time that he had made, the money that he had brought, Mr. Beck took all as a matter of course and then looked at him with a manner of speculation; and on succeeding days Mr. Beck seemed several times about to say something, and forbore, until Jeffrey trembled lest his dismissal hung upon those fat, evident lips.

At the end of the week, Little Platt having gone up to the drying room one morning, Mr. Beck leaned to Jeffrey with a manner of confidence adroitly touched with the casual, and spoke.

"I don't s'pose," said he, and combed his beard with the fingers of that veined hand, "that your folks have got a couple hundred dollars that they'd appreciate investing in the business?"

Jeffrey looked up, eyes round, mouth a bit puckered — in one of those little boy expressions which return unaware to the "big" boy.

"Now that you're in the business," Beck continued, "I could give 'em the chance, as it just happens. *Providing*," he said, nodding, "they take the chance before some money comes in that's owing me."

Beck leaned in his best manner of confidence to the adult.

"Flower and Flower," he said, "they owe me Three Hundred. Due pretty soon now. After that, I couldn't take in a two hundred investment— shouldn't need it. Tell you how it is — you interested?"

"Oh, yes, sir!" Jeffrey said.

"Well, good. I'm goin' to enlarge pretty soon — got to get better quarters to accommodate the trade. If you could put in a couple hundred, tell your folks I'm in a position to guarantee six per cent."

"Put it in — in this business?" Jeffrey asked.

"In *our* business," Beck said, and winked.

Jeffrey flushed and gasped. "Thank you," he mumbled.

"Well," said Beck, "it'd make you a sort of a secret pardner, wouldn't it? Think it over. Tell your folks."

And at noon, as Jeffrey left the office, Beck overtook him and walked with him to the corner, and returned to the matter as it had become more and more nearly possible. "Yes, such an arrangement'd cinch your job — in a way of speaking." He smiled kindly, parted from his employee absently.

Jeffrey bore home these tidings, which he had no idea how to treat. He was of the general impression that any one who had two hundred dollars need never work any more.

Mis' Hellie listened, kindled.

"Say," she said, "the insurance is here any day now. I could clap the thousand in the bank, and invest the two hundred that way, nice as a mice. Six per cent — why, I'll only get thirty dollars on the thousand, and I'd get twelve on just the two hundred — my-O! And then, if it'd help you—" None of this was clear to Jeffrey, but he was thrilled by the possibility of the act.

"He said," Jeffrey explained, "that it'd make me a sort of member of the firm. Secret, you know."

"Sure!" said Mis' Hellie. "And six per cent."

These being the only aspects of the matter which presented themselves to her, she duly appeared before Beck, following the arrival of Hellie's twelve hundred dollars' insurance, and gave two hundred into the keeping of this bland and casual man.

"It's a small matter," said he airily, "but you're making no mistake, Mrs. Copper. And that adopted son of yours is born *and* cut for the dyeing business. Already I can see that. . . ."

When she had left him: "He's a complete gentleman," Mis' Hellie declared of Beck.

Of Arthur Hoey's hints about a darker Beck, Jeffrey had said nothing. That Little Platt's desire had been to warn Jeffrey of the same thing was clear, as the days passed. Jeffrey had not been at the dye works a fortnight when he and Little Platt hurried Beck into the back room away from some innocent customers who were uncertain how to treat with the jocund gentleman, who insisted on singing instead of showing them samples of color for dyeing gray lady's cloth.

Jeffrey collected and delivered for the dyeing establishment, when there was anything to collect and deliver; and he filled out slips in the office, had a gradual hand in the tenuous bookkeeping of Beck, went for the mail, waited on customers, cashed occasional checks at the bank. On the day on which Mis' Hellie brought her two hundred, Beck permitted Jeffrey to draw a check for five dollars and to sign "Beck Dye House, per J.P."

"Must learn all sides of the business, pardner," said Beck, and winked in secret, Little Platt being present.

Jeffrey and Little Platt struck up a friendship, and Jeffrey grew in the surprising knowledge that here was a chap with whom the fellows had nothing to do, who was still a good deal of a chap and even almost a "regular fellow" — a term whose flattering import shows something of the depths of uniformity to which sheer pressure tends to reduce. Other standards were changing for Jeffrey; his dream of being a great artist had modified. Just now he was far more interested in filling his savings bank — a pink fish, with "Thrift" on its tail.

In the course of the winter came the word from Pitt.

Jeffrey had been for some time at the Dye house when Mis' Hellie's special delivery letter reached its destination far up the Yukon. She received one letter written before Pitt had her news. Like those earlier, this letter said not a word about a return to Burage, and mentioned no plans at all. "This is a fine country," Pitt wrote, "but not to stay in. I enclose draft."

"You know," Mis' Hellie said with candor, "he just makes me mad. What can be keeping him like this? I can't think of enough things."

Pitt's reply to her letter about Hellie put his sympathy in few words, but plainly he had labored over these. That the letter had been copied was betrayed by the repetitions of words and even lines. He went on:

Now about Jeffrey, if he wants to leave school and help you some, he best do it. As soon as I come home he's going to get the best there is in the way of school, and a year or so now won't hurt him. I figger on about a year more here, that's what I figger on now. The fact is, the thing I been waiting for is right here now. We got every chance of big money. I didn't intend to tell you yet but think best so's you'll know. A fellow and me have got two claims side and side that you can't beat. It's a sure thing this time and I'm right down lucky to be in on it I tell you. So no more now. Looks like more snow today, had quite a blizzard yesterday. . . .

and so on, with the usual exhaustive treatment of the Alaskan temperatures.

"Well," said Mis' Hellie, "I thought mebbe that little man had gone and picked himself out another wife, someway, and didn't like to show his face. But instead o' that, it looks like he'd had some luck at last."

5

The tremendous life of the little town went on. Gas appeared. Daughters working in the city were not told, and when they came home for a holiday, they walked from the "depot," entered the sitting-room, were puzzled for a moment by the triumphant glances of the rest of the family, and finally looked upward and saw the high burners, both lighted for the occasion and one a Welsbach. This house was momentous, and the touching delight of the family did honor to an occasion taking its place in a long line of advance. In this hour the pioneer, the hewer of trees, man himself in his discovery of fire were very near. But the daughter from the city merely had supper, unpacked her little gifts from her suitcase, and the gas was turned out; and all as quietly as if here were nothing notable.

City water was acquired, and on summer evening you no longer heard the rhythmic sweep of a whetstone sharpening a blade, or knew of somebody's yellow rose bush cut down by accident. Lawns became green and tended. Here and there remained a wire fence whose owner resisted the nagging advances of the women of his household, seeking to have the fence removed "like other folks." But fences in general had remained for fifteen years after cattle had ceased to roam the highways. Nor is that genius memorialized who at last arose and challenged the reason for fences, and boldly took down his own. But there must have been many who said: "Now, what in the world . . ."

A ten-cent store arrived, persisted, perished. Mark and Arum tore out the front of their store, and put in windows large enough to hold full length wax figures. The twenty-seventh saloon in Burage was opened, with kittens, puppies and rabbits in the windows. Every one was talking of fireless cookers. Automobiles, little launches on the canal, telephones which no longer need be plugged when there was a thunderstorm — all these came on. Furnaces became general in "the residence part." There was mail delivery. High school graduates went to the state university. ("My land, would you think they could afford it? Sending their children off to school when they live in a little tucked-up house like *that?*") One or two possible geniuses arose in the town — a boy who would do nothing but draw, in spite of all that they could say to him. ("Let him go into the store first and prove there's something to him. And *then* if he gets ahead, his folks might listen.") Lacking a slender area of initiative, he goes into the store and stays there. ("He ought to have made something of himself. Why, he can just draw anything.") And simple joys went on, and simple plans. Hope went out and came again. Triumph, bitterness, the love of God, Burage knew them all. And old Mrs. Slater's complaint was no better.

Always the little town breathed, thought, talked, watched, grew like any being.

After that quarterly letter from Pitt, his year passed in since. Not a word came from the vast north where, to Jeffrey and Mis' Hellie, the figure of Pitt roamed, unsupported by background or known accessory. No letter, no money. That huge whiteness, having wakened for him, might have yawned, might have devoured him, and then slept again.

With her frank preference for tragedy, Mis' Hellie occasionally stated her belief in his death.

"Foolin' around God-forsaken countries never done no good to nobody," she said, in a disregard for her forefathers which is witnessed by many enemies of the untried. "*I* think he's dead in a snowdrift, with another one over him." But this she never said in the presence of Jeffrey, who looked every day for his father's return.

All the boy's stirring passion for romance was not in this mysterious absent father, who had ceased to write. As with many middle-class American boys, his emotional life lagged. This is especially true in the small towns, with their gossipy publicity. But with Jeffrey, his postponement of sex-romance was partly because he was of the elusive breed which ripens slowly, matures late. These are not to be distinguished by the casual witness, and who shall say what they foreshadow? Perhaps some richer hour of the race when scrupulous choice shall become a factor in romantic love. Moreover, Jeffrey's religious and artistic bent in early life had oriented his expectation of romance toward mystery and beauty, and these still occupied him. It is not the richest natures which "fall in love" early. It is those without other sources of magic, who must make magic for themselves, love offering the way. Jeffrey's thought about women consisted of the exquisite and ambiguous word *She*. Of course he waited for her, with faith. Occasionally, in some first flash, he thought that he saw her. But *She* was an experience high, and remote in time, and to appear from outside Burage. . . .Meanwhile, reaching out to lay hold upon its proper food, his desire for romance, for magic, fed upon the thought of the unknown father, in a white, unvisualized North.

His principal approach to imaginative experience was made in those idle hours when he drew upon the backs of things, evolving figures, copying facades, contours of all that he saw. Rarely faces. The aspect of the natural world absorbed him more than did that of his fellows. He thought little about people. He was concerned with appearances in the world of objects, of color, of light. And with his future. In keeping his intention to be a great artist it was true that he made little opportunity for serious work, but then he was always about to find time, and his confidence remained warm. Some of Mis' Hellie's friends learning from her of the boy's hope, took bungling means to encourage him.

One morning Flo Buckstaff appeared at Beck's and asked for Jeffrey. The old inn keeper, known in those parts as a "veteran hotel man," had triumphed over both rheumatism and asthma to bring some tidings.

"Say," said Flo, "there's a picture man to the hotel."

"Selling picture. . . ." Jeffrey comprehended.

"Selling nothing! Making 'em!" Flo cried, as if those who made would never be expected to sell. "I was tellin' him about you—"

"Oh, me!"

"Shut up," said Flo. "I told him you'd come to see him. So you come."

"See him — what for?"

"Why, you little fool, so's to—to—to—well, how should *I* know?" Flo cried. "I should think you'd know, though. He'll be there half past twelve."

Jeffrey did not say that this was his dinner time. He bought a sandwich, and later appeared before the picture man—Jeffrey had all the capacities for sacrifice and endurance, gifts too often relied upon instead of developed.

The picture man, Dartsey, proved to be that which Chicago knows as a "commercial artist" — an originator of advertising illustrations. He was a little, taut, red-haired man, who held his neck stiffly, wore broad cuffs, and spoke with a manner of constituted authority.

"Draw, do you, m—m?" said he, eyebrows high admitting the possibility.

"Not much," Jeffrey said.

Dartsey frowned. "Oh, so you're one of those false modesties, are you?" he commented. At this he was so pleased with himself that his smile appeared good-natured.

"I've never studied," Jeffrey explained, blushing.

Dartsey waved a bluish hand with a rolled gold third finger ring and announced: "Study spoils you."

"It does!" cried Jeffrey, wrenched free of all his old admissions.

"Absolutely. The advertising game isn't looking for highbrows. Life is good enough for us."

Jeffrey was fascinated. He had never heard talk like this. He spent twenty minutes with Dartsey, listening to news of the art world.

"Come down to Chicago and call in on me some time," said Dartsey. "I'll put you wise to this art game."

"Oh, I'd like that!" Jeffrey cried.

"I know the ropes," Dartsey confessed, "and the ropes do the trick."

He gave Jeffrey his card, which the boy took reverently and cherished in a slit in the lining of his coat.

Later he went to Flo Buckstaff and said stiffly:

"I'd never have seen him if it hadn't been for you."

"Thought I didn't know that, didn't ye?" Flo growled; and Jeffrey departed awkwardly.

Of Flo's passionate interest in the lad or of Jeffrey's great gratitude to Flo, there was not a visible trace. Not because of self-control, but because the average Burage emotions never came forth. They either burst forth, or else lie hidden.

But within, new suns rose now for Jeffrey. Chicago and Dartsey! Jeffrey began to plan for the day when both should dawn.

Meanwhile he lived the life of countless of his kind and time. He woke at six in this chamber with sloping ceiling and yellow bed and a washbowl and pitcher with a lady painted on the side. (Rachel's "Holy Grail" was still on a shelf, now with an Indian's head, a stein and a string of rattlers.) Mis' Hellie had breakfast ready, her dark blue gown smelling of griddlecake smoke. Every morning these two said substantially the same thing: Of the plaster which was going to fall presently if something wasn't done to it; of the loose blind which banged in the night; and didn't it beat all how the hens acted about laying. Often they quarreled a bit, having missed each other's meaning and failed in patience, or else having received each other's meaning and failed still more sharply. Mis' Hellie adored Jeffrey, but her own bright comment and analysis creased when she talked with him, and she became merely anxious and admonitory. As for Jeffrey, he bullied her with tenderness, teased her fondly. This attitude between them passed for their show of affection. In any serious expression, he was shamefast. At no time did he give her the respectful attention which he gave to Beck.

Yet by this time, in spite of that respectful attention to Beck, Jeffrey had for him definite contempt, and for his drunkenness, absences, debts, indifference to the straits of his wife who was without credit at grocer's and butcher's. She would bring her little girl, and sit in the shop waiting for Beck to return so that she might ask him for a few cents to buy meat for their dinner, and Beck would send her to ask to have her purchase charged. And when she failed, he would berate her, in the presence of Jeffrey and Little Platt, for failing to charm the butcher.

"That three hundred dollars from Flower and Flower," Beck was always saying to them all, "it's due now—I can't think what's holding them up. Be along any day, and *then*—"

Jeffrey could not leave him because of Mis' Hellie's two hundred dollars, over which the boy felt that he must keep watch. Toward the end of the year, this investment began to reveal its nature.

On Jeffrey's arrival at the Dye House one morning, Little Platt told him that Mr. Beck wanted to go up to the drying room. There Jeffrey found his employer sitting on a broken chair and holding in one hand a black bottle and in the other a white china mug. He had been there, Little Platt confided later, when he opened the shop that morning.

Beck looked up at Jeffrey and spoke with solemnity: "I've had a blow, my boy. I don't mind telling you, it's taken me clean off my feet."

He bade Jeffrey close the door, beckoned him with a show of confidence.

"Not a word. This is strictly between you and I. You and I." He indicated the two persons by a gesture whose impressiveness was modified by indicating himself at "you" and Jeffrey at "I." He continued: "You know that three hundred from Flower and Flower?"

Jeffrey was weary of this three hundred, which had now at length fallen due.

"They've put me off," said Beck heavily. "I don't know what I'm goin' to do. I'm livin' a dog's life."

He regarded his china mug. It was a child's mug, with a blue border and "Forget Me Not" in gold letters. This legend he read and re-read, sighed, drank.

Jeffrey had no idea what to say. He was deeply disgusted by Beck, and yet honored by his confidence.

"They're sure to pay up some time," he said, without knowing anything whatever about it.

"Some time, yes," said Beck, "but I'll tell you straight out what's bothering me. I've got some interest due. Mis' Copper's interest and — and some more. If the Flower and Flower check don't come, I ain't going to be able to meet m' interest. Not *any* of it," he impressively finished.

Jeffrey was startled. Mis' Hellie had been counting on that money, counting with an excluding intentness.

Beck went on: "We'll hope for the best, my boy — you hope, and I'll hope, and you tell her to hope. I'd like," said Beck, with an air of candor, "to pay her. I give you my word I would."

Jeffrey was silent. His bent head and downcast eyes gave him the look of the culprit whom Beck's mournful eyes seemed to be accusing.

"I do think she needs the money," Jeffrey said at length, and turned red with all that this cost him.

"I shouldn't be surprised," said Beck. His manner was flatteringly reciprocal, his tone lavish with intonation. He sighed again. Jeffrey found himself feeling sorry for him, for that wandering, trembling way with his hands, for his whole wretched figure.

"Bad heart," said Beck, lifting the bottle. "Slow pulse. Low vitality. To do my duty to my work, I must stimulate my strength." He absently drank from the bottle itself, set the cup on the floor as being of no more use to him, and combed his black beard with his great fingers. "Singular thing, singular thing," he was murmuring.

"You think," said Jeffrey timidly, "that it may come — so that Mrs. Copper can have her money—"

He dwindled away. He had no idea how to deal with these things.

"I shouldn't like her to lose it," he tried it again, and gave it up. He could no more urge money from Beck than he could express his gratitude to Flo Buckstaff.

Beck looked at him with grave appeal.

"It may be here," he said, "it may be. But I can't raise false hopes, you understand. False hopes, they're—they're—they're immoral."

He made that word to behave like a mass of soft substance, in the act of being pulled out like candy.

"I know," said Jeffrey desperately, "that — she hasn't hardly anything." He was crimson at this confession, and felt a little sick.

It was true that Pitt's failure to send Jeffrey's money had crippled them, even with Jeffrey's small earnings.

Beck rose carefully to his feet.

"I sympathize," he said with gravity. "The money may get here — who can tell? I hope so. You hope so, won't you, son? And you — you tell her to hope so."

When Jeffrey repeated this conversation to Mis' Hellie, she was stupefied. She had heard of losing capital, but it had not occurred to her that interest ever goes unpaid. She sat silent, exhausted, giving all the appearance of having had some vital onslaught. But at intervals she murmured:

"I'm dumb with my fool head."

And then on the Saturday night Beck greeted him at closing time with a smiling face, a lordly manner unimpaired, and no pay envelope.

"Wretched management," said he, "but if the folks expect you to run on air, what can you run on but air? Not a soul of them paid up today. Every bugger of 'em would step in — step in. What business men ain't sick to death of that. Sorry, Jeff, my boy — Monday, at latest—"

"It's all right," said Jeffrey, with that diffident turn of head, that hunted upward look which met the embarrassment of another as readily as it announced his own.

It was, of course, not "all right." Jeffrey wondered what he should say to Mis' Hellie.

"It ain't as if," said Beck, "you and I didn't know that that three hundred was due from Flower and Flower. That covers us — it covers us."

Not Monday, and not all the next week, was there anything for Jeffrey. At noon on the following Saturday Beck took him aside and told him that he should have to ask him to "share his own embarrassment" once more. He hoped this accident — accident was the word — did not inconvenience Jeffrey too much?

Jeffrey, with his smile, said no, no, it didn't matter. Just at first, to assume this magnificent disregard to the incidence of pay pleased him as much as could the pay itself. He left the shop feeling agreeably patronizing. Beck had contrived to make him sure that they two shared the perils of the situation. On the Saturday of third week, he spoke of it as participating in the risks of the business, and referred to that secret partnership of theirs.

At the end of a month of this as Jeffrey was leaving the shop on a night of warm rain, he was aware that Little Platt was hovering on the walk, inobviously waiting for him.

"He hasn't an umbrella," Jeffrey deduced, and offered to share. But Little Platt, turning up his collar and turning down his hat, walked by Jeffrey's side, but out of shelter.

It was a few minutes after six o'clock, and the Burage business world was going home. But Hoey's, the barber shop, the bakery, Tait's billiard hall, and all the twenty-seven saloons remained indifferent to the hour, their guardians standing in doorways, one foot, toe down, heel up, crossed negligently over the other. The west broke, and a shine of pale light made a lovely surface on the cream-brick fronts and lay yellow in the puddles on the cedar blocks. There was the tramp of feet. "Nice little rain," everyone said.

Just before their ways diverged, Little Platt spoke.

"Say," he said, "I wanted to ask you: Had I ought to keep on working without my pay, or hadn't I?"

"Without your pay? Good Lord, haven't you been getting your pay?"

"It's nine weeks now," said Little Platt.

Jeffrey banished the particular meanness of unwillingness to seem to share the predicament of the boy. Perhaps this triumph was solely because of a desire to talk it over.

He grinned. "Same here, for four weeks," he said.

"What do you make it?" Little Platt had an appearance of his own to maintain, it seemed, and drew down his brows like a man of affairs. "What do you make it?"

"I'll be jumped up if I know," Jeffrey said.

They stood by Tait's billiard hall, and consulted. This social center for the youth of the town was under the barber shop. Standing by the iron railing, one might look down through the window tops into the hall itself, see the greet tables, the moving figures, smell a stimulating musty odor. Always in passing there was to be heard the click of the balls and the slipping of the markers. The fascination of the place was still the clandestine. Tait would have been sorry to lose that.

Little Platt stood facing this well of brightness. Suddenly he said: "Look there."

Together they looked down on the nonchalant figure of Beck: A Beck who wore his hat on the back of his head, who smoked, who bent the knee and shouted boisterous approval of a stroke of his own; a carefree Beck, at his pleasures. The man looked like a vulgarized replica of the Phidian Zeus — a Zeus with clustered hair wet beneath a soft felt hat, a column of throat rising above a soiled collar, old clothes worn well on what had been a magnificent frame before the flesh mounted. His motions were quick and pleasant, his face was laughingly intent upon his game, his thick red mouth showed in his beard; and that beard he continually combed with those huge fingers. As he played, there was something terrible in his naked eagerness. One ought not to have been looking.

There was laughter, a relinquishing of cues; one or two left the hall. Little Platt would have moved away, but Jeffrey held him.

"Let's wait," he said.

So they were there when Beck came up the steps. He was with the night clerk at the Halsey House, and Beck was saying:

"In time—in *time* I shall become the champ-een billiard player of the

Northwest."

The clerk left him — some edge and definiteness gone from the man marked him the loser; and Beck confronted Jeffrey and Little Platt.

"Hallo—allo, boys," he tossed at them, lifting his hand and keeping on. "Have a game with me?" he threw back.

"I guess our game with you is a losing one, Mr. Beck," Jeffrey said clearly. He always wondered how he did that.

Beck stopped short, pursed his lips, squinted his eyes, combed his beard with his fingers.

"Been comparin' notes," he said. "Damn it, you kids," he said abruptly, "I don't want to do you! If I could ever get enough ahead, I'd pay you up. On my honor, I would. I think a lot about it — it keeps me awake."

Out of great depths spoke up Little Platt.

"You can bet I think about it," said he.

Beck stared. "Where's your manners?" he inquired, brows lifted. "Expect me to take this up with you Monday. At the shop."

He left them, and lifted a hand to greet some passer.

"He'll never pay any of it," said Little Platt wistfully, "and I don't know what under the devil my mother's going to do."

"Look here," said Jeffrey, "I always keep Five Dollars folded up in my pocket, in case something awful happens. Won't you take it, till he pays up?"

To Jeffrey's embarrassment, he saw the boy's chin tremble.

"If it wasn't for my mother," said Little Platt, "I'd be licked first."

"Here," said Jeffrey.

"Thanks," said Little Platt stiffly. He turned away. He broke into running — to try to find, Jeffrey felt, some grocer whose shop was still open.

Jeffrey thought of the boy's mother, waiting for him. He thought of Mis' Hellie's two hundred dollars and her interest. And his repugnance for Beck filled him.

"If I knew how to get it out of the store, you can bet I'd do it," said Jeffrey Pitt to the universe.

The universe answered merely by the glow of the sky through the bare branches at the street's end and a smell of fresh toast from the home of the family which lived over the barber shop.

At noon one day Jeffrey observed a letter lying at large upon the cloth.

"Whose letter?" he asked.

Mis' Hellie cast it a troubled glance. "Oh, that?" said she. "It's mine."

"Any news.

"That's what I'm afraid of. I haven't opened it."

He had known her to leave a letter unopened for hours in the fear that it might contain bad news.

"It came before I went *down*town," she explained, "but I thought if it was bad news, it'd take all the tuck out of me, and I'd best do my errands and get dinner ready first."

"But why not read it now?"

"Well, if it's anything that is anything, it'll take away my appetite and I best get a square meal."

"It isn't from father, then?"

"No, no. It's from my sister. And," Mis' Hellie leaned forward, fork lifted, "I don't owe her one."

"If it's her writing she can't be dead," Jeffrey hazarded.

"But, she may be coming to visit me," Mis' Hellie said mournfully, "and I just can't afford her."

Finally she did break the seal.

"Oh, my good Scotland," she cried, "that's it. She's coming for a month." She read on. "She says she's going to help buy what we have to eat," she concluded, "and I guess I'll have to let her."

"You can't do that!" Jeffrey cried.

"Then you'll have to tell Beck you can't wait any longer."

"What earthly good'll that do? I have told him."

There had been, in fact, a sharp scene at the Dye House, on the Monday following that encounter with Beck before Tait's. Beck had promised to pay his assistants within the week. The week had passed uneventful. But both boys were chained to their places for fear of losing all hope of justice if they left. Jeffrey's bondage was double because of Mis' Hellie's stake.

"I did tell Mis' Beck," Mis' Hellie now confessed, "and she's promised to find out anything she can. But she hasn't been to tell me, and I don't like to go again."

"Oh," said Jeffrey, "I hope I haven't made you lose that money!" For all his manly desire to "take charge," he looked for a moment like a little boy.

Mis' Hellie went to the china closet and took down the red plush bag. The red plush bag was meet for the definite article, like the Constitution. For thirty years her house money, Hellie's savings, her own savings had been harbored in that bag. It had broken sides, a mended clasp, but it had appointed the thrift, the dreams the denials of three decades. It may have held no more than a hundred dollars at one time in all those years; yet that bag had measured the whole material life of the Coppers, their living, their dress, their travel, their leisure, their gifts. It was a terrible bag.

When she had counted: "Yes," she said, "I'll have to let this month's bills go, till your money comes in. And I haven't let them go once since we were married."

She wept.

Close upon her letter Mrs. Kittredge arrived — Mis' Hellie's sister, the one whom all Burage knew that Hellie had wanted to marry. Et Kittredge had led an easy life, and she was abundant, mild, tender. A possessing magnetism which, as a girl, had drawn men to her, had now brought her to an enveloping presence. She was the sort of woman who, if you had no troubles, would almost cause you to invent some that you might take her comfort.

Jeffrey watched her, and felt a happy pride. Mrs. Kittredge might have been a friend of Miss Arrowsmith's. He looked at Mis' Hellie with a new respect. He put on his "other" suit to wear to work.

As he was leaving the house a day or two after Mrs. Kittredge's arrival, Mis' Hellie beckoned Jeffrey into the pantry.

"You've just got to get something out of Beck," she whispered. "Et wants to have a party."

"Don't whisper. I don't know what I can say to him that I haven't said," Jeffrey returned.

"S—h. Whisper. She says she wants to pay for the party herself, but I just can't let her do it all."

"Well," said Jeffrey loudly, and like man of affairs, "I'll have a talk with him and come to some understanding."

"I tell you," said Mis' Hellie, "I'll invite Mis' Beck to Et's party. She didn't know her, but she won't care. And then I can find out what's what."

"Oh, she doesn't know anything," said Jeffrey. "*Don't* whisper."

"Well, I'm going to try it. What you got your best suit on for?" she demanded abruptly.

"*S-h-h!*" said Jeffrey, and went.

The party Mis' Kittredge was preparing to have at once, as a kind of announcement that she was in town, and open to engagements.

"We can get a livery and drive around in the afternoon," she said, "then we can give the invitations at the door, see everybody for a jiffy, and have a nice drive, same time."

This party was to be for Jeffrey unforgettable, though not on account of the festivity itself.

There were thirty guests. Those who, in Mrs. Kittredge's Burage residence, had naively belonged together, but had since been resolved into strata, were now reassembled. There were, of course, Mis' Monument Miles, Mis' Barber, Mis' True; above these ladies were others, ladies as long in Burage, but with more of tradition; complacent, elderly, Episcopalian. And then the married daughters of many of these, now miraculously social contemporaries: Mrs. Hugh Ames, Mrs. Jack Stubbs, Mrs. George Hudson and Mrs. Malcolm Brewster — who were still the highest stratum of all. There were two or three trying to struggle into his stratum, but there was not enough silver in their quartz to mark them true geological peers. Also there were the Unmarried Middlings, partaking of all these classes, patronized by them all, but belonging to nothing. Fossils. No one could say exactly why, but every one had the label ready — women who, in cities, might even then have been in useful occupations, were, at this period, in the little towns, still awaiting excavation. And usually resisting the sound of pick and spade as not meet for womanly ears.

Here and there sat those women who move in every society and who do not classify, for another reason. Women before whom all these standards fall away — women gentle, still, listening. There are a few in every town. Their emphasis is dissolved, their positiveness shot through with questioning and wonder. They have ceased to vibrate like useful springs; it is almost as if they were making ready for some new birth, not of the flesh. In them is no struggle. They yield, they listen. But these women have never constituted a book. When all beings have attained to such quietude, fiction and drama will disappear. But music, painting, poetry, architecture will persist, for already these do not depend upon conflict. Or we may have a new fiction, a new drama. . . . But with that the guests at Mis' Hellie's party will not be concerned.

There were one or two guests from out of town whose hostesses, on being invited by Mrs. Kittredge, had said: "No, I'm sorry. I won't be able to come. I've got company." And had let the silence fall and had looked unconscious; and had brightened to reply: "Really? *Could* I? She wouldn't be crowding in? Well, I'd just love to and she'd be real pleased, I'm sure. There hasn't been much going on since she came." As these stranger ladies arrived at the party, Mrs. Kittredge conducted them in turn round the entire circle, and during the presentation, everyone kept a respectful silence.

It was the habit of the ladies of Burage to bring to their parties a new piece of work. If it was something never before made or used in the town, this was a distinct ascendancy. If it was carried in a bag, fashioned after a new pattern, this too was a triumph. And then they said: *"Haven't* you seen this before?"

On that day it was Mrs. Jack Stubbs who came with a "novelty" bag of fresh rosy ribbon and blue. And when it had been admired, she drew from it a piece of the new shadow embroidery. Mrs. Stubbs still lived to produce sensations. She had a third:

"Have you heard about the woman in this town who is going to leave her husband? You haven't? Well, I sha'n't say a word. None of us know her very well, but it's horrid, having it happen in the town. It'll all come out in a day or two. . . ."

They all speculated. There had been more than one woman who had suddenly risen, packed clothes and wedding presents and with her children had gone to the train at night, driven by houses oblivious and uncompassionate, houses waking in a day or two to say: "So *that's* what made her look as she did." Who was she now? As if this She were some immemorial figure, her garments forever blown by the wind of that going. Who was she now? Mrs.

Jack Stubbs would not tell.

Down all those years since Barbara had been impressed by her, Mrs. George Hudson had been trying in vain to bring the talk about her to literary levels. When gossip was introduced, she made it a point to sit silent, and then to mention some similar situation in fiction. The rich values of human adjustment among her neighbors disturbed her as unseemly. The betrayed Burage wife always brought her to Amelia Sedley; the forsaken Burage maid to Little Em'ly; and as for the Burage woman who revolted, "Well, there's Nora in the *Doll's House*, by Ibsen," Mrs. Hudson would say. "You remember how her husband took her at her word and *sent* her away."

She said this now, and Mrs. Hugh Ames instantly cried:

"Oh, no, he didn't! Why, don't you know how she comes back?"

The eyes of those who read little consulted the faces of those who were known to "keep up."

"Why, I thought she left for good," said two or three of these.

"Oh, no, indeed she didn't." Mrs. Ames, in her late forties, still bent from the waist as she talked — a waist grown wider, and it may be deeper, but still permitting the plump shoulders to speak from side to side. "Indeed, I saw the *Doll's House*, by Ibsen, played in stock in Chicago. Nora *did* come back at the last. Don't I remember how her husband forgave her, and the little children came in, in their nighties, to be kissed good-night?"

There was silence. "In stock" was a term more or less vague to many, and it seemed to deserve conviction. Mrs. Hudson did not speak for a moment.

"Well," she said, "George Hudson always says I read too fast, and that he knows I must skip. But I usually read the endings. And I certainly would have said that Nora would never be allowed to come back to that man."

"Oh, Mis' Hudson," said Mis' Monument Miles comfortably, "reading as many books as you do, I don't see how you *can* keep track how they all come out."

"That's true," Mrs. Hudson admitted with complacence.

It was terrible to see how little, in these years, they had changed.

Jeffrey came home early to "help with the freezer," and Mis' Hellie met him at the door of the kitchen, where she had spent nearly the whole afternoon:

"Mis' Beck can't be coming or she would have come," Mis' Hellie said sadly. She could juggle her tenses and still keep her meaning in sight.

"Beck hasn't been near the office all day," Jeffrey informed her.

"Maybe it's him that's keeping her home," Mis' Hellie hazarded. "Look here," she said, "why not run up there, Jeffrey, and tell her Mis' Copper wants to know if she got the day wrong? Tell her to come along for some *ice* cream, anyway. I'll save her a big saucer. How'd that be?"

Jeffrey grumbled a bit, in deference to his dignity, and went.

Outside the crisp December day received him, as if he had been a prodigal, recaptured from some area alien to the high, delicate blue and the pouring gold. He drew a great breath, bearing some exquisite perfume of the cold. He threw a pebble into the blue where it disappeared, knew the ecstasy of seeing it re-emerge, and whistled, flatting horribly.

The Becks lived near the bridge, in a little rented house which, as Jeffrey stepped to the low porch, he was extravagantly amazed to find empty. Curtains were down, and walls stared out blankly from a room having bare floor and walls.

To make sure of what he feared, he walked once round the house. A neighbor was picking up a pan of chips. This woman called to him.

"She went last night," she said, and came to the fence, desiring passionately to tell all that she knew. She was in a broken straw hat belonging to some man, she had no front teeth, and she continually rubbed her freckled fingers on her chin. "Yes, sir, Mis' Beck's been getting her things together for days. I see her. I told my men folks something was coming. Seems she'd got everything fixed. 'Bout dark last night the dray backed up and took out everything. I went over and peeked in the window. She's gone, all right. I'd of went before."

Refreshed, the woman went back to her task. In her enjoyment of her recital, there lingered something of the delight of the ancient ballad singers — "thus spake they, say they, tell they the tale." She was touching fingertips with some shadowy ancestor who, over a peat fire, detailed the diversities of an imaginary heroine. To the woman of the broken hat, this flesh and blood heroine imparted the emotion of the creative storyteller. In her hands the incident became a creative work. It would grow.

In the hands of Mrs. Jack Stubbs, too. In Mis' Hellie's parlor, Mis' Hellie told this news and passed about the single fingerbowl, where a geranium floated in the water at which all the guests touched and dipped, as if here were a loving-bowl. There was a chorus of expression. But Mrs. Jack Stubbs sat serene, with lifted chin. She was slightly smiling.

"What did I tell you?" she asked, in five ascending notes, a matronly hand outspread on her matronly breast.

Was it Mrs. Beck whom Mrs. Jack Stubbs had meant? Oh, it was she. . . . Mrs. Beck was the woman who was leaving. . . . Mrs. Stubbs nodded, once, lips tightly compressed, eyelids briefly lowered.

They took this, and tore it. But in them all was something of the innocent storyteller, the ballad-man.

Next morning Jeffrey was early at the shop. Little Platt was already there. The two boys had held a conference the night before, had inspected Beck's empty house, looked in each other's blank faces, and spent a night as sleepless as that of any other financiers on the edge of ruin and darkness. Little Platt's face now looked sharp and waxen.

"I think," he said, "somebody's been in here. I think—"

He glanced toward the desk. Jeffrey went to it, unlocked it, stared at the scattered contents.

"The books are gone!" he cried.

Of the informal bookkeeping of the Beck Cleaning and Dyeing Establishment, there was not a reminder.

"Well," said Little Platt, "now what? Pitt, can they come on to us. . . ."

They talked it over, and arrived at nothing, because they had no precedent, no knowledge. In the end they concluded to go on with the work in hand, which was considerable. In spite of their anxiety, they were young enough to delight in their freedom. As the day wore on, they actually proposed to each other to run the business. Bill collectors arrived and were seated in the front room, where they chatted contentedly. Two small checks were in the mail, and these Jeffrey cashed, as he was accustomed to do only at Beck's direction. But the teller at the bank received him in matter-of-course manner, and Jeffrey came away feeling agreeably his own man. He paid a few dollars on two or three debts, as he had seen Beck do.

At noon Arthur Hoey arrived, and asked for Beck. On being told that Beck's whereabouts were indeterminate, Arthur looked startled.

"Anything else been doing round here?" he inquired.

"Anything *else?*" Jeffrey repeated.

"Well," said Arthur, "my dad's tired of waiting, that's all. And there's more that's tired too. I come over to see the fun."

They were in the back room of the shop. When they returned to the room in front they found it occupied, not to say filled, by a large, gray, elderly person. From this person's unperturbed countenance, Jeffrey and Little Platt turned and stared at each other. It was the sheriff.

"You boys keep out," said this man, "till we see what's what. Somebody from Mark and Arum's is going to be receiver, 'round here."

7

The old postmaster at Burage was named Zeri Wing. He looked like a faded photograph in a very old album. And the one who showed the album would say there was Uncle Zeri Wing, and they would all look at his hair brushed forward and looping out a little above the ears, and at the cross roll of his under lip, and at the scar where the colt kicked him.

Zeri Wing seemed already faded, like that photograph, as he moved about the Post Office, on the morning after the Beck Cleaning and Dyeing

Establishment had been closed by the sheriff. And he suggested not only his own forgotten likeness, but his very grave-stone — a little, thick headstone, it would be, in an obscure corner of the cemetery, almost as far as the creeping tide of the open meadow grasses and the Bouncing Bet: "Here lies Z. Wing" — since tombstone carvers were paid by the letter. Looking at him now you might already hear them saying, on a Sunday afternoon to come:

"He used to have the Post Office, and he had a scar on his forehead where something kicked him. . . ."

How unimportant then would seem the forgotten letters which Z. Wing had distributed to boxes bearing names of those who also would have "gone."

Yet those letters moved through his hands that morning, contemporaneous and important: The marriage, the mumps, the order, the arrival, the loss, the dun, the death — all, all modern and important. Zeri Wing treated all the letters with deference, too, scrutinized the superscriptions as he distributed, and let the entire line outside wait on him while he broke the seal of his own letter about that set of new grates that hadn't come yet. When, ultimately, the delivery window was opened, it was wonderful to see him, without a word spoken, recognize each Burage face presented at the aperture, instantly recall the number and position of its box, and deliver. A highly specialized occupation was this, and beneath the husk of his face went on something still more highly specialized: Sympathy for Mrs. Wegg, whose daughter wrote but never came; for Gene Hackett, whose son never wrote at all; anxiety for Sam Howell, whose wife was at the hospital; pity and hope for Lily Johns, who was still advertising for a job, though Lily had long ago dropped from "Young Lady Desires Position At Once," to "Wanted, a Situation." Zeri Wing was functioning in various fashions there at the window; but to Burage he was only old Zeri Wing, and they would have been astonished to be asked to think about him.

A large, elderly, unperturbed man made his way into the Post Office, accepted as his due some deferential nods and stooped to thrust his face almost into the window. A fat man, with forward-hung head, unchanging expression, little, smooth, hairless hands. He was the sheriff. A man or two in the Post Office wondered if he knew anything of Beck, whose shop he had closed, and whether it was true that Beck had disappeared and taken the books. But the word had hardly found its way about.

Zeri Wing left the window and returned with a bundle of papers and a half dozen letters. These he laid down on the sill, and was at no pains to push them toward the sheriff. This man stood still and ran through the letters, oblivious of the impatience of the line behind him on its way to work, and,

"You got Beck's mail in here?" the sheriff inquired.

Zeri's mind was slow — it did not occur to him that the sheriff was amusing himself by an excess of officiousness in the interval before the appointment of Beck's receiver. Zeri Wing had never thought as briskly as that about anything. Moreover, the misfortunes of Beck were merely rumored. And Zeri Wing answered, without looking at the sheriff:

"You got your mail, ain't you?"

Then he caught sight of Collie Foster, dancing on his toes and singing softly from one corner of his mouth, and retired for Collie's letter.

"Gimme Beck's mail till further orders," said the sheriff, and moved on. He had an air of importance which he must have maintained at the sacrifice of many realities.

"Who said so?" Zeri Wing muttered, bending to the Foster box. "Who said so?"

He brought Collie a pink envelope from Maiden Rock, and winked at him, magnificently. At Maiden Rock Collie had a "girl."

Zeri Wing had hated the sheriff for forty years. Forty years ago, Zeri Wing had been twenty years old and ambitious to get his father away from Chicago, where he was driving a dray and coughing himself to death. When father and son had saved a hundred dollars, Zeri walked up into Wisconsin, "looking for an opening."

The ice was breaking in the little rivers, and Zeri had drawn a pussy willow through his buttonhole and tramped the roads, his rough, warm clothes covering a happy heart. His father was one of those bewildered dwellers in cities who find themselves driving drays, answering bells, collecting fares without the least idea how they came to be there, the least inclination to continue or the faintest notion how to diverge. But his father could wish, and his wish took the form of a little truck-garden, with Millie—Zeri's mother—perpetually feeding perpetually downy chicks. He had seen some hollyhocks on a calendar, and they were in his wish, though he did not know what they were called. Then there was a small sister who pined in the city smoke. Reflecting on the freedom which he was to insure for them all, Zeri had a happy heart.

He had found his truck garden, he had made his bargain, and he was to meet the owner in Burage in the early afternoon, sign the papers, and pay his money down. He went to the place appointed, a farmers' hotel, with a dingy bar and a waiting-room filled with women, all nursing little babies, among crewel-and-cardboard mottoes on white walls. There he sat because he had no money to spend in the bar. Every few minutes he would run to the door, thinking that he had heard the truck gardener enter the bar. And at last the women had grown impatient of the draughts and had told him sharply that doors was doors. So he had slipped without and waited in the street.

The day was raw, and a fine sleet began driving in. Two hours passed. At dusk the truck gardener appeared, and as he walked, he lurched. With him was a man of twenty-five. Now, this man was afterward the sheriff.

These two went into the bar and Zeri followed. The truck gardener ordered drinks and shouted at Zeri that here was somebody who wanted to buy that garden and was willing to pay Fifty Dollars more for it. Zeri had no knowledge of how to treat this. He blurted out the word "promise," and stared down at a glass of something steaming hot and odorous. He was shaking with cold. He drank. And the man who was to be sheriff proposed that they two should match dollars, two out of three, for the chance to buy the truck-garden. They matched. Zeri lost. It was proposed to scratch this outcome, and to match five-dollar bills. Zeri lost. Ten-dollar bills, and Zeri lost. Again, and Zeri lost. Again and again and again. Always his new friend would give him another chance. It was rare sport. Zeri's brain began to laugh. It was rare sport. Even when he went out in the cold again without his one hundred dollars, he was still laughing.

Zeri's father, his coat falling in folds from his humped back, had kept at his work until, one day at the wharves, he blurts a blood-vessel and died on his dray. His mother married a teamster who kicked Zeri out of the house. His mother and little sister had never had either chickens or hollyhocks. And for forty years Zeri had hated the sheriff.

"Who said so?" Zeri said to the sheriff now, and left Beck's mail in its box. Beck had a half dozen letters that morning.

Toward ten o'clock, the old postmaster took up a finely snarled bunch of dark blue string, and went to the doorway for a moment of fresh air. He leaned there in the cold sunshine, his fingers busy. Zeri loved to untangle string and to melt up used sealing wax and to smooth out tin-foil.

Jeffrey Pitt, lounging downtown, made directly for the Beck Cleaning and Dyeing Establishment. As he had expected, the shop was locked, and now on the door a padlock was affixed. He stared at the blank windows, crossed the street and stood staring. It was as if some brisk, intelligent animal had fallen down in its tricks. The defection of Beck was an incident. But the store to fail one! Jeffrey thought of the drying room, the irons, the pressing tables, the vats, and it seemed to him as if their withdrawal had left him dangling. To his surprise he turned away, with a feeling of homesickness.

He looked in at Hoey's, wandered down Cook Street, and caught off his cap when he met Mrs. Malcolm Brewster, who, after all, never looked at him. She was with Mrs. Hugh Ames, and was saying: "Mine was spongy. . . ."

In his confusion at having made an elaborate bow which no one had seen, Jeffrey turned up Wisconsin Street toward his home. He passed the Post Office where, in the doorway, Zeri Wing was fingering a tangle of dark blue string.

"Hi!" said Zeri. "Hain't you comin' for Beck's mail?"

There were six letters. Jeffrey walked on, looking them over. He knew nothing of the ways of a receivership. To him Beck's mail was still his charge. There was Mark and Arum, objecting to the bill for having the counter cloths cleaned. Wadleigh, he wanted the suit of clothes returned which he had written for once before. Miss Hill at the high school desired — she never wanted, she desired — that stage curtain delivered. Two bills — they were unmistakable and had been sent bi-monthly of late, with a yellow slip attached. And there was another letter.

The clean snow of the streets flowed about Jeffrey in a tide when he had opened this letter. It was from Flower and Flower. It contained that for which Beck had so long gone sighing — the firm's check for three hundred dollars.

Jeffrey instantly returned the check to the envelope. He stood uncertain, wheeled, and started slowly back down the street. Zeri Wing still stood in the doorway. Now he was winding the string, and whistling "The Belle of the Mohawk Vale." Curious how a man of that age would hang around in the cold without an overcoat, Jeffrey thought.

Here in this envelope were Mis' Hellie's two hundred dollars. The other hundred would not cover his salary and Little Platt's salary, unpaid. The check was made out to the House. A dozen times Jeffrey had cashed checks for the House. . . . Somebody'd get his neck broken if somebody didn't sprinkle sand on that ice in front of Tait's door. It was there that Minnie Arkwright had broken her wrist. No, it was on that ice by the wood-yard.

Would there be danger in cashing this check, supposing that they would cash it for him? How could there by any danger, when the money was Mis' Hellie's and Little Platt's and his? But would it be right to cash the check? This query had come second in order, but its answer was more emphatic. The money was Mis' Hellie's and Little Platt's and his — and more money too. He kicked a banana peel under a wagon, leaped a keg which they were rolling across the walk. But someone punched him lovingly in the back before he realized that Bennie Bierce had been shouting at him. Automatically he hit back at Bennie Bierce, and then entered the bank.

In a hand whose letters always staggered a bit, like the figures in the border of an Oriental rug, Jeffrey endorsed the check for the House.

He pushed it under the grating. And, desiring passionately to seem at ease, he set his front teeth together and drummed upon them with his fingertips. Meanwhile, he examined minutely a calendar showing a horse with his nose in some sugar extended to him by a young woman, standing in a cerise opera cloak in the sun.

The young man at the teller's window was engaged with a little mirror, in trying to run down an eyelash which had gone astray. Reluctantly he laid down the little mirror, and took up the check. Jeffrey felt suffocated when he saw the teller begin counting out the money. The teller did count it out, methodically and without comment, but keeping one eye shut, on account of the eyelash. This young man had heard nothing about Beck's contretemps of the evening before. He knew that Beck was shaky, but as the bank had always refused to loan Beck anything, Beck's shakiness was nothing to the teller. The check was faultless, he was accustomed to Jeffrey who had endorsed as usual for the House, per his own name.

The bills were pushed toward Jeffrey. He seized them, forced himself to seem to count them. He longed intolerably to duck and run for it. Instead, forced by who shall say what far-flung protective cunning, he looked up at the teller with a smile.

"Most money I ever had hold of," said Jeffrey ingenuously.

"Me too," said the teller, and good-naturedly grinned and went on in his pursuit of the eyelash.

Jeffrey slipped upstairs to his room. In the dining room below he could hear Mis' Hellie speaking to an accompaniment of clinking. She and Mrs. Kittredge were cleaning the silver. Their talk came up to him as he counted the money. Mrs. Kittredge was relating:

"And I know that to be a fact," she said firmly in some conclusion, "because there has to be a judge in these cases. And *this* judge happened to have a wife. And it was her told me."

"That's as straight as angels," Mis' Hellie accepted it. "My, my, what folks are."

A judge of what, Jeffrey wondered. A *judge.* . . .

"What became of Mate Riley?" Mrs. Kittredge demanded, in one of those intoxicated irrelevancies with which reunions abound.

"She's a old maid," her sister informed her, rising inflection.

"What became of Hal Buck, that was so in love with her?"

"Oh, he's in business in Seattle — he's a habber-dabber, or whatever it is they call it. Say, do you know anything about Joey? Joey Hardlock?"

"He's in business. Where's that Carrie Cox he used to be engaged to?"

"She's married." (Rising inflection.)

"And her sister — the pretty one — Jule. Where's she?"

"She's a old maid." (Rising inflection.)

Economic tidings of the men. Of women, the nuptial news. . . . Surely, surely it was all right, or the teller wouldn't have paid him the money. He had relied entirely upon the teller, he reminded himself. But then why hadn't he asked the teller, told him the whole thing. . . .

He knew why. Emerging now from its place where it had never really been formulated in thought at all, rose the simple fact of the other creditors. Well, but this was his good luck, that was all. Everybody knew there
was luck. What else could he have done with the money? If he gave it to the
sheriff — a phrase which he had heard somewhere came to him for comfort:
"Throw it into the courts and it's good-by anyway. The lawyers get it all then."
No, sir. He was within his rights. It was luck. Everybody took advantage of
luck. He went through it again.

"What!" Mrs. Kittredge's voice swelled. "She? Why, I thought she
was a old maid, sure. She was cut out for one."

"I thought so too," Mis' Hellie said. "I guess at first them she wanted
wouldn't have her, and them that wanted her the devil wouldn't have. But
after a while she hit it mejum."

"I always *intended* to be a old maid myself," Mrs. Kittredge owned.
She diffused a flavor of "There must have been something about me—"

Jeffrey was thinking: "What if I go down and tell them the whole
thing?"

He felt not so much in need of advice as under the bursting necessity
to brag to someone. He dropped down the stairs headlong, as was his custom, and fell upon the room.

"Look here," he said, "I want to ask you about a thing."

They looked at him, work suspended. He came and leaned over a
chair-back, and laughed nervously.

"Well," he said, "everybody seems to think we've heard the last of Beck
we'll ever hear."

"Won't he be made to pay?" Mis' Hellie cried. "The sheriff'll make
him pay, won't he?"

"I don't think," said Jeffrey judicially, "I don't think he's got a sou."

He had no idea how much a sou might be.

"Ain't that just terrible?" Mis' Hellie demanded, her woe expressed
in a curious system of dimples appearing in her forehead in moments of stress.

"Well, look here," said Jeffrey, "there's a chap owes Beck three hundred dollars. If I get a-hold of that, couldn't I — couldn't we — keep it?"

"Yes. You get a-hold of it!" Mis' Hellie jeered, and picked up the silver
polish.

"I've got it now!" cried Jeffrey. "I've got it up there in my room."

"My good Scotland!" Mis' Hellie cried.

Jeffrey leaped up the stairs, and the women followed. He threw back
the covers, and showed it where he had thrust it — greenbacks, lying on the
blue-and-white ticking.

Mis' Hellie's eagerness was indecent as she cried:

"How'd you get it? How'd you get it?"

He told. And she relaxed and she began to beam.

"Keep it?" she cried shrilly. "Well, I should think you can keep it. Didn't the bank pay it to you?"

He frowned, pressed his lips, looked out the window, hand on hip; wagged his head as if of course he had aspects to consider of which women could know nothing.

"There's other creditors," said he.

"But they didn't get the check!" Mis' Hellie cried.

No, he admitted it; they didn't.

"If they had, they'd have kept it fast enough."

Jeffrey was silent. These, after all, had been his own processes.

Mrs. Kittredge now spoke, and on her lovely, maternal face was a look of shrewdness.

"Of course it's *right*," she affirmed. "But if the sheriff finds out, what then?"

"He won't find it out!" cried Mis' Hellie.

"But this Beck — he's sure to try to collect his money, and he'll find it's paid," her sister pointed out.

"Then he'll think the sheriff got it. And the last man he'll want to see'll be the sheriff. Why, he's dodging him!"

Jeffrey listened. Again these had been his processes.

"Why," cried Mis' Hellie, "how can anybody think it ain't right — that I should have my money and Jeffrey his pay? Of course it's right. I'm so glad I could cry!"

Jeffrey's heart grew warm when he saw her tears shine. She had put the money in the business to help him on. She must have it back. And Little Platt, with his anxious mother—what fun it was going to be to share that other hundred with Little Platt, even though Beck still owed them uncollectable sums. Here was Mrs. Kittredge, of experience, of knowledge of how other people did things; and she thought that his action was right. Of course it was right! Jeffrey's spirits lifted, and he smiled in the homely, reassuring faces.

He went into the street, with Little Platt's sixty dollars in pocket.

As soon as he was alone, his excitement now somewhat stilled, he was aware of a kind of physical nausea. As if he had gone into cold water up to the pit of his stomach. He was breathing hard, and his head was in confusion. A curious confusion. Conflict, pressure, urgency, a violent imperative already full-fledged within when he became conscious that it was there at all. Not a voice now, but voices, clamoring throughout his flesh, as if the cells were organs of intercourse. Voices which mounted and strove with his reason, which had settled it that all had been well done. It had been long since he had received that word with any clearness — the warning against Beck had been the last sharp inhibition, and this he had disregarded.

He had never yet been offered guidance like this which spoke to him now. It was the supreme vocative, importunate, crying the critical, the instant.

Jeffrey stood still in the snow, and his reason turned and looked at him. Take away Mis' Hellie's two hundred dollars now? Turn back from Little Platt?

"If it's wrong, I'll take whatever's coming to me," he said, and felt a kind of heroism, as if her were laying himself upon an altar.

Over his dinner in his kitchen, Zeri Wing was relating to his wife how he had got the best of that smart sheriff. But his wife was very deaf, and by the time that he had made her understand, he was querulous, and the zest had gone from his narrative. Also, his potatoes had cooled. He ate, looking sullenly out the window, and his scar showed red where the colt had kicked him. And Burage would have been astonished to be asked to think about him.

C hicago and Dartsey. Jeffrey now thought about both with passion.
He collected his sketches, pored over them. But instead of working at them, he sat idle and speculated on all that Chicago held for him. These plans were a kind of refuge, and kept his mind form the old round of argument about the check.

"You won't have to be there long," Mis' Hellie told him. "You can just show what you've made, and then this Mr. What's Name can probably help you to get some orders, and you can set home here and do them."

Mis' Hellie mused on such a life, devoted to art.

"And I can get a good hot dinner and be sure you won't keep it waiting."

Art did have its points, in her estimate, though she doubted anyone actually living by it.

"Likely folks piece out art with odd jobs, you'll find," she said shrewdly.

"I don't imagine," said Jeffrey, drawing down his brows, "I don't imagine I'll get any orders right away." This opinion gave him an agreeable sense of his own conservatism, not to say of his modesty.

"Well, I don't know," said Mis' Hellie brightly, "there's an awful lot of pictures on folks's walls, when you come to think 'em over. Somebody must paint 'em." And added as an afterthought: "Though of course the most are made by machinery."

"My line's going to be commercial art, though," Jeffrey reminded her.

"Yes, and I'm glad of it," Mis' Hellie replied. "I don't know what it is, but it sounds safer than just *art.*" That's a little stubbed name for any business that *is* a business."

Yet from day to day he delayed his going. He had the money for the journey, safe in that pink fish — enough, he thought, "to look about Chicago." And still he delayed the time of going. He even took a temporary position with Orcutt and Miles, stone cutters, at the "Monument Works."

"My land," Mis' Hellie cried sharply. "Don't you *want* to be a great artist?"

"Oh, there's time enough," Jeffrey said.

He had none of the urge with which he had attached that first work of his at Beck's. It was as if the air of his world were easy to penetrate with volitions toward business, and hard to press aside for the less abstract pursuits. Or it was as if old channels in his flesh knew how to lead to market, but were not yet worn deep enough for the stronger currents, rushing on to unknown seas, bearing unknown barques.

One day he was passing the Halsey House, where a group of men stood on the veranda. They were listening to the voice of one of their number who was talking with that unction which proved him either a leader or a successful monopolist. At first it was not evident which he might be, and therefore whether he was listened to from choice or from constraint. But he had a bawling tone.

He was interrupted, whoever he was, by a little man at the edge of things, who was gratified to make an opening to participate. This man cried:

"There's young Pitt that you was asking for!"

They made way for the talker — a man with a rolling manner to match his rolling voice.

"It's Stebe Golithar," they said to Jeffrey. "Home from the Klondyke."

Stebe Golithar's features were molded in rolls, wrinkled rolls; he was near-sighted, and with all these features he squinted.

"You young Pitt?" he wished it verified.

"Yes, sir," said Jeffrey, his face flushing, the hunted, upward look of him kindling with excitement.

"Well, say! I see your father up in Nome."

"My father! When?"

Stebe proceeded in his own way. "He had a leetle pup under one arm. Somethin' had stepped on it, and he was takin' it somewheres."

"When was that?" Jeffrey cried.

Stebe Golithar computed. By various private milestones he advanced, counting toward the time. At last he had it:

"'Bout five months ago. I wouldn't swear to it. Might have been six. Might have been four and a half. . . ."

"Was he well?"

"Well? Hell! You don't get sick in the Klondyke. You either stay on your pegs, or else you die. They ain't no half way."

The men laughed immoderately. Golithar had never been regarded as of great account in Burage, but sixteen years and more of absence, in California and Alaska, had mysteriously multiplied him. And perhaps it had.

"Yes," Stebe went on, with the air of the traveler, narrating, "he was same as all the rest of us. Goin' to strike it rich next minute or two. I never heard he done it. Us, either."

Again the men laughed enjoyably. They, too, had not "struck it rich, either," and they were indefinably pleased to hear that nobody else had done more than they.

"But say!" Golithar cried. "Your dad hit it for home before me. I thought mebbe he'd be here now, sitting round with his feet up."

Golithar scanned the streets, as if Pitt might be seated anywhere about.

"He's coming soon," Jeffrey said carelessly. "We've been expecting to hear, any time now."

"How long's it been since he was here?" Golithar asked.

"Since I was a kid," Jeffrey replied, and tried to move on.

Stebe Golithar himself had been gone from Burage since Jeffrey was a baby.

"Let's see," said he now, "what become of your mother? She living?"

On the knot of men a silence fell, and the silence pierced the boy. He stood on the lowest step, and looked up at them. He was defenseless before their pity.

Flo Buckstaff made an audible effort to shut up the returned traveler. He offered him a cigar, trying to talk about the brand; and Golithar accepted it, and continued:

"Lives here, does she?"

"No. We don't know — where," said Jeffrey.

There they stood on that street down which a dray had once come faring, bearing an empty baby carriage at which the bystanders had already laughed and mocked.

But the boy's head was lifted. He was meeting the eyes of the men. His face was burning, but he said:

"Won't you drop into Mrs. Copper's some time and tell us about my father?"

"Why, sure!" said Stebe Golithar, and made everything worse by earnestly adding: "No offense, you understand."

Jeffrey kept on up the street, and he was crying to himself:

"Offense for what? Why did they all keep so still? Why haven't they told me where my mother went?"

It had been Mis' Hellie's policy never to speak to him of anything that had "anything of a tang to it."

The 'bus was rattling through town to the Halsey House. Six or seven passengers looked out indifferently on the soggy street of the quiet town. They saw that group of men, and the boy moving away. This appeared to them as might any group, casually met and idly talking.

Golithar did drop round to Mis' Hellie's, but there proved to be nothing that he could tell. He had seen Pitt, and Pitt was coming home. Had left, as Golithar understood it, just before he himself left. And Pitt looked "good." Further than this, Golithar was as inarticulate as on the day of his birth. Save for that "leetle pup," the movement, background, detail of the scene in which he had met Pitt were not for him. Of all the rest, Golithar thought in flat surfaces, remembered without pictures, was color blind; and even his few words he could not relate to life.

Still, his one fact was dramatic. Pitt had actually started toward home.

At this news Jeffrey was fired. He had never doubted that his father was alive and would sometime come home again. But he was on the way! The fact that he had not written was forgotten. He must have had some good reason — doubtless he was filled with other concerns. This sense of preoccupation with many matters enhanced Jeffrey's respect, and deepened the illusion about his father.

Obscurely Jeffrey felt that he must do something in preparation for this return.

"I'll go to Chicago Monday, I guess," he said to Mis' Hellie that night. (In Burage most journeys are begun on Monday. This "gives you the whole week.")

He stood strewing his sketches about the dining room table, with a boy's uncertain movements at packing up.

"What started you off?" Mis' Hellie asked incautiously.

Jeffrey brought to bear that faint manner of importance which he had lately acquired.

"Well," he said, "I ought to know what I can do before my father gets here."

It was as if the unknown figure in the North had leaned and touched the boy, afar off, kindling him to action.

The Olympian goes east through Burage at six in the morning. "The Olympian," we say, without troubling to add "express" or "limited" to modify the great name. The train comes from the Pacific Coast and indeed, when its fifteen yellow Pullman and baggage and express cars roll into Burage, on time to the minute from the seventy-two hour flight, and the gigantic locomotive stands panting as if it had made the whole distance itself, then "The Olympian" is the only possible title.

If any passenger is awake when the train passes through Burage, he looks languidly on the town without troubling to know its name. As if he were turning the pages of an encyclopedia and came on: "Burage. Pop (1904) 5600," and fluttered over the leaves without even reading about it.

That ruddy line of apples in the Fox House windows, what do these folk know of the orchards in the Caledonia Hills where those apples reddened; or of Montello, where the cantaloupes grew, here displayed on the Eating House sill?

No, if they are awake at all, the passengers sit, showing a curve of sleeve and shoulder, and they read, more absorbed in the figures of their pages than in the live beings on the platform. Yet on that platform is Lot Norman, come with a basket of breakfast for her father in the express car on the Olympian, and she is telling him how the mother seems, who dies of cancer up the hill. And there is Wedge Haring, who was given two hundred dollars back pension three months ago, and is still receiving congratulations. And old Canute Nelson, the baggage man with a wooden leg, would love to show them all the picture of his daughter, singing in the music halls "somewhere." But the passengers do not attend.

For that matter, Burage is oblivious of the Pullmans. Does it ever think that great men and women may be riding there? If Bernhardt and Duse travel from Chicago to the coast, they may ride on the Olympian. Once a special train bearing the Metropolitan Grand Opera Company rolled into the Burage station toward midnight, and the baggage man and the telegraph operator told each other that it was a theatrical troupe; and the town never knew of its presence at all. Plancon, Nordica, the de Reszkes, at our thresholds. Burage is oblivious of the majesty of this train. And though there are those on the platform who remember when the road only ran as far as Watertown, and now it extends to Puget Sound, and though something of the whole triumph of engineering and of transportation is in the Olympian whenever it roars into Burage, yet it is to all merely the 5:55, and they take it to Milwaukee for trivial ends, as if they bestrode a titan to look for sugar plums.

It was to the day coaches that Jeffrey went, with his sketches in an old sample case. The day coaches were hot and crowded, and he could not find a seat beside a window. When he had traversed the coaches, he sat down beside a hatted man, asleep. This man now groaned as if one more burden had been added unto many.

At once the boy was obscurely impressed with the intimacy of American "day-coach" travel. Here he was in a car bearing a hundred others, and nearly all were either extraordinarily tense or indecently relaxed. Many had come through from the coast in these day coaches, and their windows and the cushions were littered with the jetsam of the journey. These slept, or lolled, stared, sunk in lethargy. Irritated by unwonted food and lack of exercise, some were loudly peevish, but most were the patient, good-tempered American crowd, expecting little and suffering long.

Jeffrey was thrilling with the excitement of taking his place among them, of being there alone. For the first time he was abroad in the freedom which is the birthright of the bird and the cub, but is long denied the human child. To be in that train with no enveloping presence, no one to suggest, in any way to modify his movements! If he should elect to alight at the next station, there would be no one to deny him. Here now for the first time, he was his own man and he felt almost dual satisfaction, as if some other were there to felicitate him.

Oconomowoc, Okauchee, Nashotah — all his life the Indian names had been familiar to him, but he had never seen the bodies of these towns, now coming to meet him in the winter darkness. He did not know that it was the dignity of the little places — so faithfully carrying on existence like any one — which moved him. As the light began to open to him the land, he had his first sense of his state — Wisconsin. The errands of the folk in the train seemed trivial beside the fine earnestness of the fields. Deep in their breasts lay their history, the romance of Indian, pioneer, trapper, fur trader; the retreat of the redskins at the gallop of the regulars; the tread of the early woodmen and tillers of the soil. He thought not at all of these, but he felt the schoolboy loyalty which sees its own state better than other states, that provincialism bred by the scarlet lines on maps. He tried to make a song, but when the words came they were nothing. Wisconsin! That was all. Three hundred little lakes lie in his state, and no one ever takes the trouble to say so. Their very names are unknown. The great forest reserves of the north, the Brule, the peninsula, the shores of the two mighty inland seas — he tried to remember all that he knew of this state in whose face he seemed to be looking. He could not remember enough, but he felt his own ego leaping about the more, and resolved into his intention to conquer Chicago.

As he neared the town his mind centered on what they might say to him. He liked to think about this. The burden of Jeffrey's thought concerning the reception of his sketches was: "I bet they'll be surprised." In the shell of a great humility and indifference, Jeffrey carried an egoism which was usually stirring. This was no certainty of greatness. It was a mush of impressions that everything with him would be all right. This is the unfounded assurance of youth, as it is the last spiritual fruit of old wise men.

The address which Dartsey had given him was that of an obscure printer and engraver on North Clark Street. When Jeffrey presented himself, Dartsey was at lunch. Before a dirty window Jeffrey waited, his sample case against his legs. And he looked on Chicago.

He was appalled. His cosmic egoism shriveled. Already — and this was more serious — his self-respect was gone because he had been obliged so many times to ask his direction, a necessity at variance with the secret assurance of any man. So it was like this! He thought in terror of presenting his sketches. He became poor-spirited, he felt as he had felt when he had first unsuccessfully sought work in Burage. Burage had not known that he existed.

But this place seemed organized to crush him. A legless man went by, walking on his hands. Everything was possible.

When Dartsey entered the hot and inky room, Jeffrey turned to him with the eyes of a friend. Here was something which would recognize him.

Dartsey did recognize him — after Jeffrey had told him who he was. But he recognized him casually, as some will say at the telephone "Yes?" and wait for the message, instead of the expectant "Yes!" — the affirmation for which, in some form, all the world perpetually waits.

"Sure," said Dartsey, who was not quite so dapper as in his Burage descent, showed less white cuff, in fact had dirty hands. "I'll take you to Sweeney and you can show your stuff. Can you wait a minute or two, though?"

"Why, certainly!" Jeffrey replied warmly. He had the violent emphasis of the provincial who is in addition ill-at-ease.

He followed Dartsey up some steps, and was left in an office built like a box and hanging on the side of the wall. The place was littered with proofs of advertisements, every one bearing a pen-and-ink sketch — roses, lilies, greyhounds, staircases, palms, ballet girls of 1890, fruit, kittens, cornucopias.

"Well!" said Jeffrey to himself. When Dartsey reappeared to take him to Sweeney, Jeffrey was at ease. "I've brought some sketches, yes, sir," he said to Sweeney, as one who should say: "And you wait till you see them."

Sweeney was bald, and rectangular to a degree. He yawned unabashed and persistently, so that his mouth was a vast dark oval. He rubbed the bare dome of his head with a hand nearly square. He was a gentleman geometrically contrived, and one might feel certain that his mind ran on a straight line and never met the line of any one else's mind.

Jeffrey spread out all that he had brought, and as he did so he suffered another relapse. They looked so unlike, so utterly unlike the work which he had ranged round the dining room at home.

Sweeney, talking all the time about the office having retrenched and advertising having slumped — Sweeney looked at the sketches with the aid, it might be, of a quill tooth-pick.

Prospect Hill from the Pumping Station; the Fox river at twilight; the Canal, filled with little launches; the new bridge; the Levee. He had meant to show the Prospect Hill sketch last — with the small islands in the river and a sunset sky, for it was his best work; but he anxiously produced it first of all, and looked form Sweeney to Dartsey.

"Look here," said Sweeney, "this ain't any use for advertising, and never could be."

Jeffrey was startled. But they were better than those things about Sweeney's desk which his eyes involuntarily sought.

"You ain't any good for commercial work," Sweeney enlightened him. "You're too heavy — you're too darn' serious. What made you think you was any good for commercial work?"

"I didn't know," said Jeffrey, and dared not look at Dartsey.

"I thought we might see what he had," Dartsey said, negligently. "I didn't know but what . . ."

"He never told me I could do it," Jeffrey hastened to say. "He never saw what I'd done at all."

By this Dartsey was evidently relieved, and looked not grateful but complacent.

"You know you said," Jeffrey reminded him, still defending him, "you only said you'd put me onto the art game here in town. And I thought . . ."

Dartsey blushed.

"Oh, the art game!" he said, "Yes. Sure."

Sweeney interposed. "Lemme advise you," he said. "You trot up Michigan to the Art Institoot. You don't need an introduction. Pike right in."

"Oh. . . ." Jeffrey said, and his eyes went to Dartsey's.

"That's it," said Dartsey. "That's where you want to go. Show 'em your stuff up there. Tell 'em what you want."

"Who—who? . . ." Jeffrey tried to say.

"Oh, you'll find the right folks," Dartsey assured him. "Any of 'em up there. They're all nuts on art."

Sweeney nodded. "That's what you do. You do that," he said. "Did that zinc plate come over for the bicycle folks? . . ."

"Yes, it did," said Dartsey. "So long, kid. You'll find everything you want up there. Call in again."

So the street once more — vehicles, bells, shop windows, signs, motion, haste, intolerable haste, people, people, people. . . . Jeffrey had in his eyes the look of Jeffrey, the little boy, on his way up the school aisle to speak his piece.

Where was the Art Institoot? *That?* Even if he could ever cross the street to it, how could he find courage to enter?

He crossed the street, he entered.

And as he entered, he left someone behind him. Not only that one whom he had been, confident, impudent, casual; but that one whom he had just become, trembling, hopeful, daring to test himself by others. He met the world within those walls, and the tremendous silence took him. He was little, he felt as the little feel.

An artisan and his family had entered just before him. Jeffrey was near them, kept near them with some sense of protection in their presence. For what if any one should speak to him? The squat man had a great nose and huge pores. He walked looking down at the little girl whom he was leading, and she was continually picking up infinitesimal bits of colored paper which she dropped. The mother, a soft woman, pregnant, patient, led a little boy. She looked up at the sculpture with a pathetic line of wide, lifted eyes, up-turned nose, and parted lips.

"What's that? What's that? What's that?" continually demanded the little boy.

"Hush," said his mother.

"But what *is* that?" the boy persisted.

His father shook him by the shoulder.

"Don't you be like that," he admonished him. "How do we know what these things are — say?"

"What do I know about this?" Jeffrey also thought.

For hours he walked about the rooms. He became a chaos. Nothing was as he had supposed. Now he trembled before some beauty, now he was overborne by some great room filled with the unknown. For the thousand questions which beset him he had no answers. All this was overwhelming. He had imagined nothing like this. He heard the speech of cultivated folk in the gallery, he listened, resented, yearned, despaired.

And nothing might rose within him and shook its wings.

Instead, his heart grew icy. He looked, he loved, and he saw for his own feet nothing but the deep. Room after room — would they never cease? He saw nothing objectively. All was seen in relation to his own power to create it, and he saw his power fail even to make its beginnings. He became ill. He smothered.

He fled out into the air. The ugly stones and the gray walls without received him. The bustle and noise offered their reassuring commonplace. The terror and strangeness of the streets were less terrible and strange than those halls which, at a stroke, had reduced him to nothing. He was nothing — he did not exist. His future collapsed before him. Everything went.

His throat was tight, his breath caught within his breast as if he had been sobbing. He ran from the place. He had not spoken with anyone there.

On a side street he came upon a restaurant where were no table, but chairs, having broad arms, ranged round the room. In the window was food, nakedly ticketed with prices. He read the figures, chose, entered.

Among the silent men and boys he took his place, and they all ate with the deadly earnestness of the cheap cafe, where crumbs count. Beside him sat an unshaven man, eating baked beans and a roll. A youth who was mopping the tiles was being scolded by the proprietor. The homely smell of coffee held the air.

The squalid comfort of the place soothed him. But he ate with a sense of haste. He must get his train.

He had no need to choose his course. He was going back to Burage.

To be sure, flowing about him was that old, faint urge, like a wistful voice, inhibiting his intention to return. "Stay, stay, stay!" (It said no more.) He put it aside, in his misery he was but dully conscious of its delicate importunity. He must get back to Burage where, he said, he belonged.

He sat in the Union Station. It was true that he had seen almost nothing of Chicago, but now the city had changed its form. It was no longer the place toward which he had journeyed that morning. It was alien, hostile, incomparably remote.

His mind was quiet, and his attention occupied itself gratefully with the crowd in the station. The dingy upper waiting room was filled with its night folk, some tensely expectant, some settled down to monotonous hours. Men sat, dressed for the exceptional, their hands on market baskets bulging with the unimaginable. Occasionally a red-capped boy came for a woman's bag, and every one thought that she was of a higher estate, since she had the ten cents to spare. A whole family returned from the restaurant, and it was absorbing to figure out how much they must have spent, even if they were careful. A group of Southern Europeans entered, the women hatless, the men with bundles. They sat waiting, so brightly, so expectantly, so buoyed by some hope. But one among them was old, and he was looking down, eating something.

Jeffrey thought the he should like to sketch the old man. Then he remembered. . . .

A little delicate girl now began distributing pieces of paper to every one on Jeffrey's row, and as she did no, and collected, she spoke to some. "How's your sore foot?" she inquired politely of the man with the crutch. "I think you've got a nice, fat baby," she said to a woman. "And oh, the nice kitty-fur!" Every one stopped talking and looked at her, she was so friendly and so grave, and her hair was long and bright. "That's a funny satchel," she said to Jeffrey, staring at his sample case.

"It's full of pictures," he told her, and added: "Would you like to see some?" repenting when it was too late. She climbed on the seat beside him, crying "Oh, yes. Oh, yes."

He showed the little girl his water colors. She looked absorbedly, pointing out the objects that she knew. She caressed a smiling face, patted a sketch of a patient wreck of a horse. He showed her the study of Prospect Hill, with the small island and the sunset sky, and she took it in her arms and hugged it. This was his best picture, for which he had hoped all things. He was grimly pleased that she liked it.

"Do you want to keep it?" he asked.

She cried out, ran with the water-color to her mother, a fleshly woman, with pleasant eyes, who said:

"Yes, pet. Now take it back to the young gen'leman."

"It's mine. It's mine! He says so!"

Jeffrey nodded his awkward confirmation.

"Why, the idea! Well, what did you say to him? Now don't get that paint on your clean dress," the mother said.

Jeffrey fastened the sample case. His smile was sufficiently grim, but his heart was lighter. He was glad to have given away Prospect Hill.

He got his train and in the day-coach he slept, his hands limp and undirected, his lips apart. He looked like a little boy, and yet there he was detached, faring about alone, expected to behave as an identity. He breathed like a child, his hair stood up at the back, his hat fell off.

His career as artist was ended. For he was as absolutely lacking in resilience as a long-plucked string. An earlier generation may have teased some chord, and lo, its looseness lived. Or some energy had been withheld from the boy and here he was without its motion. He was minus persistence as another is minus a musical ear.

9

Jeffrey sat in the lobby of the Halsey House. It was nine at night, and nobody was there save a salesman or two, dozing before the plate-glass window. The lobby of his old hotel was a pleasant place. The presiding taste had selected for the walls pictures of that which the locality could offer in beauty and interest—the Dells of the Wisconsin, Devil's Lake, the natural bridge, and photographs of the animals in the circus which wintered near. There were a hanging fern and a singing canary, and Flo Buckstaff had a bull-dog which slept on a braided rug, a rug which bore a homely, farmstead look.

Flo Buckstaff himself, rheumatic, asthmatic and bankrupt, was keeping the place open somehow until somebody wanted to "buy the location" and he seemed, on the whole, rather relieved not to be badgered by the hope of making money. All that was done with. Now he was the host only, remembering every good story that ever he had heard; and if he told one to a guest twice, that merely proved that the guest was worth it, and felt flattered.

Through the open door at the back of the desk, Jeffrey could see Flo moving about the bar, and now Flo beckoned to him. The puffy little man was grave and goblin-eyed.

"I was just-a-thinkin'," he said, "seeing you set there — about the night your pa first come here."

Jeffrey looked at him with attention.

"He come down stairs there," said Flo, pointing, "and out onto the stoop, were I was setting, trying to cool off. He begun askin' me questions. He talked along, and I never once see till after*wards* where he was driving at. After*wards* I rec'lected how he'd kep' asking and kep' asking about who lived in the house at the top of the high steps. Twenty-year ago," said Flo, "and him not above ten year older than you must be now."

Flo sat down at a table in the empty bar, and as he talked, he polished with his elbow, at the oil-cloth.

"The day they was married, he come a-bursting in here for his valise,

and the rig waited out in front, with the young folks a-playin' Ned. I rode
down to the depot on the step." He paused, remembered the dray with the
cook-stove and the baby-carriage, and said no more of that day. But as he
polished, he looked down and chuckled. It seemed very funny to this man
that there had been a baby-carriage on that dray, and here now was this tall
lad — here he was.

"Mr. Buckstaff," said Jeffrey, "was my father honest?"

Flo turned a fat, startled face.

"Who?" he said. "Your father? Bless you, yes. I never heard a word
against *his* character."

The emphasis caught the boy. He flushed. He glanced over-shoulder at the sleeping salesman or two in the lobby. But one was awake and was
lifting his hat and laughing at two Burage girls, strolling by.

"Do you know why she went?" Jeffrey asked low.

Flo answered without lifting his eyes from the table top which he
polished: No, he didn't know.

Jeffrey brought out his next question.

"Did—she go alone?"

"Oh, like enough, like enough," said Flo, and made of his emphasis
the affirmation which his words themselves did not carry. He chattered on,
much as he had chattered to Pitt, on the steps of the Halsey House. Flo had
seen Pitt racing through the town on the day of Jeffrey's birth; but this the
innkeeper had long forgotten.

Jeffrey pondered and harked back. "Did—did you ever hear of anything dishonest that any of—of my folks did?" he abruptly asked.

Flo considered this impartially.

"Never," he said. "Never. Lemuel Ellsworth run through with what
he had, like a deer — and your grandfather, young Lem, was left with next to
nothing. But he was dead honest — just as honest when he was alive as he
was dead. Paid as he went. Debts worried the life out of him. Oh, they was
all honest." He stressed it, trying to make up for anything that he had left
unpraised in Barbara.

"Many's the time," said Flo dreamily, "that Lemuel Ellsworth has
stood here drinking at this bar. No, that was the old one. But it was in this
room. Why, say!" cried Flo. "And your father calcimined this bar. Sure he
did. They ain't ever been a coat on it since."

Jeffrey looked at those walls. A stenciled border of green leaves showed
dim. His father had set them there. . . .

A voice shouted for Flo, and Jeffrey sat alone in the empty room.
Honest . . . all honest. Every one of them. Decent people, trying to get along.
All save his mother — and him. They two, among so many.

Yes, but he too was honest! That money of Beck's was his and Little
Platt's and Mis' Hellie's. He frowned at his paradox.

Decent people, trying to get along. . . . And his dream of being a great artist and even his hope of helping Mis' Hellie were gone. And what work was he to do now? His one attempt had failed him. He was prepared for nothing. He felt naked and unsupported. The crisis had eluded him, because he thought that it was something else. In art he was a failure. And he was "not even" honest. Then he began again to justify himself.

Flo came back from the lobby. He was fastening up a sleeve, his look intent on his lifted arm.

"Well, sir," Flo was saying, "I don't get *rested* between kicking myself for being a darn fool. . . ."

Jeffrey laughed hilariously. Of course! Everybody made mistakes. What of it? The door opened.

"Thunder," said somebody. "If it ain't old Pittsie, drinking himself blind."

There was Bennie Bierce. Benjamin Bierce now, working in a Chicago bicycle factory, wearing improbable clothes, mentioning his superior salary, hinting his superior information. He set his hands upon his sides, well above his waist, let his cigarette droop from his lips, and looked down at Jeffrey.

"Come and have a drink," he said.

They sat together at the table which Flo had so painstakingly polished. "Well, you old muff," he began, with a rolling manner of ease, and explained that he had been under the impression that Jeffrey had reformed.

"Not me," said Jeffrey proudly.

"Regular devil, ain't you?" said Bennie, and roared.

Jeffrey colored. It was true that he was not a devil, and that whenever he aped one, he could deceive nobody.

"You wait till you hear," Jeffrey darkly said.

Thereafter he talked mysteriously, intimating his sorrows, luxuriating in having something to brag about to Bennie.

"Come off," said Bennie, in mighty patronage. "I don't know what you're up against. But a fellow works because he has to, and one job's as bad as another. And as for girls, well, there's slews of girls around."

"That's a lie," said Jeffrey generically. But when Bennie laughed at him, he laughed too.

They went out in the street together.

At intervals during that night, Jeffrey was detached from his operations and sufficiently objectified. He realized, for example, that he had not the least interest in what he was doing. He wondered why he was doing it at all. He concluded that it was because Bennie so much desired to him that he should drink and be merry. Moreover, Bennie's good fellowship was a refuge.

An immense carelessness of the future overtook him. Some old sense of restraint fell away, and he perceived that he had been burdened by something which did not exist. How could he have thought that he was wrong about that check? He told Bennie about it, and Bennie shouted. "Smooth? Well, rather." Jeffrey felt himself a fine fellow. And that art business. Jeffrey told Bennie about that, and Bennie said, What! He hadn't meant to go there among those muffs? And starve? If he wanted to come to Chicago he ought to try for an opening in the bicycle business. There was a future, now!

Jeffrey perceived that the world was a better place that he had imagined. He understood everything.

Hours later, lying clothed upon his bed, Jeffrey was struck by the appearance of something on his wall, and it shining. He fixed it, tried passionately to remember what was there, to divine what this might be.

It was Rachel's cup of silver, which he had been wont to call the Holy Grail.

It shone upon him, and he could not name it.

He fell asleep, in a child's fear of that shining.

When he woke, the sun was surging within the room and cold air poured in at the window. In that blinding light Mis' Hellie stood beside his bed, and in her hand a letter.

She had been looking at him for a long time, and her eyes were filled with tears.

"You'd better get up," she said only. "Your father — he'll be here to-night."

Father and Son

1

Jeffrey had thought of his father as big and burly, as all boys think of absent fathers. There was no picture of him — it had probably never occurred to anyone to want Pitt's photograph. Jeffrey's recollection of his father was indeterminate, but it was with that big and burly image that Jeffrey went to the Burage station to meet the Six-ten "Through." Lest some one should ask him what he was doing there at the station, he strolled down to the baggage room where Canute Nelson, the baggage man with a wooden leg, wrote in a wide book which in summer he rested on top of his stove. This stove looked like the small-station and switchmen's stoves the world over, and they must mint them in the clouds and drop them in the spots predestined for them, for no human eye ever falls on them, native, in a shop.

Old Canute greeted Jeffrey and went on writing, beginning to swear aloud contentedly at the Burage dray-man who was not present. Old Canute perpetually shut both eyes to keep them from pipe smoke, so that it was a miracle that anybody's trunk was ever checked to its destination.

"What you up here for?" he demanded.

Startled, Jeffrey blurted out his surprising truth.

"Huh?" said old Canute. "Go on. Your pa? Go on!"

On hearing that he was probably coming to live in Burage now, old Canute took his pipe from his mouth, whirled, and shook the pipe at the doorway of his vile little den.

"Right there," said this man, "right there I stood and see your pa and ma start out on their weddin' trip. Say! This hull platform was full of young folks, racin' and shoutin'. They t'run rice and swarmed onto the train, and raised hell everlastin'. And down there stood the Granger carriage that they'd come in, horses with plaited paper on their ears. An' back there was the dray full o' truck the young folks had loaded up to play Ned — say! If it hain't like yesterday."

"The Granger carriage," said Jeffrey. "Is that what you said?"

"Why, sure," said Canute, with wanton emphasis. "You know your pa and ma was married to the Grangers'. Everybody remembers that."

Jeffrey hesitated between his pride and his desire to know.

"Canute," he said, "did my mother *work* at the Grangers'?"

"Work? Work out? Lord, no! Wan't her grandpa Lemuel Ellsworth?" He elaborated upon the wedding. "My wife was helpin' in the kitchen," he added with pride. "Huh!" he shouted, and fell on a pink man who stood in the doorway, rubbing his nose with the back on his hand. The pink man was the dray-man.

Jeffrey went out on the platform, and stared down the track. Thus early and thus remote from the world, its standards had crept upon the lad and claimed him. He was glowing at the knowledge of that wedding — at Miss Arrowsmith's! Why had no one ever told him? That visioned figure of his father (big and burly) took on still more romance.

Tillie Emerton, home from Teachers' Convention. Lena Sholes, back from her weekly visit to her little branch milliner store down the line. Rob Riordon, traveling man, "making" Burage as usual. Other traveling men, accepting invitations to the open buses in the raw wind. Among these men no great, burly figure, such as Jeffrey sought.

Among these men a little man of forty-seven or eight, with evident ankles, a light coat which seemed to blow about in no relation to him, and a hat a bit too large. He carried a huge valise and his long wrist showed, and he leaned far sidewise with his burden. Jeffrey looked over him, scanned the steps of the coaches, saw that all had now descended. The little man was standing still, looking uncertainly about him, with a manner of extreme eagerness. He caught Jeffrey's eye and began to move toward him.

"Is it Jeffrey?" this man asked.

"You're — you're not Mr. Pitt?" was Jeffrey's greeting.

The two walked down the Burage main street. Jeffrey was stupefied. This man? Why, he was no taller than he himself and look at his muscle. . . . Even Jeffrey's unpracticed eyes took in the ways of his clothes. There was probably no man in the world who looked less like a father than Pitt.

As for Pitt, at first he could say nothing. He tried to look at Jeffrey, but Pitt had a sense of being suddenly too near his boy, so that he could not see him at all. He trembled, his breath caught in his throat. His being sang with thankfulness. He tried to express it. And what he said was:

"Say but everything looks fine and natural as day!"

"I suppose it does," Jeffrey replied.

"Only you," Pitt said, and turned his eyes upon the lad. "My—o. It don't seem possible. Little Jeff."

Jeffrey said nothing. His father repeated this at intervals, all down the street, and every time Pitt finished the observation with hearty laughter.

"How's Miss Arrowsmith?" he inquired once.

"She's in Europe," Jeffrey said. But he was thinking of nothing save: "This man my father. . . ."

"Well, well!" Pitt kept saying. "Well, well, *well.*"

He mentioned this Burage name and that, without waiting to hear of any. He began sentences and left them unfinished. He was beside himself with excitement and delight. He took Jeffrey's arm, which the boy then held stiffly down, the hand occasionally trying to get back to its pocket. "Little Jeff." What if any one should hear that? What if Bennie Bierce should hear? Pitt talked on at random. He mentioned Hellie Copper. It was so strange — it had meant death to Hellie and the cessation of being as he had known it, yet it was no more than something sad to tell, as they walked by the quiet houses. And Pitt hardly heard.

At Mis' Hellie's door his excitement was uncontrolled.

"Hi yi! Well, sir. Well, sir!" Pitt cried. "Ain't this what's what?" He happened on the phrase and kept repeating it, as something tidy and to the point.

In Mis' Hellie's warm welcome was hidden her compunction. She had been saying to herself of late, that for sixteen years Pitt had missed the joy of that boy. This compunction she had expressed by doing the utmost that she knew for a guest for "supper." She had killed a chicken.

Beside the window in Mis' Hellie's dining room, Pitt's quality was more evident. Seated and without his hat, he seemed to emerge; and there were his dog's eyes lifted, and there was his wistful, deprecatory smile. He sat with his head slightly drooping, and that liquid, upward look of his waited upon all. If he could have been thus true to himself his quality would have been more often evident. But instead, he wore always that forced heartiness, that note of good fellowship and camaraderie which suited him not at all. He was like a friendly little dog of which people tire because it is perpetually jumping and wagging.

He hardly turned his eyes from Jeffrey. He wanted with passion to talk to him, to get near to him. He clapped his son on the shoulder.

"Now then!" Pitt cried. "Let's hear all about it!"

"All about what?" Jeffrey asked, and took a step away. Jeffrey's smile was as pitiful as was Pitt's eagerness. They boy was groping, thrust out of the reckoning of years.

"Everything!" Pitt cried explosively.

"It's all right, I guess," Jeffrey said. "I'll—I'll have to get a pail of water. . . ."

In the dusky yard he stood holding the pail and staring at nothing. He felt ill, he felt a kind of homesickness. *His father!*

"Land," Mis' Hellie said to Pitt at dinner, "you got all the rest of the time to stare at him. Tell us what you been doing."

Well! Pitt had done different things. He recalled random bits, from Colorado to Alaska. A story of expectation, incredible endeavor. He said what he could, dismissed a year of toil with a phrase, a heartbreaking journey in a sentence.

"But why didn't you write all that time?" Mis' Hellie burst out at last. "'Most a year and not a word!"

"I know," said Pitt humbly. "But I didn't have the money."

"The money! But why didn't you write — and let us know you wasn't et up by them polar dogs?"

Pitt looked mild surprise. "I never thought of writing, because I didn't have the money," he repeated. "You see. . . ."

A year ago had come his great chance. He told about it, relaxed in his chair, his hands idle and heavy on his knees. He told it as another would have told of some day's dealing which had just missed consummation.

". . . another fellow and me. Side and side the claims was. We hung on through one winter. And then I ast him to trade. I donno why. I always fancied his'n, and I always liked to trade. I guess that's why. So we done it. I took his and he took mine. Well, sir, and I never got a dollar out o' the claim that come to me — not a dollar. But I hung on a year more. And he—I guess he won't come much short of a couple of hundred thousand — mebbe more. Ain't that the funniest thing?"

And at Mis' Hellie's clamorous exclamations:

"Seems queer, don't it?" said Pitt, and laughed heartily. It was in that year that he hadn't written — had thought for a while, as Mis' Hellie guessed, of never coming back at all. About this he was inarticulate, as always, but in his look was the story. When his eyes were not watching, they were speaking.

"But didn't he offer to give you part of it?" she cried indignantly. "Why, seems as if—"

"Oh, yes," Pitt hastened to say. "He did — Bart's all right, I tell *you.* Why, he paid my whole fare home, the whole way here. . . ."

"Well, but didn't he offer to divide up. . . ."

"Oh, it was a square trade," Pitt assured her. "Business is business! 'Course, I wish't I hadn't traded," was the most that he said. "Some fellows seem to get right along. I never got the hang of it." He laughed amusedly.

Jeffrey sat staring at him, judged him pitilessly by exteriors. Even renouncing the romance of a father home from the gold fields, the boy's judgment was hardly kinder. Applying the standards of the world as Jeffrey knew it, this was not the way a fellow's father ought to be. Look at Bennie Bierce's father — a hustling, red-cheeked, ready-to-wear garment representative. Look at Otie Adams' father — a doctor. And Hellie Copper had given a sense of security and background in which this little man was utterly lacking. Jeffrey wished that things might go on as before his father came.

"I've got my eye," Mis' Hellie was saying, "on the nicest little house for you — the old Brackett place. Remember?"

At these words Pitt's eyes went to his boy's face.

"For rent," Mis' Hellie went on. "Four rooms and a nice little garden and a hen coop. Cheap as breath, and I guess you can get 'em to come down on it besides. . . ."

Pitt said nothing. He continued to watch Jeffrey. Jeffrey was eating and he may not have hard.

"Your stuff's all up in the attic, waiting for you," Mis' Hellie went on.

At the mention of the furniture which had been Barbara's, Pitt seemed to forget Mis' Hellie, to forget Jeffrey.

After supper, while Jeffrey was bringing in the wood, Pitt went to Mis' Hellie and said, with his upward look:

"You ain't ever heard one word?"

"Not one word," she answered, "nor you?" And added "T—t—t," and then compressed her lips and turned her head and not her eyes.

Entering, Jeffrey caught this, divined that they were speaking of his mother, and was ashamed; but why, he could not have told.

At breakfast Mis' Hellie returned to the subject of the Brackett house. Again Pitt said nothing, his eyes on Jeffrey's face. And when it became evident that the boy would say nothing, Pitt made his chance to speak to him alone. He followed Jeffrey to the gate when he, with his young assumption of importance, started to his work. He had arranged to go back to Orcutt's.

"You want I should stay here, Jeff?" Pitt blurted.

"Why, you're going to, aren't you? I thought of course you were," Jeffrey said.

"Well, I didn't know. I thought I'd see how—" with that apologetic, protective past tense.

"Maybe you don't want to?" Jeffrey was ashamed of the faint hope that flickered up.

"Not unless *you* say stay."

"Oh," said Jeffrey carelessly, "I say so, right enough."

"But I'm so afraid you'd say so, even if—"

"Why, we've thought for years you'd be coming home to stay," Jeffrey said.

"Have you?" cried the little man, and lighted at the word.

He walked with Jeffrey to the corner. The strong light fell on the small figure, which looked old because its buoyancy had long died from it. He was without a hat, his hair blew about; he was smiling that faint, wrinkled smile of old, which never reached his eyes. Nor did it so even when he laughed heartily, saying loudly: "All right then! *That's* settled!" as he did when Jeffrey left him.

Pitt went hurrying back to the house.

"Look here," he said to Mis' Hellie, who was in the pantry. "I want to ask you something. You know Jeff — do you think he's going to like me?"

"Like you?" Mis' Hellie cried. "Why, ain't you his father?"

Pitt stared out the window.

"I know," he said, "but — well, folks ain't never like me very well, you know. And if Jeffrey shouldn't—"

"Shucks!" Mis' Hellie cried. "Why, if you don't like your own folks, who you going to like?"

This simple reasoning did not altogether satisfy Pitt. But his desire was intense. And he was like a beaten thing, safe in cover. To perform the simplest offices of wood and water about the house, to be in the presence of commonplace things, gave him a touching joy.

"I ain't afraid but I can get back to work," he said, straightening. "I've got years in me yet."

At length his decision to stay was made, but for many nights he lay awake, wondering. . . .

"You see," he said once to Mis' Hellie, "I might have come back with two hundred thousand. And I might have found Barbara to give it to. And they didn't either of 'em happen. Ain't it the *funniest* thing?"

But then he cried: "Look at Jeffrey though — alive! And me alive! Ain't that luck enough for any one man?"

Two days later Pitt came from Mis' Hellie Copper's with a clothes-basket filled with fag-ends of his belongings, drawn from storage in her attic. The rest of his humble goods were already at the Brackett house.

Jeffrey lent a hand with the basket. They went down the street in the strong sun, the variegated burden between them. Tumbled yellow paper flowers and a red-glass lamp were to be seen.

They passed the house with the steep flight of steps leading from the street, but Jeffrey did not notice. He was observing a man who was shaking rugs at the Granger house across the street, and wondered whether Miss Arrowsmith was at home.

"Who lives there now?" Pitt asked, looking back at the little house at the top of the steps.

"There? Fellow named Meyers. He was in my class," Jeffrey explained, with disregard of the rest of the family.

After a pause Pitt asked: "Ever been inside?"

"Heaps of times," Jeffrey said, proud to affirm any experience, as if affirmation were all. "We made our herbariums in that little shop place out back," he added.

Pitt was silent. He did not know what an herbarium might be, but it was a sharp arrestant to think of Jeffrey playing — he assumed it was playing — in that room.

"You was born in that house," he said at length, as if due were not being rightly given. "Your grandfather died there," he added. Of Barbara he said nothing, and then this seemed to him unfair. "Your mother lived there," he added with dignity.

"Oh, yes," said Jeffrey with superiority. "I know that."

They said no more.

At the Brackett house the furniture had arrived. The man and the boy began to arrange it. The Brussels-covered couch which used to stand back of the stove in the sitting room of Pitt's home, the marble-topped table of which Barbara had been so proud, the chair with sagging springs, the pictures. Before a cheap print of the Hudson highlands Pitt stood, preyed upon by his remembrance. He remembered *warm*, as of something which had happened to himself. And Barbara's dishes in the cupboards, Barbara's tins, Barbara's earthenware. The persistence of the physical things filled Pitt with obscure resentment. That kitchen mirror with the wavy lines, that kitchen soap-dish with the nick. . . .

Jeffrey was unpacking the clothes basket of odds and ends.

"Here's an old calendar," he said. "I'll chuck all such things out, shall I?"

Pitt picked it up. It was torn to the month and the year on which he had left the house down the street.

"Chuck it out!" he said suddenly.

"Here's an old hotel bill," Jeffrey pursued, and tossed it after.

It was the menu of the Chicago hotel where they had dined on their wedding day — ham and eggs, celery on the branch, lemon pie. . . . On the card's back was the notation which Jeffrey had made at the dictation of Strain, the paper-hanger, out on Michigan Avenue. Pitt threw the menu after the calendar.

"Chuck it out," he said.

Struck by his own firmness, he looked resolutely about his house. The truth was, he was going to begin over again. He and his son were going to make a home. They were going to be happy. Pitt said it over to himself several times: "Happy."

In a night or two he joined the procession of tramping feet, passing the Brackett house as they passed all other houses, on their way to the town, in the warm dusk. Pitt did not go with Jeffrey — after supper Jeffrey seemed to have affairs of his own, so Pitt strolled forth alone. He smelled wild grape-vines and faint bonfire smoke, nipped an end of a cedar bough and tasted it, heard the laughter and the low humming, saw a light or tow carried in from kitchen to sitting room for the evening. Yes! It was Burage. And here was he with his son — *his son* — and he must work for that boy. Already he had put out before their home a little sign: "Pitt: The Paper-hanger." In his hand was a letter written to his old firm to order samples and "make connections," he thought importantly. He should be "back at his old tricks in no time," he said to himself.

He dropped in at Hoey's, and picked up a *Burage Daily*, lying out-spread on the cigar stand. The local column chronicled that "M. Pitt, for-merly a home businessman in the papering line, had returned to Burage after an extended sojourn in Alaskan parts, and would again take up his residence here. The *Daily* extends its greetings, along with the many old time friends with whom he was seen shaking hands." Pitt bought the paper, and later cut out the item and cherished it in his wallet. Now he returned to the street and looked about him, relaxed and watchful, ready for old faces. As a matter of fact, fifteen years is not long, and Burage remembered, and newcomers were told. "Funny he stayed away from his boy so long, I think," they had been saying. And "Wonder how they'll manage about the cooking," the women said.

He found a grocery store where the same proprietor presided, for-ever grinding coffee, or coming in from the back room with a little keg sup-ported on the stomach. This man wanted to talk about a refrigerator, which did not interest Pitt, but it gave him the sense of conversation and comrade-ship. On the Ellsworth house veranda sat Flo Buckstaff, but Flo was now filled with grievances against the Wisconsin government, which he said was goin' to the dogs, tinkerin' with folks's rights, mussin' up the railroads and what now, and he insisted on talking about all this. Pitt had never been interested in politics, beyond liking to say, "Yes, sir, we got to have a change. Them fellows have had things their own way too long now." It was not until Jeffrey rose to leave that Flo began to ask about Alaska.

"What kind of a place is it, anyway?"

Well, it was cold, Pitt said. Alaska was cold.

"None too much gold layin' round loose up there, I guess."

Pitt laughed amusedly. No, sir! Not too much. Not *too* much.

"Folks go up there much now, as they used to?"

Well, Pitt could not say. Wouldn't say as they did, wouldn't say but they did. Hard to tell.

"Glad to be back, I bet?"

Oh, sure. Sure. Sure.

"Advise anybody else to go?"

Well, Pitt didn't know as he would, didn't know but he would.

"Many blizzards up in that country?"

Blizzards? Well, *say*. . . .

Of all that store of colorful companionship in the wild, the still nights, the starry black and white, the flat, low-lying shadows on strange figures and uncouth act, Pitt could say not a word. There were some things which he would have liked to tell, too. But nothing which he had been through seemed to matter. There was one thing which he started to tell, but the 'bus came from the Local, and Flo thought that the story was done.

Out of the 'bus came Buck Carbury, back from a day in Milwaukee, and he shouted in a way which made Pitt think how, after all, he had missed Buck, all these years. Buck was going to leave his parcels at the hotel and go to see his mother before he went home, and Pitt walked on with him. Buck, now a thickening figure, with flat, red cheeks, had the tact of an ox, and in his inquiries trod about among delicate nothings, but Pitt forgave him all. And Pitt might have been heard saying:

"No, sir. I've never heard one word. Not one word. Ain't it the funniest thing? . . ."

Walking about the Carbury lawn was one in a cerise "tea-gown," and she yawning, and plump, and painted. Mrs. Mayme Carbury Hanson (he had deserted her, but she kept it all) spied Pitt, pounced and hovered, diffusing magnificence, an odor of *chepre*, and a kind of accent, at which she was working now.

"You must come to see us! We can amuse each other. Mamma will be delighted. . . ."

After totally neglecting her mother's protection during youth, now, in maturity, Mayme had at length conceived her mother as a factor in the life and action of good society, and produced her own at every opening.

On the other hand, Buck had increased in sincerity and said, as Pitt was leaving:

"You must see *my* two. And the little woman. We'll have you round some night to supper." (Even as he said it he was shot with a pang of fear that he might not be able to bring it off. Nor was he able. When the matter was presented to the little woman, she replied that with two babies on her hands and all the housework, she was not going to have any company, and he needn't think it. Romance in Buck's household was at that stage.)

But it warmed Pitt to see them both, and he went back down the street, happy, as the sad are happy.

Now the tide had ceased to flow toward the town, and the time was in the lull before their return. They were in the motion picture houses, or visiting, or walking. Most of the stores were closed. But opposite the Ellsworth house, and farther down, Pitt saw two wide plate glass windows, flaring with light and a sense of color.

"Let me see," Pitt thought, "that'll be Billet, the tailor. How he's branched out. . . ."

He neared the windows, stood across the street from them, then was drawn across the pavement to stand before them.

Rose-colored damask, tapestry-patterned paper, lengths of shining grass cloth, and a glass and gilt sign: Designs Executed to Order. What did this signify? He stared up at the sign above the door — a great gilt and black sign, solid, fixed, like a sign for the Bank of England: Weilbarren and Harding, Decorators.

"Say!" said Pitt aloud. *"Say. . . ."*

For the first time his fifteen years of absence rested full upon him.

Left to himself, minus the ministration of women, the middle-class man of the United States would subsist exclusively on a diet of baked beans, bacon, fried potatoes, American cheese and coffee. Occasionally this diet would be enlivened by a bag of bananas, a can of sardines or a soup bone. For Pitt and Jeffrey these were the farthest excursions, save when Mis' Hellie brought in hot corn-bread. Of pie and waffles the two thought lovingly, but as those who long without hope. It was strange to hear these two, at their haphazard table set in the kitchen, talk of business prospects exactly as if the town regarded them as integers in its business life.

"Kind of hard gettin' back in harness," Pitt admitted, a month after his return. "Seems like I'd been away an awful while, now I'm back."

"Why, it was a good while," Jeffrey said, looking down the years.

"Yes, some ways. I wouldn't have believed Burage would change that much, though."

Jeffrey reflected on this. Privately it seemed to him that there had been ample time for Burage to turn itself inside out.

Having grasped that what he called the high class trade had gone irretrievably to this cloth and silk chap of the bright windows, Pitt had decided to put in a little sideline of cut flowers and potted plants. He had lately glassed in the side porch at the Brackett house and bought a modest stock; but he had now heard that people were charging him with taking from Paulina Dart, the widow and cripple who had sold flowers for years to deck the living and the dead. The cloth and silk chap had superseded him, and he had superseded Paulina, and he suffered because of both. It was extremely puzzling, but he accepted all and thought that no doubt things would look up.

He had been wanting to question Jeffrey about his plans, but the boy was nearly inarticulate; and so, as always, was Pitt.

"You must be getting hold of things pretty good by now, to the works," Pitt offered. This was Jeffrey's third month with Orcutt, the stone man.

"Sure I am," said Jeffrey, who had never learned those charming, deprecatory hypocrisies, nor mounted to self-depreciation itself.

"Hard for you, is it?" Pitt asked.

"Well, I should say not" — scornfully.

"Still like your boss?"

"Oh, I don't know." (What was the use of talk like this?)

"Well, you work hard and try to please him—that's all there is to it."

No reply. (What did his father think he *was?*)

"I s'pose he don't give you much what — you — might — call — responsibility?"

"Why, sure he does."

"I didn't know," said Pitt. "Say, Jeffrey, one thing: You'll get along pretty good if you don't never answer him back."

Jeffrey's reply was indistinguishable. And now Pitt asked, with delicate hesitations:

"Do you want to work that line? I mean — is that what you want to be?"

Jeffrey hitched about — his shoulders, his very looks hitched.

"I don't know."

"Ain't you never — never give no thought to what you'd like to be, when you grow up?"

"Well, sure I have!" Jeffrey exploded. Along obscure highways, that explosion was traceable to the words "grow up" — irritating, supererogatory words. But neither was conscious that these had anything to do with the moment.

Pitt wondered what it was that his boy would like to be. It seemed a reasonable subject for curiosity on his own part.

"What is't?" he asked, flatly.

"Why, I wanted to be an artist," said Jeffrey, crossly, to hide his embarrassment. "But I'm never going to be," he added. And to escape further inquiries, he went off to work earlier than he was expected. Why he was squirming from head to foot could not be told. Nor why Pitt, touching about among the dishes in the kitchen, going hopefully to the Post Office to see if there was any mail with an order — why Pitt should have felt heavy and restless and immersed in something with which he did not know how to deal. *Artist. . . .*

A thin red line in a gray sky, beyond a dead field; and in the foreground, bare trees and the figures of country men, the color of the soil. Pitt knocked the water-color to the floor from a shelf in Jeffrey's room. Restoring the sketch, he was struck by another, giving an aspect of the Burage bridge,

in winter. This he lifted, and was faced by Mis' Hellie's likeness, in her familiar blue calico. Well! Then they were not chromos — his appellation for all
unframed pictures. He caught a touch of their unprofessionalism, looked closer,
and found Jeffrey's name on the margins of every one.

"Say!" said Pitt aloud. "*Say!*"

He pored over them. He had no notion of their worth, but he had
pathetic respect for all manifestations of art. He found none of this work squar-
ing with his idea of prettiness, but he was quick to make allowance. The point
was that, all this time, Jeffrey could draw. He fell back upon the terms he had
used in his son's babyhood: The little scalawag. The little *skeesics*.

When Jeffrey came home, Pitt confronted him. Well, sir! So that was
what he had meant by being an artist. He was a deep one! Here he could
draw all this time and had never let it show. Jeffrey accepted this modestly,
smiled, lifted one shoulder. Oh, well, he said.

Before this gift of his son's, Pitt was humble. Of course, the father
said, he himself knew nothing about art — never had given it any attention,
in fact — never had had the time; but *he* should say that these were fine, just
fine. He had been once to the Chicago Art Institute. These paintings made
him think of some of the things he had seen there.

"They aren't paintings," Jeffrey said shortly. "They're just sketches."

"Sketches," Pitt corrected himself.

"Water-colors, you know," Jeffrey said.

"Oh, are they?" said Pitt, and lifted his brows and nodded. He had
never observed a water-color, as Jeffrey divined; nor was Pitt trying to seem
critical; he was merely trying to find all the common footing possible with his
son. "I guess they're real nice," said Pitt cheerfully, "when anybody knows about
them."

At supper he returned to that which he believed to be the subject,
and attacked it brightly.

"I went to a show once," he said, "where a fellow was drawing with
colored chalk. My, but he was a good one. He made a duck like lightning,
right before your eyes." He told about this. "He was a great artist," he concluded. "I don't know what all he made a week."

He looked fondly at Jeffrey.

"I wish't you'd been with me," he said. "We'd have gone up afterwards and showed him some of yours."

"Oh, those fellows aren't artists, though," Jeffrey brought out.

Pitt's face fell. "They ain't! Why, this chap was on the circuit, so much
a night and a steady job. I don't know anything about it," he added, "but I
s'posed he must have been one of the best."

Jeffrey felt uncomfortable. He felt a little sick. He wished that his
father would talk of something else, and he asked about the plants. In the
silence which fell, Pitt felt dimly that he had been lacking; and at last he

observed that, speaking of pictures, that was a nice one in the Sunday supplement. After supper he hunted it out and brought it to Jeffrey.

"It says it's by Thomas Gainsborough," Pitt said, reading. "Is he one of the big guns?"

"Of course," Jeffrey said.

Pitt again took up the sketches. He wanted passionately to say more about them.

"Jeffrey!" he cried. "I wish you'd let me see you make one. Couldn't you — now?"

"In this light?" Jeffrey was amused.

"Oh," Pitt said, "I s'pose you couldn't, could you?"

Jeffrey's discomfort was the discomfort of one who has taken advantage of something defenseless.

"I'll make one some day," he promised, "when I feel just like it — and you can watch me, if you want. It isn't much to see," he added, self-consciously.

He went about the room on an imaginary errand, holding his head rather stiff, as was his wont when attention was fastened upon him, and whistling. He was haunted by the feeling of having left his father, in some fashion, unattended.

"Going down town?" Jeffrey asked, hoping that he was not going.

"Why, I wasn't," said Pitt, "but I can walk along down with you, I guess."

They went into the twilight.

"I s'pose you get points while you're walking round like this," Pitt said, "and then go home and paint 'em out."

On which Jeffrey cried rudely: "Oh, don't let's talk about *that* all night."

The man who had been beating rugs at the Granger house had known what he was about. And now the house was opened, and Mrs. Granger and Miss Arrowsmith, the *Burage Daily* announced, "had returned from an extended pleasure trip to European parts."

Pitt wanted to go to see Miss Arrowsmith, but also he dreaded to go. Now he forgot himself, and without Jeffrey's knowledge he took the sketches there one morning, and asked for her.

Rachel had a genius for the casual. You would have thought that it was she who had been absent, and Pitt there all the time. And instead of taking him to the living room where he had met Barbara and where he had been married, she led him to the library, where he had never been, asking him en route what to do with mirrors whose backs had collected moisture.

Pitt replied that he did not know, and absorbingly spread out Jeffrey's sketches. No graces, no inquiries about herself or her mother, no taking account of the years — which was, after all, a grace. He was served in no better stead by Rachel's manner than by his own tremendous and darling preoccupation.

"Look here," he said, "Jeffrey made these. Painted 'em. Water colors, he calls 'em."

He tried to show them to her all at once, searching anxiously, too, for the one which he like best — and this meant the one having the most rose color. He scanned her face.

"You seen a lot of picture galleries, I expect," said he, "and you'll know how these compare. Of course," he added, "I know these ain't as good — I don't mean that. But I wanted you to see if you thought—"

Rachel took the sketches and her heart tightened queerly. Jeffrey had made these. . . .

Night after night, on deck alone, under the stars, she had been wont to imagine beside her the lad whom he might have been — listening to her, questioning, revealing. . . . In places of beauty, in the mountains, on the Rhine, at the expositions, he had often footed it beside her, a slim, viewless thing, growing in the measure of that stature which she had set for him. When, now and again, she had seen the awkward, sensitive reality of him, she had been haunted by the old, aching regret, by the weight of the irrevocable. Now in this revelation of his effort to express something of beauty, of sight, that little lad of hers had come by, groping for his own.

She looked at the sketches in silence, the frank gray fields, the quite relevant rose of the west, the huddled, ambiguous farm hands. Here was something which he had seen, and had selected to get into paint. He had seen something and had uttered it, in a broken speech, but with power. In the bridge sketch, he had painted water as he had seen water painted, leaves as he had seen leaves painted in cheap prints; but in all he had also painted directly something which he himself saw, as he alone saw it. This was all that Rachel could have asked. She was silent so long that Pitt became alarmed.

"Of course," he said, "these may not be so very good. But if he can do these as good as he has, maybe, if he learnt better—"

"These are extremely interesting, Mr. Pitt," she said. "Yes, I am sure that he can go on."

He stood motionless, and his lips did not smile, but his face grew bright to its depths.

"Say," he said, "I knew it! Of course, in my line — there ain't much comparison — but you do get to think lots about colors. . . ."

He scanned her face to see if he had been ridiculous. She was quite grave and intent — evidently he had not been ridiculous.

"I shouldn't wonder," she could not help saying, "if you had helped him — long ago — to care for color."

She was unprepared for the vivid light which swept him.

"Do you s'pose that?" he asked, and turned his eyes to think it out, his face still lifted, his lips still parted. "Me — messing in paints and things when he was little. . . ."

"Why not?" said Rachel.

His extreme, credulous happiness at this ideas was the only touch of egoism which Rachel had ever seen him wear. An egoism constituted of the hope that just possibly even he might have given something to the boy.

Rachel too, all that was maternal in her rose into feeling. That old desire to mother Jeffrey woke again at sight of these partial transcriptions. Here was probably no great talent, but enough, perhaps, to liberate him. Out of this incredible stone-cutting establishment and away to Chicago to the Institute she could help him now at last.

"Have you talked with him about these?" she asked.

"As much as I could," Pitt said. "It's kind of hard — I don't know exactly — you see, I ain't much up . . ."

"What does Jeffrey want to do?"

"He don't seem to think he can do much of anything."

"That's good," said Rachel. "I mean," she explained, "that isn't at all what he probably does think."

"I can't seem to get at him much," Pitt said. "I thought — I wondered if you would talk with him?"

"Of course. But you talk with him first. That would be better, wouldn't it?"

Pitt looked troubled.

"You see," he said, "I don't believe I know how to do things like that. I ain't been his father so very much. . . ."

"Well, talk with him as if he were a friend."

"I'd like to!" Pitt cried. "You see, that's how I feel. Why, I know how *he* feels. I feel that way too! I mean about everything. When he's going around, doing little things—" Pitt did not know how to say what he had in his mind. "I don't feel any older than him," he said earnestly. "But he — you see, he don't know that!"

This Rachel understood — the anomaly of Forty and Fifty which feel Twenty, while Twenty feels itself so outdistanced.

"You know," said Pitt, "I've wished I knew some men that had boys. I've asked several men if they had — but their boys are either girls, or else older, or else little kids. Only one chap. He had a boy. But he didn't know what I was driving at. . . ."

"What were you driving at?" Rachel could not help saying.

Pitt colored. "Well," he said simply, "I fell down once. And I wouldn't want to fall down again. With Jeffrey. . . ."

She understood. The little man was wondering how fathers act.

"And then especially," Pitt said, "when he's got this art in him." He meditated. "I s'pose you ain't got a book," he said, "about a chap that had a boy that had art in him. . . . No! You wouldn't have. . . ."

"I don't believe you need a book," Rachel said. "Get him to talk with you."

"But I always say the wrong thing," Pitt muttered. "I notice that." He looked up at her with appeal. "Sometimes," he said, "he acts kind of the way Barbara used to. Not cross — *patient on purpose!* That's a terrible thing. . . ."

"Still," Rachel said, "if he wants to study art, and you can get him to say so, that's all, isn't it?"

He caught her confidence.

"I guess so," he cried. "I'm going to see, anyhow. If you think he can do art, I guess the rest's all right!"

"Talk with him first," Rachel said. "And then, if you think well of it, send him over here. Of course I want to see him, anyway."

"That's what I *will* do!" Pitt said brightly. He seemed a bit ashamed of his fears.

As he was leaving, the door was pushed open and a little dog came into the room. Burage had never seen a Pomeranian, and that was a Pomeranian — a beautiful little creature, with eyes not unlike Pitt's eyes. The small thing came and stood before Pitt, and regarded him. Pitt made a caressing sound in his throat and lifted the tiny animal.

"He won't like that," said Rachel quickly. "Jep — be good!"

The dog looked at her languidly, wagged his splendid tail, and laid his nose in the curve of Pitt's arm.

"Just like a baby," said Pitt, laughing. "Ain't he — ain't he? Now look at that."

"He doesn't usually do that," Rachel said, as owners of expensive dogs will always say.

"You see," said Pitt, "he don't know enough not to like me!"

He was rather proud of this comment, and said it again.

"My!" he cried, "what a day. This about Jeffrey — ain't it grand? And now this little fellow for a friend. Say!"

Pitt went away, happier than he had been in years. Rachel saw him shutting the gate carefully, his long wrists, his over-large hat, his short, thin coat which blew when no wind was blowing. . . .

At supper that evening Pitt could not eat, but sat smiling at his son. The little man was looking at Jeffrey with the dignity and benignity of a god, about to open a door to man. He had thought out a way for Jeffrey. However, Pitt brought out his proposal like a happy child.

"Son," he said, "how would you like to go to school and learn art?"

All his starved paternity, his long hunger for family relationship, were by way of being satisfied. Here he was, the father, able to offer some instruction in art to a gifted son.

Jeffrey went on eating.

"Not me," he said.

But Pitt thought nothing of this. Jeffrey usually took the opposite side of every question. The father set himself patiently to explain.

"I'll tell you what," he said. "You can draw — anybody can see that. You color things nice — I guess that ain't just what you call it. . . ."

Jeffrey had certain delicacies, but the family relationship seemed to wear them away. He forbore to put his father at his ease, and merely kept silence.

"Well," Pitt said, "I mean you got a lot of ability for art. And I want you should make the most of it. I want you should go to the Chicago Art Institute, Jeffrey."

"Yes!" said Jeffrey, derisively. "We have the money for that, haven't we? Why don't you send me to Europe, dad?"

Jeffrey laughed good-humoredly, but Pitt colored, said, "You may get there yet!" and continued to praise his work.

"But those things of mine are no good, really," Jeffrey cried. "I *know!*" he added, the memory of that Chicago trip of his stinging.

"So do I know!" Pitt cried merrily, with Rachel's judgement safe in his own.

"Well," said Jeffrey, crossly, "there's no use talking that."

Pitt was patient with him, tried to tell of Jeffrey's future as an artist — the returns, the friends, the honor. Service to art had for Pitt its middle-class interpretation of fame, nothing more that he could put in words. But from some unopened chamber of his being there had rayed out the news of fairer regions than those wherein he walked.

"Even if I'd go — where'd the money come from?" Jeffrey at last put it point blank.

"That's all right about the money," Pitt informed him with an air of happy importance. "Don't you worry about the money. If you want to go to Chicago and learn art, you can start of tomorrow morning. Jeffrey — you'll go, won't you?"

Before the bright confidence in his father's eyes, Jeffrey could not bring himself to divulge the circumstance of that earlier trip to Chicago. He continued to say nothing, save to disparage his work and emphasize his disabilities.

After three days of this Pitt appealed to Rachel, and she asked Jeffrey to dine.

"Oh," she said with confidence, "we'll talk him round. I can't think he's *that* obstinate."

"I thought," Pitt returned, with ruminant eyes and a faint frown, "I thought you might be able to put it. I can't seem," he added, "to put it." He laughed a little. "I guess I ain't much good at talking," he told her.

It was four years since Rachel had seen Jeffrey. When he came up to the lighted veranda that evening, she scanned him with a kind of ear. Suppose he came slouching, awkward, maladroit, caught in the sad net where so many Burage youth forever struggled. Then that would be her handiwork. She thought of his exquisite childhood, steeled herself to see him struck down to some lower level of being by her own failure. Again she laughed at herself: Was she then so sure that she could have saved him to himself by her tutelage. . . .

He stood before her and gave her his hand in a grasp a trifle too relaxed. He flushed. She caught the self-conscious lines tightening about the small mouth. In all his movements there was irresolution. But she was struck, as she had been struck in his babyhood, by a certain definite quality in his face. This quality she was always able to recognize in others, but had never been able to define — a certain beautiful transparency, a strength which was not the strength of old standards; and overall a look as might be surprise.

"Well, Jeffrey!" she said.

"Great to see you back," he said boyishly.

She liked his straightforward greeting, in spite of its short unnecessary laugh. But when he sat down, she felt a kind of terror. No quick, nervous movements, no bright light in a roving eye, no sharp concentration of faculty in the moment of this delayed meeting with her. Instead relaxation, a kind of Oriental quiet, a waiting to be approached. In this temper, which is the crown of a mature life, she saw the peril of the youthful life relaxed and open to every influence, alike the fine and the fatal. Here was the possible prey, close to type. Or, on the other hand, here was the potential god.

At table she began: "What do you find to do with yourself here in Burage?"

They were alone, and Rachel was now at an age when delicacies possible to the process of probing were quite neglected by her. She had grown that terrible directness of the woman of forty-five who is so sure of her own nicety of feeling that she can afford to disregard it.

She saw that his mind instantly became a blank. What *did* he do there in Burage? He could not think of a single thing. He tried to speak of his work at the stone-cutter's which, for Rachel's purposes, was precisely as if he had used a mask.

"Do you like it?" she wanted to know.

"Oh, no," said Jeffrey in surprise.

She noted this with approval. In social intercourse, then, he did not go so completely out of his mind as to reply the obvious, which might be also the untrue. Thus all went together: His lack of facility in movement, in initiatives of talk, these left him free to be reflective in reply.

She regarded him. If he had remained with her, they would be sitting thus, but in an accustomed manner, he very likely at home from college. He would not be holding his fork like that. He would not give that startled, interrogatory look when she addressed him, or when a dish was handed. He would have had a tailor. She saw that within its confines, his taste was good. She had accepted his cravat, his waistcoat, his hose, his shoes. His hands were acceptable, his hair fine, docile, well-cut. He was presentable. He had rather a nice vein for companionship, he had humor, and a good little grin. The only point at which he failed her was an occasional error in his estimate of a moment — he placed the emphasis where Rachel had not intended it, was caught by an auxiliary to her main fact. Rachel herself might have been wrong, but this would not have occurred to her.

"He seems to have a new set of subtleties," she thought, resentfully.

As the years passed, it had not presented itself to her that subtleties, like their laws, evolve, and that her equipment, even in its delicate, individual advance, was not eternally to be sufficient. Rachel, at forty-five, was the lovely *idea fixed* of herself at twenty-five. She judged Jeffrey inexorably by her own standards of *nuance*. These were immortal, to be sure, but she had forgotten that they were also not incapable of growth.

"I thought," she murmured, "that you would have been an artist."

"So did I," said Jeffrey, low.

To his naive surprise, it was not unpleasant to talk of this, with Rachel. He had got over all that, he assured her. He thought he should be a businessman — "some kind of businessman," was what he said. All the time Rachel had her pang: If only she had trained the taste which she had divined.

She thought that she saw it all — Beck's failure, the money loss, the lack of opportunity — out of these had come distrust of himself, discouragement, dry rot.

"What now?" she asked. "What kind of business?"

"Stone-cutting — or dye works," said Jeffrey. "I think I'd like to cut designs," he volunteered, "or to mess in the dyes — I don't care which."

"Don't you see that's the submerged artist in you, trying to get out, in stone work and colors?"

Jeffrey looked important. He had not thought of that.

"Oh, no" he said, pleased.

"I'd better own up," she said. "I have some of your sketches here. Your father loaned them to me."

Jeffrey was irritated, felt trapped. So that was why she had invited him to dinner.

"They're extremely interesting," she said. "Not really good, Jeffrey — but really promising."

"They don't interest me," he said.

"That's good," she assured him, cheerfully. "Then you can do something better."

After dinner, as they sat on the lighted veranda, Rachel, in her formless wrap of bright wool, was like some sibyl expounding multiple futures. Her fine hands moved among some books of youthful artists' adventures in London. She told him much of the student life there and in Paris. She had brought out her photographs of the Italian and German galleries. She told him of artists whom she had known.

It was the only house in Burage where one might hear talk such as this. Rachel's table was covered with the new reviews and with that which they reviewed. But from Burage main street, the lighted windows of the Brewsters and the Ames's and the Hudsons looked as bright and promising, though their tables carried only the illustrated weeklies. And under the eternal democracy of intellect, which appears so grossly undemocratic, there was Rachel Arrowsmith, going delicately to seed, just as surely as the takers of drugged milk, behind those bright windows. Also here was Jeffrey — the only youth of his age in Burage whom Rachel could have interested with this talk of hers — and he was planning for himself a life like that of Otie Adams or Bennie Bierce.

She said: "If your father gives you a chance to go to Chicago to study art, you'll go, won't you?"

"I'm not in that class," said Jeffrey. "I couldn't do it — not now."

These two words echoed in her like a bell of death: "Not now." That was it. Where had she been down the years when the fiber in him might have been stiffened for its attack?

Later, Pitt dropped in, his hair brushed erect, his shoes obviously donned for the occasion, sat on the edge of his chair, and his lips moved as he followed what Rachel was saying.

"Miss Arrowsmith really think there's anything in you?" he asked Jeffrey, and laughed heartily, but did not succeed in covering his wistfulness.

"Me?" said Jeffrey, flushing. "Oh, she's jollying me. I couldn't do anything with art — not now."

There it was again — "not now." The eyes of the little man, wistful, ill-equipped, met those of Rachel, which had seen so much. Their joint failure, it seemed, had brought the boy to this — failures how differently conditioned.

The tramp of feet toward the town had now begun: There went light gowns, baby carriages, go-carts; snatches of song were heard, laughter, and a whiff of tobacco smoke rose, vagrant, or the spicy breath of a joss stick, lately introduced in Burage and affected at evening, on porches and in the street. There went Burage, looking for wonder, and overhead flowered the planets and the suns which Burage could not have named. Up in the leafy Fifth ward the German band began its practice, faintly audible. There was a rumble of thunder, sounding old-fashioned and worthy of regard, not casual and intrusive like city thunder.

Mis' Hellie Copper, Mis' Miles and Mis' Nick True, returning early from town and some legitimate errand, came up to the screen door of the veranda.

"Can't stay a secunt," they said, as they entered and sat down.

"Here we come along in without any invitation whatever," Mis' Miles observed. "Well, I can't be bothered being formal or using frizz-papers any more. I'm too old."

Mis' Miles was now stout, breathless, complaining. Her thin white skin looked floury and the sagging muscles of her face had left her eyes somehow exposed, with flat mats of shadow. Something within her had been worsted, for she was completely absorbed in externals.

Mis' Nick True rose from her seat as soon as she had taken it.

"What on earth's that?" she said, pointing to a photograph of the Victory in Rachel's hand. "Victory! I shouldn't call it much of a victory if I'd had my head knocked off my shoulders. I s'pose that's just the name of it."

"Well," said Mis' Hellie Copper, "if it's pictures of *any* kind, with heads or without, Jeffrey's happy. Ain't you, Jeffrey?"

"That's what I tell him," said Pitt brightly. "Jeffrey, he's all pictures, I tell you."

Jeffrey cast an appealing look at Rachel, who laid on Mis' Hellie's knee a handful of photographs of Italian architecture.

"Perhaps," she said, "these will amuse you. I've just brought them back with me."

"I do love pictures," Mis' True declared, with generous stress.

"*I* like pictures," Mis' Miles agreed, with an air of invincible originality.

"Yes, but mercy," said Mis' Hellie, looking at a print of the cathedral at Milan, "what'd they put so many stick-ups in its bonnet for?"

"Oh," Mis' True cried, "that's easy enough in a picture, so. All they had to do was just make a mark."

They stooped to the pictures, and Rachel picked up one of Jeffrey's water-colors.

"You know, Jeffrey," she said, "I wanted to find fault with your hills a bit, in this one. I wish you'd try dissolving them more — do you see what I mean? — they're too naked, too near. . . ."

"My land," came Mis' Hellie's comment on a Florentine fresco, "if they're going to paint, why don't they paint so's you can see it? I'd just as soon have my brown veil on as try to look at this."

"Oh, I s'pose they're pretty old," Mis' Miles added. "They're faded pretty bad, like enough."

"And then," said Mis' Nick True, "they didn't take photographs in them days to compare with now. Awful dim, the old ones get. That one makes me think of one I've got of Aunt Lausanne — can't hardly see it. Eighty years old that woman was, and not a gray hair in her head nor one that wasn't curly—"

"—that was what I meant about color," Rachel was saying. "Your hills there — a warm gray, just out of neutral toward blue — don't you see? — instead of so much blue?"

"The one with the pink front door!" Mis' Miles exclaimed. "Sure enough I remember Aunt Lausanne. I hadn't thought of her for years. Why, she was the one that—"

"Here's the Roman Forum!" Mis' Hellie exploded, to punctuate for Mis' Miles. "Why, say. That looks funny for a church. Where's the minister stand?"

"It wasn't a church," Mis' True explained with superiority, "it was a circus. Of course. Where the gladiators killed the Christians."

"Oh, I remember now," Mis' Hellie said humbly.

Rachel's voice went on. "You see, we hear people speak of blue hills, and when we come to paint them, we *remember*, instead of merely looking for ourselves. So the hills are not your hills, not natural, as we say, and it's an excellent word. . . ."

". . . buried in her bonnet," said Mis' Hellie, lifting a death masque of a De Medici. "Just like Great-aunt Mate Pixley. After she died, not a soul could do up her hair so's it looked natural. So they put a bonnet on her, and a knit shawl to match, and she went in that to the tomb. Real appropriate, I always think. I think they dress corpses much too light to seem fitting. I wonder if that's why they left this lady's bonnet on her. . . ."

"It's real warm in Rome, though," Mis' Miles objected. "Why, you know, they didn't use' to wear much of anything there, one while."

"Look at here!" Mis' True cried ecstatically, over a print of a Borgia. "The photographer tinted her cheeks — just like they did mine. Well, I'll tell 'em I'm real Roman style. . . ."

"I believe," Rachel was saying, "that composition is going to fascinate you. That's all locked to you yet — see there, if you had brought that line on down, to lead to this rock mass. . . ."

"I don't care if that is Augustus Caesar," Mis' Hellie said, with great positiveness. "It looks like my mother's oldest brother. Only Uncle Lute got a scar on his eyebrow, felling a tree when he was only sixteen, and then a hornet stung him on the other eyebrow to match. . . ."

"My land," said Mis' Miles, "I've got to go home and set bread sponge. I can't set here talking art."

Pitt, who had been listening alternately to both conversations, drew a breath of content.

"I guess," he said, "you don't know what it is to be where you can't hear talking going on like this. I was just thinking how nice it is, sitting here, hearing nice talk. . . ." He laughed, and looked from one to another, to see if any had understood him.

"Well," said Mis' Hellie, as they rose, "you're just like Jeffrey. I always thought he was cut out and born to be an artist. Have you ever thought of going back to Chicago to try again, Jeffrey?"

A silence fell. Pitt looked at Mis' Hellie questioningly. She went on, patting the photographs to a neat pile:

"All the matter was, you didn't half try. Went into the Art Institute and came away without ever seeing a soul, mind you! I wish't I'd gone with him, that day. I'd have walked right up and told 'em that from the time he was a little thing he never was really happy unless you give him a cardboard and some paints to smool with. Well, good night, all!"

The others said their good night, and went into the dark. A full moon, just rising, struck through a little "popple" tree and they stepped down a narrow corridor of that light.

"There," they heard Mis' Miles say, "I never showed Miss Arrowsmith my sample, now. Navy blue or green, I can *not* decide. . . ."

Their talk of color died down the soft gloom of the street.

"What'd she mean?" Pitt was saying in excitement. "What'd Mis' Hellie mean about you going to Chicago?"

Rachel, hoping to prevent the moment, rose with some word about something to drink. But she paused on Jeffrey's answer:

"Well, that's it. I *have* been. And I know now that I can never do a thing that is anything. That's why I won't go again. But I hated . . ."

"Who'd you see?" Pitt put the question, leaning forward, his face lined with his eagerness.

"Oh, a commercial artist chap. And then I went to the Art Institute. . . ."

It came out. He told them how he had seen nobody. He was not looking at Pitt or Rachel as he talked, but at the floor, or anywhere. When he had finished, he was astonished to find his father smiling.

"There!" cried Pitt. "There, sir! Now that's all I want to know. You did want to go all the time! Ain't it the luckiest thing I come home just exactly when I did?"

He was looking from one to the other, eager, happy.

"Here I come along right off — not two months afterwards! Ain't it the *funniest* thing? And now you can go — Jeff! You was just holding back because you thought you hadn't ought to try again! Don't you see that's just what you'd ought to do?"

He appealed to Rachel.

"You see? He didn't want we should be disappointed from knowing how disappointed he'd been! Well, but what's once? You must go up there and stay a month, Jeffrey — two months! Till you see what you can do. Six months!"

He was reckless, and shining. He paced the veranda, his coat hunched over his collar, his shoes squeaking horribly.

"Say!" he said. "I don't mind telling you what worried me was your not caring to go. A son of mine, I thought" — he said this again — "a son of mine, not caring to take a chance like that! But now I know you did care I don't think of any of the rest. Of course you cared! And back you go. And get to be a regular artist in no time. Won't he? Won' you, Jeffrey?"

Rachel had kept silence. When she spoke it was in order to uphold Pitt rather than to lighten the moment for the boy.

"It really was considerate of you, Jeffrey," she said — and if she spoke a trifle dryly, Pitt did not know that — "not to let us hear of that trial of yours. It was no trial at all, you see. *One* day . . . that's nothing."

"I'm no good," was all that Jeffrey could say, miserably.

"Come on!" Pitt cried. "Come on home. I'll give you the week out at Orcutt's, and then off you go. Ain't it just fine!"

He looked at them with that peculiar sweetness of mien which was no smile of mouth, but of eyes, the head thrown a little back.

"Well said!" he exclaimed. "If I could just have known this, some of those days up in Alaska, I wouldn't have been quite so willin' to die, would I?"

Beside his glowing confidence, Jeffrey made a figure negative, even alien, as they said good night.

"Never asked for the little dog!" cried Pitt, from the steps. "Say, don't tell him I forgot him, will you? Next time I'll come to see *him!*"

He was overflowing with friendliness, with good feeling, with his joy. He laughed, and as they went through that white place of moonlight, Rachel saw that he drew Jeffrey's arm though his own.

She did not hear what Pitt was saying. This was:

"Son! I'll tell you what we're going to do. We're going up to the city together and try it again!"

3

Crossing the lawn, vivid in the strong sun of the next morning, Rachel saw Pitt coming down the street, a tall hydrangea nodding in his arms. She remembered that she had told him to bring her a hydrangea; it was evident that potted plants were not drawing many to the Brackett cottage. Those that Pitt did sell he delivered himself, carrying about crimson ramblers and calla lilies shaded by a huge discolored umbrella, which shielded his burden now. Rachel picked up Jep, who was pattering at her heels, and waited for

Pitt at the gate. She was in yellow, and Jep matched her brown garden hat.

"Do you know what I was thinking, comin' along?" said Pitt, without preliminary. "I was thinking I owe you and Mis' Copper the most of anybody in the world — next to Barbara."

"You don't owe us a thing," Rachel said shortly. She wanted to add: "And heaven knows you don't owe Barbara anything. Don't you know it too, by this time?"

"And now look at," said Pitt. "Since last night Jeffrey had stopped saying he won't go. There it is again!"

He stooped to Jep and touched him with a forefinger. Jep wagged, regarded the finger, licked it languidly.

"Say!" said Pitt. "He ain't human. He's better than human — like flowers."

He looked up at his big hydrangea.

"They's things about flowers we don't know, either," he said. "I donno but the little buggers come stickin' up from some other world, layin' inside o' this one. *Inside*—" he repeated, frowning for the right word. He laughed heartily. "Jep here — he's just more than somethin', ain't you, Jep?"

"Mr. Pitt," Rachel said, as they walked to the house, "I want to talk to you about Jeffrey. I've been wanting to tell you — I hope you'll let me provide the means for him to go to the Institute."

"You mean write to somebody about him?" Pitt's face was bright. "Well, I was just wishing I could ask you for that! Just look at! Don't I get 'most everything?"

"I meant that too," Rachel said. "But to send him — to furnish him the money — that's what I want to do." She added: "To help to make up to me for all of him that I didn't have."

"Say!" Pitt said. "*Say.*"

He set the hydrangea on the porch, depositing it with anxious care even in his agitation. Then he stood up, the old umbrella which he had now lowered casting its reddish light on his bright face. He took off his hat, and he seemed to droop and soften before her, as if he were under some lovely influence.

"It's your wanting to do it," he said, "wanting to do it for Jeffrey. I tell you, you don't know what it means. . . ."

Rachel became her most casual. Her high head, finely freckled nose, smoothly parted light hair seemed in themselves to become casual. It pierced her intolerably when the little man was like this. He accepted the universe which he had never even glimpsed, save darkly. And for some far, reflected splendor he was so unbearably glad.

"It would be my pleasure," she said indifferently. "The hydrangea — I think we might have it on the left of the door. . . ."

He paid no attention to the hydrangea.

"It's — it's a regular present to have you say that about him," Pitt said earnestly. "But, you see, I couldn't — I couldn't do that. I—I want—"

He stopped, embarrassed to be caught at wanting himself to provide for Jeffrey. He shifted it.

"You see," he said, "I thought of a way so's Barbara — she could have her share to do."

Rachel regarded him. Other folk suffered a loss and in fifteen years it dimmed. But Barbara seemed still vivid, importunate, *there.*

"That three hundred dollars," he said, "left from the house? Her house? You know it's been in the bank for her — there it is, and all the interest. And I don't believe now she'll ever—"

He stopped, perhaps because to say the words made their prophecy possible.

"—well, I thought she'd want it to go for Jeffrey — in case she don't want it — ever — for herself. Don't you think she might? . . ."

"I'm sure of it," Rachel said instantly. "Yes, of course — that is the thing to do."

So it was to be Barbara, after all, who would do this for Jeffrey, and not she herself. Later perhaps they might need her. . . . When she said so, Pitt shook his head.

"Barbara's money'll get him started," he said. "And then I can keep him going. Oh, I know I can. Things are going to look up now. Ain't they, Jep?"

He had the little being in his arms. When he did not sufficiently regard him, the dog pawed imperiously at his lapel. This demonstration went to Pitt's heart.

"Nobody every paid as much attention to me before!" he cried, and laughed heartily. "Barbara liked little dogs," he said. "That's one of the things I used to wish I'd done for her." He meditated. "You know," he added, "how you can think of more things to bother you in the night than when it's light — with folks around? Well, I think it's that way with Alaska. My! But the things I use' to could think of up there. . .that I hadn't done. . . ."

"But there's only Jeffrey to think of now," Rachel said. "You've told him about his mother's — about the money?"

Pitt looked troubled. "Just this morning," he replied. "I don't know whether he understood. He didn't say any too much. . . ."

"Jeffrey never says much," said Rachel. "It's one thing I like about him."

"Pitt set down the little dog, tenderly, as if it were Jeffrey himself and he a baby. He came and stood before Rachel, his absurd umbrella bunched awkwardly in his hands.

"I guess I can't never tell you anything I mean," he said.

"Nonsense," said Rachel, too abruptly. But it was either that or to find her eyes misted, as were his. She called to Jep, and mounted the steps. Jep, however, elected to accompany Pitt to the gate.

"Little *skeesics*. Little scalawag. My stars! My stars!" said Pitt all the way, and made ridiculous sounds with his tongue.

On Cook Street they were putting in sewerage. Not that there had occurred to Burage a certain disparity in the absence of sewerage in a town which registered eighty-odd automobile licenses, but that an advantageous contract was possible, and so the reform can about creaking. And civically disposed ladies thrilled as at a spiritual advance. Which it was, assuredly.

Pitt stood watching the men dig up the wooden blocks before Mrs. Granger's house. To these wooden blocks, which it had been widely prophesied would send the town into bankruptcy, many were yet unreconciled; and whenever, as now, these had to be disturbed, certain passers-by said, "Now see?" Two workmen, laborious with pick-axes, evidently shared the general low opinion of paving, and complained that there ought to be more men on the job.

"Who hires you?" Pitt asked gently. He had to say it twice before any one heard him.

"Druse," said the man, and leaned on his spade. "But you got to slip him something to give you the job."

"How much do you get?" Pitt wanted to know.

"Two," said the man, "and he has the first day's pay."

Pitt walked on, thinking. "Kind of nice, no worry, no counting up, nothing but taking in Twelve at the end of the week. Fifty at the end of the month." His thought shifted uncomfortably. Twelve at the end of a month was about his own recent average.

Of late he had applied for various jobs, here and there. But he applied for a job as another would accept dismissal. Even those needing help, on seeing the bald, hesitating little man who looked fifty said, No, they thought they could get along. All the way home, now, he kept thinking about the men who dug there on the shady street, at Two a day.

He was thinking about them that night, when Jeffrey came home to supper — so that Pitt even started guiltily, as if Jeffrey would know his thought. At sight of Jeffrey's face his father's attention wrapped him. Jeffrey was frowning, and almost at once he opened his mind.

"Father," he said, "I can't use that money."

"What money?" Pitt asked stupidly.

"You know. That in the bank. Hers."

Pitt looked up at him fearfully. Why? Why not?

"Well, a nice thing it'd be," the boy held, "if she should get sick or something, and want it."

"I tell you," Pitt said steadfastly, "she's dead. Don't I know for sure that she wouldn't have stayed away from you all these years if she hadn't been dead?"

"You don't know," said Jeffrey obstinately. "Nobody knows. Anyway, I'm not going to use that money — that's flat."

Pitt walked to the open door and stood there, his head thrown back. Pitt never held his head up as in challenge, but rather in a kind of helpless, ruminant way, like a child thinking. As Barbara had cruelly thought: Like a frog.

"Miss Arrowsmith has offered to send you," he said at length.

"She has? Well, of course you told her we couldn't do that."

"I told her," Pitt said with dignity, "that you were going with your mother's money."

"Why should I? Even if she never does come back — why should I use her money? What interest has she ever taken in me?"

Pitt turned and looked at Jeffrey in horror.

"Why," he said, weakly, "for two years you and her went round together."

"I couldn't use her money," said Jeffrey shortly.

Pitt considered. "Then — then you let Miss Arrowsmith start ye?" he asked.

"No!"

"Just for a loan, of course?"

"And have to come back and face her with the news that I'm no good. I tell you, I know it now — without spending all that money."

"Well, you wouldn't come back like that. But I don't like it, either — her letting you have money. No, sir! Jeffrey — you ain't thinking straight. It's your mother's money that ought to send you. Jeffrey — it's mama! Can't you remember. . . ."

Pitt searched his face. It seemed impossible that Barbara's son should remember nothing of her, should think of her as of some strange woman, should not be willing to take her help.

"I tell you, you might as well drop it, father," Jeffrey said. "I never shall do it. Leave me alone!"

They sat at supper in silence. Still in silence, Jeffrey went away after supper, and Pitt brought his chair to the locust tree, by the kitchen door. Here he could watch the procession on its way to the town, discern the few whom he knew. Once, when an old acquaintance lifted his hand to him, Pitt half started up, waved his arm, nodded, smiled, and continued to smile when the man was out of sight. Pitt sat with his back to the west, which was lighted to ocher and peach and dove. He knew that it was there, but in his later years he had ceased to consider intimately these aspects of nature. They were there, but he had put them by, said to himself that he would pay more attention when he got time, thought of all this as for some other occasion, like prayer.

For two hours Pitt sat there. He had two little pieces of celluloid and these he kept brushing and clicking together — Pitt like to make little noises like this. Sometimes his hands drooped, and he would stare into the dark, or watch the bracket lamp on the kitchen wall, and then he would sigh and take up again the motion and the clicking.

Jeffrey came home early. And having no wisdom — none — Pitt followed the boy into the kitchen and clapped him on the shoulder, with that affectation of camaraderie which sat so strangely upon the little man.

"Now he's thought it all over!" Pitt cried. "And now he's going to behave himself — like a sensible boy!"

Obscurely irritated, Jeffrey tried to edge away, smiled, yawned with some stress, and said that he thought he should go to bed.

"Four hundred and forty-one dollars and a little more, Jeffrey," Pitt went on. "That'll keep you a long time in Chicago — long enough to learn all the picture painting they've got there, *I* should think."

"Don't, please, father," Jeffrey said, edging toward his room.

"Say you'll go," Pitt said. "There's a good boy."

At "good boy" Jeffrey cried: "Don't go over it again, father. I've told you I'll never use that money. That's flat and final. Don't talk of it again, please."

Something of his secret sense of superiority, usually so carefully guarded from his father, flared up in his words. It is certain that Pitt did not recognize them as bearing this import, but his nerves reacted. He cried:

"Can't you see I'm trying to save you from the kind of a life I've had?"

Arrested, Jeffrey stared at his father. Pitt's pale eyes were fixed upon his with an intolerable sadness.

"Look at me," Pitt said. "I've dogged it for 'most fifty years. I didn't have a show — I didn't have a soul to tell me. Don't you s'pose if I'd had a silver of anything to crawl out on, the way you have, I'd have done it?"

"I tell you," Jeffrey said, "I've got nothing either! Only I've got sense enough to know it."

"Well, you can try, can't you?" Pitt said ardently. "Can't you try? What's the reason you can't try?"

"It isn't honest, when I know I can't do anything," Jeffrey had not thought of this before, but he flung it out with authority, and walked across the room, holding his head stiffly. Pitt followed him.

"Am I older than you, or ain't I? Ain't I had some experience — say, ain't I?" he put it wistfully.

"In art?"

"Not in art — no! But in gettin' along. That's the real experience — gettin' along. I want you should get along!"

"But just because you want me to do something is no reason why I can do it."

"It's a reason why you should try, ain't it?"

"Not with that money."

"What kind of a way is that for you to feel? Jeffrey — you tell me?" Pit said sorrowfully.

"Well, what kind of a way was that for a fellow's mother to act?"

"Jeffrey!" Pitt cried. "You're talking against *mama!*"

"I don't know enough about her to talk about," Jeffrey returned. "But I won't touch her money."

"Oh, oh," Pitt cried. "What's this we've said? Jeffrey!"

"Don't let's talk about it, father."

Pitt groped about the kitchen. "Can't you take my advice?" he cried. "You're going it blind. I want to see you look whereabouts you're going. Not blunder into the first thing handy. . . . Can't you take my advice?"

"Why should I?" said Jeffrey, with cutting emphasis.

Pitt did not catch his meaning. "You're throwing away your life," he said.

A throng of voices beat at Jeffrey, beseeching him not to say the thing which he was to say. All these he put aside, and his words came with bitter force:

"You say yourself you've made a failure of it. Then how do you think you can tell me. . . ."

On this very point of his own toil Pitt had been making his argument, and Jeffrey's injustice stung intolerably. Pitt stopped short, and in his eyes was death. At length he looked at Jeffrey as if the boy were unknown to him.

There were no more words. When Jeffrey had flung away to his room, Pitt sat down in the kitchen, against the wall, under the high bracket lamp. He felt heavy, sick, old, pierced with a new grief. He understood that some veil had been torn — it was as if some distance were now bridged for the convenience of evil spirits; as if the channels of his flesh and of Jeffrey's — of Jeffrey's — had been opened to forces which should never have entered. What had Jeffrey said to him? He blamed himself, he tortured his hands in his passion to undo whatever he had done which made the boy speak to him like that. He covered his face and sat motionless. When he looked out, the oil-lamp was burning low. It filled the kitchen with its odor of greasy burning. Hour after hour he sat in the darkness. He put his hand on his two little pieces of celluloid and sat clicking them together. Long before dawn he knew what he would do.

Jeffrey slept soundly, woke late, found his father's room neat and vacant, breakfast hot on the back of the stove, and no one about. Hurrying down Cook Street, he glanced with indifference at the men working at the sewer ditch. He father he did not see at all. Pitt was picking up wooden blocks just before the Granger house, and he kept stooping, with his head turned away, as Jeffrey passed.

4

Pitt was one of the oldest of the twenty men who worked in the street. They were in blue overalls and their irregular motions were pleasant against the chocolate earth, from which they flung up deep yellow sand. In other yellows the sun surged through the bright green maple leaves and glossy cottonwoods, glistening, as glistened the tin dinner pails piled on the green parking. Golden glow and red hollyhocks bloomed in the Granger garden. An occasional oriole flung his orange sharply against the blue. But Pitt's lift of spirit was not so much from these things as from the pleasure of physical exercise. He worked as briskly as the brown young giants about him.

The broad shadow of the Granger house fell upon him. He did not think about the day when he had first fared down that street, and opened the iron gate. The gate and fence were gone now, and he had not missed them. Once, when he stood to rest, he looked across to the little house at the top of the steep steps. A woman was in the doorway, watching the work. Pitt stared at her and at he house, and he wondered what had become of those little black pigs which he remembered. It was this that he was trying to recall as his pick-ax worked away at the wooden blocks across which Barbara's feet had trod, where they had crossed on her wedding day, where she, and then he himself had brought Jeffrey to leave him with Miss Arrowsmith. . . . Now he remembered that it was Cal Arum, of Mark and Arum, who had bought the little pigs for his farm. Pitt wondered what Cal had sold them for, and if they had all lived.

Most of the time, however, he thought about Jeffrey, and computed. Fifty a month for two months. With what he could save from this, Jeffrey should make his start. This work would last for four months or more. After Jeffrey left, Pitt need spend nothing on himself. Before cold weather came he meant to take his remaining plants in a push cart and go from door to door. Those that he did not sell he would give to Paulina. . . . But why in the world the boy wouldn't use his mother's money — that was the funniest thing. The *funniest* thing! Yet Pitt had explained it to his own heart: Jeffrey didn't want to take the money from him.

When the brickyard whistle blew at noon, the men sat under the trees. Pitt sat among them — he had not wished to risk discovery by returning home at noon and meeting Jeffrey. When Jeffrey passed, Pitt was lying down, with his hat over his face.

"Never saw me!" Pitt thought, looking fondly after him. "Say! I can go along this way for four months, having fun with him!"

When he was torn by his recollection of the words spoken the night before, he planned the hour of Jeffrey's surprise as the money was given to

him. It was the old happiness with which he had earned for Barbara the paisley shawl money, the insurance, the mortgage.

From the Granger house Jep came down and barked at the spectacle
of men eating on the ground. Pitt called to him. The little dog listened, advanced, doubted, was lured by a bit of meat, come close, sniffed, barked joyously and sprang to lick Pitt's face. The insignificant creature wished to be
aristocratic, but was overcome by friendship and by meat. Pitt fed him from
his dinner pail. The expensive little thing sat on Pitt's blue overalls, waved his
splendid tail and was the closest approach to bric-a-brac that the men would
ever see. Pitt held him in his arms, brooded over him and at the end of the
hour carried him to the Granger door, at the risk of detection, and laid him
on the mat. The contact left Pitt warm. He whistled and thought about nothing.

Toward four o'clock Miss Arrowsmith emerged and walked down
to her carriage, waiting at the end of the street, a carriage driven by the coachman, Henderson, of Pitt's wedding day. She did not know that if she had
gone to drive on the afternoon of a hot day nearly twenty years previous, one
of those blue figures would not have been there on the street, pickax in hand.
Nor did this occur to Pitt, looking after her. But he thought that her black-
and-white gown showed well in the maple shadows, and then he wondered
proudly whether noticing such things might not mean that he knew something about art. But this he dismissed as improbable and kept on with his
plans for Jeffrey when the money should be earned.

"I wish't I hadn't traded claims," he thought once, but without bitterness.

That night he reached home, hid his blue overalls, and had the supper ready when Jeffrey returned. Their meeting and their memory of Jeffrey's
words of the night before were erased by the comfortable chatter of Mis' Hellie
Copper, who arrived with a custard pie:

"Me?" she said. "Oh, the rheumatism's all over me. I declare I can
hear it crack in the joints of my brain when I try to think. How're you? Oh,
you always say that."

Pitt looked up brightly, lips parted, hands hanging from his stiffly-
held wrists.

"Back's kind of stiff," he volunteered, and for no reason which they
could divine, shook with quiet laughter.

"I don't see the fun in that," Mis' Hellie said. "Well, I'll run along.
I've got a boarder that acts like the world was down on him personally if his
victuals ain't served up when the whistle blows. You'd think he had to use the
six o'clock hand for a knife, while it was straight."

Between father and son talk about this boarder endured through the
supper, though neither knew the man. And neither referred to the last night's
conversation, and there was no mention of art in any form.

Late that night Pitt, still dressed, went with a lamp to Jeffrey's room. The boy did not waken. He lay with his head thrown back, his straight, thick hair spread about his face like the wind-blown youths in Italian paintings. Pitt saw that he was pale, that there were channels of shadow of his temples and his throat. His hand on the coverlet looked frail — the hand which should have told all the creative gift legible there and legible, too, that weak grasp on physical reality. Pitt went to the shelf where lay the little pile of water-colors and carried them away with him.

He took them to the kitchen, and spread them on the oilcloth of the table. For the life of him he could not see that they were not as fine as any pictures that ever were painted. He meditated sending them to the Chicago Art Institute, foresaw the enthusiasm of the letter with which they would be returned, Jeffrey summoned to the Institute, his way paid, honor and success to follow, perhaps some such engagement as that chap who drew like lightning, right before your eyes . . . he checked himself, remembering that Jeffrey had said this chap's work was not art. What was art, anyway?

He thought of taking the studies himself to the Institute. He could walk round till he found somebody. But all this he dismissed. That which pierced him was Jeffrey's own lack of effort, of hope.

From an envelope there slipped a half dozen pages of rough paper covered with vagrant design — conventionalized flowers, flame, fern, crystals, a breaking wave, hanging moss, cloud forms, musical instruments, vines.

"Looks kind of like wallpaper," Pitt thought.

Then he thought: "Why, it would do for wallpaper!"

He examined the sheets, and was shaken by his fresh hope. Hadn't he always envied the designer fellows who made the paper which he hung, and what if Jeffrey could be one of these! It might be that this was what he could do, all the time. And if this was true. . . .

"I give it to him!" Pitt said aloud. "I done that, sure as you live. If he can plan wallpaper, he gets it from me. . . ."

He closed his eyes. Barbara, Alaska, the lost claim, the dull toil . . . all, all had meaning if only he had given Jeffrey this gift.

"Think of me — _me_ — workin' in wallpaper till he got the trick of it when he was born. . . ."

Pitt felt like the mother, as if he had stamped the child before birth. He was flooded by the extreme creative joy, in its moment of belief in the authority of that which it has conceived. Why, wallpaper designers, they must be only the best. . . .

Next day he faced Jeffrey with his expectation. Jeffrey grudgingly conceded that he might be able to do something with those things, after a long time, when had practiced and studied up . . . oh, no. There was no use hoping anything from these, but perhaps some time—

"Yes, but if you don't do it, you won't do it," said Pitt, expertly. It was marvelous how experience with Hart, Hollow and Orr, Pickle and Fruit Products, and in Alaskan mines, should have given Pitt a formula valid for creative art, and to be hurled at one who disregarded a faint voice. "You'll never do it if you stay at Orcutt's. You got to get right after these things. They won't come to you—" Pitt was trembling, flushed. He spoke in a kind of inspired knowledge, born of his desire. "Jeffrey! Take mama's money and go up and give it a try, with some wallpaper folks. . . ."

"Father! I—"

"You see, I could write you a letter to my folks in the business, there in Chicago. Don't you see? It'd be like mama and me sending you there. . . ."

"Don't ask me to take that money," said Jeffrey. "I'll see about the other — later," he added; and went about the room as if he were burdened with innumerable concerns of which (his father must understand) this was only one.

🐚

In a fortnight more Jeffrey found out what his father was doing, and faced him. Orcutt had told him, vast, genial Orcutt, who had lived in Burage all through Pitt's life with Barbara. Being a stone cutter, he had contempt for what he would have called common labor. And when Orcutt spent an idle moment watching the paving work, and there recognized Pitt, he went away shocked and saddened and, in that genial sadness of undertakers and executors, commented to Jeffrey on his father's course.

"It must have been someone else," said Jeffrey. "My father's helping Weilbarren and Harding."

"If it wasn't him," said Orcutt, "I'll eat my headstone."

Orcutt always said this, varying it by "masticate my monument." Ghoul-like figures, both, with bore conviction.

At night Jeffrey left ten minutes earlier than was his wont, went round by the sewer workers, saw his father throw down his shovel when the whistle blew, and then grimly attached himself to him, as it were, red-handed.

All the way up the street Jeffrey held forth, and Pitt said nothing. It was curious that the line which Jeffrey's argument took was, "Father. You're disgracing me. They'll all think I shouldn't let you—" and so on. This Pitt noted, with a whimsicality rare in his estimates. ("I'd like to know who the hell'd back he thinks is aching, anyway," Pitt said to himself. "His'n?") Aloud he said nothing until the boy's indignation — an odd blend of altruism and pride and filial notions — had spent itself. Then Pitt said:

"We don't seem to like each other's business, Jeffrey. I'll tell you what we'll do. I'll give up the street work if you'll go and learn art."

Jeffrey raged, Pitt held his point. When they reached the back door of their home, Pitt dropped down on the steps. He was tanned and perspiring. His hands, roughened, hung heavily between his knees. His shoes were covered with earth. Earth soiled garments, worn face, weariness marked him, but his eyes were blue and quiet and thinking, and he was the master of his little temple.

"I've worked like a horse my whole life," he said, "and I've never liked any of it. You're going the way I've went. I've wasted what was in me" — it was the first time that he had said this — "and there was something in me!" It was the cry of the soul, which always recognizes its infinity, glimpses its own wings. "But I couldn't do only what I done. You could do more. And I'll do what I'm doing and earn the money for you to go to Chicago — unless you'll take that money in the bank, and go like you'd ought to go. . . ."

His words trailed away. Pitt rarely finished a sentence and let it stand. He pecked at it until it lost its outline. He now added a few indistinguishable words. He rose and turned indoors.

"But I tell you I won't have you doing work like that for me—" Jeffrey followed him, and there was in his face genuine distress as well as his pride.

"Hush up!" Pitt said, very gently. "Do as I say, and I'll do whatever you want. Till then, quit your talking to me!"

He struck his fist on the table. But there was in the gesture no authority — you knew that he was forcing it from himself; it was as if he had flung down a velvet glove, empty. However, like all weak men, Pitt had an obstinacy which, once aroused, was unassailable. It was his saving, and losing, substitute for firmness. Nothing that Jeffrey could say impressed him.

"I made a mistake," Pitt said to himself. "I made a mistake. I'd ought to have stayed away, where I didn't worry nobody."

But he said this to keep down the thought which was causing him his greatest misery: That he had not come home in time.

In a night or two he went to lay all before Rachel. It was a night of rain, and Rachel was in the small room at the hall's end — the room where they had gathered before Pitt and Barbara were married, the room where Barbara had her news from the old doctor, the room which, remote from Mrs. Granger, Rachel had meant for Jeffrey's nursery. Pitt was in that heavy winter suit which was his "best," and he sat relaxed, as always, but on the chair's edge, ready to get out of the way if there was "company." "Got company?" was his first question, on the threshold. Rachel wished that this were one of the nights when she had not dressed for dinner.

"You see," Pitt said, "I thought at first Jeffrey could get to be a real artist — like that Thomas Gainsborough one in the Supplement, and some of them. But he don't seem to want to. So then I wondered how it'd be if he made wallpaper patterns."

"Wallpaper patterns?"

"Yes, and I wondered," Pitt ventured, "whether you'd write up to Nickett and Reeve about it. And see if they'll look over some of the patterns

Jeffrey's made."

"Patterns. . . ."

"Yes. The different patterns. I think if you wrote—"

He hesitated, and flushed.

"I—I have wrote," he explained, "but my spelling or something — I guess they think they won't be anything to it. I ain't had an answer. Of course," Pitt added, "they wouldn't remember me."

Rachel threw out her hands. "Pitt!" she cried — as everyone called him. "I can't bear it. What have I done? Why don't you hate me?"

He stared at her in intense astonishment.

"You left him with me. I've simply let his life slip through my fingers."

"Well," said Pitt, "that's just exactly what I done. To think of your saying that. Ain't that the funniest thing. . . ."

"All my worst crimes," Rachel said, "are the things I didn't do."

"Why say," said Pitt in concern. "Say! Don't you go and feel like that. I give you my word, I never thought of that. You! Why, it was me."

She stood up in the ugly, old-fashioned room, on which her modern touches showed ineffectual and assumed. Her Persian rugs and her prints were dominated by the pier glass and by the chandelier hung with prisms. So her own modernity, her sophistication had been sucked in, nullified by the dead hand of that house. She was that remnant of the patriarchal age, the woman with the mind of tomorrow, born of today, and enslaved by yesterday.

"If Jeffrey doesn't make the most of himself, as we say," she said, "it is I who am to blame. I saw his possibilities, but the worst of it is, I made no choice. I didn't even decide not go accept the responsibility of him. I let him go to Mis' Hellie's, and from year to year I have fooled myself, saying that I meant to take charge. . . . What he is now, I have made him. . . ."

Pitt twisted his hands, his distressed face lifted.

"Oh," he said, "don't you! Don't you! If you feel bad, then it's my fault for asking you to take him that time."

She laughed then, and resumed her normal manner, relaxed, distant, contained.

"The fact is," she said, "our organism can't live up to us. We *are* more than we can do. We injure one another even when we do our best — the machinery doesn't work — yet. *There ought to be something that can make it run. . . .*"

This Pitt did not follow. He sat, with his liquid, upward look, and that pitiful cheer of his abruptly shone out.

"Say!" he cried. "Don't you worry. Why Jeffrey, he'll come out all right. This letter to the wallpaper folks'll start him right in."

On this they parted, and Rachel went to prepare her mother's milk. Mrs. Granger liked it at a certain temperature and in a certain glass.

Nickett and Reeve replied to Rachel's letter that they would be glad to have these designs submitted. Jeffrey was at his work at Orcutt's when the word came in that his father was outside. Pitt, in his overalls, stood in the passage — it was just before noon — and told his news. In spite of Jeffrey's curt nod, his father knew that he was pleased. But Pitt was disappointed that the "patterns" might not be begun at once. Some work in the country kept Jeffrey for several evenings, and it was a fortnight before he had three designs ready to submit. At the work, Pitt hung over him until Jeffrey asked him to go away.

"It seems to me like it was me doing it," Pitt explained in apology, and sat down at a distance.

When Nickett and Reeve accepted one of the designs and asked to see more, Pitt's happiness made him articulate, as his misery had done in the old days. He went about telling everyone what had happened. He told the sewerage contractor and the superintendent and the baker, and held up the line in the post office while he told it to Zeri Wing. As he dug on the street, he talked about it with the men.

"My boy's got a wallpaper pattern taken by the art folks that makes wallpaper. . . ."

He went to Weilbarren and Harding on a Saturday evening and related all to them, and tried to draw the "pattern" on the back of a hand-bill.

"Something like that," he explained, "only more like a face and done better at the corners. . . . You know, I was thinking: Burage folks can have it on their walls and tell their company a Burage boy thought it up. . . ."

On one occasion, Jeffrey heard his father say this. And one of the boy'd old delicacies arose and would not let him complain. In the large relationship, Jeffrey could trample. In the little, he was constrained to niceties, as if in his flesh there played the softness of Barbara's old compunctions.

Mis' Copper came over and praised him, said that she wanted to bring Mis' Miles and Mis' True to see the "pattern." And they all urged him on, and scoffed when he said, as he was beginning to say, that he didn't believe he could make any more designs. Not the aspiring soul who fails is the tragic soul, but the soul which, having power, will not venture, but is still surrounded by its faithful group of those who seek to kindle it, to help it in secret, to confide in others a belief in its ultimate triumph. These tragedies live in every town. The hearts of kinfolk bear their certainties of what might have been, and now and again these certainties have ground.

These days of expectation which Pitt was powerless to open into action, resolved themselves on a chance word.

One night Jeffrey joined the tremendous nightly procession of youth and romance footing under the maples toward the town. It was now September, the dusk fell early, and yellow and blue light netted the leaves, gemmed by the suns and the planets. The world of Burage walked together toward the town, their feet tramping in the after-supper measure of the little towns of the world, marching toward dreams and toward the unknown. Jeffrey went, imagining nothing, but restless under the touch of that haunting purpose which made him scan the faces of girls and look away. It was little more than that word *She* in his consciousness, but the consciousness was there, and powerful.

A new parrot hung before the bakery, and spoke to the crowd and was teased by the boys. That which at this period was called a talking machine gave out from some saloon its raucous, nasal challenge:

"I leave it to you, genl'man, if she was not the peachiest little queen that ever pattered down this pike, a-ha. . . ."

The aimless adventuring of the warm evening took the street. About the post office an hundred men and boys assembled, and down the lane which they made, the Burage young women in bright attire threaded their way, exchanging nods, signals. And more than one of that light crowd which years before had gone to the tent show on the market square, now passed by, faded, unlit, absorbed in technicalities of house and child, as if nature should announce victoriously: "Even these I assimilated." But there must have been some star to reply: "Ay, but too often as yet you first smother and then assimilate." For at the distance of a star the processes of smothering and of planting bear a resemblance. No wonder then that these processes are mistaken for each other at closer range.

Otie Adams strolled by. Otie was in a bank, dressed well, went about with the daughters of the Brewsters, the Hudsons and the Ames's.

"Hello, Pitt," he hailed Jeffrey, and halted.

By some protective cunning functioning in old channels, Jeffrey tried not to look too pleased.

"How's business?" Otie inquired, and rolled a cigarette.

"Good enough," Jeffrey said, "but not as good as yours, I guess."

Otie lit his cigarette.

"How's your father like his?" he asked, and looked in Jeffrey's eyes.

Jeffrey flushed. "Don't know," he said. "That's *his* business."

"Long as you didn't lose your job. . . ." said Otie. "Have a cigarette, or don't you roll them?"

Jeffrey went home that night and found his father lying on the Brussels couch asleep. When Jeffrey struck a light, Pitt opened his eyes. Jeffrey came and stood over him.

"Father!" he cried with violence. "I'll go into the city. I'll try anything so you'll get off this infernal street work."

Like a spring, released and quivering, Pitt sat up. He was collarless, his hair was rough, and there were great circles beneath his eyes.

"And use the Four Hundred in the Bank?"

"As much as I have to," Jeffrey said, walking away. "I—I can't stand it to have you grubbing like that. . . . I can't stand it!"

Pitt came and stood before his son. Pitt was hunched and his clothes were crumpled, but his face had a kind of swift, inner shining, and there was a mist not alone in his eyes but in some inexplicable way attending his face and head.

"Oh, Jeff!" cried the little man. "I didn't know I could feel so glad."

In the night, when he was thinking about going to the superintendent to give up his work, Pitt speculated:

"I wonder what Jeffrey thought was the matter with my job, anyway?"

5

Jeffrey was in his room making ready for his journey. The room was bare, bare floor, white-washed walls, and for counterpane, a pink patchwork quilt which Barbara's mother had made. On two shelves were his sketches, half a dozen books, and Rachel's loving cup — the "Holy Grail." The cup was dull and needed care.

Pitt came in. Over his arm he had his own best suit of clothes.

"I wanted to ask you," he said, "it seems a shame to travel in these." He looked doubtfully at the clothes which he was wearing.

Jeffrey drew down his brows.

"What's that for?" he asked.

"Well, I thought I'd ought to look as good as I could."

"You're not think of going?"

"Why, yes," Pitt replied. "I thought that's what we said."

"There's no need of that," Jeffrey declared. "None in the world, father. Well! Can't I take care of myself?"

Pitt stood before him and looked up at him.

"You didn't before—" he murmured.

Jeffrey flushed.

"I've told you I'll show them my stuff this time," he said shortly. "It won't take long!"

"Yes," Pitt said eagerly, "but I meant — there's Nickett and Reeve, you know. I thought I could kind of get you started right, there."

"Oh," said Jeffrey, "don't you bother — and spend all that money. I'll be all right."

Mis' Hellie, who had arrived early to assist in these preparations, tried to catch Jeffrey's eye from the doorway, behind Pitt; but Jeffrey was reiterating the needlessness of Pitt making this journey. Jeffrey himself may have thought that this was from delicacy, but it was a delicacy which flushed his father's face and silenced him.

"Why couldn't you let him go?" Mis' Hellie ventured, when Pitt had left the room.

"Why, what's the use?"

"But I think he'd like to go. He ain't had much fun, going round with a son."

Jeffrey reflected. "I suppose," he admitted, "I don't want to be led into Chicago by the hand."

Mis' Hellie sniffed.

"Pride went to the fair," she remarked, "but love got the prize."

Jeffrey laughed, then whistled, then went away with an air of profound and absorbed importance.

Toward six o'clock Mis' Hellie went home to prepare supper for her meticulous boarder. According to her custom, she entered her house by the kitchen door and did not go into the "other" part of the house until evening. Then she opened her front door and found the letter.

It was a letter curt, typewritten and arrogant in its indifference to the tragedy which it culminated. As she read, Mis' Hellie went a thick white, as if something definite, like death, had overtaken her. She said, "Oh poor soul, poor soul," and ran from her house and turned toward Pitt's house. She held her letter, saw no one whom she met, and now she was crying.

Mis' Barber was standing at Mis' True's gate, and they called to Mis' Hellie as she passed. She poured out to them some broken part of her news, and they came into the street and hurried with her, three dun-colored figures against an orange sky.

"Who wrote?" one asked.

"I never looked," Mis' Hellie said.

"Chicago?"

"Chicago."

"When was't wrote?"

"I never looked."

"What'll he do?"

"What'll he do?"

"What'll he do?"

Pitt was in the kitchen. He had laboriously written and rewritten a letter introducing his son to Nickett and Reeve. At supper he had shown the letter to Jeffrey, who had thanked him and, unaccountably to Pitt, had flushed.

As they sat at supper, Pitt had turned many things in his mind and as they rose, he said:

"Look here, Jeff. I guess you better not use that letter."

Jeffrey asked guiltily "Why not?" and wondered whether his father had guessed that he had not intended to use it.

"Well," Pitt said, "of course I knew 'em, but I was never any great shakes 'round there. And you look so fine — you don't look like you belonged to me." Here Pitt laughed loudly. "I think you'll be better off to brace up to 'em on your own hook."

"Oh, well, I can see how it goes," Jeffrey replied, and strolled away. He felt uncomfortable. It is true that he had regarded his father's awkward letter to his former employers as distinct handicap.

Jeffrey went out the side door and down the side street. The three women came hurrying to the front door. Pitt saw them standing against the smoky green and silver of the maple leaves below a blue arc lamp. He would have cried out some hearty banality, but he caught their look.

"Pitt," Mis' Hellie cried. "Oh, Pitt. . . ." and her features seemed to fall out of drawing.

It was not so much that he divined their news, as that all those years he had never ceased to expect that any letter, any message might be from Barbara. Therefore now he spoke Barbara's name.

"She's sick," said Mis' Hellie. "She's in the city—"

"*In the city!*"

"She's sent for me. . . ."

She held out the terrible letter. "Mrs. Barbara Ellsworth" it said, asked that she be summoned to the hospital which it named.

He tried to read it, gave it up, and they saw him shaking. His face was a sickly, solid color. He kept trying to get words.

"Sent for you!" was all that he said.

"She give 'em my name, I expect—"

Pitt cried out terribly: "She didn't give my name!"

"She must have known you wasn't here for so long," Mis' Hellie thought to say.

"We'll go," Pitt said, "we'll go. We must go tonight. . . ."

"I thought you'd do that," Mis' Hellie said.

"And Jeffrey, he'll go. He can go tonight instead of tomorrow—"

He was moving through the house, and the women were following. He went to the kitchen, the room in which he was most at home. He looked about him, as if there was something which would have helped. It was dusk, but it did not occur to him to light a lamp. He sat on the woodbox. The three women moved about the room, vaguely looking for matches. Mis' True and Mis' Barber were murmuring indistinguishably comfort, suggestion, grief, which no one heard. At last they asked about Jeffrey, and the two women went off to find him.

It was not until that hour that Pitt was ever actually without Barbara. For he had said to himself that if she were alive, she would have come back, not to him but to the boy. She would have tried to see Jeffrey. And since she was dead, she could not be far away, after all. But she was not dead. *Barbara was not dead.* The shock came in the news that she was living. That she had been somewhere, not far distant, for fifteen years.

The old anguish was in him, tearing him. All his fault. Whatever had come to Barbara, he alone was to blame.

Mis' Hellie talked on — arrangement, speculation. He said nothing. After a long time, when she had at last found a lamp, she looked at him fearfully, his head on his chest, his hands heavy and limp. She had asked some question about the train, and waited for a reply. And after a silence he said:

"I didn't know how to be married."

He had heard nothing that she said. She fell silent. They were sitting so, under high bracket lamp, when the women returned with Jeffrey. The boy looked harassed, driven, hunted, but by no means grief-stricken.

"We'll go in at eleven, Jeffrey," Pitt said.

Jeffrey stood awkwardly before his father. He would have liked to go to him, but the women were there. However, at his father's words, the boy straightened.

"I'll wait now, I think," he returned.

"What!" Pitt cried.

Jeffrey's voice rose. "How do I know she wants to see me? How do you know, for that matter?"

"Why, Jeffrey—"

"It's all right," he said, "you'll do as you please, father. But I'll not go, till I know."

"But you was going tomorrow anyway."

"That can wait."

The women looked from one to another. They had no particular power of thought, but the motions of existence had given them something and they turned to Jeffrey in troubled silence.

"Jeffrey! Mama'll want to see you!" Pitt cried.

"She'll be wanting to see you more than to see either of us," Mis' Hellie said.

"Then she must say so," Jeffrey answered.

"Oh, poor thing, poor thing!" Mis' Hellie cried, and could not go on. Mis' True wept. Mis' Barber spoke out sharply.

"It's your ma," she said.

The boy replied: "She ought to have reminded me of that before."

He would like to have been softer with his father, on account of his father's grief. But the three women annoyed him. "Why don't they get out?" he thought. "A lot of women looking on. Why don't they go home?"

But when they had gone, Mis' Hellie to make ready to take the train with Pitt at eleven, it was no easier for Jeffrey to speak plainly to his father. In the little that they did say, each missed fire, was not quite understood in some significant shade.

Pitt fell silent, went in the parlor and found some pictures of Jeffrey as a baby which Mis' Hellie had given him. These he meant to take, and he looked about the house, trying to find other things. Finally he went out in the garden with that old red glass hand lamp and picked a bunch of scarlet salvia. This he shut in the suitcase. But he did not know what he was doing. He was in a shell, as after great grief. *Barbara.* This that he felt was no realization of her, but a mere background to the terrible truth that for fifteen years she had been alive.

He left the house for the station an hour before the train was due to leave. When he saw Jeffrey preparing to accompany him there, he cried:

"Jeff! You're coming too?"

"To the depot."

"All the way!"

"No. I can't do it."

A moment later Pitt appeared in his bedroom door, and his look was soft and liquid.

"Jeffrey, *I* see! You're going to stay here to get the house ready for her. That's it, ain't it, son!"

Without waiting for his reply, he went on — suggestions about the room, the bed, food.

"That's best," he said. "I'll bring her right home, as quick as she can come. And you can have everything nice for us. . . ."

Jeffrey said nothing. And on discovering that it was beginning to rain, Pitt insisted that Jeffrey should not go to the station as there was only one umbrella, and Mis' Hellie must be called for — the only time that Pitt was ever effective was when he was refusing to let someone be at trouble for him. He went off alone. And Jeffrey sank miserably down and wept. "Daddy!" he sobbed, as he had never said since he was a little boy. Pitt would have liked to hear him say that.

Pitt went through the black streets. He was not thinking. He was quivering, smarting, weighed down. When he passed the Grangers' and the little house with the steep flight of steps, his pain burst bounds and he talked to himself.

"What's that?" asked a man, passing in the dark.

"Nothing," Pitt said. "Nothing."

The next day as Jeffrey sat alone at his supper, Mis' Hellie Copper walked into the kitchen.

"You're back?" he stared at Mis' Hellie. "Where's — father?" And looked toward the door by which she had entered, as if he expected to see some one else standing there.

For once Mis' Hellie seemed to have no words. She stood trying to speak, her face puckering queerly.

"He won't be here till tomorrow," she said. Then: "Jeffrey—Jeffrey! She's dead. Your mother, she's dead."

"Dead!" Jeffrey cried — but it was not of her that he was thinking.

He put his question with a break in his breath, but not for her. "My father! Did he get there in time?"

Mis' Hellie broke down.

"No," she sobbed, "no, he didn't, Jeffrey. He didn't get there in time."

Barbara had come to the hospital, a stranger, with a handbag, and a little box and money enough for her first needs. The sole address which she gave was Mis' Hellie's. She had refused to let them notify Mis' Hellie earlier — until, in fact, they told her that she would not recover. And Barbara had died just before the two had left Burage — in that hour when Pitt had walked to the station alone.

"Did you see her?" Jeffrey asked.

"Yes," Mis' Hellie said, and fell to sobbing. He asked nothing more.

They were to arrive at five that afternoon and go straight to the cemetery for the service, which Mis' Hellie was to arrange.

"I donno," she said severely, "how much you'll want to have to do with this, Jeffrey. . . ."

With his head held very stiff, Jeffrey said that he could take charge, and seemed to be rather hurt that Mis' Hellie had hurried back for that purpose. Death is creative. It not only removes differences. It creates the spiritual.

It was Mis' Hellie who had to meet the questions of Burage, but she cut them off sharply with "We don't know much." It was noticeable that all, without exception, in repeating the name, said "Barbara Ellsworth." Pitt, it seemed, had been an interlude, forgotten. Yet there was their son, standing in Mis' Hellie's dining room, trying to think what else there was to do for Barbara Ellsworth.

At noon Mis' Hellie and Mis' Miles, Mis' Barber and Mis' Nick True toiled up to the cemetery and covered the mound of earth with evergreen and lined the grave with green. Mis' Hellie, as was the Burage custom, got down into the grave for the purpose. ("No use paying out money to the undertaker for such things," Burage said.)

While they worked, the women speculated.

"Say, where do you s'pose she's been all this while?"

"Land knows."

"But she must have lived *some*how."

"I'm not so awful sure Pitt never heard from her. I bet he knows more'n he lets on he knows."

"Him? *No*, sir. He'd have told it before he hardly had the news."

"Not if it was some kind of news, he wouldn't."

"Yes, but if it was that kind of news, he wouldn't have had it."

"And it *wasn't* that kind of news, or else would he ever have gone tracking off to meet her today?"

The speaker had them there. They tacked in silence around that home where Barbara would lie with the truth hidden.

"Anyhow," said Mis' Monument Miles, gathering up scattered tacks when their work was finished, "there ain't never anything happened that couldn't have happened some different."

The three women laughed and went back to Mis' Hellie's carrying tools and tacks and a length of white cheesecloth left over. And as they went, they were stopped by those who had heard the news and were eager for details. These were invited to be at the cemetery when the party arrived from the Through, and it was clear that they would be there partly for an exchange of news, not to say views. And yet the fact that love is now motive in the race was evident, for all spoke with sorrowful faces and none with flippancy or recollection. Of course if Barbara had returned alive, love might not have been so motive.

At the hour when the three trains left Burage the little party waited that afternoon in the crowded Burage station.

Now it was for Barbara that they waited, and they were to close her history. Yet nothing happened which marked the hour from other hours. The minister and the bearers and Mis' Hellie and Jeffrey looked as if they were going to take the train, and all the others in the rooms looked as if they were going to take the train. Perhaps, then, they too had histories, about to be closed, or still open. The minister held a hot-stemmed bunch of coreopsis and the bearers wished that they had thought "to bring a posy." These men tried to talk with Jeffrey, who said nothing of his own accord. There were three observations as to the train being late, and the combinations of seven men and three observations are mathematically enormous.

Outside Flo Buckstaff was entertaining a group of commercial travelers, telling them who would be on this train. "I been right in on the whole thing and now here I am and there's her hearse." Flo said it several times as if with these words the gate of destiny yawned and thrilled him. But one of the commercial travelers said: "Jocks, I'm goin' over here and set down in some shade."

Barbara and Pitt reached Burage after six o'clock. Pitt had been sitting in the baggage car and got stiffly down. In him excitement now absorbed all other emotion. He did not greet those who waited, but ran to meet the approaching truck, insisted on helping to lower the coffin, shouted directions, so that those who did not understand this man laughed and exchanged glances. It was no wonder that they laughed — he looked for the hearse and did not see it and when his eye first fell on his son, Pitt cried querulously: "My God, where's the hearse? Didn't it wait?" — as if the vehicle had trotted busily off on its collections. Pitt, it seemed, was ridiculous in all tragedy.

When he saw Mis' Hellie he went to her with the air of a child.

"Barbara's there. She's there," he said piteously, and stared at the truck. How it all shook and jarred as young Nicky True trundled it across the platform — Nicky was assistant baggage man now. When Pitt saw the six men, "Well, sir," he said, "I never thought of that part." And before the minister — "Of course, the parson!" he said, as if he had just thought of him. "I'm glad to see you here," he added earnestly. It was not until he looked in Jeffrey's face that his mouth quivered.

"Mama died," Pitt said to him.

Then he pushed by them and went with the bearers and the gentlemanly undertaker to the hearse, himself closed the doors, and came hurrying back.

He did not observe that it was Miss Arrowsmith's carriage which he entered, driven by Henderson. He sat forward on the edge of the seat, between Mis' Hellie and Jeffrey. Pitt's derby hat was on the back of his head, he wore those best winter clothes of his and perspiration laved his face. He began excitedly to tell about the incidents of his journey. His story, repeated and amplified, occupied the whole drive to the cemetery. Besides his heaviness, and an indeterminate sense of disgrace, Jeffrey now felt a definite shame of the little man.

Beautiful light and outstretched shadows were on the tended grass under the oaks. There Barbara's rebellion and her passion were hidden away, with her secret, and the forgotten lure of her.

When father and son came home that night from Mis' Hellie's where they had had supper, Pitt lingered outside the door, as if he could not bear to face that house of his. Beyond their little yard lay a low vacant lot, and here frogs chorused. A child was crying, and the smart closing of a door cut off the sound; the door opened and they heard once more, then it closed again. They stood there facing Capella, sparkling above the maples, but this they did not know.

"Six weeks in the hospital, and none of us knew," Pitt said. "Just think — walking round here like we done — and didn't know."

"Wasn't anybody with her?" Jeffrey asked.

"They said not. I wish they had been — no matter who it was." Pitt repeated it. "No matter who it was."

Suddenly he sat down on the step, his whole body drooping.

"Not five hours," he said. "There was so much time — all the while you was a little shaver — and Alaska — and all that. And if I'd just got there five hours quicker, she would have talked to me."

Jeffrey said nothing. The child beyond the vacant lot cried out sharply and said something not to be distinguished.

"And now we don't know — nobody knows." He mused. "Mis'

Hellie's boarder — if he hadn't been so particular about havin' his meals on time, she says she'd have gone to look for the mail before she got supper. I could have caught the Six, then. And yet I don't know that chap — and he never heard of me. Ain't it the funniest thing?" Pitt said. "The *funniest* thing. . . ."

After a silence he said:

"There's a little box of things she wanted Mis' Copper to have. When that gets here, mebbe then we'll know. . . ."

Jeffrey wondered if his father had seen her, and how she had looked, but he could not ask. He never asked.

"There's one thing," Pitt said, after a time. "That's the money. It's going to take quite a little money. There's some to the hospital — and then the funeral. . . . Of course that's hers, anyway. But, Jeffrey, I guess you'll have to wait a little bit before you get your art started, now."

"You know how much I care," Jeffrey said to this, and repented when he caught the pain in his father's motion. "That can wait a while," Jeffrey put it lightly.

Another silence, and the child still crying ⁻ a lonely crying, as if he were alone in the dark.

"Before," Pitt said, "when — when she. . . ." His words trailed away. "You was just a little chap," he said. "I held you on my knee."

"When she—" what was the rest, Jeffrey wondered.

"It seems funny," Pitt added heavily. "You don't remember her even a little bit, do you, Jeffrey?"

"No," Jeffrey said, "I don't. I don't know anything about her." In spite of himself his voice rose a little.

"She was an awful good woman," Pitt said.

Jeffrey could bear it no longer, knowing how these next days would bring talk of her. He thought of Otie Adams.

"Father," Jeffrey said, there in the dark. "*Was* she good?"

Pitt started as if these words had physically smitten him.

"Who told you that?" he cried.

"Told me what?" Jeffrey asked.

"I don't know what you mean," Pitt answered.

"Well, I don't know what I mean!" Jeffrey cried. "But nobody tells me anything about her. I know she went — and you didn't go away together. I wouldn't ask Mis' Copper. When you came home, I thought you'd tell me. But you didn't tell me. You ought to tell me — was she? Was she?"

Pitt continued to look up at him in the gloom.

"She's your mother," he said. "I don't see what difference anything could make."

"You think that!" Jeffrey cried — and laughed.

Pitt got up from the steps, and he moved like an old man. He went close to Jeffrey, and the finger that he pointed trembled.

"Look here," he said, "and I'll tell you what you say I ain't ever told you. Why should I tell you? I never thought I needed to tell you. Your mother was an angel. She was so good and so pretty that I'd ought to have known I didn't have any business to marry her. I'd ought to have known she wouldn't never have looked at me if she hadn't been lonesome. She took me into the house she owned. She give me her father's wallpaper business. And then she tried to get me to help her to be happy. But I was such a dub I couldn't do it. She couldn't stand me — I don't blame her, I don't blame her. I've always known it was my fault she went off. She was good — she was good. She wasn't nothing else, I tell you, but good."

There was a moment's pause, then Jeffrey went close to his father.

"Tell me one thing more," he said. "I thought — I heard somebody say once — *Father!* Did she go away alone?"

Pitt looked down at him as if from some enormous height. He seemed tall, he seemed glorious.

"Yes!" he cried. "She went alone."

6

Every afternoon now Pitt went to Mis' Hellie's to see whether the box from Barbara had arrived. They did not know whether it would come by express or post, and every day Pitt went to the Post Office to ask Zeri Wing whether he had see anything of a box which ought to be there. But he did not tell Zeri from whom the box would come, nor why it would be addressed to Mis' Hellie Copper, as once he would have explained. He was suddenly silent in these days. And there is nothing which leaves a garrulous person more terribly isolated than to be deserted by the need to talk. It was difficult to attribute this silence to mere grief. Everyone felt that Pitt was intimating that he wanted to be let alone. Yet in all his lonely life Pitt had never so passionately wanted companionship.

He would go to a certain flour and feed store, a hardware store, a harness shop where there presided men known to him in his old days. There he would sit, saying little, happy if he could get them to talk to him. And if their talk became reminiscence, so that Pitt was, as we say, "carried out of himself," he would try to prolong the hour by many innocent arts.

He had read almost no books of fiction, but one day he wandered into the library and looked along the shelves. Of the titles he could make nothing, but he examined them with earnestness. At last he went away with nothing. He thought that someday he would ask Miss Arrowsmith what was a good book. She would know.

For the first time he found himself looking with longing at the theater and motion picture house announcements. He saw that if he could go there for a little while, he would cease to think. It had never occurred to him that these temples thrive not upon homage to art but upon the need to forget. The people who went there he saw with new eyes.

He thought with longing of the days in Alaska, when physical toil left no time for remembrance. He understood why folk go away on journeys. Travel and the theater he could not afford, of books he knew nothing — from all the inheritances of forgetfulness he was cut off. He understood that the means to forget are expensive.

Thus Pitt turned to Jeffrey with a passion which made the boy the symbol of the world. He was Pitt's world. Pitt lived for him, was happy only when he was with Jeffrey, in him found forgetfulness, found a future, found a life. He did not return to the street work because this made Jeffrey unhappy. But that future at the study of art became Pitt's obsession. He became frantic to make money. While he waited for some promised work with Weilbarren and Harding he took his plants in a cart and with his upward, liquid look, appearing at doors. But he soon saw that they did not like to refuse him, that they bought, and then counted out the change taken from a clock-shelf, from a drawer-corner, from a bowl in the cupboard, and he guessed that this would be money saved for another purpose and diverted to him, not in trade, but in sympathy. So at last he dragged his cart to Paulina's house, and gave plants, pots, cart and all to her. And Paulina thanked him although it was (she said) a little late to do much with them *now*.

So a month passed. It was now late October, copper, ocher, gold. Still the box from Barbara had not come. Still he went every afternoon to Mis' Hellie Copper's, to ask about it. And still Weilbarren and Harding had not sent for him. Pitt hunted out some old-fashioned paper which he had at hand and hung it upon the walls of the parlor at the Brackett house. Not that he and Jeffrey ever used that forlorn parlor; but it was essential to have a task.

One day Jeffrey went out in the country with another man from Orcutt's, to deliver and set up a stone. They were not to return that night and Pitt, dreading the evening, made his work last long. It was nearly dark when he ceased and went to the side-yard to clean his brushes.

Out there he heard the front doorbell ring. It was a cracked and rusty ring, a poor broken wave of sound, a very lost soul of sound, fleeing in the spicy dusk. Save by agent or collector, the bell had not been rung in months. Pitt hurried round the house.

"Mebbe it's somebody I can ask to stay to supper," Pitt thought. Pitt often tried to think of somebody whom he could ask to supper, but this was hard, since nobody but Mis' Hellie ever invited him and he feared to rebuke them by a summons of his own.

On the porch, against the faintly yellow west, stood a man who, to Pitt, looking up at him from the walk, seemed tremendous in size and importance. Pitt hurried forward with his air of bright expectation. The little man always liked to be asked for; it struck him now that this important-looking stranger had doubtless got the wrong house. Pitt greeted him warmly: "Good evening! Come in — come in!"

"Evening," said the visitor. "This where Jeffrey Pitt lives?"

His affirmative Pitt gave with real delight, explained with anxious regret that Jeffrey would not be at home that night. "But come in, couldn't you?" Pitt urged.

The stranger uttered a disappointed exclamation. "I've come to town on purpose to see him," he volunteered.

Well! Pitt's expectation mounted. Good luck of some kind for Jeffrey, maybe.

"Come in, come in!" cried the little man.

The visitor stood on the porch and pulled thoughtfully at his beard — made a peculiar motion of combing his beard with his fingers.

"Stay to supper!" Pitt cried.

The man hesitated. Pitt threw open the door, urged the guest within, led the way to the dining room, found alight and turned and surveyed his guest with delight. It was as if he had said: "Company at last."

"My name is Beck," said the guest. "Jeffrey used to work for me."

"Mr. Beck!" Pitt cried delightedly. "I'm Jeffrey's father. I'm regular glad to see you — stay to supper!"

"I really shouldn't," said Beck. "I'm in a tree-menjous hurry. I'm here just between trains," and sat down.

He was a changed Beck in appearance — a pale Beck, a Beck who started when a door shut smartly, but a Beck with his manner of patronage and tolerance unimpaired. Under such toleration, Pitt's manner of anxious homage became nervously eager.

"I'll be quick," Pitt said. "I'll get us something or other — I'm my own cook—" Pitt laughed heartily, "but if you can stand it—"

Beck didn't know, he didn't know but that he could manage.

There was no selection of best dishes, for there were none. But Pitt put on their tablecloth, gave the guest the cup which was not nicked, the plate without a crack, and three-fourths of the bean soup, in a thick bowl. And the host kept thinking:

"If it's about paying Jeffrey the wages due him, why couldn't he tell me?"

Until he had eaten, Beck was not disposed to talk at all. He ate ravenously and was unabashed by his frequent returns to the bread and coffee. Pitt could not have analyzed it, but his guest's enormous and uncontrolled appetite made the little man less in awe of him. At last Beck leaned back with a sigh: "That's better. Much better," and glanced at the clock. Pitt caught the glance — and risked it.

"I was thinking," Pitt said mildly, "whether I couldn't do the business for Jeffrey."

Beck centered on Pitt, for the first time seemed to take in the little person who was so eagerly intent upon him.

"What makes you say *business?*" he inquired.

Pitt flushed. "Well," he said, "I didn't know, Jeffrey working for you—"

Beck studied him and shot his question, suddenly frowning.

"I want to find out," he said, "whether Jeffrey knows anything about a check that was supposed to be sent here to me, after — after I left town."

"A check," Pitt stupidly repeated.

"Check from Flower and Flower. A check for Three Hundred Dollars."

"Three Hundred Dollars!"

"Swear they sent it. I never — I — that is, I wasn't in a position to — ah — inquire about it, till lately. But they've shown me what they claim is the stub — sent April 16, last year. Claim it was returned, properly endorsed—"

"But Jeffrey wouldn't know—"

"That's what I wondered. He was around the office for a few days after I went, I hear. . . ."

"But he couldn't cash—"

"Oh, yes. He often cashed my checks."

Pitt laughed. "Oh, well," he said, "he never cashed that one. Why, he never even mentioned it to me."

Beck grinned and Pitt flushed.

"Why don't you inquire at the bank?" he demanded. "They might know. . . ."

It was Beck's turn to flush.

"I'm not running in and out of that bank every day," he said curtly.

"But I know Jeffrey never had the check," Pitt said. "Why, he told me you left owing him money."

"Well?" said Beck slowly.

Pitt understood and sat staring at Beck.

"Look here," Pitt said, "that was before I got back from Alaska. But I tell you who we can ask — if *you* want to make sure. We can ask Mis' Hellie Copper."

"Oh, no," said Beck hastily. "No."

"Sure. She'd know all about it."

"No," Beck said. "I'd rather not — I — in fact, there ain't time. But look here. Jeffrey's honest, I know that. I thought mebbe he cashed that check to pay himself back and was keeping the rest for me. You give him my address — I'll leave it. And tell him I need the money so dog-goned bad that I'm done out if I don't get it."

Beck delivered this word with his head up, and his own manner of lordly superiority. It was as if he had said: "I will do what I can for you." Beck was the patron, though the suppliant.

"Well, he never cashed it or saw it," said Pitt tolerantly. "I could swear to that." He found all his courage. "Could — could I say anything to him about what you owe him?" he asked, and blushed.

Beck stood up, in over-shadowing dignity.

"That," he said, "I shall negotiate in good time. When this is settled up, perhaps. Meantime," he hesitated, "if he *did* cash that check, for his own payment, or for — for any purpose," he looked significantly at Pitt, "the law won't pay no attention to what it was for. Not in forgery."

Pitt rose, his eyes fixed on Beck's face in distress and horror. He did not know what to say. He rubbed his wrists, his lips parted, moved, and he tried to smile.

"No offense," said Beck. "Much obliged for a good supper. Here's my card—" he scribbled a number on an envelope. "I shall expect to hear from Jeffrey, couple days. Good-by, Mr. Pitt, I'm sure. No offense."

"No. No. No," Pitt said. He followed with the lamp. Beck went away with a casual goodnight.

Pitt said to himself that he would say nothing to Mis' Copper. He wondered if he should even say anything to Jeffrey. The thing was preposterous, took no vital hold on Pitt, but still he found himself returning to the probabilities. When he woke in the night, the thing awaited him. But in the morning he laughed at the idea and put it from his thought as he pasted in the sun. Before Jeffrey returned, Pitt had dismissed the matter almost entirely, and his mind engaged in its routine of sad speculation about Barbara.

It was dark when Jeffrey arrived home the next night. Pitt had supper ready, and his delight in having his son back took unto itself form in a rain of maddening questions: Had the stone been heavy to handle? Was his help any good? Hard on the horses, wasn't it? How much would a stone like that cost, now? And what was the wording?

And almost every day, since a hint of Mis' Hellie's about Jeffrey's pallor, Pitt asked the boy how he was feeling. It irritated him, and he let his father see that it did. Only Pitt never saw.

At any rate, Jeffrey was looking almost handsome. That brown skin, reddening mouth, and thick, straight hair, those ruminant eyes and nervous hands would have made him almost exotic, in spite of his fine body, had these not been dominated by the lovely transparency which Rachel had noted and loved. That faintly luminous look, attributable to his glance, to his smile, to some atmosphere of gentleness, made it seem impossible that the boy was not of exquisite sensitiveness. He looked the sensitive, the developed. But there had been some arrestment, for he was querulous, irritable at these attacking questions, quite capable of silence or of an ironic curl. Nature's sound intent was evident enough in Jeffrey; but her hired servants, including Jeffrey himself, had not elaborated.

It was at last in some pathetic eagerness to interest the boy, to arrest his attention and give them a common ground that Pitt said when they were seated:

"Well, now, I've got a joke to tell you."

Jeffrey had not found that his father's sense of humor was often his own; but the boy was trying desperately hard to help his father through these days.

"On me?" he asked.

Pitt reflected. "Well, no," he said, "I rather guess it's on me. Anything that — well, anything like this *would* be a joke on me." He laughed. "It'd be me that would be come up with," he said. "You'll see when I tell you. It's the *funniest* thing."

Jeffrey said nothing.

"You can't guess who was here last night," Pitt said.

Jeffrey said nothing.

"For supper!" Pitt went on, "with me."

Jeffrey said nothing. At that moment he rather wanted to affect silence and superiority — he could not have told why.

"Guess!" said Pitt, trying to prolong the moment.

And after a pause Pitt announced it triumphantly:

"Mr. Beck!"

Jeffrey turned a terrible white, shadowed, ghastly. His eyes flew to his father's face, like a little boy's eyes, seeking some assurance.

"W—what'd he want?"

Jeffrey's lips were trembling, he jaw hung loose when he had spoken. Then he pulled himself together and tried to smile.

"Old Beck," he said. "How's — he?"

"Jeffrey!"

Arrested as he was about to go on with his story, Pitt rose, and his plate clattered on the table. He began to breathe hard, and as if breath exhausted him.

Jeffrey lifted his eyes without moving his head — a terrible gesture for the eyes of a human being.

"You had that three hundred."

"What three hundred?" Jeffrey frowned, looking in his cup.

"You know. You had it. You show you had it."

Jeffrey threw back his head.

"It was mine. And Platt's. And Mis' Hellie's. It was all ours — and more."

"Yours. What does that mean?"

"It means Beck owed it to us. And more."

"You got the check after Beck had gone!"

"Yes, but—"

"You cashed it."

"Well, but—"

"And never told him it had come. Oh, Jeffrey, God."

He said the names as one.

"Listen to me!" Jeffrey shouted. "He owed Mis' Hellie two hundred dollars that I'd got her to put in — owed her that and a year's interest. He owed Platt Sixty. Well, I paid them back, and kept what was left, but it didn't half pay up what Beck owed me. Now do you see? It was ours."

"Didn't Beck owe anybody else?"

"Yes, but—"

"Then you stole from them. You stole from the other creditors."

"Nonsense. Any one of them would do as I did — if they'd got the chance."

"Oh, God," said Pitt. "Then you're rotten right through."

He whirled and ran to the outside door, closing it violently behind him. On the step he sank down, his body shaking.

Jeffrey sprang up and lowered both window shades, as if to keep something out. As he turned, the homely look of the kitchen — the table, the porridge pot on the stove, the singing tea kettle, seemed to smite him to some sense of a faith outraged. He stood looking this way and that. Then he sat in his chair at the table, buried his head in his arms and burst into sobs.

After a time Pitt heard him. Out there in the darkness, Pitt faced something keener than his grief for Barbara. But now the two griefs were fused in the sense of his own failure. He had blighted Barbara, killed her (he said) and had begotten a son who did not even recognize his own baseness. Pitt stood in the naked egoism of flagellation.

When he thought he heard the boy's muffled sobs, he hurried to the door — if only Jeffrey saw what he had done, if only he cared. . . . Pitt opened the door, and instantly Jeffrey threw back his head and turned toward him a sullen face.

"Jeffrey!"

"Well?"

"I want you should come with me."

"Where?"

"Come!"

Pitt was commanding. Jeffrey moved to the door. On the street Pitt cried:

"I want you should come with me to Mis' Copper's. We'll talk this thing out."

Jeffrey's confidence kindled. Mis' Hellie would make him see.

The night was chill and starry. They joined the procession tramping toward the town, the tired women, the baby carts, the strolling couples marched with them. There were laughter, a little boy's whistle, the smoke from a bonfire in an alley, all the common places of the time. The two went in silence.

Mis' Hellie, setting bread-sponge in the Summer kitchen, by the light of a lantern hung on the wall, was startled by the two who stalked in at her door, unsmiling.

"I've come to ask you something," Pitt said without prelude. "That Three Hundred dollars that Jeffrey took from Mr. Beck — can you show me how that was the right thing to do?"

"The right thing to do!" Mis' Hellie looked puzzled.

"Jeffrey seems to think you can prove it was right," Pitt said. Mis' Hellie looked at him in wonder. How strangely he was talking. Was this Pitt?

"Right!" she said, and leaned on her pan. "It wasn't only right. It was smart."

"Smart!" Pitt shouted. "Smart!"

Mis' Hellie stood up and rubbed her hands on her apron.

"Well, my land. Beck owed us the money. And we'd never got it any other way."

"What about the other folks he owed?"

"That was their look-out, wasn't it?"

Pitt laughed. Pitt was a man who laughed often and heartily in his embarrassments. But this was another laugh. It was as if somewhere within him another voice shook out its terrible mirth.

Jeffrey, his comfort returning under Mis' Hellie's vindication, looked at his father with a show of confidence, and:

"Anybody'd say so," Jeffrey said.

"That so? What did Miss Arrowsmith say?" Pitt shot at them.

Jeffrey shifted. "We never asked her. We didn't tell the whole town."

"I should say not!" Mis' Hellie cried shrilly. "If you know you're right, then go ahead, *I* say."

"Sure enough," Pitt said, "sure enough. Well, listen to me," he cried trembling, "for I say you done dirt. Dirt."

Mis' Hellie reared her head, an effect impaired by a streak of flour on her cheek. "The idear!" she said.

"Come along, then — come along!" Pitt called out — so that some in that procession on the street turned their heads at the loud voice, saw a man against the dim light of the summer kitchen door and wondered. "Come straight to Miss Arrowsmith and put it up to her. Come along *now!*"

"Law, I'd leave my bread to do that," Mis' Hellie cried good-naturedly. "She's got sense enough to see that, I know. Though what difference it makes now," she added, "I don't understand."

Pitt said nothing. The three went out in the street. A fog was creeping about. An occasional strain came from the Burage band, practicing in its room in the engine house. Mis' Hellie had thrown on a knit shawl which smelled of the dye.

Rachel was walking up and down the strip of walk which led from her house to the gate. She did this frequently at evening and would have liked to do it by day, but it had taken Burage ten years to understand this habit in its Catholic priest and Rachel was not minded to load them with another burden.

"Come in!" she cried. "There's some ice cream from dinner. . . ."

"No!" said Pitt. "We want to ask you something."

His voice was pitched high, she caught his air of excitement, marveled at his leadership of this little party and wisely said: "At any rate, come inside. It has grown cold."

They followed her into the lighted parlor. She sat down in that room where had been enacted so much of the drama of this father and this son, and Mis' Hellie was seated also. But Pitt stood, poured out the circumstances, and put his question. Before he had finished, Rachel had grasped all.

"Yes, but—" Jeffrey essayed.

"Wait!" Pitt cried. He stood erect, he pressed his hair back from his forehead, his eyes blazed. No one had ever seen him look like this.

"She understands," he shouted to Jeffrey. "Miss Arrowsmith! What do you think of this kind of doings — say?"

"My dear Pitt," Rachel said, "mustn't you try not take this so seriously?"

Pitt stood pierced by her words. He was motionless, staring.

"The boy is young," Rachel said. "He was without experience — he didn't know. You must make allowance for all this. He—"

"He stole!"

"No, no!" she cried. "Why, you are using the word that we'd use if he had embezzled — taken money for his own gain."

"He took money that wasn't his. Ain't that stealing?"

"Surely you see a difference?" Rachel said quietly.

"Well, I should hope so!" Mis' Hellie shrilled.

Rachel was moved by Pitt's suffering, by the appeal in the eyes of Jeffrey, but Mis' Hellie's swift complacence annoyed her. Rachel moved toward Jeffrey and laid her hand on his arm. The boy was not sullen or defiant. From head to foot he was trembling.

"Oh," she said, "things are not so simple as this, Pitt. It is all so complex — everything — that one cannot condemn like this. . . ."

Pitt continued to regard her. "But," he said, "he done the other creditors out of their share of the money. He stole from them."

"Yes — unintentionally. Unconsciously."

"Unconsciously!" Pitt's voice rose. "He's got sense. Jeffrey's got the sense to see what he was doing."

"Undoubtedly. But try to see it as he saw it when he did it," she begged.

"Well, I do. And I see it as Beck saw it, too. Look how he acted to Beck," Pitt cried.

"Look how Beck acted to me," Jeffrey muttered.

Rachel frowned, but Mis' Hellie's erect head and double chin stood indignantly. "Well, I should think so!" her irritating emphasis descended.

Pitt turned upon the three the same look of despair. Rachel's need to measure values, his simple code classed with Jeffrey's guilty defense, and with Mis' Hellie's shrill complacence.

"All of you. . . ." Pitt said, with a strange, ragged gesture.

Abruptly upon Rachel the clear misery and loneliness of him smote, as if she were indeed standing with them and against him. She tried again.

"You can't judge him like this," she said, "you must make allowances—"

He stopped her with a word.

"Why?" he said.

He turned upon the two women, and his look held them, and counted them together. He pointed to Jeffrey.

"It ain't all him," he cried. "Look what you done! You—" his finger found Mis' Hellie, "made me go off and leave him. You said I didn't know how to keep care of him right. And I went. I left him to you—" his hand dropped, but his look lay upon Rachel, "and you left him go to her. And I guess it's just as good, seeing you both agree on him. And he's turned out a thief, that don't even know when he's stole. And now you both try to cover him up. I wish to God," Pitt shouted, "I'd never left my boy!"

He took a step toward Mis' Hellie, and the woman paled at the look which he held upon her:

"How do I know," he cried, his body shaken, "but you was just as crazy wrong when you advised me to leave him? My God in heaven, fifteen years stole from me. How do I know you didn't think just as crooked about that as you do about this — say!"

Mis' Hellie took up her little shawl.

"I've heard enough," she said. "My land — him that I took care of like my own and of course you paid regular but you can't know all! And I'm sure I tried my prettiest to sew him and feed him proper and right like his own mother. . . ." She burst into angry tears.

Pitt threw out his arms.

"Like his own mother!" he said loudly. "Yes! And if he'd had his own mother here to teach him, things wouldn't have been like this."

He held his Barbara against the substantial respectability of Mis' Copper and the delicacy and sophistication of Rachel.

"His mother was honest!" he cried. "She was honest about every penny she ever had and every penny she ever owed. And she knew stealing when she saw it."

He turned to Jeffrey in his exceeding triumph.

"Your mother," he said, "she'd have hated and despised what you've done. She was as far above it as heaven — thank God!"

He seemed to sweep back all three of them.

"If she'd been here," he cried, and his voice rang with the victory of this for Barbara, "if only she'd been here it never could have happened — no, nor nothing like it—"

He broke off abruptly, and Rachel, who would have spoken, was held silent by a sharp new torment in his eyes. He seemed to droop and to shorten. When at last he spoke, he was looking away from them. His voice was thick and torn:

"And he *would* have had his own mother to teach him, if it hadn't been for me."

"Ah, don't say that. . . ." Rachel begged.

"It's true," he said monotonously. "I'd ought to thought. Here I was, laying the whole thing on the both of you women and on Jeffrey. And it's my fault Barbara went away."

He was de-magnetized, he looked up at them piteously, he began that old absurd mopping movement of his hands upon his wrists. He held his hands so and moved toward the door. "Oh—" he said, low, like the voice of a woman, and the tone wavered and went down.

From the passage, as the door was opened, Jep bounded in and sprang upon him, but Pitt seemed not to see. The little dog ran after him, barking joyously, but Pitt did not hear.

"You must go with him," Rachel said to Jeffrey.

Already Jeffrey was following. He wanted to thank her, but something held him, and the look which he turned upon her shifted. Rachel, too, rather avoided his eyes, as he went.

Mis' Hellie alone abounded. She reared her head, adjusted her shawl, bore an air of elation.

"Well, we certainly stood up good for Jeffrey, didn't we?" she cried heartily.

Rachel did not answer.

"My!" Mis' Hellie said, "I tell you I was glad you see it the way I did."

"But I didn't see it the way you did," Rachel said shortly.

"Well, it come to the same thing," Mis' Hellie comfortably concluded. "We was both for Jeffrey, and we both thought Pitt come down too hard on him. And we made Pitt see it, too! I'm glad o' that."

She went away, one of her shoes dragging a bit at the heel. Rachel stood in the doorway, looking into the darkness where, somewhere invisible, Jep was crying for Pitt.

7

After lunch next day, as he passed Mis' Hellie's corner on his way to work, Jeffrey heard his name. Mis' Hellie had been watching for him and she held high her short-sleeved arm, and beckoned.

"I was going down to Orcutt's if I missed you," she called, before he reached her. And when he was at the gate she whispered, though there was not a soul in the street: "The box has come."

"The box?"

"With her things in. Your mother's! See here. . . ."

He followed her, and in strong excitement she showed him the band-box which she had already opened. It contained a decent black gown of some thin materials, shell combs set with brilliants, a red feather fan, a lacquered box of handkerchiefs and cheap lace, a white plume, a pink feather boa and an empty suede bag with a blue glass clasp. All bore a faint odor of camphor and kid. The old Barbara was speaking here, or perhaps that mother who had wanted to wear in her coffin the blue bow, kept in the box with a kitten on the cover.

"But this is the thing!" Mis' Hellie cried, and handed a little packet on whose wrapping was penciled: "Marshall Pitt."

"I was crazy to run right straight over there with it, the minute I took it out of the box," she said, "but after last night I felt I just couldn't do it. So, thinks I, I'll watch for you on your way home for noon. But I missed you — I was frying steak for my boarder and I had to keep running to the kitchen—"

Jeffrey was turning the packet, and he hardly heard her until she said with earnestness:

"But, Jeffrey, your father'd ought to have that box right straight off — no matter what — all he said to me, I hold to that. Can't you run back home with it?"

"I'll be late as it is," Jeffrey said. "I'm sorry. I'll put it in my pocket and give it to him tonight, unless—"

He glanced at her, but she shook her head.

"I can't take it over," she answered his thought. "He don't want to see me."

But she followed Jeffrey to the door.

"Look what it'll mean to him," she said, "after eighteen year. I declare I'd ought to take it to him—"

She let Jeffrey go away with the box, however. He slipped it in his pocket and ran.

He was thinking: "But those things in the box look so young—"

And at his work at Orcutt's all that afternoon, with the box in his pocket, Jeffrey wondered if his father thought of his mother *that* way—as young and with a red feather fan. . . .

It was not of Barbara at all that Pitt was thinking that afternoon, but of Jeffrey. Pitt was holding imaginary conversations with his son. For though they had had a few minutes together the night before, Pitt had not found himself able to say anything that he tried to say.

On the way home from Rachel's, Jeffrey had not overtaken his father. But seeing the house dark, Jeffrey had lighted the kitchen lamp and come outside again, and there found his father moving above the edge of the dooryard. Jeffrey had wanted to make some tremendous concession to that grief in his father's eyes as he had left them, and the boy's most tremendous concession was, it seemed, an air of the casual.

"Ready to go to bed, father?" he asked, and was vexed to hear his own voice sound like that of another.

Pitt came toward him. Jeffrey longed for a commonplace reply, but Pitt's mere presence seemed to convey some unaccustomed vibration of all his small body.

"Jeffrey!" Pitt cried.

Jeffrey tried desperately for some hackneyed bit of talk.

"Lamp smokes pretty bad there in the kitchen," he observed. "Have to get a new wick, won't we?"

"Ye—es," Pitt said. "A new wick."

He came into the area of the light falling from the doorway. There he stood, a huddled figure, ill-equipped, unfurnished.

"Jeffrey!" he said again.

"In the morning," Jeffrey went on hurriedly, "I'll see about that wick. Only you'll have to put it in, you know — I always make ears on 'em."

"Oh," Pitt said, "you mean the wick? Yes — sure enough, the new wick."

He entered the kitchen, and Jeffrey followed, locking the door noisily, stamping off to the parlor to look at the lock there. And they went away to bed without saying anything of importance. Then, having prevented him from speaking, Jeffrey wondered what his father had wanted to say. But he himself had stood all that he could stand that night, he told himself. He lay for a few minutes sleepless.

"Tomorrow," he thought, "I'll tell him I knew I did wrong by Beck — and I'll tell him I guess I knew it all the time. He'd feel better if he knew that. . . ."

But in the morning Jeffrey was hurried in getting off, and his father had seen that the time was wrong for talk, and had let him go. And at noon he had made an unfortunate beginning. As soon as Jeffrey sat down at the table, Pitt, from the deep of his own forenoon of reflection, had said abruptly:

"Now — when you was a kid, Jeffrey, you understood about good things. I see it then. Mis' Copper, she sees it. She said you give her the creeps, you was so knowing about God. Well, now, what happened — that's what I want to know? What happened?"

"Oh, gee!" said Jeffrey. "Nothing happened."

In that moment he was all boy, feeling himself put upon. Pitt persisted methodically:

"Something must have happened. They must have done something to you some of 'em."

"No, no. Of course they didn't."

"I don't mean I blame 'em," Pitt said. He pushed back his chair and sat leaning forward, rubbing at his wrists. "It's my fault — the way I said last night. I wasn't right to your mother, Jeffrey, and that's why she went off. I done the best I knew, mebbe, but I wasn't right . . . and if it's spoilt you—"

The appeal in his eyes was terrific. But his voice rose shrilly, and it was the voice alone which reached Jeffrey. Jeffrey was thinking "I wish he'd waited. Why didn't he let me get dinner first?" He was hungry, and he put away that intention to tell about his understanding of what he had done to Beck.

"You see," said Pitt, "I want us to try to get back there, Jeffrey — to when you was a good boy. . . ."

Jeffrey flushed and laid down his fork.

"I can't eat dinner like this," he said shortly.

Pitt fell silent. He heart was passionately addressing the boy but he did not know how to go on. Jeffrey said to himself that after all there wouldn't be time to tell him that he knew himself to have been wrong about the money — he would wait until night. He had brought home the new wick for the kitchen lamp, and he tried to talk about that. Pitt said no more, and Jeffrey left his father putting the new wick in the lamp.

That afternoon Pitt tried to think it through. He had known evil men, dishonest men, lying men; and naturally that which they did was wrong. But when you tried your utmost and yet did wrong, when you could not measure up to the simplest situation. . . .

"Something awful must have been the matter with me in the start," poor Pitt thought.

Not for one moment did he accuse life.

He had made a little bench under a box alder, the only tree in his yard. He sat there, and it was as if all the paths that he had walked ended at that bench and now lay beyond. There was the money to be earned to help Jeffrey to pay Beck — but how to earn that? There was the money to be earned to help Jeffrey go up to the city with his "patterns." How to earn that? It came to Pitt that perhaps his days of earning money were done, and that was bitter. Deep in him was his intolerable fear of Jeffrey's spirit; and that was more bitter than all.

He whispered about it:

"I done everything wrong from the first."

Then he came back to his great problem: How to bring Jeffrey to the level of his little boyhood. He whispered about those days:

"He use' to pray so nice. He use' to play God was in the room. He use' to feel terrible when he done wrong. I know he wanted to do right then — I know it. He could get like that again, if only he could remember back. . . ."

He looked about at the dying leaves, the empty sky, the indifferent street.

"Ain't they something that could tell a person how to get along right — if they could get a-hold of it. . . ."

After a time he saw Rachel drive up the street and he tried to discern Jep beside her in the carriage, but he could not see him there.

"That little dog," Pitt thought, "he don't know what I am. He likes me anyway."

He thought about Barbara, and went back to the affairs which, as he had now fixed them in his mind, he might have managed otherwise, and so might not have lost her. He thought about the night on which he had left Jeffrey. He thought about his claim, and the bleak Alaskan trail on which he had stood when he gave his word to exchange his claim for that other. Curiously, and for the first time in years, he thought about his own little boyhood, with a rush of pity for the only little chap whom he remembered. Why, he had wanted to be good, and had cried behind a certain door when he had done wrong. And now this was all that it had come to! He himself had done everything wrong, and Jeffrey had done everything wrong. He could make nothing of it. And how he had hoped to get on, at work for Hart, Hollow and Orr. And that had come to nothing. Now, if Jeffrey, too, came to nothing. . . .

"He will be something," he thought passionately. "He will! He will!"

It was almost prayer, but this Pitt did not know.

At last in the mellow air, he slept, leaning against the tree. Some dream visited him, a dream whose only remnant when he woke was a sense of strong sun. He sprang up, for a moment forgetting all but that bright air.

So the afternoon passed, and toward six o'clock, he went to look for Jeffrey. Without arriving at any conclusions, Pitt felt that he now knew how to talk with him. He was in a happy impatience for Jeffrey to be there. They were going to talk and Jeffrey was going to understand.

Pitt peered down the street, but Jeffrey was not yet in sight. Earlier in the afternoon, Pitt had planned their supper. Now it occurred to him that

Jeffrey liked best the nights on which there were flapjacks, and Pitt changed his menu to these. He might wait until Jeffrey reached home before making them ready, and thus might walk down now to meet the boy.

On no more than this decision, Pitt stepped into the street.

8

That afternoon two country girls, named Waxer, previously unknown to any one in this history, came to Burage to "work out" and were recommended to Mrs. Granger. Both presented themselves, hoping to find a home together. Mrs. Granger wanted only one, and her custom being herself to engage her servants, she sent for both girls to come to her room.

Lottie Waxer was vigorous, capable, definite, and Mrs. Granger would have preferred her. But Lottie had a felon on her thumb and this felon, with its white and evident wrapping, offended Mrs. Granger. So she engaged Gertie and sent Lottie away.

An hour later, Gertie went to the kitchen to heat for Mrs. Granger her milk. Mrs. Granger had not had a cup of tea in years, as she was fond of telling you, but every afternoon, at five, she had her cup of hot milk, salted. This Rachel usually prepared, but that day she had gone to a glen in the south woods where there were said to be closed gentians, and the task was left to the new maid. Intent on pleasing her new mistress, Gertie lighted the gas stove and, her mind on the milk, tossed her match into a waste basket in a corner where the cook had been cutting carpet rags.

For a time the match smoldered, then it reached a trip of cotton, blazed up among the rags, caught at the reed basket and the dimity "draw" curtain. The cook was in the basement, making sage cheese. Gertie Waxer was with Mrs. Granger. And Lottie Waxer, who might have been more scrupulous with her match, had meanwhile been engaged by a woman who had not even observed the felon.

The alarm was turned in later, and by the time that the first of the volunteer fire department arrived, the south wing, where were the kitchen and the servants' rooms, was in a tide of smoke, blown down about the walls. The engine and hose cart appeared, the gray horses galloping reflectively and as if they had done it before. They came down the main street, but it was found that the alley would be better, and more time was lost while they galloped round the block to the alley. Meanwhile, the old clapboards were blazing red and high.

Folk sprang from the earth and arrived, running. But it was seen that the wing could not be saved, and so everyone stood back to watch. There was the luxurious emotion of settling to watch a fire which could not be quenched. All save the department could enjoy with a clear conscience. The portable furniture downstairs in the wing had been carried out, and some belongings from the upper closets, but there was no use in

trying to get down anything more from above. The department said so —
already the roof was blazing.

Mrs. Granger was borne downstairs, and her chair set in the garden.
Her room was not near the fire, but no one could tell what was to happen.
She looked out of place, hunched in her pillows over by the salvia bed — as
irrelevant as a sea-shell in the parlor.

Pitt came down the street on his way to meet Jeffrey. Pitt had heard
the fire-bell without curiosity, his thoughts being so far remote. But the smoke
above the trees, and the look of the black, disquieted groups down the street
quickened him, and he arrived running. The crowd parted to let the fire chief
through, and Pitt — who had never made his way to a choice vantage place
in his life — followed this man and found himself near Rachel, who had just
returned from her drive and, here hands filled with closed gentians, stood beside her mother by the salvia.

"Why, Miss Arrowsmith," Pitt said in concern, "how'd it catch?"

She was serene, detached.

"I haven't seen anybody," she said. "It isn't going to spread, though.
The wind's right."

"Well," said Pitt in distress. "*Well!*"

He craned to see, his lips parted.

"Can't anybody *do* anything?" he inquired brightly.

"Everybody," Rachel said, somewhat dryly, "is at liberty to try."

He moved uneasily about.

"Say," he said to one or two who stood nearest, "can't anybody do
anything? It seems awful." This he repeated at intervals. "It seems awful."

He was invaded by a new possibility.

"Got everything out?" he asked anxiously, eyebrows lifted. Those about
smiled and exchanged glances. They were like the group in a public waiting
room all of whom have tried in vain to lower a window and now watch an
officious late arrival who attacks the matter with a seasoned confidence.

"I think they've selected some things to carry outside," Rachel said.
Pitt hardly ever annoyed her, but his bright approach, his banalities, his utter
uselessness, did now irritate her.

"Say," said Pitt, "say! It does seem awful."

"Perhaps it seems worse than it is," Rachel said cheerfully, seeing the
red end cave in.

"I hope so," said Pitt, with a bright look, as it were, of imagination.
"I do hope so, really."

Mrs. Granger was crying, but without emotion, and with an odd
appearance of crying because she had nothing else to do in order to be a participant. Pitt saw her, and she added to his distress.

"It *is* awful, ain't it?" he said to her, conversationally. She did not reply.
This was the only time that Pitt ever addressed this woman, whose house-

hold shaped his destiny.

Pitt went down the line, watching the flames.

"That's an awful thing — awful," he informed them all. "My goodness, who would have thought it? I came in here just last night, and everything was all right, and now look—"

Once he went back to his favorite formula in catastrophe:

"I never thought of such a thing. Did you?" he appealed to one and another.

He returned to Rachel and took up his post again.

"I declare," he said, "it does seem too bad."

Rachel moved away. Running toward her across the little open space close to the burning wing, she saw the new housemaid, Gertie Waxer. This girl's face was blackened by falling soot, and her eyes were wide with some besetting horror.

"Oh, Miss," she called, "your little dog — they say he's in the cook's room."

"What's that?" It was Pitt's voice, and he shouted.

"She's bound to go up after 'im — they're holdin' her back — if you could come and not let 'er—"

The girl sobbed, bending from the waist and throwing her arms — not because of the dog, but because of the fire.

Rachel cried out and ran with the girl. At her side Pitt ran. He ran unevenly, absurdly, with open mouth and wide-stretched fingers. He began to call the little dog.

"Jep! Here Jep, here Jep, here Jep. . . ."

The cook, an elderly American woman, was struggling with a fireman. She was crying that she could get to her room, she knew she could, and sobbing indistinguishably about "the little fellow."

"Keep her here," directed Axel Golithar, the fireman. "The blaze'll burst through there any damn minute. . . ." He ran for a ladder.

"Which room?" Pitt asked the woman, with attention.

"Right there!" she cried. "Them two windows — oh, my God, there he is!"

Beneath a yellow shade, which had been raised a trifle crookedly, and beside a potted pink geranium, there appeared the anxious face and silky ears of the little animal. They saw him bark, though they could not hear him — saw the little red mouth and, as it closed, the tongue, saucily protruding.

"Here Jep, here Jep, here Jep!" Pitt called furiously, and bent his knees and snapped his fingers and whistled. He stared about at the watching people, and they did not help. He looked at the doorway, saw the red stair, its belching smoke lifting to show the banister, the homely carpet, and the eating red. He looked at the window, at the little dog beside the pink geranium, beneath the crooked yellow shade.

"Say," he cried, *"Say!"*

Then he stepped forward, broke into uneven running and disappeared in the red doorway.

They were bringing a ladder, but a ladder did not occur to Pitt.

A sound of terror went up from the people. The word was carried by methods of its own, and all the people came running forward, fighting for place. The firemen herded them back as they pushed and trampled on one another's feet to try to see. But they made way for Rachel, now shaken from her calm disregard as by physical blows and buffeting.

"Oh, why did you let him go?" she cried, so that all the people heard.

They fell silent, watching that window where the dog held his place. The flames had tossed along the shingles until they were above the window. The cornice caught, and the blaze came creeping — little Jep looked up and watched it, and they saw him bark again, as at some new kind of bird. Then he turned his head and leaped from the sill.

As he disappeared into the room, some uttered cries. This must mean that Pitt had opened the door of the room. It did mean this, because at once a faint red glared beyond the glass. He must have left the room without shutting the door behind him and the draft was fanning the flame. The ladder was at the window at last, but when a fireman ran up, smashed the glass and peered in, he found the room empty.

Rachel, her arms folded, had torn at her thin sleeves until they were tattered upon her bare arms. The cook and Gertie Waxer were sobbing and speaking through their sobs, like children. The eyes of all were on that red stairway, which yet held.

The stream was withdrawn from the roof and directed to the doorway. With all its force, it struck the stair. As it did so, the smoke parted, and they could see a mass of white descending. The stair collapsed.

But the outside walls still held. Two firemen charged through the doorway, fell upon that mass of white and dragged it from the ruck and out at the door. They carried Pitt, and in his arms was a white marseilles spread in which he had swathed the little dog. The spread was burning, Pitt's hair was burning and the thin cotton of his shirt was all burned away about his throat and breast, and blazed upon his shoulders.

They laid him on the ground, and the people beat out the flames As the fire was quenched, there was terrific motion in the white marseilles spread. Out leaped Jep, not a silken hair of him singed, and he snapped indignantly at having been caused intolerable inconvenience.

Not Rachel or the others noted the dog. They were about Pitt, or making room to move him back. Some ran for water, for a physician, some fanned him. When the roof of the wing crashed in on the red ruins, those nearest looked briefly over-shoulder and then resumed the effort to help or to look on Pitt.

Jeffrey was coming home from his work, and he saw the people and the havoc. But the spectacle of Mrs. Granger, never before seen, humped alone in her pillows by the salvia, gave him a sharp sense of the moment. He ran across the lawn to the crowd before the ruined wing. And he heard them say:

"Hush. Here's his boy."

"What is it?" Jeffrey cried, pushing his way, and no one answered. But he heard a man's voice lifted in excited speech to his neighbor, and saying:

"Well, but of all the fool things. For a *dog*. . . ."

The doctor did not know whether Pitt had a chance — the doctor said so, with a lack of importance which caused them all, save Rachel, to distrust his skill.

"He don't really act like a doctor, my idea," Mis' Miles said. "I bet he don't know much. Anybody can understand *him*."

They were all there in Pitt's kitchen — Mis' Miles, Mis' Barber, Mis' Nick True. With their instinct to apply to a stricken household their best gifts, they began to sweep the kitchen, arrange the shelves, polish the lamp chimneys. Rachel was with Mis' Hellie in Pitt's room. None of them left him. In the little house where he had wanted company and had tried to think whom he could invite, they lit the lamps and made movement and cheer, but he did not know.

Jeffrey seemed to himself like someone else, and his father seemed like someone else, and the place like another place. Jeffrey would have liked to take his father's hand, but he never had taken his hand, and he felt unable to do so. And now in any case, he might only have touched his father's wrist, for both the hands were bandaged.

Once they hear Pitt whispering. He was saying something with terrible intentness and absorption. When they went to him, the whispering stopped. He looked at them, but his old anxious look was gone, and the ready, eager smile. He closed his eyes and lay quiet, but more than once they heard him whispering.

Then at dawn he opened his eyes full upon the room. It was lit by the naked flame of an unshaded lamp, and in that unwonted light, at that unwonted level, there may have seemed many people present. An odd, thin-drawn sound broke from Pitt, and he threw up his hands in their shapeless bandages.

"Say!" he whispered, and the words came like whistling. "Am I going to die — like a fool?"

Their deceiving answers seemed not to reach him. He said nothing more. He lay quiet, and now the whispering was not heard again.

Within the hour, his breathing ceased.

Mis' Hellie's voice, with its terrible lack of restraint, filled the house.

"He's gone," she cried; and again and again, as if no one would listen. "Why, he's gone!"

Jeffrey ran and looked. The little figure lay in intolerable stillness. The wrist was warm, but there was that stillness.

Then Jeffrey shouted out, as if he could send the word after:

"*Father!* Why, father! I wanted to tell you—"

He whirled upon Mis' Hellie and sobbed:

"How could it be so soon?"

Something of ice and of iron came weighing on the boy and choked him. There was no end to that weight, pressing outward, as if it would rend his flesh.

It was hours later, while Mis' Hellie and Jeffrey were together, trying to make the simple plans, that she said:

"Oh, I wanted to ask you. What did your father say when you give him that box? I hope *that* was something nice for him, anyways—"

At the look on Jeffrey's face, she stopped. He groped in his pocket and brought out the little package.

"I never thought. . . ." he faltered.

They opened it. Within lay the necklace of seed pearls which had been Pitt's gift to Barbara on their wedding day. Upon the pearls lay a folded bit of paper:

Marshall and Jeffrey — love — Mother.

9

The tramp of feet toward the town had set in early because of thunderheads in the northwest. The most severe storms came thus, against a southeast wind, and bread or yeast or tobacco must be ensured before the clouds spread. It was unseasonable weather, hot and wet and sullen. The air was thick and bore an odor, the river was low and all day the shore mud steamed. And now this mutter of thunder brought its boding. And the tramp of feet toward the town was hurried, lest bright frocks suffer.

For the first time in the week since his father's death, Jeffrey joined the procession toward the town. He had meant to open his father's trunk that evening, but his courage had not been adequate. The house was almost empty now, and having dragged the truck from the foot of Pitt's bed, Jeffrey had abruptly turned and rushed into the street.

They were not all merrymakers on their way to the town that night, it seemed. Not all those who sought the positive magics. Here, for example, went Paulina Dart, the widow, the cripple, the florist whose trade Pitt had injured. She went swinging along on her crutch, perhaps to get away from her melancholy little house — but the house pursued her and held her and you saw its air in her pinched face. Axel Golithar had lost his cement-block business, and he went slouching down town as a relief from figuring on the backs of envelopes. Mayme Carbury Hanson, in black and red, came walking the streets, no longer looking for adventure, but to escape the loneliness of the old house, smelling of its carpets, where she lived alone, resourceless. It was difficult to tell when, for so many, that nightly search for magic had slipped into this need for some escape. Now the procession seemed made of these and not of the young folk who attended, giggling.

Jeffrey went toward the town. The street sloped, and at its curve he could look down the length to that block of brightness which was the only common gathering place for the people. This spot offered so much and held so little. It gave glamor, with no body. For the first time, Jeffrey looked toward it without expectation. He was filled with the sense of his own loss. It smote him with surprise that he could not get away from this that had happened. It was there. He felt as some women feel in pregnancy and as they feel in wartime.

He entered Hoey's store and stood over the magazine rack, turning leaves. There were pictures of men fighting, hunting, loving, exposed to perils of the sea; but all seemed to him less than his own hour. The talk of the people in the store and the street sounded indifferent and external.

Beyond the paper palms, two men came and leaned at a counter— Nick True and Stebe Golithar. And their words went over the store with no concealment, and held Jeffrey.

"Sure," said Steve. "Sure. Sure. No two ways about that."

"Just plumb oodle-headed, I call it," said Nick.

And Stebe contributed: "Sure. Sure. Sure."

Nick went on with it, in the manner of one who has said the thing very often and yet derives flavor from every repetition:

"The place wa'n't only burnin'. If the place had been burnin' that would have been bad enough. But the place was *burned*. Down any minute. Down *that* minute. A straw o'sense, a grain o' sense, would 'a' kept a man out of it. S'pose it kept him out? No, sir. Why not? Because—" Nick paused, and his voice lifted, "because he didn't have the grain o' sense. No, nor he never did have."

"Sure he didn't. Sure he didn't," Stebe went on agreeably.

"What did he do?" Nick inquired. "Walked right into the place, brass-nosed. Took his life in his hand and t'run it on live coals — like that. Might just as well — just exactly as well offed with the kitchen griddle and laid his head on the grate. Say!"

"Yes, *sir*," said Stebe, varying his assent with unexpected resource. "Yes, *sir*. Yes, *sir*."

"Heroism?" Nick interrogated in four tones. "Call that heroism? Don't you call that heroism to me."

"*I* don't," said Stebe, with a manner of independence, even of revolution.

"Does anybody?" Nick asked. "Don't we all call it just that same silly? Which it was. No doubt about it. No doubt. Not a sliver."

"Not," said Stebe, "a sliver."

Some one joined them — Matt Barber, by the asthmatic breathing. When he talked he coughed, but this did not deter him.

"Say," he said, "I've heard some say he wasn't so silly as he seemed. Ain't you heard anybody say that?"

"Say what?" said Nick, irritably. Nick was that species of gossip which discounts everything it hears, and then repeats it as a fact.

"I've heard some say he did know what he was a-doin', just. Knew it and done it anyway."

Matt's cough really seemed needlessly extended, as if it were a means of inducing suspense.

"Done it a-purpose," he gave forth finally. "I've heard it more'n once, from different folks."

"Wh—at?" cried Nick, in an extreme register which his eyebrows must have tried in vain to reach. "You don't mean—"

"Suicide," said Matt Barber. "That's what I mean," and forgot to cough.

"Shucks," said Nick, "he didn't have that much spunk."

"Mebbe not," said Matt, conscious now that he had gone pretty far.

"Hardly," said Stebe Golithar, judiciously. "Hardly."

"No — he never knew what he was a-doin' at all," Nick maintained. "S'pose he'd have walked into that place if he had stopped to figger out that he might not walk out of it? No siree! That man never knew what he was doin' at all."

"Well," said Matt, "I donno but what that's right. He always was a little out of his senses, and mebbe he just went out plumb."

"Yes," cried Nick, "and mind you. Mind you! For a dog. Pipe that. For a *dog!*"

The men laughed. They moved to the door. They went into the street, still talking.

Jeffrey stood quietly looking at the cover of a magazine. The illustration showed a girl, with sugar in her lips, feeding a bright bird in a gilded cage, beside a huge jar of chrysanthemums. For a long time Jeffrey looked at this picture. The bird was too small for a parrot. Jeffrey wondered what bird it was. The bird blurred and went out. To his horror his tears overflowed and his breath was shaking. As Arthur Hoey came to speak to him, Jeffrey fled from the store.

So that was what they were saying. That was what everybody was saying: That his father was a fool. . . .

He found himself opposite Rachel's house. A light shone behind the thinning vines, and her gown being visible on the veranda and no voices to be heard, he entered swiftly, disregarded her greeting, and burst out:

"They say my father was a fool to do what he did!"

"They would," Rachel murmured, but he did not hear.

"My God," he said, "are people like that?"

"They are," said Rachel Arrowsmith, "like everything possible."

She did not try to comfort him or to dismiss what he had heard. She was a wise woman, who understood how much is both true and false and makes its own adjustment.

"They cannot change what your father did," she suggested only.

"No, but they can take away what he did," Jeffrey cried, and added passionately, "He never had anything!"

"He never had anything but you," she corrected.

These words pierced him.

"Look at the way I acted to him," he muttered.

"Well," she said, "and how are you going to act now?"

Of this thrust he seemed not to be conscious. "Now?" He spoke vaguely, as if the present were his last concern.

She regarded him, and wondered whether this was the time to say that which she had to say to him. She had been waiting to tell him something.

"Your plans," she said at length, "what are they — do you mind my knowing?"

"I'm going back to Mis' Hellie's," he replied indifferently.

"And keep on at Orcutt's?"

"For a while."

"'For a while' means too long," she said sharply. "It lasts most intolerably, that."

This did not touch him. "Well, I don't know what I shall do, later," he murmured.

She leaned to him, her face on her hand, her eyes reading him.

"You mean," she said brutally, "that you are putting off your decisions, so that they will make themselves."

Her terrible directness, her insolence in sitting above minor delicacies and disregarding them, was like the insolence of the members of a great family, who offend with safety and carry off that which in others they would not tolerate.

Jeffrey quivered and made a base reply. It was too soon, he said, to decide anything. It is true that he was still bewildered, but he was hiding behind that bewilderment.

"Jeffrey," said Rachel, "come and live here. And let me send you to Chicago to try what you can do with the designing."

His lifted eyes held amazement, dawning gratitude, but no fire. She went on rapidly:

"It isn't only that you're wasting yourself at Orcutt's — as you are. It's that I want the interest, the pleasure. Come along, right away. Tomorrow! Go down to Chicago as soon as you like. I want you to do this."

"Why, Miss Arrowsmith!" Jeffrey cried.

She leaned her elbow on her knee, and shaded her eyes.

"You see, Jeffrey," she said, "I'm a good deal of a failure. I'm the kind that has always been going to do something and never has done it."

He looked at her, startled. It had never occurred to him that she should have done anything. She was Miss Arrowsmith.

She went on: "I could do so much decently that I've never done anything really well. I've never done anything enough — never wanted anything enough. I've thrown everything away — that's it, I think exactly. I've had every gift in my hand, and I've let them all go."

She threw herself back in her chair, and the light smote her face and gave it all its line and shadows.

"I suspect," she said, "that most people do that. And even if they'd done things differently, still the case might be no different, after all. However, it hurts one none the less."

"But you—you—" Jeffrey stammered. It was as though an element, or some other fundamental which he had regarded as sufficient, complete, were to talk like this.

"The other day," Rachel said, "I realized that I shall never do anything more than I've done. I'm forty-six years old. Some women are at their best after that, but I've wasted too much. I relied too much on my superiority—"

She broke off, and began again with passion.

"Jeffrey! It isn't only that I want to 'save my soul.' I'm accountable for you. I and my family. . . . If it hadn't been for an impulse of mine on a hot day, to give a struggling creature a cup of tea, you wouldn't have been born at all. After that I — we — changed your destiny when we sent you to Mrs. Copper. And now we — we've killed your father."

"Oh, no, no!" Jeffrey cried.

"Think of it," Rachel said. "That morning of the fire, I went to the kitchen for a bit of string to tie a bundle of useless letters. In the kitchen the milkman's wife was leaving some cream. She had a closed gentian in her belt — and she told me where they grew. If I hadn't gone for the string and then for the gentians, Jep would have been with me—"

She stared at him.

"Your father's death," she said, "his marriage, and your existence have all depended on a whim of mine. Could anything be more shocking?"

She threw out her hands.

"What do you make," she said, "of a universe like that? I ought not to be talking to you in this way. Why not? Is it because we're all in a conspiracy to dignify the thing — keep it going?"

Jeffrey felt giddy, felt on some height from which he ought not to look down.

"I felt an impulse," Rachel said then, "not to go for the gentians. I overcame that and I went. Then Jep came running after me, and I sent him back — and felt and denied some sort of urge to take him with me. What does it mean . . . or does it mean anything at all? Did something try to get through, to tell me. . . ."

She held her hand to her eyes, and dropped it.

"Who knows?" she cried. "I'm talking nonsense, am I not . . . But in any case, I feel responsible for you, Jeffrey — and I want to be so. You must let me send you to Chicago. And I owe myself something — you must call this house home."

Jeffrey said a strange thing.

"Do you think," he asked, "that my father would have liked that?"

"He left you with me when he first went away," Rachel reminded him.

"Yes, but now—"

"You know what he wanted about Chicago. Why, any man would like to see his son so provided for, wouldn't he. . . ."

"My father was different from most men," Jeffrey said, low.

He was conscious of a sense of pride, such as he had never before known, in speaking of his father. He thought about this, while Rachel talked on about his future. At last she said:

"You're not listening."

It was true — he had not been listening. He had been thinking of his father as he had often looked, sitting here on her veranda, on the edge of his chair — his best shoes from which, with his handkerchief, he anxiously flicked the dust; the thick winter clothes, the parted lips, the anxious eyes, the bright, ready smile . . . but now, in his absence, Pitt was for the first time really present to Jeffrey. For the first time the boy felt his father's quality, felt his soul.

"Thank you," he now said heavily, "I'll have to think. I wish," he added, "I could have talked it over with him."

He left abruptly.

The figure that had so often waited up to hear about an evening, to ask irritating questions, to make unwelcome suggestions Jeffrey would have given all to see on his bare porch.

Instead, there was the trunk, waiting beside Pitt's bed. Jeffrey carried the lamp to the bureau — that old, deformed bureau which had been Barbara's — and threw up the trunk lid.

The house and yard were still. The storm, after all, had moved round to the south, "gone to Madison" Burage said, in comfortable dismissal. In the vacant lot the crickets were crying, insisting that they meant it, whatever it was. The time was like that of that first evening, when, after his father's funeral, he had contrived to slip back to the house. He had locked himself in, given way to his grief, weeping without restraint, like a little boy. But then, and since, he had been conscious that he was keeping something from himself, holding it back lest it should prove to be more than he could bear. And now this influence, still nameless, came at him with the opening of the trunk.

Beneath the few neat clothes, folded on top, lay a woman's blue calico gown, a common "house-work" gown, and an old gingham apron. There was a little smock of embroidered muslin, a girl's smock, still threaded with faded ribbon. Then came a box of articles looking as if they had been swept from some bureau — a shell, vials, a broken japanned box, a mirror with curled celluloid back. He lifted a nosegay, some blossom, frail like petunias, with crumbling rose-geranium leaves, wound and tied with thread. There was a flowered calico curtain, like a Burage kitchen curtain, and with it a turkey wing, such as they use in brushing a hearth. Jeffrey stared into a thread box where lay a bit of fine hair in worn tissue, wrapped with newspaper and marked: "J's first hair-cut." Here was something from a life which he had regarded as exclusively his own, treasured by someone else all these years. There were also a calendar of fifteen years before, and a bill-of-fare from some Chicago hotel, and both he thought that he remembered throwing away when they came into the Brackett house.

In a tin box was a sum of money in bills marked "Funeral," on yellowed paper — the dignity of this shook Jeffrey intolerably. Beneath lay a thick envelope postmarked sixteen years earlier. It contained six pages, laboriously written on lines, and headed "The Little Boy at Our House." And folded within was a printed slip from a great magazine declining the manuscript. With this were some manuscript verses, three stanzas, called "Love's Sympathy," or, "Her Answer," and at the end, Pitt's name and Chicago address. He found a dozen or more letters from various firms — wallpaperers, plasterers, grocers, department stores, briefly declining his father's applications to serve the firms. There remained only a Bible, with a leaf turned down and a heavy mark at:

Bring up a child in the way he should go.

And an old wallet, empty save for a three-line notice, cut from the *Burage Daily*, about Pitt's return to the town and his "shaking hands with old friends."

These things gave the last poignancy to that which Jeffrey was suffering. He suffered as if he were the little boy who prayed, who had waited on the stair landing for the blessing, who had worn his cap inside-out and called himself Galahad. Veil after veil was rent away, ways of use and wont which had obscured Pitt were now dissipated and memory showed only the lonely and the large. How alone he had been . . . the gamut of the boy's torture went down to his impatience when Pitt had tried his best to talk about art; and ascended to that which tore him — the wistfulness of his father that his boy's life should be better than his own. He had slighted and mocked those attempts of his to be proud and hopeful of his son's "art." That in the boy which gave him his love of beauty now turned and lacerated him with a fierceness greater than its strength for giving joy.

For the first time Jeffrey saw that Pitt's heroism had not consisted merely in fulfilling that last impulse of his.

"I wish I was dead," the boy thought, and now he shed no tears.

He lay on his bed. The room was faintly lit by a young moon. He was sleeping, waking, dreaming. He was conscious of nothing save pity and remorse. He lay quiet in pain which weighed upon his breath, his center of being. Conscious, he dreaded to move lest he should come to full consciousness and so to sharper sorrow.

Everything was there — his own childhood, Mis' Hellie, his first mornings at work, Beck, with his promises, his slithering, his veined hand combing at his beard, his shouting voice; masses of color, designs on stone, his sketches; and dancing figures and lines never incarnate for him. And his father, everywhere in the room went his father, wistful, watching him for some sign which he could not make.

Jeffrey turned, sighed, and his sigh shook him like a sob. He opened his eyes. The room seemed to him full of over-lapping presences which left him nothing to breathe. What were they? He knew that they were all his father, as if his father had been infinitely multiplied and had come with some claim. He found himself listening. He felt himself over open darkness and upheld only by these thronging presences of one man. He was in unspeakable isolation, remote from voices and echoes whose import he tried to catch. Of these the words mingled with the words of Nick True: "Heroism? Don't you call that heroism to me." But mingled too, with words which he used to say in school. They reached him:

Lest these dead shall have died in vain. . . .

What dead? The answer was only those thronging presences of his father.

And as sleep came, he was pierced by a thought of inexpressible sweetness: What if he could do something so that his father should not have died in vain?

What would that be? He slept, his whole being open, relaxed to the question.

He woke to a thin singing within him. The languor, the nausea of these days were there still, the heavy head, the throb of his flesh in sudden movement. But there was too this thin singing. It was as if he had something to do that was pleasant. This he tried to recover, and it was already there. It was something that he was to do for his father. He had thought that it was too late, and after all it was not too late.

It was a day of pouring sunshine. It was an affirmation, and it drew from him his affirmation. He had a sense of being embarked on a program, as if he had entered a corridor of many doors. For one thing, he said to himself, that wallpaper fellow who had wanted him to send more designs — he must have them at once. He dressed in urgent haste. This could not wait. His mind harped on its purpose and vaguely questioned its surprising vigor.

"I must have figured this out in the night," he thought with satisfaction.

He felt alive with some streaming consciousness of energy. He felt driven.

"I must hurry," he found himself repeating.

In the background was the stimulating companionship of Rachel's offer.

He went downtown for drawing paper. He went briskly, his line of vision somewhat above the first story of the buildings, where the eye most often rests. So observed, cornice lines instead of thresholds, green branches instead of tree trunks and bricks, the town presented an aspect of which he had been unaware. It now lay fresh from its night's cessation, wrapped in that same web of quiet which nets the human being in the morning. The vivid trees, the commonplace houses, the preoccupied streets wore an air of surprise, as if the stars were still somewhat upon them.

All Burage on its way downtown stopped at the post office, just before the carriers started out. Though Jeffrey expected nothing, he too stopped at the post office.

Since that morning on which he had received the three hundred dollars at that window, Jeffrey had seen Zeri Wing countless times. But now before the window, the memory of that other day attacked Jeffrey, so that attention became emotion. Jeffrey stared at the old man until he repeated his negative with irritation, and craned his neck to recognize the next in line. Several greeted Jeffrey, but he returned their greetings without seeing them, and went into the street.

Beck! He had forgotten Beck's money. . . . The thought had moved close to him and was waiting for him.

He returned to the bare house where he had still a few days to stay. He sat before his drawing board and began some design of urns and peacocks which had teased him. As he worked there grew for him an idea the like of which he had never known: The idea that there may be many unseen forms of beauty created by the good and the evil. He wished that he might have been taught as a child that to be "good" would create this and this beautiful line and color. He thought that the wallpaper in children's rooms might be devised to tell something of this. . . .

Three hundred dollars. If he was to return it, he would return it to Beck — the miserable little business, without assets, had been promptly closed out and the receiver discharged by the court. And if the three hundred was returned to Beck, Mis' Hellie must never be told. She should not lose her two hundred in any event. And Little Platt must not be told — he must not lose his sixty. Little Platt had a sweetheart. Jeffrey had often seen them walking on Sunday afternoons. Little Platt looked happy. Jeffrey sighed.

Below the urns and peacocks he set some design of conventionalized leaves. He closed his eyes, and beneath the red-black within there, he watched the clustered leaf-shapes assemble and dissolve and form again — but some escaped him.

How should he get the money to Beck if he did return it? He thought that he should prefer to take it himself. To take it to Chicago, see Beck, explain all. Perhaps, Jeffrey thought candidly, Beck might refuse to accept it. He mused awhile on such a Beck.

He made a border, this being the age of borders: A row of peacocks. He thought how once there were no peacocks in the world, no birds, no flowers. He wondered if sometime there would be other forms of life, now unknown, and if they would be beautiful. What if the living spirits within each one were some day to become visible — oh, beautiful, inconceivably beautiful in form, in color, in light. Ways of color and of light not yet imagined by us. . . .

If he took the morning train to Chicago he would be there by nine, and have time to see Beck and take the wallpaper designs himself to the house to which Rachel had written. Therefore he must have a number of designs finished before he went. And he must hurry, because it seemed to him that it was important that he go soon.

Above the peacocks, white on the white, he drew in a faint hint of turrets and arbors, as might be above green lawns and little groves. If there were people in such places, what beautiful people they would be. What if some day the world were to be peopled only by those who are beautiful and busy with beauty. . . .

He laughed aloud. "Well," he said, "I never thought about that kind of stuff when I was down at Orcutt's. My new job must have gone to my head."

Was it to be his new job, as Rachel had proposed? To live in her house, to be clothed, fed, to have a little money to spend, to go to Chicago as his father had wished and study design — that "art" which had so puzzled and eluded Pitt, but for which his reverence had been authentic.

"Couldn't you leave me see you do some work like that, some time?"

"Couldn't you make me a picture right here? I s'pose not. . . ."

"I could have taken you up to that cartoonist. I guess he was one of the best artists going."

Pitt's inconsequential words came back to his boy and thrust him through. For these were not now the words as Pitt had spoken them. Instead of vexing Jeffrey, these words filled him with anguish. In the thought of his dead father, an old shell of words fell away and inner signs peered out — faint, frustrated meanings once thwarted but now alive and plain. Jeffrey remembered the little things — smiles unattended, bright looks that had died for lack of looks that answered.

His father's life had gone by, years of toil and of loving had reached to nothing that he had dreamed — his toil of no moment, his love outraged. There remained a trunk full of useless mementoes, a sacrifice on which, it seemed, the town frowned, and a case of seed pearls with a message — when Jeffrey thought of that case, that message, he breathed the air of the tomb.

But in all was lifted Pitt's meaning, clear now like some beautiful figure, that longing that Jeffrey's life should be lived at its best.

Like some beautiful figure. . . .

What if this decent living, this fine living upon which Pitt had been so intent for him, did indeed proceed in some beautiful design, such as he knew a little how to draw. . . . What if that same impulse which told him how to guide his pencil could tell him the ways of that other "pattern" — as Pitt had pathetically called design.

Jeffrey closed his eyes. With no vision and upon no ear of his, he was yet conscious that *the guiding impulse was there.* Not only urns and peacocks and turrets and arbors did it create. It created too that Beautiful Figure which is father had wanted his son to trace. And in the Beautiful Figure — Jeffrey knew it clear — the next line should lead him straight to Beck.

It was so that a flash of wisdom came to him, as if he were again the little boy whom once he was, and painting his idea of God in a wash of pale blue.

Jeffrey felt a glow of certainty and a freedom from some weight. He finished the border, delicate leaf in delicate arch; and he rose, stretching.

"Well, sure," he cried boyishly. "It's to Beck's, then — tomorrow!"

10

H e did not see Rachel before he went to Chicago. He left next morning, having closed the door at last upon the Brackett house. The few things which remained in his room Mis' Hellie was to take away. He left the house unlocked, and went with no feeling of finality. His illusions usually saved him from a sense of the irrevocable. These had failed him only in that naked catastrophe of his father's death.

He carried four new designs for the wallpaper firm, and in his pocket, folded with the address which Beck had scrawled, was Pitt's "funeral" money, from his trunk.

It was barely dawn, and Jeffrey saw no one. Burage lay in her yellow autumn dress, and of the glory of blood-red vines flung indifferently over veranda and shed she seemed as unconscious as were her people. The trains which flashed by Burage were as negligible to her as to a city, sunk in larger solicitudes. Of what does a town think, lying so absorbed? . . . It seemed to the boy, faring through the little streets, that he and his father were now utterly disregarded by all. Until the week before, he and the town had always seemed to him in some faint alliance against his father.

Again the day coaches of the early train to Chicago were vast, public bed chambers, where everyone slept industriously, as if sleeping were in itself an occupation, a tense and sustained positive.

Among the sleepers Jeffrey sat down, raised a window and forgot them. His own affairs absorbed him as emotions. They were emotions. They came palpitating, and among them that strange hour of the night, when he had found what he was to do. But all had been with a kind of recognition, as if matters had been so decided for him before.

The morning was opening from some silver distance which bore gateways of unknown ore. Above Swan Lake and the fields, the clouds were thrown up in soft borders whose parterres slowly bloomed.

Watching this glory gain its prominence and shine down, Jeffrey remembered how, when he was in doubt as a little boy, he had listened. He recalled how he had done that: He had buried his chin in his collar and *listened*. Listened for something to tell him what to do. It came back to him now: If it was saying "yes," he felt a kind of light. If it was saying "no," it felt the same shape, but dark. But not quite that, either. For it was not like seeing or hearing or knowing — oh, not in the least like anything to know. Indeed, that which he knew would often tell him to do quite the opposite. Rather, this was something to feel. And though he hadn't always obeyed it, it always came out the way that it said. He had noticed that. What a funny little boy he had been!

Then there was the time when it began saying something more. Mis' Hellie was going to meet him at Mark and Arum's, in the carpet department. He had been a little late and was crossing the street to Mark and Arum's quite ten minutes after the time that she had told him to be there. And suddenly it had said: "She is not there yet." He had been so certain that he had joined Bennie Bierce and they had "chosen" the whole window full, apportioning every object before he had seen Mis' Hellie coming from the station.

"Poor little boy," she had said, "have you been looking everywhere for me?"

"No," he had rejoined proudly. "I knew you hadn't come—"

But even as he spoke he had felt a sharp stab of warning, and had known that he must not boast of having been told in this way.

So he had never told about it, but it had kept on telling him. When he first went to school it had gone too. There, on several occasions, it had told him when to answer "no" and when "yes" in class, and he had been almost ashamed of that and wondered if it was cheating. But after all, it was in this way that his wallpaper designs came to him; and now he thought that perhaps color and line and music wait in this way for their expression no more than do all knowledge and all goodness — not needing to be dug out, then, but only welcomed. If one knew how!

All this went through his mind vaguely and at loose ends; but he felt a bit proud of himself for thinking of it and looked with some superiority on the sleeping hundred about him. The dawn's great moment had arrived, and it shone on the faces of these sleepers. The heavens were so open that from distant north to distant south there rolled dawn upon dawn, and deep in the east came manifold dawns to flame and pass. His the only watching eye in those great fields of sky and stubble, Jeffrey had a sense of overflowing all boundaries, and of himself joining in the surge and color of the hour. The lawless motion of the train half-freed him from space. He felt some power never known to him. He thought in excitement:

"There. *That*. If I could feel as I feel now, I'd always know what to do. . . ."

What was that? If it were always dawn or if there were always beauty, he wondered whether *That*, whatever it was, would be near, as it was now. But he knew that it was something greater than beauty.

There was no surprise when at last he thought what it was that pressed upon him. It was as if he had known for a very long time, but was now first feeling it. No surprise, but an intense excitement which shook him. Because this presence, gentle, silent, was right here in the midst of people, and in him himself. And of late he had thought that God was far away.

He remembered how, a night ago on his bed, he had questioned into the dark, had gone to sleep waiting to know what to do, and had wakened knowing. Then he had found himself singing, sure about his work, sure about taking the money to Beck — and yet he himself had decided nothing. Perhaps it had been like prayer and an answer. Perhaps he had *listened*. He remembered the voice which had warned him away on the day when he had first sought work with Beck. But was it so simple, when everyone thought it was something hard?

The hundred sleepers were beginning to waken, in hunched and horrible ways. He looked away from them to the east, now falling into a level glory of flat gold, expressionless. God there! God in the coach, too. . . .

He thought of his father — had he known? Jeffrey said to himself, oh, no, his father never thought about anything like this. And yet at last he recalled how, in one of their talks during which he himself had been so eager to escape, his father had said:

"I've never known how to do anything right, seems though. *Ain't they something that could tell a person how, if they could get a-hold of it?*"

Was it this sense which is father had caught? This sense, which would speak straight through all inequalities of intellect? This sense which, putting away all pride, must be used as Jeffrey had used it when he was a little child. . . .

He thought of Rachel. "What do you make," she had said, "of a universe like that? Your father's death, his marriage, your existence, dependent on a whim of mine." *Whim.* But if the guiding impulse was there, and always there, whim would come no more. His soul was in sudden, passionate amazement. Was there this simple connection with the great dynamo? Was conscience, as we say, not only for right and wrong but for all possible action?

All this presented itself to the boy not in consecutive thought, but in flashes, which came, and closed.

He looked down the coach. Did any of these know? At any rate, they all *could* know. He felt a new interest in them. He brought a cup of water for a woman with untidy hair and scowling face. Then he went on thinking about his own affairs, as emotions.

Toward noon he found Beck's flat on the extreme south side, above a Vienna Bakery. The door was answered by Mrs. Beck, and Jeffrey thought that she looked alarmed when he asked for Beck, by his naked name.

"Mr. Beck," she said uncertainly, head lowered, eyes lifted, neither lip dropping while the teeth remained together, hand folded and working at her wrists, "Mr. Beck. Well-a, who is it wants him?"

"Why, Jeffrey Pitt of Burage, Mrs. Beck. You know me."

"Let him in!" came Beck's big voice from within.

He appeared, without coat or waistcoat. He was in worse condition than Jeffrey had ever seen him — unshaven, blotched. He presented the spectacle of the man who would have been willing to stoop to anything for money, but who had never been clever enough to know when to stoop.

"We ain't receivin' today," said Beck, combing his beard with those thick fingers, "but we're home to you, let me state. How are you, my boy? Your father told you about my tender inquiries then?"

He expressed noisy concern at Jeffrey's news. Mrs. Beck had slipped away. Jeffrey took out Pitt's old wallet. On the bills Beck's eyes fastened with an eagerness which was physical. Jeffrey drew out the money which Pitt had cherished. He put it in Beck's hands, since there was no table and since Beck's hands were so terribly outstretched to meet it.

"Flower and Flower did send the three hundred," Jeffrey said.

"My God!" cried Beck, and Jeffrey started as at some terrible violence which he would not have recognized until that day.

"I gave Mis' Copper her two hundred," said Jeffrey, "with no interest. And Platt his sixty. And I kept forty of what you owed me. When my father knew — he didn't know when you saw him — he said I ought not to have done that on account of the other creditors."

Beck stared. "The other creditors!" he cried, with an oath. "What about me?"

He walked about the room, both hands filled with the bills.

"Here I've been starvin'. And kept out of money that was owed to me. Wha' do you think of yourself?"

"But you owe Mis' Copper—"

"To be sure I do! And that'll be settled, so much on a dollar, all in good time. But my money was due *me*, for value received, see? Why, you young blackguard, how'd you come to get hold of that check anyway?"

There was no one to explain about Zeri Wing's lost truck garden, fifty years before. Jeffrey said again that he had taken only that which was owed to him and to the other two.

"I s'pose you know, you scallywag, that I could put you behind the bars for what you done? I s'pose you know that?"

"But the money was ours—"

"Not much. A receivership is one thing, all due and regular. Appropriatin' a check is another. You could be locked up for signin' the firm's name without my orders. You'd ought to be locked up. When do I get the rest of this, may I inquire?"

"When I can earn it," said Jeffrey shortly. "But what about our money—"

Beck roared. "Don't I tell you you'll be traded like all the rest? But as for helpin' yourself, say!"

Jeffrey looked down. After all, that was what his father had said. Jeffrey signed the note for the remainder, which Beck laboriously drew up, grunting. When Beck had examined it, he turned on Jeffrey.

"You're a young crook," he shouted. "It's well for you that you come a-sneakin' back to me with this money. It'd 'a' been found out, and then I'd 'a' made it hot for you, I can tell you."

Jeffrey stood, his throat swelling, all his pride in his noble action brought down, his anger mounting. He cried:

"I've heard about folks like you, but thank God I never saw any others!"

He whirled to the door, opened it blindly, tripped ignominiously in the passage, and got down the stairs. He heard Beck shouting and he went out into the street, burning with wrath, wrenched, shaken, worsted.

And this within the half day in which he had made sure that he should dwell and move without cessation in that gracious knowledge which had opened to him.

The remainder of the day was better. He found the wallpaper man occupied and curt, but he accepted one design out-of-hand and kept two of the others for examination. And Jeffrey had a talk with someone in the department, about its needs. They made it plain to him that they had no desire for him now, but that if he cared to come down and be on the ground, he would find it an advantage.

It is necessary for one to have known both success and failure before a great city reveals itself. Now Jeffrey caught something of the steady throb of that city which is the West. With his wallpaper design accepted, Jeffrey understood these humming cables, these roaring plants, these congested highways.

Should he stay? Should he be "on the ground," and take his chances? When he thought of it, he was aware of a positive energy pulsing through him like some resistless "yes." Go back to Orcutt's? His whole consciousness drooped and lessened.

Was it only that he had succeeded ever so little with these designs, and that his confidence had come? Or was something telling him what to do? He remembered the quiet, steady inhibition against his return to Burage, when he had come there to Chicago before. That time it had spoken to him after failure! If he had heeded, perhaps he and his father might now be living safely in some corner of the city, together, he himself already established at his work and his father happy, proud. . . .

Down the welter of Wabash Avenue it seemed to him that he could see his father: The small figure traversing these streets, looking hopefully for this job and that, expecting something better tomorrow. He saw him going home to some lonely room, saving food, saving car-fare, so that he might send the money to Mis' Hellie for his boy; going about these very walks, planning for him, wishing to be with him; hoping, too, to meet the woman with the seed pearls, who had come home to be a wife and mother for the hour of her burial. She too had walked these streets. Now Jeffrey was sorry for his mother, whatever she had been.

He crossed to Michigan Avenue and came out before the Art Institute. All his life, the sight of any building or process of art would bring back to him that enormous, blind respect for "art" which had fired his father, that "art" which he had tried to have Jeffrey talk to him about, together with deeper things. Why had he not talked with him? For the first time in years Jeffrey recalled that morning of his little boyhood when his father had stood with him on the Burage railway platform and just as the train come in, had stopped with that hurried whisper:

"Jeffrey, don't you ever let anybody make you ashamed of God."

Through Jeffrey there burned a fire of comprehension. The great gray building blurred, the blue of lake and sky flowed about all. And in his ears came beating the voice of the Chicago streets, the invitation, the command. Oh, somewhere there lay life, his life. . . .

Yet Jeffrey never definitely decided to stay. It was as if he had been given over into the hands of some re-creating energy which was acting for him. And in him that potency had its way more definitely than evil has its strong will in a fallow place. He had become fallow to some lovely efficacy, some vigor acting for him, and at last with him. . . .

And it was an energy, it seemed, which did not disdain the human ministries but was nourished by them. Once in the day a girl in checked black and white came toward Jeffrey, looked, passed. It was not her dark hair, her evident eyes, the rose upon her hat which Jeffrey saw. But in the fact of her presence there went for him reminders, the step and touch, the very *She* who moved so dim in the depth of him. *She* might be here, her voice in this voice of the city. . . .

Side by side with his father who had given all for him, this unknown girl in black and white, whom Jeffrey was never to see again, appeared for a moment, supporting, cooperating. The rush and flash of a fire engine, the sparkle of the lake, the thunder and throb of Chicago, all these came sustaining Pitt, in his old desire to call Jeffrey into complete being.

It was as if the primal energy itself, recognizing its own impulse to perfection, had functioned through the inconsiderable figure of that little man who had tried so passionately to play his part, and had failed in all else.

11

Once more Rachel made ready a room for Jeffrey, the room which had been in readiness for him more than fifteen years before. That time she had sent him away, and with him had gone something of herself, never reclaimed. Now it was he who disposed, and his news came to her as she was happily arranging that untenanted chamber.

". . .and so I know," his letter said, "that I ought to stay here. And,

Miss Rachel, there's something else. All that time my father was here in Chicago, he didn't have any help, and he paid for me besides. And so I am ever so much obliged to you, but I would rather not have you send me here. . . ."

Rachel laid her head on the pillow which would never be Jeffrey's and wept. But her tears were not all for the loss of him.

She returned to her mother's room. That room was unchanged, but change was on the pale woman, pillowed in the deep chair. From her, life had receded until the eyes looked out upon another plane.

Abruptly, Rachel was aware of a need to run to her for comfort, a surprising need such as she had not known in years.

"Oh, mother!" Rachel said, and dropped beside her, her head on her mother's knees.

Mrs. Granger regarded her tremblingly, burst into tears, said nothing. At length:

"Rachel!" she whispered. "You *want* me!"

For a flash they were lit by the relationship which they had never known. The wings of some beauty fanned the air of the room. Their lives opened and met. Richness which they had not claimed flowed about them. This was not alone the richness of the mystery of their human relationship. It was as if it were the Mary, mother of spirit, who stirred, rising by simple means. Loving, like prayer, is a power as well as a process. It is curative. It is creative.

This moment came late. In these two, the years had settled as into wood, ingraining a pattern, ringing it round. But for an instant they saw one of the substances of life, shining like a soul in the body of earth's accustomed death.

A fortnight later Jeffrey was obliged to come down to Burage for a day, and arrived in the haze of an Indian Summer afternoon. Burage lay like a cat asleep, now and again showing a glimmer of interest beneath a drooping eyelid.

The eyelid of Mis' Monument Miles, for example, who, when her work was finished, had run over to Mis' Hellie Copper's and had sacrificed changing her shoes in order to get there early. For she liked the rush rocker in the bay window. And sure enough, Mis' Nick True and Mis' Matthew Barber arrived just behind her and had to be content with the camp rocker, and the spring rocker — which went of *ping!* whenever anybody sat in it.

"There goes Mayme Carbury Hanson," their afternoon of observation began. Mis' Miles said this name like lightning, and with ironic emphasis on the last word.

"What's she stopping for?" Mis' True wished to know, peering.

Mis' Miles gave an experienced glance at Mayme, who had slowed, paused and was examining her purse.

"Forgot her sample," she diagnosed.

She must be getting old to start down town without her sample. They had begun to develop this, counting back, when Mis' Hellie sprang up with:

"There's Jeffrey!"

He was with Rachel in the car and could not come in until later. But he ran to the door, and Mis' Hellie walked with him to the "horse-block," and he stood between the two women — their most intimate hold upon the morrow.

"Going to stay in the city and be a great artist!" Mis' Hellie incautiously burst out.

He looked at her without irritation, with eyes of intelligence and adjustment.

"Going to make some decent wallpaper, I hope," he said.

They lingered there, talking happily, and as if something large and pleasant were before them all.

The three in the bay-window were watching.

"Say," said Mis' Barber, "did you ever see anybody pick up the way Jeffrey has since his father died?"

"Ain't he?" said Mis' True. "I've thought of that myself."

"Why, my land," said Mis' Miles, "he's a different person. It looks like what he'd needed was to get rid of that little man — honestly."

They wove this in small patterns, and when Mis' Hellie came back they all reverted to an old design.

"Jeffrey ain't a bit like his father, is he?" Mis' Hellie observed with satisfaction.

They gave their negatives without restraint and Mis' Monument Miles took up the whole story, from the first, rocking slowly and looking out upon the Burage Street.

Bibliography
Works of Zona Gale

Novels:
Romance Island (The Bobbs-Merrill Co., Indianapolis, 1906)
Mothers to Men (The Macmillan Co., New York, 1911)
Christmas (The Macmillan Co., New York, 1912)
Heart's Kindred (The Macmillan Co., New York, 1914)
A Daughter of the Morning (The Bobbs-Merrill Co., Indianapolis, 1917)
Birth (The Macmillan Co., New York, 1918)
Miss Lulu Bett (D. Appleton & Co., New York, 1920)
Faint Perfume (D. Appleton & Co., New York, 1923)
Preface to a Life (D. Appleton & Co., New York, 1926)
Borgia (Alfred A. Knopf, New York, 1929)
Papa La Fleur (D. Appleton-Century Co., New York, 1933)
Light Woman (D. Appleton-Century Co., New York, 1937)
Magna (D. Appleton-Century Co., New York, 1939)

Short story collections:
The Loves of Pelleas and Etarre (The Macmillan Co., New York, 1907)
Friendship Village (The Macmillan Co., New York, 1908)
Friendship Village Love Stories (The Macmillan Co., New York, 1909)
When I Was a Little Girl (The Macmillan Co., New York, 1913)
Neighbourhood Stories (The Macmillan Co., New York, 1914)
Peace in Friendship Village (The Macmillan Co., New York, 1919)
Yellow Gentians and Blue (D. Appleton & Co., New York, 1927)
Bridal Pond (Alfred A. Knopf, New York, 1930)
Old-Fashioned Tales (D. Appleton-Century Co., New York, 1935)

Poems:
The Secret Way (The Macmillan Co., New York, 1921)

Essays:
Portage, Wisconsin and Other Essays (Alfred A. Knopf, New York, 1928)

Biography:
Frank Miller of Mission Inn (D. Appleton-Century Co., New York, 1938)

Plays:

Neighbours (Walter H. Baker Co., New York, 1921)
Miss Lulu Bett (D. Appleton & Co., New York, 1921)
Uncle Jimmy (Walter H. Baker Co., New York, 1921)
Mister Pitt (D. Appleton & Co., New York, 1925)
The Clouds (Samuel French, New York, 1932)
Evening Clothes (Walter H. Baker Co., New York, 1932)
Faint Perfume (D. Appleton-Century Co., New York, 1934)